OUTSIDER

AN OUTSIDER NOVEL
BOOK ONE

MICALEA SMELTZER

Copyright 2012 Micalea Smeltzer
All rights reserved. This book or any portion thereof may not be reproduced or used in any manner whatsoever without the express written permission of the publisher.
This is a work of fiction. Names, characters, businesses, places, events and incidents are either the products of the author's imagination or used in a fictitious manner. Any resemblance to actual persons, living or dead, or actual events is purely coincidental.

Cover design by Regina at Mae I Design

PROLOGUE.

It was amazing how your whole life could be split apart by a few simple words. Everything that I had known to be true was anything but. They were asking me to believe in the impossible. Not only that... they were telling me that I was a part of it. I didn't want to believe. Stupidly I thought that if maybe I blinked my eyes rapidly this would all go away. But this wasn't a dream. It wasn't even a nightmare. It was harsh reality. It was real. Deep down in my soul I knew what they spoke of was the truth. I was a werewolf. No, that wasn't the correct term. Shifter. I was a shifter.

But there was something else that I knew that I didn't want to admit to myself.

Caeden.

Caeden Williams was my mate, my destiny, my future. The love I felt for him frightened me more than the harsh reality that I was shifter. I wanted to deny my affection, to fight it, but fighting it was impossible. Thoughts of him consumed my every waking hour and even the ones when I was sleeping.

But to accept being a shifter meant I had to accept Caeden as my mate. Accepting Caeden as my mate meant accepting my destiny as a shifter.

Was I ready for that commitment?

My heart and soul screamed yes while my mind said no.

What does one do? Follow their heart or run from it?

ONE.

"Daddy, I'll be fine really. It's not like you're sending me to live with Satan. This is Gram. Everything will be fine. You worry too much," I said as my dad loaded my last suitcase into the back of my brand new white Honda Pilot. It was a gift from my parents for always putting up with moving. My dad was in the military and all we had ever done was move. We were back in the states now, Indiana, but my dad was being transferred to Germany. I had friends, which were more like acquaintances, all over the world. We didn't stay in one place long enough for me to make a lasting friend. But this time was different. My parents knew I was sick of moving all the time and decided since it was my senior year that I could move in with Gram. My Gram lives in a small town in Virginia. I had been there a few times and it was just a quaint little place surrounded by larger cities. In other words it wasn't very exciting but it would be a steady solid home and that was just what I needed.

"Sophie, you're my only child. It's my job to worry about you," he closed the trunk.

My mom chose that moment to come out of the house with a bag in her hand and a tissue held to her face.

"Sweetie, I'm going to miss you so much," she grabbed me into a hug.

"Mommy," I hugged her back, "I love you."

She pulled away but held me at arm's length. "Promise you'll call every day."

"I promise mom." She nodded as if my answer was good enough for her.

"Don't worry about her honey. My mom will take good care of her," my dad said. He wiped his brow with his hand. My dad had thick dark brown hair and hazel eyes.

"I know. But she's my little girl."

"She's my little girl too," dad rubbed her back

"Um… Little girl standing right here," I said. It always drove me crazy when my parents acted like I wasn't standing right in front of them.

My dad laughed his good belly laugh.

"Alright, Christine, we've got to let her get on the road. She has quite a drive ahead of her."

"I'm not ready," my mom dabbed at her eyes with a tissue. She had her honey brown hair pulled back into a sloppy pony tail and her makeup was starting to run as her dark brown eyes pooled with tears. I had my dad's dark hair that was slightly wavy like my mom's but sometimes wanted to hang like limp noodles and I had my mom's brown eyes. My features were a mix of both of theirs. I had my dad's long straight aristocratic nose and my mom's full lips but unfortunately my top lip was slightly larger than the bottom. Luckily, I hadn't inherited my dad's widow's peak.

They each gave me a hug and then my dad handed me my car keys. He pulled me in for yet another hug.

"Take this for gas and anything else you need while you're with Gram. This is for emergencies only though. No shopping sprees," he joked as he slid a credit card into my hand. My dad knew I wasn't into clothes and therefore had nothing to worry about. I had learned a long time ago that the less I owned the less I had to pack.

I got in my car and backed out of the driveway. Looking in my rearview mirror I could see my mom and dad standing on the driveway waving. He had his arm around her but then I saw the FOR SALE sign and it shattered the image. If they weren't moving I wouldn't have to do this.

I sighed and turned up the radio. A loud pop song was on but for once I didn't mind; anything to keep me awake. I had a long drive ahead of me; almost ten hours and I wasn't looking forward to it.

Familiar sights flashed by me. Our neighborhood, my school, the 7Eleven where my friends and I always hung out. The sights didn't bother me as much as it might someone else. I was used to leaving. Leaving I could handle but I wasn't so sure if I would be able to handle staying.

I got onto the highway and the car hummed pleasantly. The traffic was heavy and I became increasingly irritated. After driving for four hours with no stops I finally pulled over and filled the car with gas and used the bathroom. There was a Wendy's next door so I walked over and got something to eat. It was twelve o' clock and people were out milling about. I couldn't help but envy them and their simple uncomplicated lives.

I got back in the car wishing that I was already there. Depending on traffic I had another five to six hours ahead of me.

I had to stop again another four hours later to get something to eat. I grabbed a drink and sandwich and ate it in the car. I had five missed calls. Three from my parents, one from my friends, and one from Gram. I took a bite of sandwich and decided to call my parents back first.

My mom answered on the first ring. Was I fine? Yes, I assured her. Was I getting close? Yep, almost there. Would I call when I got there? Yeah, definitely.

I hung up and called my friends back. Hopefully they would be able to cheer me up.

"Hey," I sighed into the phone.

"Oh my god, Sophie, it's only been twenty-four hours and we already don't know what to do without you!" said Anna. I could hear the sounds of Katelyn and Jess in the background.

"I'm sure you'll be fine without me," I said with a smile tugging at my lips.

"We'll never be the same! You're the life of the party!" sounded Jess's voice.

"Well I can't argue with you there," I laughed. I was far from the life of the party. I was the quiet timid girl in the background. Being the center of attention was more Anna's scene. I knew I could count on them to make me laugh, though. "I better go," I said, wanting to finish my calls so that I could get back on the road.

"Okay," said Anna, "We miss you!" all three of them said in unison before hanging up.

Before calling Gram back I got out and threw away

my trash. Climbing back in I dialed her number but all I got was her voicemail.

"Hey, Gram it's me Sophie, I'm almost there. I'm going to be about another hour to an hour and a half. So, I'll see you when I get there. Bye," I hung up. I couldn't wait to finally get there. My legs were stiff and my butt was starting to hurt from sitting so long.

I got off of I-81 onto my exit and relief flooded my body. I was here. I had done it. The trees were tall and bright green. I could see mountains. There were no mountains in Indiana. Everything here was new and different. It was wonderful.

I turned onto the back road and seeing my gas gauge swivel closer and closer to the big E I decided to fill up before I officially arrived at Gram's. I drove down to the Handy Mart that I remembered being close to Gram's house. A bunch of kids my age were hanging out in the parking lot. I assumed they went to the local high school and would be my classmates. School didn't start for another three days. My schedule and everything was already in order. I got out of my car and swiped my dad's credit card. As I was pumping gas I noticed that pretty much everyone was looking at me. The kids that had been hanging out laughing were now staring right at me. I looked down at my feet but I could still feel their eyes on me. I heard the little click that said the car was full so I replaced the nozzle and jumped in my car as quick as I could. I looked back at the crowd of kids and saw their eyes follow my car. It looked like school was going to be awesome.

I pulled into the neighborhood and quickly found Gram's quaint but cute pale yellow house. As I pulled up I could see her sitting on the little white front porch rocking in a rocking chair that she got one summer at Cracker Barrel. Seeing me she jumped up and waved enthusiastically. I pulled into the driveway and hopped out of the car. I ran into her welcoming arms like a little kid. She kissed the top of my head and then held me at arm's length.

"Wow, my child, you're taller every time I see you! What are you now six foot?" she said.

I laughed, "No, gram. I'm actually five-ten."

"Close enough," she gave me a huge smile, "Sophie it's so good to have you here."

"It's good to have a home."

She got a sad look and said, "Remember Sophie, it's the people that make the home not the place."

I gave her a small smile, "Then this should be the best home yet."

"That's the spirit," she patted my shoulder.

She helped me carry my bags in from the car. We put it all in the guest room that would now be my room.

"Your dad called and he told me to tell you to go ahead and use his card to buy some stuff to fix up the room to suit you."

I smiled, "That was nice of him but it's your house. I doubt you want me changing stuff."

"Oh no dear, go right on ahead. In fact I got you a gift card to the hardware store down the road for you to get some paint. I doubt you want this color. And just so you know I was planning on redoing this room anyway. So, now I don't have to pay for it. Just don't tell your dad," she laughed.

"You're the best Gram," I said. Looking around the room I was grateful that my dad was going to give me the money to fix up the room. The walls were an old faded blue that was peeling in places. There were leak spots on the ceiling. The bedspread was old and had been there for years. At one point it had been white but now looked yellow. There was still a nail polish stain on the wicker dresser. It needed work. A lot of work.

"I made your favorite for dinner," Gram said.

"You mean," my eyes took on a dreamy glaze, "Your famous spaghetti?"

"The one and only," she said.

"I love you," I ran to the kitchen. I could immediately smell the heavenly scent of Gram's own spaghetti sauce recipe. My mouth began to salivate. "Can we eat now?" I asked.

"Of course," she smiled.

We sat down at the table together. Everything was just as I remembered it. From the yellow walls to the rooster salt and pepper shakers. This was the only place that ever felt like home to me. We moved around too much for me to permanently get too attached to one place. Moving never got easier but I did get used to it which helped. Whenever we moved I knew we probably wouldn't stay for more than six months. The most we ever stayed in one place was a year. But every summer I would come and stay at Gram's house. I looked forward to it every year. I hadn't spent the whole summer here this year because I wanted to spend as much time as I could with my mom and dad. I probably wouldn't get to see them again until graduation. The thought saddened me but I knew living here was for the best.

Spooning spaghetti onto my plate Gram said, "I'll need you to work at the shop while you're here. After school and a little on the weekends. I just really need the help and of course I'll pay you well," she smiled.

Gram owned her own little store not far from here. It was called Lucinda's. Lucinda was my Gram's first name. Her specialty was cupcakes. Gram made the best cupcakes in the world. Actually, Gram made the best of everything. But she also sold little sandwiches and had the store set up for people to sit and read or write or just hang out.

Sprinkling cheese onto my food I said, "I love working at your shop Gram. It's so magical and special. It's my second favorite place in the world," I said taking a bite. "Oh my God this is so good," I moaned.

Gram laughed, "Glad you like it," she nodded to my heaping spoon, "So what's your favorite place?" she asked.

I shrugged, "Here of course."

She laughed, "What's so special about here?"

"I don't know," I said, "You're here. And promise not to laugh?"

"Cross my heart," she said.

"I just... I don't know... I feel connected to this place. Like- like I belong here or something. I know it sounds silly but it's the truth."

Gram's face became very serious as she listened. Her eyes darkened and she became grim, "There's nothing silly about the truth, my dear."

TWO.

That night I settled into bed. I was extremely tired and I knew that I would have a rough couple of days ahead of me with preparing for school and my new life here. Pulling the blankets back from the bed I climbed in and scooted under the covers. I thought for sure that I would fall asleep as soon as my head hit the pillow but that didn't happen.

First I heard the howling of wolves. Then one wolf. The lone wolf sounded like it was right outside.

But wolves don't live in Virginia.

Then I heard something scraping at my window.

I tried to convince myself it was a tree blowing against the window but I knew better. There was only one tree in Gram's back yard and it was nowhere near this window.

After that I heard the breathing. Heavy, shallow, desperate breathing. My heart rate accelerated. I squished my eyes shut and covered my ears with my hands. But that just let my imagination take over. I felt like a little kid who thought there were monsters under her bed.

"Calm down, Sophie. It's just the wind. You're getting worked up over nothing," I said to myself.

Then there was the banging at the front door.

I screamed bloody murder.

"Oh my God, Sophie. Are you okay?" asked Gram flying into my room.

I clutched at my chest my breathing ragged. "Do I look okay? Who is at the door at this time of night?"

Gram gave me a funny look. "Sophie, there's no one at the door."

Now I gave her a funny look, "Are you kidding me? It sounded like someone was trying to break the door down."

Gram sat down on the edge of the bed. She tucked a piece of hair behind my ear. "Honey, I think you were dreaming. Just go back to sleep."

"Dreaming? But it was so real," I said to her in disbelief.

"Some dreams are," she stood up. "You've had a long day. You're tired and your brain just took advantage that's all."

"Yeah, I'm sure that's it," I said, but I felt like she was hiding something from me.

She left; closing the door behind her.

I could have sworn I heard her open the front door and talk to someone but I was too tired to get up and investigate. After all it was probably just my over active imagination taking over.

I pulled the covers tighter against my body.

This time I did fall asleep. My sleep was restless and dream filled.

Golden eyes watched me from the darkness. They were always there. I could not escape their glare. I couldn't tell what creature the strange golden eyes belonged to but I knew that it wasn't human. Anger rolled off of it in tumultuous waves. The instinct to run flowed through my body but my legs were leaden. I couldn't move. I couldn't breathe. I was frozen by the golden eyes. I knew I should run but even if I could move my feet the result would be disastrous. If I tried to flee I knew the creature would lunge out of the darkness and attack me. It probably would even if I didn't move. This creature was malicious and it wanted me. All I could see of it was its strange eyes but I tried not to show fear. This creature fed off of fear. I would not be afraid. I had to be strong.

I felt like the dream would never end but eventually it did. I woke up to the feeling of eyes glued to me. Goosebumps began to cover my arms. I was starting to question my move here. I hadn't even been here a whole day and I was already becoming paranoid. I hoped my paranoia was without reason.

I could smell the delicious melody of crackling bacon coming from the kitchen and decided to jump in the shower before I had breakfast. I towel dried my hair and let my natural soft waves roll down my shoulders. I pulled on a pair of jeans and a t-shirt and put on some make up to hide the dark circles under my eyes, normally I wore little to no makeup. Deeming myself ready I headed to the kitchen.

I kissed Gram on the cheek. "Something smells delicious."

She smiled. "Good morning, Sophie," she deposited some eggs and bacon onto my plate.

"Thanks. You didn't have to make breakfast."

"Oh, I know," she said. "But I have someone covering the store this morning. I'll need you to go in though around twelve o' clock. I have some things I have to take care of."

"Okay," I took a bite. "You have got to be the best cook ever," I moaned in ecstasy.

Gram laughed. "From what your dad says you're a pretty good cook yourself."

I blushed. "I learned all I know from you."

"Oh, I doubt that," she settled herself into the chair across from me. She had her gray hair pulled back into a bun. Laugh lines framed her eyes and mouth but she still managed to look young. She seemed to exude this aura of peace and tranquility.

I finished my plate and then cleaned it. "I'm going to start unpacking before I head over to the store."

"Alright," she said, now reading the newspaper.

I began filling up the closet with my clothes and then used only one drawer of the dresser. I sighed and put my hands on my hips. The beauty of not owning much was that it didn't take long to unpack. I left my room and headed out to the living room. I flopped on the couch and started flipping channels. I still had thirty minutes before I had to leave the house.

Gram came out of her room, smiled, kissed my cheek, and told me she'd see me at dinner.

Finally, I couldn't sit still any longer so I grabbed my car keys, the hat and shirt I was required to wear, and headed out the door.

The store was only two minutes from Gram's house, across from the drugstore so it took no time at all to get there. I pulled around back and parked next to a shiny black motorcycle. The door to the back entrance was unlocked so I went right in pulling my hair back into a ponytail as I went. I put on the black shirt and baseball cap that said *Lucinda's* in flowy pink script. As I was pulling my ponytail through the baseball cap a guy came around the corner.

He took one look at me, his eyes went all misty, looking at me like I was his own personal sun, or the only thing holding him to this Earth, and then dropped the tray of cupcakes he was holding on the floor. Icing splattered across the floor and onto our shoes.

I noticed that he was extremely good looking with tan skin, dark brown wavy hair, and dark scruff covering his cheeks and chin. He looked to be about six foot three and had a well sculpted chest and arms. He looked to be around my age, maybe older. His blue eyes were captivating. They were endless shimmering pools and I knew immediately I wouldn't mind drowning in them. I'd go gladly.

He looked down at the mess and then back up at me blushing profusely. Somehow, his flaming cheeks only added to his looks. He bent down and began cleaning up the mess.

"Don't worry. I've got it," I bent down.

"It was my mistake I'll get it," he said.

"I can get it. I'm sure you probably want to get out of here," I smiled.

He smiled back and I thought I would melt.

"Why don't we do it together?" he suggested in his sweet caramel voice.

My heart thudded erratically in my chest and I blushed. "Sounds like a plan," I dumped several of the ruined cupcakes in the nearby trashcan. "I'm Sophie by the way. Lucinda's granddaughter."

"Caeden," he said. "I didn't know you were coming."

"Should you have known?" I asked quirking a brow.

He dismissed my question with a wave of his hand. "I

didn't know anyone was coming and as you can see you gave me quite a fright," he motioned to the spilled cupcakes. But I felt like he was lying about something. Hiding something. The way he had looked at me? It was like a blind man seeing the light for the first time and then to act like he had the right to know I was here? It was all a bit strange to me but I chalked it up to the fact that he worked here and the only other employee was Gram and some older lady so it probably was a shock to see me come in the door. He probably would have looked at any girl who came through the door like that. I was nothing special. I had brown hair and brown eyes, plain and normal.

I wiped off the floor and then washed my hands. When I turned around Caeden was standing there with that same strange look on his face like I was everything he ever wanted.

"So," I said. "You can go now."

He shook his head like he was clearing it. "I'll go after I make some more cupcakes to replace the ones I dropped. You can cover the front."

Just then the front door chimed.

"Okay fine," I muttered. "Show time."

Like promised Caeden made more cupcakes before leaving and it was a good thing because the front was extremely busy and there was no way I would have been able to make more while manning the front. At six o' clock I was finally able to lock the door and clean up. Gram's little store had apparently taken off. It had never been this busy on previous times I visited. In the past it had been all she could do to hang onto the small little cupcake shop.

Once everything was sparkling clean I headed out. I locked the door behind me and went home. Gram's car was still gone. I wondered what she could possibly be doing this long.

I grabbed the front door and went to open and then realized it was locked.

"Shit," I moaned.

A neighbor sitting on their front porch glared at me. "Sorry," I sent them a sheepish glance and my cheeks burned.

I pulled out my cell phone and rang Gram. She didn't answer so I tried again starting to panic. I didn't want to have to sit outside all night. She finally answered and I sighed into the phone. "Gram, I'm locked out. I don't have a key."

"Oh, you poor child don't worry," she hung up.

I sat down in the cracker barrel rocker and waited. I had a book in my purse so I pulled it out and started to read. I didn't know how far away Gram was so I might as well get comfortable.

A few minutes later the rumble of a motorcycle disturbed the peace. Peeved I looked up to glare at the person only to find that they were pulling in my driveway. I stood up and watched the person climb off the bike. He went to pull of the helmet and I immediately realized who was here. Caeden.

"What are you doing here?" I asked.

He shook a set of keys. "Rescuing a damsel in distress. Doesn't everyone do that in their spare time?"

I laughed. "You must think I'm pathetic. Wait, how do you have a key?" I asked.

He chuckled. "It's a long story. But the gist is that your grandma trusts me."

I crossed my arms over my chest while he opened the door. He held it open for me so I went in and tossed my purse on the hall table.

I turned around to thank him and found his chest only inches from my face. I gasped and his woodsy scent filled my lungs. I must have staggered because suddenly his hands were on my arms to steady me. They were warm and calloused and felt wonderful. Tiny zings pulsed through my body at his touch.

"You okay?" he asked.

"Yeah," I breathed. "Thanks," I said. "For unlocking the door," I added.

He chuckled and then deposited himself in one of the

flowery arm chairs. Noticing my raised eyebrow he said, "Lucinda asked me to stay with you." He put his hands behind his head and leaned back in the chair, sighed, and turned the TV on.

"I don't need a babysitter," I snapped at the gorgeous boy that seemed out of place in Gram's flowery living room.

He chuckled. "I'm not about to cross Lucinda so you can take it up with her later."

Exasperated I threw my hands in the air and stormed into the kitchen. I quickly decided that I better make the most of having this gorgeous guy in my house so I called out to him, "Are you hungry?"

"Starved," he said.

I looked through the refrigerator and saw some steaks that were getting close to going bad and decided I would make those. I was sure Gram would be hungry whenever she got home.

I mixed up my special marinade that kept the steaks from getting dry and then started the grill. I stuck some baked potatoes in the oven and mixed up a salad with homemade dressing. Deciding I couldn't avoid the living room anymore I took a seat on the couch.

Fox news blared through the room. I laughed. "You watch the news?" I asked.

"Doesn't everyone," he said in his silky voice.

"I just pegged you for more of the football, chest pounding, type," I said with a laugh, pulling my legs up and making myself comfortable.

He laughed. "Don't get me wrong, I love football, but I'm kind of a nerd."

We sat in companionable silence until the timer for the steaks went off. I got up and got them and was pleased with how they turned out. I fixed us each a plate, put one in the microwave for Gram, and set out some toppings for the baked potato since I didn't know what Caeden liked.

"It's ready," I called.

For someone as big and muscular as Caeden was his

steps were practically silent. He sat down and I appraised his reaction. He inhaled. "Mmm, smells delicious."

"Thanks," I tucked a piece of hair behind my ear.

"But I don't eat salad," he pointed to it. His large smile made the words less cutting. "Anything green is not a part of my diet. I'm a man not a caterpillar."

"It's good for you. Try it. Just one bite and I won't bug you," I used my fork to point at him.

He scrunched up his face, picked up his fork, and speared a piece of salad. Dramatically slow he moved the fork towards his mouth. Finally, he took a bite. He chewed and then swallowed. A slow smile spread across his face. "That's actually pretty good," he took another bite.

"So," I said. "How old are you?"

He chuckled. "Why? Do I look old?"

I blushed. "No, that's my backwards way of asking if you're still in high school or not."

"In that case, yes, I'm still in high school and I'm eighteen."

"So, I guess I'll see you around school then? You do live around here, right?" I asked and took a sip of water to have something to do with my hands.

He chewed and swallowed. "Yep, you'll see me. Do you have your schedule yet?"

"I don't think so," I said.

He smiled. "You're a senior right?"

"Yeah."

"Well, maybe we'll have some classes together. At least I hope so," he got that funny look on his face again.

I blushed and looked down at my plate. "That would be nice." *Very, very, nice.*

He grinned. "School starts in two days. Why don't I take you over there tomorrow and we'll get your schedule and then I can show you around so you're not completely lost on your first day."

"That would be great," I sighed. "You'd think as many times as I've moved I'd be used to being the new kid but it never ceases to stop bothering me."

"You wouldn't be halfway human if it didn't bother you. But don't worry I've got your back. Plus, almost everyone is nice."

"*Almost?*" I asked.

He chuckled. "I'm not going to lie. There are some people there that get under my skin."

It was so easy to talk to Caeden and I found myself leaning closer to him as if pulled by some kind of magnetic energy. He seemed to be doing the same. Just then the front door opened and startled we jumped apart.

"Lucinda?" Caeden asked standing. He stood in front of me and his stance suggested he was ready for an attack.

"It's only me," she called and then came around the corner into the small yellow kitchen. "Something smells divine."

Caeden sat back down and leaned the rickety wooden chair back on two legs. I didn't know how the old chair didn't snap. "Sophie is an amazing cook." He rubbed his stomach. "She might be even better than you."

"Take that back Caeden Williams," she smacked the back of his head lightly.

He laughed and deposited the chair back down on four legs. I was amazed at their light banter. I had never met Caeden on any of my previous visits with Gram but the two acted like old buddies.

"I put a plate for you in the microwave," I told Gram and she proceeded to warm it up.

Suddenly the room felt heavy with tension and the only noise was the low roar of the microwave.

"I better get going," said Caeden. "Bryce and I have to do something. He's probably standing on top of his head."

"Be careful," said Gram, "and don't worry about work tomorrow. We open later on Monday's anyway so Sophie will cover it."

Caeden nodded his head. His face looked dark with worry about something. I wondered what was going on. It looked like something was passing between Gram and Caeden.

He started to leave. "I guess I'll see you when I see you," I called.

"Yeah," he said, not turning around.

Puzzled I turned to look at Gram. "What's going on?" I asked her.

She sat down in the seat that Caeden had vacated and then proceeded to take a couple bites of food.

I repeated the question.

"Nothing," she said. "I don't know what you're talking about," Gram added.

"Oh, I don't know maybe the voodoo mind magic going on five minutes ago?" I said.

Gram laughed. "Sophie, you're just like your father. He always did have an overactive imagination."

I sighed and went to the sink to clean my plate.

It was still early but I turned to Gram and said, "I'm going to bed."

"Don't forget to call your parents," she chimed as I left the room.

"Kay," I called over my shoulder.

I brushed my teeth, washed my face, and got in my pajamas before calling my parents. Neither answered so I just left a message and then climbed under the covers and was out like a light.

Gram was gone when I woke up which I thought was strange because I hadn't overslept. I made myself breakfast and then showered and got dressed. I put my cap and *Lucinda's* shirt by the door so I wouldn't leave either here by mistake. I noticed before she left Gram had attached her house key to my key ring. I smiled to myself. If she hadn't done that there would have been no doubt that I would have locked myself out. I might have even done it on purpose just for the chance to see Caeden.

Sometime later a knock sounded on the door scaring me to death. I put a hand to my racing heart. I had never been so jumpy before. This place must be messing with my head.

I slowly opened the door so that, if necessary, I could slam it shut quickly.

But to my relief Caeden stood outside. He looked flawless in a pale blue t-shirt, which brought out the cobalt of his eyes, and his motorcycle jacket.

"Hey," he said. "I didn't mean to scare you."

"I wasn't scared," I defended. He gave me a look that told me he didn't believe me.

"I told you that I would show you around the school, today," he grinned at me.

"Oh right," I said awkwardly and just stood there.

"Are you coming?" he asked after a moment.

"Yeah," I shook my head and grabbed my stuff. I didn't know how long it would take at the school and Gram would have my head if I opened the store one second late.

I shut the door and saw that Caeden was holding out a helmet to me. I scrunched up my nose. "No thanks," I said. "I don't wish to be road kill."

He chuckled. "Don't you trust me? I would never hurt you. Come on it'll be fun," he said and tried to get me to take the helmet.

I clicked the button to unlock my car and it beeped cheerily. "We can go in my car," motioned to it like I was Vana White on Wheel of Fortune.

"Fine," he grumbled and put the helmet back.

I climbed behind the wheel and he got in a moment later. The radio blared on and I immediately turned it off.

Caeden studied the car and rubbed the leather seats. "*This* is your car? Your parents must love you," he laughed.

"Something like that. It's more of a bribe for being a good sport about all the moves through the years. But they do love me," I added backing out of the driveway and trying to avoid his monster of a cycle. "And hey, that bike doesn't look cheap," I jested.

He rubbed his hands uncomfortably on his jeans. "It was my dad's," he cleared his throat. "Before he died. It was going to be my graduation present but my mom gave it to me early."

"Oh," I was stunned. "I'm so sorry."

"Accidents happen," he said.

I didn't know what to say, I had never known someone with a dead parent before, so I didn't say anything at all. I pulled into the school parking lot; I had been here plenty of times with Gram to see plays, and followed Caeden inside. He held the front doors open for me and then turned to the right and went passed the attendance and office, before stopping in front of the guidance office. Once again he held the door open for me.

The lady sitting behind the desk looked up, her reading glasses perched haphazardly on the end of her nose, and smiled at me. "Sorry, sweetie no schedule changes until the second week of school."

I smiled back. "I'm not here for a schedule change. I just moved here and I haven't received my schedule yet so I was hoping you would help me," I said.

"Oh, certainly," she said. "What's your name?"

"Sophie Beaumont."

She searched her computer and then said, "Ah, here you are." She hummed to herself. "It says you live with your grandma."

"Yes, Lucinda Beaumont. My dad's in the military and so we moved around a lot. They decided it would be better if I spent my senior year in one place."

"Oh... Lucinda? That sounds familiar," she tapped her chin.

"Lucinda's Cupcakes, maybe?" I suggested with a shrug of my shoulders.

"That's it!" she said clapping her hands. "Those are the best cupcakes! Here you are," she handed me my schedule and then a map of the school.

"Thanks," I turned around and walked into something hard. I put my hands out in front of me and felt hard muscle. My cheeks flamed and I pulled my hands away like I had been burned.

"Sorry," I muttered to Caeden. I had forgotten he was behind me. He had that same enamored look on his face which made me blush more. I went around him and that seemed to snap him out of his weird trance.

He shook his head and followed me out.

"Let me see your schedule," he said and I handed it to him. He clucked his tongue and smiled. "You got Harding for Math good luck with *that*," he said. "She's the worst."

I groaned. "I already suck at math. I need a good teacher."

"Don't get me wrong. She's a good teacher as long as you don't get on her bad side. She absolutely *hates* my brother Bryce," he said as we continued to walk straight down the hall. He laughed. "She threw a ruler at him once."

I laughed too.

"Okay," he said as the hall ended and the only way was to go left. "This is the math wing. So, you're going to come down here first. It's this classroom right here," he indicated the second on the right. A plump woman with graying hair sat behind a desk. Seeing us she looked up. Then she noticed Caeden and glared.

"Is that brother of yours still here?" she growled.

Caeden turned to me and rolled his eyes. I stifled a laugh. "Yes, Mrs. Harding. He's a grade behind me. You still have to see his face every day for the next two years."

"Every day my foot," she groaned.

Caeden shook his head and shot her a charming smile. "Anyway, this Sophie. She's new. You'll be seeing her in your first class."

She turned her beady eyes on me and stabbed the air with a pencil she had been holding. "You're not going to give me any trouble now are you young lady?"

"No ma'am."

Her eyes narrowed to the point that I didn't know how she could see out of them. "I can smell trouble a mile away and *you* are trouble."

I gulped. I didn't know what to say but I finally found my voice. "I won't cause any trouble," I breathed.

"Hmm," she said.

We started out of her room and then Caeden leaned his head back in. "Oh, Bryce's head is fine by the way. Thanks for asking."

I saw her scrunch up her face and stand up.

Suddenly Caeden's warm hand was on mine. "Run!" he said.

We sprinted down the hallway and he pulled me into an alcove out of her line of sight.

I could see Mrs. Harding out of the corner of my eye. She was standing in the middle of the hallway with her hands on her hips seething. She mumbled something about annoying teenagers and walked away.

Caeden's hand still held mine. I didn't want to let go. I liked the way it felt there. Like it belonged. Once he was sure she was out of ear shot he burst into laughter.

I smacked his arm. "You're horrible! She could have eaten me!"

He started laughing harder. "I couldn't resist."

I let go of his hand reluctantly and said, "Can we finish the tour now?"

"Sure, sure," he said and another giggle escaped.

We started walking again and I asked, "How come you said that she would see him every day? Don't we have block scheduling?"

Caeden rubbed the scruff on his face. His blue eyes were glittering with laughter. "Yeah, we have block scheduling but Bryce is like a math whiz and Mrs. Harding is the only teacher that teaches the everyday advanced classes. So, she gets to see his wonderful face every day for the next two years just like she has for the last two years. Even one of his electives is Math. I actually think he might be in your class."

I laughed. "Math? An elective?"

"What can I say?" he said throwing his hands in the

air. "The kid's a freak. But he's my baby brother."

    I shook my head. Caeden finished showing me around and told me that he'd meet me in the parking lot on the first day. This reminded him that I needed to buy a parking spot first. I bought the spot right next to his.

    I drove back to Gram's to drop him off and then headed to the store. I had some time before the store opened so I started baking fresh cupcakes. The spicy and sweet scents permeated the air. Guiltily, I snatched a cupcake and moaned in ecstasy. Gram's recipes made the best cupcakes.

Before I knew it the day was over… and the next. The first day of school was staring me in the face and I was so not ready.

THREE.

I groaned into my pillow as the alarm went off. Finally I couldn't take the incessant buzzing anymore and turned it off.

A light knock on my door, a shed of light, and then Gram's head finally emerged. "Rise and shine!" she chanted. "First day of school!"

I groaned and covered my eyes with arm. "At least it's the last first day of school," I mumbled.

"That's the spirit!" she said. "Now get that toosh out of bed and get ready. I've already started breakfast," she tried to entice me with her cooking.

"It's dark out," I grumbled. "That means it's time to sleep, not eat."

She put her hands on her hips. "Get. Out. Of. Bed." She said in her serious voice. You didn't mess with Gram's serious voice.

"Fine," I grumbled. "I'll get up and I'll go to school and I promise to hate every minute of it."

She tapped her foot. "Sometimes I swear you're your father except with lady parts. You act *exactly* like him!"

"No, I don't," I grumbled.

She threw her hands in the air. "Oh, please. You have the same eyebrows and you even swallow the same."

"My eyebrows are fine," I said but self-consciously tried to smooth them down.

"If you're a man," she said. "Come on," she said pulling me towards the bathroom. "Take your shower and when you're done breakfast will be ready."

Her joking banter was beginning to rub off on me. "So, now you're telling me I stink?"

"No," she said and looked at her watch. "I'm telling you that you're wasting time."

I shook my head and closed the bathroom door.

I dressed quickly and dried my hair. I dabbed on a little mascara. Like Gram had promised a feast befitting a king was waiting for me. Homemade pancakes were stacked on a plate.

"Gram, you're too good," I said digging in.

She smiled at me across her own plate. "I am quite amazing," she said. "I'll need you to work after school. Just come straight to the store. Caeden will be there too. He usually comes in a little late but you'll need his help. We're usually really busy once school starts."

"Okay," I yawned. "And just so you know, the store is *always*, busy. I hardly get a break."

She chuckled. "You'll see."

I finished my breakfast, grabbed my backpack, and headed out the door. It should be illegal to have to go to school this earlier, I thought to myself. I was shocked at the long line of cars at the stoplight and resolved to not waste so much time in the mornings.

When I finally made it through the light a man directed me to my left and into the student parking lot. I remembered my parking spot number and repeated it in my head like a mantra. But it was pointless. Caeden waved to me from where he was standing next to what looked like a younger version of him. I assumed it was his little brother.

I parked next to him and found myself smiling.

"Hey," he said as I jumped out of the car.

"Hi," I smiled.

We must have just standing there staring at each other like goofs because all of a sudden the other boy whistled and waved his hands in the air. "Hello? Earth to Caeden and new girl."

We both shook our heads and I blushed. His cheeks were flaming too.

Caeden tossed his thumb over his shoulder and then stuck his hands in his pockets. "This is my annoying brother, Bryce."

Bryce smiled. His brown hair was shaggy, and like his brother, his eyes were a bright blue. His face was more round compared to Caeden's chiseled features. With his floppy hair and easy smile he reminded me of a lap dog.

Bryce extended his hand to me, "Bryce," he said. "The unfortunate younger brother of this one."

I smiled. "Sophie."

Bryce stepped back and lovingly rubbed an old green Jeep. "And this is the love of my life, Stella."

Caeden punched his brother. "Dude, you are so weird."

Bryce laughed and danced away. Walking backwards, towards the school, he said, "I never claimed to be normal Caeden. You know that."

Caeden narrowed his eyes and I would swear for a moment they flashed gold. A small growl escaped his throat.

Bryce turned completely around and sauntered away. Caeden shook his head. "Ignore him. I do."

I smiled at him. "Granted, I've never had siblings but I was always under the impression that it was your job to annoy each other."

He laughed and we started walking. "That's very true."

Just then a car came screeching through the parking lot. Tires squealing, music blaring, the reckless driver swung into the parking space. The car was a shiny new Audi S5 coupe.

Caeden glared at the tented windows and visibly bristled. A tall, muscular, blond guy got out of the car, with a smirk on his face like he owned the place.

Caeden growled and took my hand pulling me in the other direction towards the gym entrance.

A deep male voice said, "Caeden my friend."

I watched Caeden's face tense. His teeth were clenched and his jaw was twitching. He moved me behind him and tuned around.

The blond guy stood with his arms crossed over his chest grinning. "Travis," Caeden rasped. "What do you want?"

The boy, who like Caeden, really looked more like a man, tried to peer around Caeden to look at me. Caeden's grip tightened on my hand to the point that it was painful.

Travis' dark eyes peered into Caeden's. "I just wanted to meet your friend." He put his hands up like he was surrendering. "Don't get your panties in a bunch."

Caeden growled and Travis smiled. "That's right, breathe, control your temper Caeden. We wouldn't want to have you exploding out of your clothes in the school parking lot, now would we," said Travis tilting his head.

Caeden took several deep breaths. "Come on let's go," he said to me.

Travis clapped his hands. "Good boy Caeden. That's right walk away. You know you'd never win."

Lighting fast Caeden turned around and with a loud thunk sunk his fist into Travis' face. Caeden quickly pulled me away from the scene, his chest was heaving and he seemed to be vibrating, or maybe shimmering was the better word, around the edges. I looked around expecting a crowd to have gathered but no one seemed to have noticed. All in all the interaction hadn't lasted long.

Once we were safe distance away, in the cover of the gym hallway, I pulled Caeden to the side.

"What the hell was that about?" I asked.

He took a couple of breaths, his nostrils flaring. "It's a long story."

"Is everything a long story with you?" I demanded my hands on my hips.

He sighed and looked into my eyes. He looked sad. "Haven't you ever had a secret that you're bound to protect?"

"No," I scoffed.

He quirked his eyebrow.

"Maybe," I conceded.

He leaned his head against the cement wall and closed his eyes. "I just can't stand the guy, okay?"

I quirked my head. "We went from secrets to you just hate the guy. I'm lost," I said.

He smiled, barely. "Don't worry your time to know will come. Just be patient."

I groaned. "I'm so confused."

He grinned. "That's the point."

"You're evil," I said.

"I'm the good guy," he whispered in my ear making me shiver.

Suddenly the bell rang making me jump. "Can you remember your way to class?"

"Yeah," I croaked and then he disappeared.

Blinking, I started down the hallway.

I practically ran down the hallways, gym was on the complete opposite side of the school from the math hallway, and somehow I made it there early. Only three other people were in the room. Mrs. Harding glared at me and I ducked my head.

Bryce came in, smiled at me like an eager puppy, and took the seat next to me.

More people filed in, Travis, the guy from the parking lot, included. He took the seat behind me.

I turned to look at him. "How's your face?" I asked. It had sounded like Caeden broke his nose but behind me all I found was smooth pale skin.

I raised my eyebrows. Travis smirked.

"Why are you asking him about his face?" asked Bryce.

I turned back to Bryce. "Because Caeden punched him in the parking lot," I whispered. "And it sounded like he broke his nose."

Bryce burst out in laughter. He eyed Travis with a smirk. "Hasn't your dad ever told you not to mess with an Alpha. You will get burned. Or, I guess in this case, punched."

A ruler slapped down on Bryce's desk making him and everyone else jump. Bryce growled. What was with all this male growling?

"Mr. Williams you should know by now that the second bell means no more talking. And you-," she said pointing to me. "I knew you were trouble." She narrowed her eyes at me. I gulped.

My back was rigid the whole class. In fact, I was scared to even blink. In part because of Mrs. Harding but she wasn't the whole reason. Every little bit Travis would tug gently on my hair or touch my back, or neck. I wanted to squish my eyes closed but I knew Mrs. Harding would accuse me of not paying attention. Bryce kept eyeing Travis like he wanted to bite him or maybe just defend my honor. I wanted to cry. His touch was creepy. It made me feel like spiders were crawling all over my body. Something inside me screamed that he wasn't supposed to touch me. At one point a whimper escaped my lips and in the silent classroom Mrs. Harding turned to glare at me.

When the bell rang I picked up my backpack and ran. I was doing a lot of running around this place.

I slid into a chair in the very back against the wall in my next class just in case Travis was in here too. Luckily, a girl with long curly red hair took the seat next to me.

"I'm Charlotte," she said. "A friend of Caeden's."

"Hi," I said politely. On the inside however, I was seething. Was this his girlfriend? I had never thought to ask. Suddenly I wanted to jump out of my desk and smack the pretty red head next to me. I had the primal thought of, *he is mine.*

"Just friends," she said as if she could read my mind. Had it shone so plainly on my face?

I smiled and looked away ashamed. She seemed content to say no more and I was relieved. I was extremely embarrassed. Since when did I act like a crazy hormonal teenager? And it was more than that, I felt like I owned him. Like no one else could have him. Once again I had the thought, *he is mine.* It was weird. We weren't even a couple. Heck, we weren't even friends. We were just mere acquaintances.

Lunch was next and despite my earlier coldness Charlotte walked with me. She held her books close to her chest and her green eyes kept scanning the halls. She reminded me of a shy, small, fluttery bird.

"Hey," Caeden called coming down the hallway. "How's it going so far?" he asked me and then nodded his head at Charlotte like he was dismissing her. She scurried on down the hallway closer to lunch crowd. Now, she was more like a skittish rabbit than a bird.

"It's been okay," I said. "Charlotte seems nice."

"She is, just quiet."

I followed him through the lunch line and then to a table where Charlotte, Bryce, and a couple others were already sitting. He motioned me to a seat and then took the empty seat next mine.

"Everyone, this is Sophie," he said. They all nodded and smiled. "You already know Charlotte and Bryce," Caeden said. "That's Bentley," he said pointing to a tall, muscular guy, with golden brown eyes. His arm and chest muscles bulged out of his t-shirt and even though he was sitting down I could tell he was tall. Probably taller than Caeden. "This is Christian she's a junior like Bryce," this time he pointed to a blond girl next to Charlotte. She had an angular face, pale green eyes, and a willowy figure.

The girl named Christian smiled at me and said, "Call me Chris. Either way I still sound like I'm a boy."

Bentley laughed. "That's because you were supposed to be a boy."

She narrowed her green eyes at him. "I am obviously not a boy."

Bentley waggled his eyebrows at Chris, "Maybe I should check that out."

Christian tossed a fry at him and everyone was laughing, myself included. I was amazed at how easily I fit in with them. It normally took me awhile to find a niche in school but somehow I fit in here. They acted like a family and embraced me like I was a part of it.

Caeden shook his head and continued the introductions. "Lastly, we have Logan, Chris's older brother."

Logan and Chris certainly looked alike. They had the same angular cheek bones and pale green eyes. But where Chris was willowy, Logan was stocky.

Logan said to everyone at the table, "At least my parents got one boy. It was quite a surprise when that *one* came out," he said rolling his eyes at his younger sister.

She stuck her tongue out at her brother. "Well, it didn't change much did it. You still treated me like I was a boy and your own personal punching bag."

"That's only because you always wanted to follow the big boys around," he said motioning to himself, Caeden, and Bentley.

"When are you ever going to stop undermining girls? We've saved your butt plenty of times," she said including Charlotte in her tirade.

Logan quirked his head. "I see I can't win here."

Chris stuck out her chin. "That's right. Never pick a fight with a girl. You'll always lose."

Logan sighed. I nibbled my food and added to the conversation whenever I could actually get a word in.

I noticed the significant glance that would transpire between Bentley and Chris. Bentley would study her, with a gooey expression on his face, and once caught would look away, and vice-versa. Their glances didn't go unnoticed by Logan either and I could tell that even though Bentley was his friend he didn't like the idea of him with his sister.

I also noticed how Charlotte, bashfully, eyed Logan but he was absolutely oblivious to the whole thing. I guessed he was too worried about his little sister to notice her affections and I knew that Charlotte was too shy to do anything about it. She maybe said one word through the whole lunch.

Bryce, around a mouthful of chicken nugget said to Caeden, "Oh, by the way Travis is in our math class," he swallowed. Caeden's fist clenched. "And he couldn't keep his hands off Sophie. I would've hit him except... well you know Mrs. Harding," he said shrugging his shoulders.

I hadn't told Caeden on purpose. Anyone could see the animosity brewing between him and Travis and I didn't want to give him another reason to punch him in the face. I glared daggers at Bryce, who put his next chicken nugget down, and innocently said, "What did I do?"

"*He did what?*" Caeden hissed at his younger brother. Once again Caeden was doing that weird, shimmery, vibrating thing.

I put a hand on Caeden's shoulder. "It was nothing. He's just hoping to start something with you by bugging me."

Suddenly Caeden was standing. "I'll kill him," he growled.

"Sit down," said Bryce and Bentley. After a moment Caeden listened.

"You're just doing what he wants," said Charlotte and I was shocked to hear her voice.

Logan said, "Travis just wants to pick a fight with you. Don't let him. Show him who the Alpha male around here is."

I rolled my eyes at Logan's term *alpha*. What were we? Animals?

The bell rang dismissing us from lunch and I was once again thankful that Caeden had taken the time to show me around because none of the others had the same study hall that I did. I started to head in the opposite direction when suddenly Caeden jogged up beside me.

"Really, I know which way I'm going. You don't have to walk me," I said.

He shook his head. "Maybe I want to."

"Be my guest," I waved my hand in a flourish.

Up ahead of us I could see Travis and in the pit of my stomach I just knew he was going to be in my study hall. Sure enough Travis turned into the classroom in which I was headed. Caeden growled.

I stopped just outside the classroom to say goodbye to Caeden but he walked purposefully into the class. I quickly went in after him, afraid he was going after Travis again, but instead he strode to one of the two-seater tables, the farthest away from Travis, and sat down. I raised an eyebrow and sat down beside him.

"What are you doing?" I hissed.

"He's not a good guy, Sophie," Caeden whispered. "Trust me. You need to stay away from him and since *he* apparently can't stay away from you I'll be right here," he leaned back in the chair. "I won't let him hurt you."

"What happened in math was nothing," I said. "He just wanted to mess with me because he thought I'd come crying to you. I'm stronger than that. I think I know who to trust and who not to trust. And despite the fact that *you* punched *him* I can tell he's the wrong sort." I glanced over in Travis' direction and he was glaring at me. Not at Caeden but at me. I shivered involuntarily. "Something about him... it's not right."

"You can say that again," muttered Caeden.

Caeden somehow managed to convince the teacher that there was some kind of mix up and he was supposed to be in this study hall. Travis' face turned redder and redder in anger. I noticed his fists clenching and unclenching

Caeden and I talked and laughed. It was so easy being with him. He was like the friend that I never had. In just a few days' time we had become friends and his friends were pretty great too. I felt accepted. Like I belonged, and with moving all over creation that wasn't a feeling I was used to, I hoped it never went away.

Caeden and I had all three classes at the end of the day together. Luckily Travis wasn't in any of those and the tension in Caeden's shoulders seemed to relax a little. But there was still tomorrow. A whole new set of classes and chances were Travis would be in one. The school wasn't large and the senior class was small so lady luck was not on my side when it came to the avoiding Travis matter. I was never one to have good luck but I sent up a silent prayer that I would be wrong.

The last class of the day was woodshop. Woodshop? I looked at Caeden and the rest of the roomful of boys. It was a small class. Only fifteen of us where most classes had thirty or more people.

How did I end up in here? I silently guessed.

"My guess," said Caeden leaning over. "Is that this was the only class with an empty slot."

"Did I say that out loud?"

He chuckled. "Yeah, you did."

I buried my head in my hands. "I may not be a girly-girl but I draw the line at saws."

"Don't worry I'll be your partner," he reassured me.

"I won't be much help," I bit my lip.

"I figured that," he laughed.

The teacher came in and gave us some basic safety instructions and said that next class we'd watch a safety video and take a test. If we fail the test we can't work in the woodshop. For a moment I considered throwing the test but looking over at Caeden I couldn't resist the urge to see those muscles in action.

The teacher, Mr. Collins, was pretty cool. He looked more like a science teacher than a woodshop teacher though. He had thick, black framed, glasses and had a lanky build but he seemed patient. Patience would be golden for me. I had no idea how I would manage to get a good grade in this class. I only hoped Caeden had enough skills for the both of us.

Mr. Collins dismissed us early and I had to practically jog to keep up with Caeden's long legged stride.

"Hurry," he said. "This place turns into a mad house once the bell rings. The parking lot is a mess."

Out in the parking lot Caeden kicked his bike to life. "I'll see you at Lucinda's. I have some things I have to do before I come to work."

"Don't worry about it. Gram told me that you're always a little late, that you have to do some things to do first," I said with a wave of my hand.

"I'll see you soon," he reassured me before putting

his helmet on. I smiled as he climbed on the back of his bike. Kids began pouring out of the school and I decided I better get a move on. I saw Bryce and he waved. I waved back before climbing in my car and following Caeden out of the lot.

Gram had been right. *Lucinda's* was packed. No more than a minute after I had opened the doors there were fifteen people standing at the counter. Gram's store was tiny and I couldn't understand how they all squished inside. It reminded me of the circus and all the clowns in the tiny car. Luckily Caeden didn't take too long in getting there. Within moments we had a system down. I took the orders and called them out to him to fill. It went this way, non-stop, until closing. Exhausted I collapsed into one of the bistro chairs Gram had for customers.

Caeden laughed. "You better get used to it."

"Is it like this a lot?" I asked.

"Yeah," he said. "It sucks for us but it's great for Lucinda."

"I guess I shouldn't complain. She was kind enough to let me come live with her. But this place always used to seem so magical. Now, all I feel is stress."

Caeden grinned and a dimple appeared in his cheek. "I've always thought this place was magical too. Like an escape. But... I've always had a really bad sweet tooth, so maybe that's why I thought it was magical?" I laughed and he continued, "But the magic is still here. You just don't see it because now you're in the real world. You're not doing this for fun you're doing it for your grandma."

I sighed. "I guess we need to clean up so we can get home."

Caeden smiled. "I've got it."

"No, you don't. If we do it together we can get it done in half the time. Toss me that rag," I said. He did. "Come on, I'm tired, let's get this done," I turned on the radio cranking the music up.

I started twirling the rag and shaking my hair, which I

had finally released from a pony tail. I sashayed my hips and Caeden's cheeks turned pink and he got that strange look on his face again.

"Like what you see?" I asked.

His cheeks turned even redder and he looked away. He started mopping the floor while I wiped off the tables and counters. I was dancing and singing along to a song when my feet hit a particularly slippery spot.

My feet shot out from under me and I landed on my bottom. "Ow," I said.

Caeden busted out laughing and couldn't stop.

"Stop laughing at me," I said but my words didn't hold much backing because I was laughing too. "Help me up," I pleaded.

He started over towards me and suddenly his feet were in the air. He landed on the ground with a thud.

"Are you okay?" I asked trying to contain my giggles.

"Yeah," he said hoarsely. "I think the only thing I bruised was my ego."

I couldn't contain my laughter anymore and it bubbled to the surface. Caeden joined in. Tears began running down my face because I was laughing so hard.

Caeden tentatively started to stand. "I think the floor's dry now," he said, but tiptoed towards me anyway. He held out his hands and I took them.

The floor must have still been wet because suddenly we were falling. Caeden somehow managed to twist his body so that he was the one that hit the concrete floor and not me. I landed on top of him though, with my hands splayed across his muscular chest. His blue eyes met my brown eyes and it was like I was stuck there. I couldn't have moved if I wanted to. My eyes moved to his lips. I wanted him to kiss me. I leaned in closer. He moved towards me and our breaths mingled together. So close, there wasn't even half an inch in between our lips. I closed my eyes.

But nothing happened. I opened my eyes. "Not yet," whispered Caeden. His eyes were closed and I felt like his words were meant more for him than me. It stung though. I had never wanted someone to kiss me more than I wanted Caeden to kiss me.

Hurt, I rolled off of his chest onto the floor, and mumbled, "Sorry."

He sat up. "What are you sorry for?" he asked.

"Nothing," I snapped standing and brushing off my pants.

"Well, I'm sorry too," he murmured.

"What are you sorry for?" I repeated his question.

"Sorry, I can't kiss you," he whispered.

"Can't or won't?" I asked with my hands on my hips. He was still on the floor so I stood taller than him and was able to glare down in to his too beautiful blue eyes.

"Can't," he sighed. "I want to. Believe me. I have ever since I saw you three days ago but I *can't*. Not yet."

"You already said that, 'not yet', what does that *mean*?" I asked.

"There are some things you have to know first," he said softly.

"So tell me," I snapped.

"I can't. I promised I wouldn't even though everything inside me screams to tell you. Lucinda wants to be the one to tell you," he said, still sprawled on the ground.

"Tell me what?" I asked in exasperation.

"You'll just have to wait and find out," he said rather sadly.

I sighed. "I don't see what this has to do with not kissing me but I'm going to find out. Mark my words, Mister. I will find out," and with that I walked out the back door without a glance.

FOUR.

Weeks passed and Gram never spoke of whatever it was that Caeden couldn't tell me. I quickly got over our almost kiss and things between us returned to normal. Well, as normal as normal can be when you have a major crush on the person that has become your best friend. I felt like a silly little school girl having a crush on the most unattainable guy and not only was he unattainable he was my friend too. I had thought that day at Gram's store that he *wanted* to kiss me but the more time passed I was sure that I was wrong. It was already October and he acted as if that day had never happened, so I did too. But that didn't change the way I felt. I saw the way other girls in the school looked at him and it made my blood boil. Thankfully, he seemed completely unaware of their attentions.

I noticed tension arise between Gram and Caeden but I didn't ask either about it. I knew that whatever it was Gram would tell me in her own time. That didn't mean that I wasn't curious though, in fact, the curiosity was killing me. When she wasn't home I had resorted to snooping. But nothing seemed abnormal.

Halloween was fast approaching, only a week away. My parents called me every day to discuss the woes of high school life. They both seemed particularly interested in Caeden. When I mentioned Travis, my dad exploded and like Caeden said to stay far away from him. His defense was that he knew Travis' dad, Peter Grimm, and that the apple doesn't far from the tree.

"It looks great," said Gram, making me jump.

I had been so engrossed in my thoughts I hadn't heard her approach. "What?" I asked.

"The decorations," she said. "I haven't had the energy to decorate in years."

"Oh," I said. I had wrapped the front porch in orange and purple lights. A mummy dangled from the tree. I had even found a couple of gravestones and invested in some zombies coming out of the ground. "I've never had the chance to decorate for a holiday before. Dad didn't want to buy any decorations that we'd later have to store whenever we moved again."

She smiled. "Well, I love it."

"I didn't go too overboard?" I asked sheepishly.

"I don't think so," she said and hugged me. "Sophie, I'm so glad you came to live here. You've done me so much good."

"Gram," I said hugging her back. "Don't make me cry."

She brushed my hair with her fingers and pulled away. With tears in her eyes she said, "Sophie, there are some things I have to tell you."

I took a deep breath. Maybe I was finally going to find out what the big secret was. I had speculated for months.

"You must be cold," she said. "Come inside and I'll make you some hot chocolate and I saved you the last peanut butter fudge cupcake," she said shaking a bag. "Then we'll talk."

I took the bag from her. "Gram, are you bribing me with cupcakes?"

She smiled. "I'm just hoping it will soften the blow."

I followed her inside and sat at the kitchen table while she started the hot chocolate. I pulled the cupcake out of the bag and devoured the peanut butter goodness. I hadn't eaten in hours, I had been too consumed by my Halloween decorating.

"This is heaven," I said to Gram.

"They're pretty good but red velvet is my favorite."

"I like that too but the pumpkin cupcake you sell during the fall is pretty good. Although, neither of those comes close to peanut butter fudge."

She laughed. "You always would eat anything if it had peanut butter in it."

"Peanut butter is a major food group," I defended with a smile, making her laugh. "While I was at the store I picked up some chocolate for the trick-or-treaters."

"Oh, thanks," she said. "I'll pay you back."

"Don't worry about it Gram," I said.

She set down a steaming cup of hot chocolate in front of me and added a dollop of homemade whipped cream and chocolate shavings, she topped it off with one large marshmallow.

"Mmm," I said sipping it. "Mom, always tried to make this for me but she could never get it right."

"It takes a grandmother's touch," she said and sat down in front of me with her own mug.

"So," I started. "What is it you need to tell me?"

"I don't know where to start," she said and stirred her hot chocolate.

I looked into my own mug and said, "Caeden's in on it isn't he? He told me the first day of school that he wanted to tell me something but he couldn't because he promised you he wouldn't. He said you wanted to be the one to tell me."

Her eyes darkened. "Caeden's a good boy but he shouldn't have said anything."

"He didn't. He said that you would tell me when the time was right," I immediately came to his defense.

She took a deep breath. "Sophie, you're special. We're special. Me, your parents, you."

"What do you mean?" I asked.

"We're… There's no easy way to say this, Sophie," she said and stared into her own steaming mug of hot chocolate.

"Just say it," I said. "Like ripping a band aid. Quick and fast should lessen the blow," I joked.

"We're not human," she said.

I laughed and spewed some hot chocolate on the counter top. "What do you mean we're not human? Of course we're human." I grabbed a napkin to mop up the mess I had made.

"We're werewolves… Well, the proper term is shifter. Werewolves are evil, unholy, where we're not. There are different kinds of shifters we just happen to shift into wolves."

"Are you off your rocker?" I screamed. I couldn't believe she was continuing with this nonsense. This was ridiculous.

"Sophie, calm down and hear me out. Haven't you ever been able to smell things, or hear things, or move faster than normal?"

"No," I said too quickly and she knew she had me.

"It's because you're special," she said simply.

"I'm not *special*," I said. "You're telling me I'm a monster."

"You're not a monster. I'm not a monster. Neither are your parents," she said calmly.

"But you're telling me I'm not human! Oh my God! Caeden! Is Caeden a shifter?" I gasped.

"Yes," she said. "He's the Alpha."

No, no, no!

"Bryce?" I squeaked. "Charlotte?" Could quiet little Charlotte be a werewolf? Shifter? "Chris? Bentley? Logan?"

"All shifters," she said. "They make up the Williams pack."

"Pack?" I said. "Wait, wait just a minute… How can I be a shifter? I've never changed before?" I said thinking I had stumbled upon a solution to my problem. I couldn't be a shifter if I hadn't actually shifted. But that would make Gram crazy. I guessed a crazy Gram was easier to deal with than me as a wolf.

"Male shifters have their first change on the first full moon after they turn sixteen. Females have their first change on the first full moon after they turn eighteen."

"You mean to tell me that in January I'm suddenly going to become a wolf?" I asked crossing my arms over my chest in a defensive stance.

"Yes," she said. "You will."

"You're crazy!" I said. I buried my head in my hands.

"You're dad become Alpha of the Beaumont Pack

after your grandpa died. But then your father fell in love with a girl from a rival pack, your mom. So, he ran away with her, it's why they've never come back here. He appointed his second in command, Roger Williams, as the new Alpha. The pack is now the Williams Pack and not the Beaumont Pack. When Roger was killed his eldest son, Caeden, became the new Alpha."

"Stop it! Please stop it!" I cried. She quieted and let me take in all the information. "Rival pack? So, you mean there's another pack here?"

"The Grimm Pack. We were once all one pack, still led by the first wolf shifter, a Beaumont. The Grimm's never liked being led. They're evil and so are the ones that choose to follow them. They don't value human life, or shifter life for that matter, they consider themselves gods. But we're not gods, we're protectors, it's our duty," said Gram like we were simply discussing politics.

I covered in my ears. "This isn't real! I'm dreaming! You're lying!" I cried.

"No, I'm not," she said simply. "You're a shifter, Sophie."

"Why tell me now? Why didn't my parent's tell me when I was younger?" I asked.

"They've renounced what they are to protect you. That's why they ran away in the first place. Your mom was pregnant with you. The Grimm Pack would never have allowed you to exist."

I decided to play along even though I still didn't believe her. "Then don't they know I exist now? My last name is Beaumont."

"They think you're adopted, that's what I told everyone to protect you. They think you're merely human. They also don't know that Garrett and Christine ran away together. They think your father married a human woman and that's why he left."

"What about my mom?"

"They think she's dead. She faked her death to protect

you. Her own parents don't know the truth," she said folding her hands on her lap.

"How do you know, then?"

She quirked her lips. "Your father and I were always close. He was my only child. I told him that I didn't care what he had to do as long as he kept me in his life. His father didn't know. He was a stickler for the rules but your father's departure from Alpha was what did him in. He was already sick and that was the last straw."

"This is crazy! You're crazy!" I said standing. Before she could move to stop me I ran out of the room, grabbed my keys, and left.

* * *

I drove and drove and drove. I knew I was wasting gas but I didn't care. I had to get away. I finally pulled into the parking lot of Target and got out and walked through the store. After three laps of the store I went back to my car and leaned my head on my steering wheel. My phone kept ringing but I ignored it.

I sobbed. I didn't want to believe Gram's words but it all made sense to me. I had always had fast reflexes and been able to hear and smell things that I shouldn't be able too. My feeling of belonging here? Caeden? Did I only like him because I sensed that we were the same? I didn't want to believe that one.

The sky began to darken but I couldn't make myself move. My chest ached and finally, to my relief, my eyes ran dry. So, I just sat there.

I picked up my phone. Two missed calls from Gram and five from my dad and one from my mom which was probably still my dad just trying a different tactic.

I sighed and leaned my head against the head rest. I didn't want to go back to Gram's. I didn't want to have to face her. I wiggled around in my seat and decided if it came to it I would sleep in my car. It wouldn't be super comfortable but I could manage.

Suddenly my passenger door opened. Shocked, I

gasped. How stupid of me not to lock my doors.

Caeden slid in and closed the car door.

"What are you doing? Get out!" I screamed trying to push him out of the car. Unfortunately my tears decided now was the time to return and streamed down my face in a torrent and all the strength left my arms. They sank like noodles to my sides.

He gave me a sad look. "I'm sorry," he said quietly.

I sniffled. "It's all true isn't it?"

He nodded his head. I cried harder.

"My whole life has been a lie," I sobbed.

He held out his arms to embrace me. At first I didn't want to find comfort in his arms but I finally ceded. He held me to his chest and pulled me onto his lap.

"I'm sorry that you're upset but it's such a relief for you to finally know," he said as his fingers tangled in my hair.

He held me until I finally stopped crying.

Embarrassed I started to pull away but he just held me tighter. "I'm sorry for being such a cry baby."

He chuckled. "If I hadn't grown up knowing what I was all my life I probably would have acted much like you. I don't like surprises. I guess it's part of being the Alpha. You like to be in control." He cleared his throat like he wanted to say more but was stopping himself. I untangled my legs from his and moved over to my seat.

"What are you not saying?" I asked.

He cleared his throat and pointedly looked out the window.

"Caeden?" I demanded. "Just tell me. My family has kept so much from me. I can't stand it if you do too."

He sighed and ran his fingers through his dark brown hair. "I don't want to freak you out."

"I'm already freaked out! I'm not human! And apparently neither are you!" I cried throwing my hands in the air.

He ran his fingers through his hair again sticking it

up in every direction. "I'll start with the easier to process."

"Okay," I said taking a deep breath.

"You're the female Alpha of my pack. For two reasons. Reason one, you're a Beaumont and it's in your blood..."

"And reason two?"

He gulped and took a breath. "You are..."

"I am?" I prompted him.

"You are my mate," he whispered.

"What," I said. "on earth does that mean?"

"It means you're my mate. It's never happened before. It's one of our legends, that a few of us find our mates, we're meant to be together. We're made for each other," he said looking into my eyes. The truth shown, like a beacon in the dark, in his bright blue eyes.

I started hyperventilating. "You're telling me that there's some kind of weird wolf voodoo going on that tells us we're supposed to be together."

Caeden shook his head. "That's not it. Not entirely at least. Don't you feel attracted to me?"

"Yes," I admitted reluctantly and blood flooded traitorously to my cheeks.

"I didn't even know what was happening at first. Like I said no one has ever found their mate before, not that I know of at least. The pull to be with you is worse for me because my wolf has already been released. It'll be harder for you to once you shift," he sighed.

I buried my head in my hands. "So, you only like me because of *this*?" I said and threw my hands in the air. "It figures! I finally like a guy and he only likes me because of this stupid wolfy mate thing!" I ranted.

He grabbed my hands and held them still with one hand while the other grabbed my chin so I had to stare into his two endless blue pools.

"I had feelings for you before I even knew what was going on. I like you for you. In fact my feelings are stronger than what the mere insignificant word *like* can encompass.

But I'm not going to push you into anything. I want to date you, get to know you; I want you to fall in love with *me* not the wolf."

"But you already know that I have feelings for you," I said.

"There's a difference between knowing something and hearing it. So… do you want to date me?" He asked and he truly seemed unsure of my feelings.

I hesitated. I had feelings for Caeden, strong feelings, that was undeniable. I wanted to be with him more than anything. But I didn't want to take his choice away from him either. That seemed cruel.

"I don't want to take your choices away," I voiced.

"You're not. I choose you. Despite the bond I would choose you. You're everything for me. You're smart, funny, caring, and beautiful, shall I continue?" he asked leaning closer to me.

I laughed. "No," I said. "I get your point. I am pretty wonderful," I said jokingly and flipped my hair over my shoulder.

He laughed. "You're perfect."

"Far from it," I said.

"For me you are. Just like I'm perfect for you. Or so says the legend. We're made for each other. You know, the vampires have soul mates so it makes sense that we should too, I wonder why it hasn't happened before?" he stated.

One word stared blaringly at me. "Vampires? There are vampires?" I gasped going into shock yet again.

"Yeah," he said. "There are shifters, werewolves, sorcerers, and vampires. I've heard about fairies but I've never actually met one," he said rubbing the back of his head.

"Vampires?" I said again.

He rubbed my arm soothingly. "I know it's a lot to take in."

"A lot to take in? Are you kidding me? First, I'm told I'm not human, I'm a shifter. And not only are there wolf shifters but there are others. Then there are werewolves, but they're different from shifters. Then you tell me that we're 'mates' and 'we're made for each other'. Now vampires and fairies?"

"Breathe," he said.

I didn't realize that I had stopped breathing and the air whooshed out of my lungs.

"This is crazy!" I cried.

"It is," he agreed. "But it's real."

"Just give me a minute," I said. He sat back against the seat and didn't say another word. Finally I looked back over at him. Gripping the steering wheel in my hand I said, "Will I get to see you shift?"

He blushed. "Not yet," he said.

"Oh," I said.

"You better get home," he said starting to get out of the car.

"Wait," I said and put a hand on his arm. "How did you find me?"

He blushed. "You're my mate. I can find you if you're somewhere close, faraway not so much," he said.

"Can… Can I do that?" I asked.

"Yeah," he said. "According to the legends there's a lot more that we can do." Climbing out of the car he turned and said, "I'll follow you home. Make sure your safe."

I knew what he was really saying; he was making sure I didn't run away again.

I nodded my head and started the car. A moment later his motorcycle cranked to life.

As promised he followed me all the way home.

I pulled into Gram's driveway and waved to Caeden as he pulled away.

Gram came storming out the door. "Young lady, I do not appreciate you running out like that! I've been worried sick! Your parents are beside themselves!"

"I'm sorry Gram. I just needed to think. But it's fine Caeden found me," I said.

"Caeden?" she said.

"Didn't you tell him I was gone?" I asked puzzled.

"No," she said. "I probably should have."

"Well, he seemed to know that I had left and that I was upset."

"He's a good boy. A good Alpha too. He's young but he's strong," she said like she was selling him to me.

"He said I'm his mate," I said.

"I know," she said.

"You know?" I asked.

"He came to me right away. I'm the head elder so they come to me for consultation. He wanted to know if it was possible. I said it is."

"But how would you know if it's never happened before," I said.

"It's happened once, as far as I know, before," she said.

"Who?" I asked.

"Your parents."

"My parents?" I asked.

"Come on, it's cold out here," she said motioning me into the house. "Shifters all had mates a long, long, time ago. When we first started shifting. Then something happened and it stopped. The mating, the bonding, moved from fact to legend. Hundreds of years passed. For whatever reason it's starting up again."

"And my parents were the first?" I asked.

"Yes, it's why they defied their packs, their whole lives, for each other," she said.

I sat down with a huff on the couch. "This is a lot to take in."

Gram came over and patted my hand. "I know sweetie. I know."

FIVE.

Wolves. Shifters.
I'm a wolf.
I'm a shifter.

I stared at the ceiling of my room and tried to make out shapes and patterns while I contemplated the nightmare my life had become. I had never considered the existence of the supernatural and here I was a part of it! It was crazy, unbelievable.

Caeden and the others had done a good job of acting normal and letting me process the news. After all, my whole world had been blown apart.

Gram stuck her head in my bedroom door. "I have to go meet with the shifter council. Can you hand out the candy?"

"Sure," I said. I sat up and looked at her. "So, is that where you go when you disappear for a whole day?"

"Yes," she said and looked at her watch. "I'm late so I don't really have time to talk. I'll be in late." She came over and kissed me on the cheek. "We'll talk later, okay?"

"Yeah," I said and plopped back against my pillow.

She smiled and left.

I couldn't get my thoughts to shut up so I decided to busy myself by cleaning the house. I scrubbed the bathroom until it was sparkling and polished the hardwood floors. I vacuumed the carpet in the bedrooms and wiped everything down. Once everything was sparkling clean I started to organize, starting with the DVD's and moving on to the bookshelf. I ate a bowl of cereal for dinner and then proceeded to scrub the sink clean. There wasn't much left that would distract my mind but just then the doorbell rang and I realized I had completely forgotten about the trick-or-treaters.

I opened the door to a chorus of, "Trick-or-treat," from a fairy, power ranger, and Darth Vader. I gave each of the kids a handful of candy and they left happy. From that moment on the doorbell rang non-stop. I was bombarded by

Frankenstein, witches, and an assortment of Star Wars characters that seemed to be the most popular.

I felt like a jack-in-the-box hopping up and down every time the doorbell rang. At least, I mused, my legs were getting a work out.

When I ran out of candy the kids moaned and groaned. I felt bad but I thought it was pointless to run to the store and get more. By the time I would get back it would be past most of these kids bed time.

I turned off the porch light and hoped that people would get the message and not come knocking anymore.

After about fifteen minutes of silence I decided that I was probably safe and no more kids would come so I pulled on some pajama pants and a sweatshirt. Gram hadn't called and normally when she left for a meeting with the shifter council she didn't come in until really late. I popped some popcorn, added butter, and put a movie on. I knew I should have been doing my homework but I figured I'd do it tomorrow. I was just beginning to fall asleep when I heard a scratching at the door.

Startled, I sat up straight on the couch, looked around, and clutched my heart so it wouldn't beat out of my chest.

I stood up and heard more scratching. I opened the door and said, "Sorry, I'm out of candy." Rubbing my sleepy eyes I realized that no one was at the door. Not a person at least.

A huge wolf sat on my front porch, its tongue hanging out of its mouth, with blood matting its fur.

I screamed and backed away towards the kitchen.

"Oh my God," I said and clutched my head so I wouldn't faint.

The wolf strode confidently into the house and collapsed onto the floor breathing heavily. I quickly realized that the wolf was seriously injured. Huge lacerations ran down the wolf's body, like claws, one was so deep I was sure I could see bone.

"Oh, dear," I said. Blood was quickly pooling on the

hardwood floor that I had just polished. I looked in panic at the wolf. "I don't know what to do!" I cried to whoever the shifter on my floor was. The huge wolf lifted its shaggy head and then plopped it back down on the floor. Its fur was a beautiful silver gray color but the silver was quickly turning red as blood oozed out of the wolf's wounds. The wolf's very human blue eyes bore into mine.

The wolf lifted its head again and motioned me back. "You want me to go into the kitchen?" I asked.

The wolf nodded its head yes. I put my hands on my hips. "I don't see how I can help you from the kitchen but fine. I'll go. Just bleed to death on my floor for all I care," I said throwing my hands in the air. "Stupid, stubborn, wolf," I muttered going into the kitchen.

A moment later a very human hand clamped down on my shoulder, startling me, and making me let out a blood curdling scream.

I turned around to face Caeden. "A little warning would have been nice," I said. "Where are your clothes?" I added noticing the fact that he was completely naked except for a blanket draped haphazardly around his waist. His chest was well defined and his biceps were huge. Unfortunately, for me, the image was destroyed by the deep cuts on his right side. "Oh my God!" I said, my fear of blood suddenly gone, I tentatively touched the skin at his side. He flinched. I could see dirt and gravel caked into the five deep cuts. "Caeden," I whispered "What happened?"

"Travis and his idiotic father," he growled and sat down in one of the kitchen chairs. "As for my clothes, when we shift, our clothes don't shift with us. When you're a shifter you have to be comfortable with nudity. It's a fact of life."

"Oh so this," I said motioning to the blanket. "Is for my benefit?"

He blushed and ignored me. He lifted his arm up and poked at his wounds wincing. "Where's Lucinda?"

"She left for a council meeting this afternoon. She

said she wouldn't be back until late," I answered him.

"*Great*," he said rolling his eyes. "I'm going to need you to help me then. I don't have much time. We heal fast, but," he said looking at his deep wounds. "Sometimes not fast enough. Go to the hall closet and pull out the large black case on the floor."

I did as he said but the box was too heavy to lift so I had to drag it into the kitchen. The lock was a set of numbers, which he quickly rattled off, and the trunk unlocked. I looked up at Caeden and I could see that his eyes were growing foggy and that he looked close to passing out.

"Let's get you to the couch," I said and wrapped my arm around his uninjured side. Slowly we made our way to the couch where he collapsed. I had to pull the heavy trunk into the living room. Caeden's eyes were closed and his breathing was abnormal.

"Stay with me Caeden," I whispered. He looked close to death and as if my heart sensed it, it began to thump erratically in my chest. Suddenly my feelings for Caeden came to the forefront of my mind. He was my mate. My mate! And I was going to lose him! We hadn't even gone on a date! I hadn't even kissed him! I had been too wrapped up in my discovery of shifters to even think about a relationship with Caeden or the fact that we were mates; we were made for each other and here he was dying underneath my fingertips.

I opened the lid of the large black trunk and found what looked like a mobile hospital. There were gloves, masks, syringes, all kinds of medical liquids, sutures, bandages, and other items that I had never seen before that I assumed were specifically for shifters.

I pulled my cell phone out of my pocket and rang Gram. It went straight to voicemail. "Gram, it's Sophie. Caeden's here. He's hurt. It's bad Gram. He seemed fine one minute, alert, and now? Gram, I think he's dying. Please get this, hurry!" I said into the phone and hung up. I only hoped she got my message soon enough.

"What do I do?" I said to myself looking into the case. I pulled on a pair of surgical gloves, grabbed some gauze, and alcohol. I figured the first order of business was to clean the wound.

I poured the alcohol into the wounds and Caeden came to life with a furry. He started screaming and cussing. "I know, I know," I murmured. "It hurts. I'm sorry. I have to clean the wound."

He growled through clenched teeth. A few tears leaked out of my eyes. "I'm sorry, Caeden, I don't want to hurt you," is sobbed.

His breath hissed in and out through his teeth. "You're doing a great job," he said. "Don't worry about me. I'll be fine."

"No, you won't!" I cried. "I can feel it," I said and touched my heart, not caring about the blood I smeared on my sweatshirt.

He looked away and then met my eyes with a steely resolve. "I'll be fine, for you." His breath hissed in and out again. "I'll make sure of it."

I shook my head. "I don't know what I'm doing! I'm not a doctor!" I cried.

He collapsed back against the couch. "Do you see that small vial of gold liquid?"

I began pulling out the different vials until I found one that was gold. "Found it," I said holding it up.

Taking a few strangled breaths he said, "You're going to need to pour that into each wound and then stitch it up."

"Okay, I can do it," I said. "What did they *do* to you?" I asked not expecting an answer.

"Normally, we heal fast, the only thing that... kills us is... an attack from... another... Alpha... or silver..."

I could tell he was fading fast so I poured the gold liquid into his wounds. The raw skin sizzled and popped. I grabbed a needle and sutures and pulled his skin together. He groaned and bit his lip. "Do it quick," he moaned.

"I've never done this before," I whispered.

He groaned.

To distract him while I stitched him up I said, "So silver? I thought that was werewolves?"

He groaned and it was a minute before he finally answered. "Silver is deadly... to werewolves too, more so, than it is to us... For shifters it gives us an injury... that doesn't heal fast... which can lead to death... whereas if silver... enters a werewolf's system... it kills them... And... for shifters... only another... Alpha's attack... can kill... an Alpha..."

"So, is that what happened? You were attacked by another Alpha?" I asked. I had the worst laceration stitched up and so I moved on to the next most severe one.

He growled as the needle entered his skin and his breathing turned rapid. Sweat drenched his body. His eyes slowly closed and didn't reopen. "Caeden? Caeden? Caeden!" I screamed and shook his shoulder. His eyes slowly opened. "Stay with me," I begged. "Don't leave me. Talk to me, please?"

He grunted and had me repeat my question. Slowly he answered, "Yeah, Travis' dad... Peter... is the Alpha of the Grimm Pack... and he did this," motioned to his wounds.

"And since you're an Alpha?" I prompted him to get him to keep talking. I was scared of what would happen if he stopped.

"It won't heal on its own," he answered. He took a couple of breaths. "In fact it wouldn't heal at all if it weren't for that," he said and pointed to vial of gold liquid.

To keep him talking I said, "Oh, really. What is it?"

"You really want to know?" he asked with a quirk of his brow. I was pleased that he still found some amusement despite the dire situation he was in.

"Yes," I said as I finished the final stitch on his the third claw mark.

It's... fairy dust."

"Fairy dust? Sounds kind of Peter Pan to me," I said starting on the fourth one.

"That was pixie dust," he said and tried to smile but it turned to a grimace.

I could see some color returning to his cheeks and his speech was getting better. His eyes didn't look fuzzy anymore. "Well, you'll have to remind me to thank the fairies because this stuff is working. You look like a new man."

He gave me a look. "Well, maybe not a new man," I conceded, "but you do look better," I said and shrugged my shoulders.

"Better's good," he said.

"Why did they do this?"

He huffed and said, "I was patrolling the woods when they snuck up on me, Travis and his dad, I was alone..." he looked at his wounds. "And you know the rest."

"Why were you patrolling the woods?" I asked.

"To keep people safe. Normally we go in pairs. Me and Bryce, Bentley and Chris, and Logan and Charlotte. But I got the bright idea to be the big shot Alpha and go out by myself. Look where it got me?" he said rhetorically.

"But why do this?" I asked. "They could have killed you."

"They did it to prove a point. That I don't deserve to be Alpha. Peter thinks that if he kills me he'll gain control of my pack. He's wrong. First, because my pack is too stubborn to follow him... and second because you're the rightful Alpha."

"Me? I know you said I have Alpha blood because of my dad but... I know nothing about being a shifter. I only found this out a couple of weeks ago. I'm no leader," I said.

"It's in your blood," he said.

"Really? Because I've had my blood tested and ALPHA never came back in the toxicology."

He tried to laugh and then winced.

"Sorry," I said. "I shouldn't have tried to make you laugh."

He sighed. "Don't worry about it. I'll be fine in a couple of hours."

I clipped the final stitch and sat back on my heels. "You're going to be okay?"

"Yes," he said. "I'll be back to normal in no time."

"Good," I said and hit him as hard as I could on his uninjured arm. I stood up and glared down at him. A few tears came cascading down. "Caeden Williams don't you *dare* do that again! And just so you know I can't stand the sight of blood."

"Sophie," he whispered and tried to grab my arm.

"Promise you'll never do it again," I said softly.

"I promise." he said and then whispered, "I'm sorry."

"You better be, Mister. I've been worried sick. I may have acted calm but I was far from it. I've never..." I paused. "...been so worried for another person... I thought I was going to lose you... I can't..." I said. I ducked my head shaking it back and forth.

His hand gently caressed my cheek and I realized that I had collapsed against the flower print couch. Silent, choking, sobs escaped my chest.

"I'm sorry, Sophie. I'm new at this... I haven't ever had someone... I mean, I know we're not together but..."

"Stop Caeden," I said. "I can feel it too. We're mates. We're supposed to be together. I can't deny it anymore. I *want* to be with you. When I thought you were..." I choked on the word, "dying, I thought I was dying too. I felt so helpless."

"You want to be with me?" he asked.

"Yes," I said. "I have ever since I first saw you. I just... I didn't want to think it was because of some crazy wolf stuff. But... I know that my feelings would be there anyway... despite us being mates."

He smiled. "I want to kiss you now," he said.

I laughed. "You almost die and you want to kiss me."

He smiled even bigger. His white teeth glimmered in the dim lighting. "All the more reason," he said and finally, after months, pressed his lips against mine.

A fire consumed me, starting at my center and

moving up. His lips devoured mine. I pressed my body as close to him as I could without hurting him. My fingers tangled in his hair.

Visions swam past me. One was of Caeden holding me, we were both crying, and I was covered in dirt and grime, my clothes torn. In the next one we were in the woods and Caeden was telling me that everything would be okay. Another was of me in a white dress walking down the aisle to a dashing Caeden. Then there was one of Caeden carrying me through the front door and into the bedroom of a tiny little cottage. And the last... in the last one my stomach was large and round and Caeden was touching my stomach with a look of wonder on his face.

Slowly, he pulled away from me.

"Did... did you see that?" I asked breathlessly.

He nodded his head, "Do you think... that was our future?"

"I think it was," I said and put my fingers to my still tingling lips. They felt warmer than the rest of my body.

"Wow," he said and settled back down against the cushions.

"Yeah, wow," I echoed. I stood up and grabbed the blood soaked bandages and other assorted pieces of trash. "I'll be right back," I said. "Don't go anywhere."

He chuckled and then winced, "Don't worry. I'll be right here."

I threw away the trash and pulled off the surgical gloves and tossed them in too. Blood soaked my sweatshirt so I took it off and tossed it into the trash, it was beyond saving. I puttered into my room and put on a long-sleeved black shirt over my cami.

"Are you okay?" I asked coming back into the living room. His naked chest stared me in the face and already I could see that his wounds were disappearing.

"I'm fine," he said and grimaced.

"Liar," I said and bent down to peer inside the trunk full of medical supplies. "How does Gram even have this thing?" I asked motioning to the trunk.

"We get injured, a lot. Most of the time we heal fast but bigger stuff takes some time, like broken bones, or this," he said pointing to the claw marks. The five lines were now completely closed, the stitches I had just put in were gone, and an angry red.

"Well, is there any pain reliever in here? You can give me the tough, 'I can handle anything', Alpha spiel all you want," I said.

"Right there," he said pointing to a bottle of little white pills.

"How many?" I asked.

"Two," he said.

"Let me get you a glass of water," I said.

He took the pills from me and swallowed them without any water. I rolled my eyes. "I still won't be satisfied until you drink a whole glass of water. Don't you know you're never supposed to take any medicine without water?"

"Sophie," he said. "I'm tired."

"Oh no, Mister, you're not getting off that easy. You know, I kind of like this. It's empowering getting to boss you around like this."

I disappeared into the kitchen and came back with a full glass of water, "Cheers," I said and handed it to him.

He rolled his eyes, downed it all in one swallow and said, "Happy now?"

"Very," I replied.

I closed up the trunk and had to push it back into the closet. The thing was either entirely too heavy or else I was entirely too weak.

Caeden cleared his throat when I came back into the room.

"Yes?" I said.

"Will you lay with me? I just… I don't want to be by myself."

"Oh," I said and paused. "I guess so."

"Thanks," he said and blushed. He pulled the back

cushions off of the couch and scooted over to make room for me. I blushed and laid down beside him, careful not to jostle him, for fear of hurting him. He grabbed an extra blanket from off the back of the couch and draped it over us. His arms snaked around me and pulled me closer. I was suddenly very aware of the fact that I was lying next to a nearly naked Caeden. My cheeks flamed but in the dark room he couldn't see it.

I must have fallen asleep because the opening of the front door startled me. Somehow in my sleep I had turned to face Caeden. My face was pressed into his warm muscular chest and his arms held me close. He snored softly in my ear. He looked completely at ease in his sleep.

A light flicked on and Gram appeared. "Sophie," she said startled.

I realized the compromising position I was in and tried to pull away but Caeden's arms only tightened around me.

I gave Gram a sheepish look. "He didn't want to be alone," I defended.

"Uh-huh sure," she said. "So what happened? I just got your message and broke about seven traffic laws on my way here. But it looks like that was unnecessary."

"Gram," I said sternly, still trying to pull out of Caeden's arms. "He was *dying*. Travis' dad attacked him. He had five really deep cuts. I had to pour some kind of gold liquid into them, he said it was fairy dust, and then stitch him up. I didn't think he was going to make it. At first he seemed fine and then all of a sudden he just… wasn't. I didn't know what to do."

She came over and removed the blanket that was covering us. Her breath hissed through her teeth. "*Peter*," she growled. She looked at Caeden and ran her fingers through his hair. "He's just a boy. How could Peter do this?" Her fingers trailed the red marks covering his side. Even in the dark I could see that they were slowly turning pink.

"This Peter sounds pretty evil to me," I whispered.

"He's a bad man," she said. "But murderer? I just... I guess I want to believe in the good of humanity too much." She paused and sat down in the arm chair. "Go on to bed, Sophie. I'll sit with him."

"No!" I said a bit too quickly. "I mean... I gave him some pain killers and he'll be out for a while. You need some sleep. I'll stay here."

She eyed his arms wrapped around me and stood. She shook her head. "I guess I'm going to have to get used to the fact that you're mates now. I can't keep you apart, and I wouldn't anyway, he's a good kid. It's just going to take some getting used to."

I gave her an apologetic glance. "I don't want to be away from him," I said.

"I know, sweetie." She said and patted my leg before covering us both up with the blanket. "It's only going to get worse now, the pull to be with him. It'll get so it's hard to fight it."

I looked at Caeden's face, so peaceful in his slumber, "I don't want to fight it. I want him."

"Get some sleep," she said and disappeared.

SIX.

Light streamed through the living room windows when I woke up. Dust motes swirled in the air like tiny orbs of rainbows. Despite sleeping on a narrow couch, next to a very large Caeden, I had never slept better. I knew that I would be content to spend the rest of my life in his arms. While he was still sleeping I reached out and traced first his eyebrows, then his nose, chin, and finally his perfect lips. His lips cracked a smile and he let out a happy sigh in his sleep.

"Caeden," I whispered and shook his arm. "Wake up."

"Hmm," he mumbled in his sleep.

"Wake up, sleepy head."

He cracked his eye open and upon seeing me broke out in a smile. "Hey," he said.

"How do you feel?" I asked.

"Never felt better," he said.

"Yeah right," I said and pulled back the blanket.

The cuts were no longer an angry red but a whitish color. Tentatively, I traced them.

"See, I've never been better. Unfortunately though, I am forever marred. An Alpha's attack leaves a scar... That is if it doesn't kill you."

"Lucky for you," I said running my fingers lightly down the scars. "I like scars. They add character."

He smiled and lightly kissed my nose.

"Lovebirds," Gram called from the kitchen. "Come get some breakfast."

We both laughed and Caeden unwound his arms from around me.

"Caeden," Gram said appearing in the doorway of the kitchen wiping her hands on a towel. "I found some of Garrett's old clothes. They're in the hall bathroom. I'm sure you'll want to take a shower to get rid of the blood."

"Thanks," he said and disappeared.

"I'm going to go get dressed," I said to Gram.

I spent a lot more time in picking out my clothes than

I normally would but then scolded myself for being silly. Was I seriously going to dress differently for a guy? So, instead of the heather gray sweater dress I had pulled out, I put on jeans and a sweatshirt. I pulled my hair back into a ponytail and applied some lip gloss, my only concession. After all, if Caeden was my mate I should be able to wear a sack and he'd still think I looked good.

I must have taken a while to get ready because Caeden was already showered and sitting in the kitchen. His hair was wet and little droplets of water dripped onto the shirt he was wearing. Gram had found him some navy sweatpants, that were slightly too short, and a gray shirt that said NAVY on it. I smiled and he beamed back at me.

Last night had changed a lot of things. For one, I was now ready to embrace the fact that I was a shifter. Maybe it was the Alpha in my blood but I had the deep yearning to protect what was mine. Not just Caeden but my pack. Second, I no longer wanted to run from my feelings for Caeden. Last night had made me realize that life was short; you never knew when the end would come. I had thought I was going to lose Caeden. I never wanted to have that feeling again. I wanted to live, be a part of my pack, and be Caeden's mate.

Only a week ago my life had been completely transformed. It seemed like so much longer. It felt like years ago. But I was ready to take my rightful place. Be the female Alpha and whatever that entailed.

I sat down across from Caeden and Gram set a plate down in front of each of us before sitting down herself. Caeden had enough food to feed three people but he acted like it was normal and speared a piece of egg. I shook my head and took a bite.

"I can't believe Peter did this," Gram said. "It's appalling."

The thought of whomever this Peter was made the wolf in my blood howl. How dare he attack what's mine. A growl ripped through my body. Startled, I eyed the other two who stared back at me wide eyed.

"How did I do that?" I asked.

Caeden smiled. "You've accepted what you are, haven't you?"

I blushed. "Maybe," I mumbled.

He smiled. "The wolf will become more prominent now. Your instincts will start to take over now."

I buried my face in my hands. "I'm not sure I'm ready."

"Don't worry," said Caeden and I felt his large hand stroke my back. "I'll be here to help you every step of the way."

"Ugh," I groaned and looked up, meeting his cool blue gaze and Gram's warm brown one. "I feel so... protective. The thought of anyone hurting you... or the others..." I blushed and said, "It makes me want to rip their throat out."

Caeden smiled and looked at Gram. Gram shook her head. "I always knew you'd be a feisty one."

"Just wait until she shifts," said Caeden with a wide grin. "With that attitude she'll be unstoppable."

"I don't want to be unstoppable. I want to be *me*."

Caeden's hand stroked my back reassuringly. "Don't worry, babe, you'll still be you. Just a little stronger."

I quirked an eyebrow. "Babe?" I asked.

He blushed and removed his hand from my back. He sat back in the chair and tried to avoid eye contact. "Sorry," he mumbled.

"No," I said and smiled. "I like it."

"Yuck," said Gram. "I'm not sure my old soul can handle all this lovey-doveyness."

"Aww, Gram you were young and in love once too," I said and then blushed when I realized I had said *love*.

Caeden looked over at me and I blushed even redder. "I didn't mean... Just ignore me," I mumbled.

"Well," said Gram. "Why don't you two do something today? Go on a real date," she said with a wink.

"And try not to get yourselves killed."

Caeden smiled and said, "Sophie is that okay with you?"

"Of course," I said. "Especially the part about not getting killed. I don't know if I'll be able to handle you almost dying again."

Caeden looked down at the table. "Sorry," he mumbled. "I was being stupid."

"Yes, you were," said Gram sternly. "You know you aren't supposed to engage alone with rival shifters. And you may be the Alpha of this pack but you're young and inexperienced. Peter has led the Grimm Pack for many years now and knows many things that you do not. You can't be cocky when you're the Alpha, you have to be smart and diligent, in order to care for your pack. Your pack is your responsibility. You must think of them before you do something rash."

Caeden hung his head. "I've learned my lesson, Lucinda. It won't happen again."

"It better not. Especially if you're, my Sophie's, mate. You have to be able to protect her."

Caeden looked up at me. "I will," he said. "Till my dying breath."

"Oh, stop with all the melodramatics you two. This is ridiculous." I looked at Caeden. "Let's go before she starts reciting the shifter laws to us."

"You'll have to hear them eventually," Gram said.

"There's really shifter laws?" I asked. "Because I was just being sarcastic."

"Of course we have laws," she said.

I deposited my plate in the sink and shook my head. "Another time, then. I'm really not in the mood to be lectured on how to be a good non-human."

"Sophie," she said. "Being a shifter doesn't make you less of a human being."

"Doesn't it? Being a shifter means I'm *not* human."

Gram groaned and looked at Caeden. Throwing her

hands in the air Gram said, "She's all yours. Maybe you can get her to understand."

"I'll try," he said standing.

I narrowed my eyes. "Can we go now?" I snapped. "I feel like I'm suffocating."

Caeden cleaned his plate and said, "Let's go."

"Have fun you two," said Gram.

Caeden smiled. "I'll make sure she has fun."

I crossed my arms. "Are you suggesting I don't know how to have fun?"

"No," he started and upon seeing my look said, "okay maybe. You need to smile more. I've hardly seen you smile at all this last week."

"My whole world's turned out to be a lie. Therefore, I find that I don't have much to smile about."

He came over to me and with his fingers tweaked the corners of my lips so it looked like I was smiling. "Ah, there it is," he said when I finally smiled at his antics. I swatted his hand away.

"I plan on seeing that smile a lot more today. I have a whole day of fun planned," he said walking out the door.

"Should I be afraid?" I asked.

"Terrified," he said with a grin, the dimple appearing in his chin.

Outside I looked around and said, "Where's your bike?"

He gave me a look and I said, "Oh, right."

We got in my car and he said, "If you don't mind too much I'd like to stop by my house to change."

"Oh, sure." I said. "Just give me the directions."

Caeden gave me directions and it took about fifteen minutes to get to his house. We came to a gate and Caeden had to slide a card through a slot in order for the gate to open. The gate opened and I had to turn down a narrow, almost completely obscured, dirt road and follow it. Driving through here I felt one with nature. The trees created a natural green canopy and the smell of dirt, rain, and decaying leaves filled the air. It wasn't an entirely unpleasant smell. Squirrels continually jumped in front of the car so I had to keep hitting the breaks to avoid them. I didn't want to have a little squirrel death on my hands. Finally, the trees receded and a large white, plantation style, house appeared. "Wow," I said. "It's beautiful."

The house looked like something out of the civil war era. Bright green vines clung to the side of the house. I could see a large garage in the back that was obviously an addition. I came to a stop in front of the house on the circular driveway. Despite it being autumn everything here was still green. I felt like I had stepped into another world, like I was in some kind of enchanted green planet. For all I knew maybe I was. After all, if shifters, werewolves, vampires, and fairies could exist, then so could paradise.

"You like it?" Caeden asked.

"It's amazing," I said. "I always did have a thing for old homes. They seem so majestic." I shrugged my shoulders, "Old homes have a history and because I moved a lot I never felt like I had one."

He took my hand. "We can make a history together." I blushed and he unbuckled his seatbelt and said, "Come on in. My mom's dying to meet you."

I grimaced, "She knows."

He knew what I was talking about and said, "Yeah, she knows we're mates and she's ecstatic. So is my whole family. We're the first mates in a long time."

"But that's not true," I said. "Gram said my parents were mates. And what if they don't like me? What if I don't meet their expectations?"

"First off it's just my mom and annoying brother, whom you've already met, not my entire family. Yet," he added. "And I never knew that your parents were mates."

"Well, according to Gram they are. My mom was from the Grimm Pack and you already know about my dad. They risked everything to be together."

"Wow," he said. "I'll have to talk to Lucinda about it

some more. I wonder why them and why us?"

"I don't know," I said. "I guess we're just special."

Caeden grinned, "Alright enough stalling. Time to meet my mom."

"That's okay," I said. "I'm perfectly comfortable right here," I said and patted the leather seat to punctuate my point.

Caeden smirked. "You could be sitting on a bed of nails and you'd be comfortable right now wouldn't you?"

"Yeah, pretty much," I said.

He laughed. "It's just my mom."

"Fine," I said grumpily.

"Don't worry," he said. "She only bites sometimes."

"Sometimes," I gulped and he winked. I got out of the car and stalked around to Caeden's side. "Does she know what happened?"

"No," he said.

"Then isn't she going to be wondering where you've been?" I asked.

"Maybe," he said. "I'm gone a lot doing shifter stuff. Roaming the woods, chasing squirrels," he said with a grin.

I smacked his arm. "So, what's with the security gate?" I asked.

"That," he said, "is to keep the Grimm's out."

"Oh," was all I said.

He opened the front door and we were greeted first by a large sweeping staircase and then by the biggest dog I had ever seen, it resembled a horse more than a dog.

It tried to make a jump for me but Caeden grabbed the dog by the collar and said, "Bad, Murphy. Sit."

The dog sat and even sitting it almost reached my eye level.

"That's a huge dog," I said stating the obvious.

Caeden petted the dog affectionately on the head. "This is my dog. He's an Irish wolf hound. His name's Murphy."

"Hi Murphy," I said and tentatively stuck out a hand

for him to sniff me. I must have passed the test because he gave my hand a quick lick.

Just then another dog came trotting in followed by Bryce. "I see you've met Murphy," said Bryce. "I myself prefer smaller dogs. This lady here is my Bailey," he said petting the beagle that had stopped in front of him.

A voice sounded from our left. "Caeden Henry Williams where have you been? And don't tell me you were on duty because I know for a fact that you weren't."

Caeden groaned and turned to face the woman standing in the doorway to what looked like the kitchen. She was short with straight brown hair. Her hands were perched on her hips. She wore khaki pants and a white t-shirt.

"Hi, to you to mom," said Caeden.

"Caeden-," she started again before Caeden threw a hand in the air.

"Mom, before you give me the third degree, this is Sophie."

"Oh," she said and a huge smile appeared on her face. I noticed that like Caeden she had a dimple in her cheek when she smiled. "I'm Amy," she said and came forward pulling me into a hug.

I hugged her back. Her hug reminded me of my mom. A surge of sadness rolled through me. I missed my mommy.

"Don't think you're off the hook," she said over my shoulder.

"Wouldn't dream of it," muttered Caeden from behind me.

She pulled away and smiled at me with the same bright blue eyes that her son had, "I'm so happy my Caeden found you."

I blushed and Caeden warningly said, "Mom."

"Are you hungry?" she asked me.

"No," I said. "I just ate but thanks anyway."

"Now where were you?" she demanded, turning to glare at Caeden.

"At Sophie's," he mumbled.

"All night?" she asked him.

"Yes," he whispered.

"Alright, man!" said Bryce and Caeden punched his younger brother in the shoulder.

"It wasn't like that," he said. "I just spent the night."

"Why did you 'just spend the night' and not call me? I've been worried sick," she said.

"She has," said Bryce, "She even wore a hole in the rug."

"Bryce, go do something productive," Amy said.

Bryce picked up his dog, Bailey, and sauntered into the kitchen.

"Caeden," I said. "Just tell her. She's your mom. She'll find out anyway. Mom's always do."

Caeden sent me a betrayed look and said, "I don't want to worry her."

"I was worried all night anyway so tell me what happened," she said waving her hand impatiently.

"Peter attacked me," said Caeden. "That's why I went to Sophie's house. I hoped Lucinda would be there but she wasn't. Luckily, despite her fear of blood, Sophie helped me."

"What did he do to you?" shrieked Amy.

Bryce came back into the foyer. A line of worry puckered his forehead.

Caeden looked at me pleadingly. "Show them," I said.

He shrugged out of his shirt and turned so that his mom and brother could see the five white scars.

Breath hissed through their teeth and then Amy growled. She came forward to touch her son's scars. "He tried to kill you," she stated.

"He almost did," I said.

Amy looked over at me and pulled me into a bone crushing hug. "You saved my son."

"Hardly," I said. "He had to tell me how to do everything."

"Mom," Caeden whined pulling his shirt back down, "let her go. You're crushing her."

"It's okay," I said. Caeden shook his head.

"I'm going to go change and then Sophie and I are leaving," said Caeden. "So, please don't crush her to death while I'm gone."

Amy let me go and patted my hand. She smiled at me. "Sophie will be just fine," she said.

"Sure, she will," said Caeden going up the stairs.

Amy smiled and pulled me into the kitchen.

The kitchen was large with white cabinets and white marble countertops. The floors were a black and white checkered pattern. There was a large island with three chairs, Bryce was sitting in one feeding Bailey pieces of bacon, and then against the far wall was a large bay window with a table and chairs that served as the breakfast nook. The kitchen reminded me of a restaurant with its industrial size refrigerator, large stovetop, and double ovens.

Noticing my perusal of the room Amy supplied, "The pack eats here a lot and with that many hungry wolves you need a lot of food. One wolf is bad enough," she said. She shook her head, "They can eat enough to feed a small army in one sitting." She giggled and pointed to herself, "Me included."

I laughed, "Will I get like that?"

"Once you change, yes. It'll happen earlier if you start working out with the rest of the pack, which might be a good idea." She felt my arm and said, "Yes, you definitely need to bulk up."

"Bulk up?" I croaked.

Caeden came into the kitchen and said, "Your arms are fine don't listen to her." He had changed into a longs-sleeved blue shirt and dark jeans. The blue of the shirt brought out his eyes.

Amy let go of my arm and put her hands on her hips, "The girl should be able to protect herself. What if the Grimm's find out who she really is? Hmm? What then,

Caeden?"

He sighed and looked at me. With a sheepish look he said, "She's right, you should know how to defend yourself especially since you still have several months until you turn eighteen."

I gulped.

"It'll be fine," he said.

"Do you really think I'm in danger?" I asked.

"No," he scoffed. "It's just best to be prepared for any situation. Don't worry we'll go easy on you."

"Sure, we will," taunted Bryce.

"It was fun chatting with you guys but we've got to go," said Caeden taking my hand and towing me from the kitchen.

"It was nice meeting you," I said to Amy.

She pulled me into another hug but Caeden kept a hold on my hand. She patted my cheek and then turned to Caeden, "Now be careful with her."

"*Mom*," he groaned.

"Caeden," she said sternly.

"We'll be fine," he said and pulled me to the front door.

From the kitchen his mom said, "No funny business like last night, Caeden, do you understand me?"

"Yes, ma'am," He conceded and then we were out the door.

I started towards my car but Caeden gently pulled me towards the back of the house and to the garage. He punched in a code and the door rose. Inside was a mocha colored, Cadillac SRX, Caeden's motorcycle, Bryce's green 1999 Jeep, and then at the far end a new dark red Jeep Grand Cherokee.

Caeden looked longingly at his Honda motorcycle and said, "There's no chance of me getting you on this is there?"

"Not yet," I said with a smile.

"Not yet," he repeated, "I can live with that." He

towed me to the end of the garage and opened the passenger door of the red Jeep Grand Cherokee. "I guess we'll take this then."

I shook my head, "A motorcycle and a brand new Jeep." I clucked my tongue, "And you wanted to talk about my car."

He ducked his head, "The Jeep like the motorcycle was my dad's. I'd trade the cars to have him back any day."

I closed my eyes, "I'm so sorry Caeden. That was so insensitive of me. Please, forgive me."

He gave me a small smile. "There's nothing to forgive." He pecked me on the cheek and then closed the car door. The car still had the 'new' smell to it. Caeden opened the door and climbed in. "Actually," he said. "Before my dad died that was mine," and pointed to Bryce's Jeep, "and if I was lucky he'd occasionally let me borrow the bike."

"So Stella was yours?"

"Hey," he said in defense, "I didn't name the car Bryce did, so go poke fun at him."

He started the car and I sank back into the plush beige leather. "So, where are we going?" I asked.

He smiled, "Georgetown." He started driving down the narrow gravel road.

"That sounds good to me," I smiled. "I just want to get away from here." I chuckled, "Pretend I'm normal."

His hand rubbed my arm soothingly before his fingers tangled in mine. "I know this has been tough on you. I can't imagine if I had grown up not knowing what I was."

"It's a lot to take in. A lot," I said.

He stopped the car when we came to the gate and had to put some kind of code in so we could get out.

He looked at me sadly, "And then there's us."

"Yes, there's that too."

He pulled out onto the road and said regretfully, "It pains me that all of this has been sprung on you." He glanced over at me, "We'll take things slow."

I smiled and blushed. "I *want* to be with you," I said

and looked out the window. Boldly, I said, "There's no one else for me. I know that. I can feel it."

His eyes were hopeful as he said, "I want you more than anything. Being away from you is hard. I wanted so badly to tell you about all this when I first saw you but I couldn't. Then when I told Lucinda that we were mates she said that she thought it would be better if she told you, rather than me telling you. But…" He blushed and studied the road for a moment before continuing. "I feel like… there's some kind of physical…binding… I have to you. It's like there's a rope connecting us. Do you… Do you feel it too? Or am I just crazy?"

I was quiet and let his words sink in. What he was saying made sense. The pull I felt to be with him was like a rubber band. It stretched around us and when we were separated it pulled back but it created a pressure to be with him, like it wanted to snap back into place, and that place was his arms.

"I feel it too," I whispered. "It's like if I'm not with you there's this pressure pulling me back to you."

"Incredible," we said in unison.

"I wish we could talk to your parents. Maybe since they're mates too they could shed some light on the situation."

"Maybe," I murmured still rubbing my chest where Caeden's heart had been beating next to mine only a moment ago.

Caeden sighed and said, "I can see this is upsetting you. I want us to have fun today. So, from this moment on let's just be Caeden and Sophie, no shifter talk."

"Sounds good to me," I said.

He smiled and we began to talk about normal, mundane, things to pass the time.

* * *

When we finally made it to Georgetown it was early afternoon. The orange and red leaves created a false sunset. Despite it being the end of October it was fairly warm. A slight breeze had my hair dancing around my shoulders.

We managed to find a parking spot along busy Main Street. Caeden got out and put some money in the parking meter and took my hand. I looked at our intertwined hands and blushed. I looked up and met Caeden's eyes. He was grinning and the one dimple in his cheek showed prominently.

"Is this okay?" he asked with a glance at our hands.

"Mhmm," I said as my cheeks flamed redder. I wished I could blame my cheeks on the cold but it felt more like spring outside so I knew I would only make myself look sillier.

"Come on," he said pulling me down the street. It was crowded but not overly busy like I had originally thought. The buildings were all older, and I quickly realized they were old row homes, but they all contained high-end shops. I saw stores like, American Apparel, BCBG, Coach, Kate Spade, and many others. Caeden pulled me in and out of different stores. He bought himself couple of shirts and some new pairs of jeans.

"When you're a shifter you go through a lot of clothes," he shrugged handing the sales girl his credit card. Her eyes roamed over him and I instantly bristled.

As the sun started to go down Caeden's stomach gave a loud growl and mine followed suit. I giggled, "I guess we're both hungry," I said.

Caeden rubbed his stomach and said, "I'm starving. I think this may be the longest I've ever gone without eating."

I laughed, "That must be quite a feat."

"You have no idea," he replied towing me towards a fancy French restaurant.

"Oh, no, no, no," I said putting on the brakes. "That's too expensive."

He smiled goofily and said, "Anything for my lovely mate," and boldly kissed my cheek.

"Really," I said, "I'm not a fancy kind of girl." I pointed to the Five Guys down the road. "I'm more of a burgers and fries kind of girl."

Caeden grinned. "I'm falling for you more and more. Could you be more perfect?"

I blushed and ducked my head so he wouldn't see. I clutched his hand tighter and towed him down the street to the red and white burger goodness.

I ordered a little cheeseburger, fries, and a drink. Much to Caeden's chagrin I paid for my own meal. As I was getting my drink I heard Caeden order four of their biggest burgers with just about everything on them and two large fries.

I snickered when the girl at the register, who had been checking out Caeden despite the fact that we were obviously together, asked, "Is this to go?"

"No," said Caeden and pointed to me, "I'm on a date." He grinned at me and I blushed down to my neck.

The girl looked peeved but then brightened. "Are others joining you? They must with all that you ordered."

"Nope," said Caeden with a smirk. He rubbed his flat stomach and said, "It's all for me and I'll eat every last bite."

"Oh," she said looking slightly disgusted as she handed him back his change. I rolled my eyes and sat down at an empty table that was slightly out of the way. Caeden got his drink, swigged it down quickly, refilled it, and then grabbed a container of malt vinegar before sitting down across from me.

"That girl was so into you before she found out you were going to eat all of that," I remarked.

"Really?" asked Caeden looking up through his dark hair with those impossibly blue eyes. "Jealous?" he asked waggling his eye brows.

"No!" I scoffed as my cheeks flamed red. I was caught.

He grinned and his dimple stood out. He pointed a finger at me. "You so are," he scolded. He sat back and folded his arms across his chest. "I kind of like you jealous." He appraised me, "It's hot."

"Stop it!" I said as my face became even redder.

He grinned. "I don't think so. I like this."

I threw my hands in the air. "So, I have feelings for you. You already knew that. Isn't it logical that I would be jealous of another girl checking you out. Wouldn't you be mad if a guy was checking me out?"

"Ah," he sighed. "I don't think I'll ever get used to you acknowledging your feelings for me it's like music to my ears. As to another guy, if he dares take one look at you, I'll rip his throat out."

I shook my head at his words but it was the first sentence that struck me. Looking into his eyes I knew that Caeden was already in love with me and I knew that I felt the same. But I wasn't ready to admit it. We had been friends since I moved here but I knew that to say, "I love you", would mean another step in our relationship and I wasn't sure if I was ready. I was just getting used to idea of us being mates, being boyfriend and girlfriend; I wasn't ready to give him that piece of my heart yet. Once I said it there would be no taking it back and I wanted it to be special to the both of us. I wanted it to be because I had truly fallen in love with him and not because my body was telling me that I loved him.

They called my order number and a moment later they called Caeden's. He stood. "I'll get yours," he said with a wave of his hand to get me to sit back down.

He came back with our food and before I had taken one bite of my cheeseburger he was already on the last bite of his first.

He swallowed, took a sip of his drink, and grinned. "Sorry, normally I'm more mannerly but I was starving."

"You should have said something," I scolded. "I'm not used to all this shifter stuff," I whispered.

He stuffed some fries in his mouth while he unwrapped his second burger. "Don't worry, I'll remember, because if it's left up to you, you'll starve me to death."

I tossed a fry at him which he deftly caught in his

mouth. He smirked and I rolled my eyes.

"You're impossible," I muttered.

"That's what my mother says," he grinned.

"Oh," I said, "so, you're calling me your mother now?"

"No," he said quickly. "But that is what she tells me."

"Probably because it's true," I laughed.

He smirked. "How else do you think I managed to get Murphy? Do you think my mom would willingly let a seven-foot dog in her house?"

"Murphy's big but he's not seven-foot," I said sarcastically.

"Wanna bet?" said Caeden.

I shook my head. "Boys," I muttered.

"Seriously," he said. "If I put Murphy's paws up on my shoulders he's over seven-foot."

"I believe you," I muttered, "The dog's the size of a horse or maybe a small house."

"Don't diss the dog," he said around a bite of burger. "He's my familiar."

"Your familiar?" I asked.

"Yeah, you know, my *familiar*," he said with a flourish of his hand as he finished his large fry and started in on his third burger. He said *familiar* like I should know what it meant.

"No, I don't know. That's why I asked, Einstein," I said rolling my eyes.

"Well," he said and swallowed. "Every shifter has a familiar. It's an animal that you just kind of, *connect,* with. They *know* you. Supposedly they can find you anywhere. They're your animal counterpart."

"Do I have one?" I asked.

"Of course," he replied. "We just have to find it. Or maybe it'll find you."

"Didn't your dad have a familiar and your mom? I didn't see any other dogs there."

He chewed quietly and said, "My dad's familiar was a

Siberian Husky named Marlo but he died when my dad died. And my mom's familiar is a Siberian Husky too, her name is Mattie."

 I gulped. "Does that mean my familiar will be an Irish Wolfhound?"

 He laughed, "I doubt it."

 "Phew," I said and let out a breath. "I'm not sure one would fit through Gram's front door."

 "It would be a tight squeeze," he conceded.

 I finished my food while Caeden polished off his last burger and ate the last of his vinegar drenched fries. He finished and leaned back in his chair, rubbing his stomach. "That was good," he said.

 "Full?" I asked, quirking an eyebrow. I certainly hoped so. I had just watched him single-handily devour four massive burgers, two large fries, and two large drinks, in just a matter of minutes.

 "Mhmm," he said thoughtfully, "I think I saved room for dessert."

 "You're disgusting," I said with a laugh.

 His dimple appeared. "I can't help it. I'm part wolf. I have four stomachs."

 "That's cows, you idiot," I said with a laugh.

 He grinned, "Moo."

 "Let's go find you some dessert," I said getting up and throwing away my trash. Caeden quickly followed suit and held the door open for me.

 He took my hand and led me down the street towards a tiny ice cream parlor. He ordered a large root beer float and got me a scoop of banana ice cream even though I insisted I didn't want anything.

 We sat down at a table by the window. Caeden slurped his float while I stirred my ice cream.

 Taking a bite I said, "How did you know banana ice cream is my favorite?"

 "I, uh, I don't know. I guess it's a mate thing," he said shrugging his wide shoulders.

"Really?" I asked. "Hmm," I said thoughtfully. "Ask me what your favorite candy is?"

"What's my favorite candy?" he asked me.

I thought for a moment and replied, "M&M's?" I asked questioningly.

He grinned. "That's right. Let me guess yours." He thought for a moment and said, "Reese's cups?"

I laughed. "You're right! This is so cool!"

We finished our ice cream with a smile. He held my hand on the way back to the car. "I had fun," I said.

"Best day of my life," he said, "because I got to spend it with you."

I shook my head and smiled at him, "Suck up."

He feigned indignation, "Sophie, are you accusing me of lying?"

"Never," I said and we laughed all the way to the car. He held the car door open for me like a gentleman and then we started the long drive back home.

He held my hand as he drove. I had noticed all day that his hand always remained toasty warm.

"Why is your hand so warm?" I asked.

He gave my hand a light squeeze and said, "Well, shifters are always slightly warmer than the normal human. Once you shift the first time you get even warmer. But we're not that much above the average temperature for a human so it's nothing to worry about. It just always feels like we have a slight fever."

"But why?" I asked. "What's the purpose?"

He shrugged his shoulders and kept his eyes on the road. "The common theory is that it's because we're outside so much. It would suck in the winter if we had a normal temperature, since we're always running around doing our watches, we would get sick. So, I guess we're warmer so that we don't end up sick all the time. Because… uh… when we shift… our clothes don't shift with us…"

"So, you're saying when you go all wolf you lose your clothes, so you're like naked?" I gulped. I don't know why I had even bothered to ask. I already knew the answer from when Caeden showed up at my house last night.

He glanced over at me and winked. "You get used to the human anatomy real fast when you're a shifter."

I blushed an unhealthy shade of crimson. Oh dear, what would I do?

"Don't worry about it, yet," he said, "there's still time until you turn and I'll be there to help you."

"That's what I'm afraid of," I said.

He laughed, "Don't worry, I won't look." He glanced at me and wiggled his eyebrows, "That is unless you want me to."

"Stop it, please stop it," I said trying to hide my flaming cheeks. We didn't need any heat in the car, my cheeks provided plenty.

He laughed and squeezed my hand, "Really, I don't want you to worry about it. If it makes you feel better talk to Chris and Charlotte. They won't turn until after you but they've always known about the whole no clothes thing so maybe they can help you cope. They don't seem uncomfortable with the situation. But what do I know," he said shrugging his shoulders. He laughed and added, "I guess we all did run around naked with each other when we were little. So, you are kind of out of the loop."

"And you're not helping," I muttered.

"I'll be quiet," he said. But then a moment later he said, "Hey, why don't you come over to my house tomorrow. Sunday is our workout day although we work out pretty much every day this is the one time we're all together. The whole basement of my house is a gym and the whole pack comes over and we lift weights and do some martial arts."

I groaned. Exercise was not number one on my to-do list. I wasn't fat but I wasn't small either. I liked my size. I thought I looked healthy. But I guessed if I was a shifter then I better bulk up like Amy said. "Sure, why not," I muttered.

"Don't sound so enthusiastic," said Caeden with a smile. "Don't worry you'll love it," he said. "Just wait and see."

"Is that your favorite line, 'don't worry,' because it's really starting to get on my nerves? Don't you know that 'don't worry', usually means you *should* worry?"

He laughed and murmured, "We're a match made in heaven."

"More like hell," I said with a laugh so he'd know I was joking.

He was already pulling into Gram's driveway before I realized that I had left my car at his house. "Caeden," I said, "my car's at your house."

"I know," he said putting the car into park. "I'll pick you up tomorrow and take you to my house. You did agree to working out, remember? Or are you already chickening out?" he asked with an evil glint in his eye.

Despite my reluctance I was not about to prove him right, "Nope," I said. "I'll be bright eyed and bushy tailed tomorrow morning and be prepared to get your butt whooped," I joked.

"I hope that's a promise," he said with a grin and I smacked his arm. "I'll walk you to the door," he said getting out of the car.

I hopped out of the SUV and followed him to the door. We stood there for a moment just gazing at each other. His hand slowly came up to meet my face. His finger, ever so slowly and lightly, grazed my skin.

My heart raced and my body involuntarily leaned closer to his. My chest lightly touched his, sending electric currents through my body, I wondered if he felt it too.

He bent his head closer to mine. His breath tingled my face causing an erratic cadence to my heartbeat. I wanted to close those few precious gaps and press my lips to his. I wanted to kiss him and not think he was dying. But more than that, I just wanted *him*.

"I want to kiss you," he whispered.

I sucked in a breath and said, "Then do it."

His hand cupped my face and he pressed his lips to

mine. Heat coursed through my body and I found my arms wrapping around his neck holding him close. His other hand grabbed my waist. His scent invaded my senses like the most delectable drug ever invented; pine and cinnamon. My fingers tangled in his silky hair as our lips continued in their complicated tango. Kisses like this didn't exist. They shouldn't. A kiss like this was dangerous. This was the kiss someone gave you when they owned your soul.

Caeden owned my soul and I owned his.

He broke away from the kiss, his chest heaving, "I'm not sure I'll ever get used to that," he said.

I had seemed to have lost control over all body functions. I couldn't move my arms from around his neck and I couldn't get my voice to work to I mutely nodded my head in agreement.

He kissed me quickly, just a peck, but it still ignited the same fire in my soul.

"Night," he said removing my arms.

I didn't say anything. I just watched him walk to his car, a light chuckle trailing along behind him.

SEVEN.

I woke up and immediately dreaded what was waiting for me. All I could think about was treadmills, weights, and other unpleasant things.

On the bright side however, there was Caeden. But a hot, sweaty, Caeden sounded even more dangerous to my senses than the normal one.

I sighed and got dressed, figuring a shower was pointless.

Gram smiled when she saw me. She appraised my workout clothes and said, "I see Caeden has convinced you to join him at the gym. What's next?"

"Torture," I suggested.

She patted my hand and said, "Don't worry I think you'll have fun."

"I didn't know the definition of fun was something unpleasant," I replied.

She smiled and turned towards the kitchen. "Want some breakfast?"

I rubbed my grumbling stomach. "Better not," I said sadly. "If I eat and then exercise it makes me sick," I said remembering a very unpleasant school year where I had lunch right before gym.

"Okay," she said. "Caeden should be here soon anyway."

I settled on the couch and listened to the news. The sounds and smells coming from the kitchen were not helping my stomach one bit. My stomach rumbled in response to the sound of eggs frying. I was just about to give in and eat something when I heard a light honk on a car horn come from the driveway.

I grabbed my sweatshirt off the coat rack and pulled it on. "Bye Gram," I called.

She didn't reply but I could hear her singing while she cooked.

Caeden was waiting outside in the Jeep as I climbed in he said, "I thought about bringing my bike and forcing you onto it but I figured I was already pushing my luck."

"You thought right, Mister," I said.

He chuckled and pulled out of the driveway.

* * *

An assortment of vehicles were parked at Caeden's house and I quickly recognized Charlotte's, Bentley's, and Logan' vehicles and figured Chris had rode with her brother. Caeden pulled into the garage, planted a quick kiss on my lips, grinned and then proceeded to tug me towards the house. Instead of going in through the front door we went in through the basement door.

Caeden hadn't been exaggerating. The whole basement was a gym. It was even equipped with girls and guys showers. Mats for martial arts littered the floor, several treadmills were clustered in a corner, and there was lots of weight lifting equipment.

Bentley was lifting weights, while Chris looked on longingly while she ran on the treadmill. Logan and Bryce were wrestling and Charlotte was doing a bunch of complicated aerial moves. I gulped. They were all in extremely good shape. The girls were lithe and graceful of build and the boys were all well-muscled, even Bryce who was only sixteen.

"It'll be fine," whispered Caeden in my ear.

"Sure," I muttered.

Caeden pointed to the different equipment, telling me what the various items performed, and then released me into his high-tech gym. I hoped I didn't break anything.

Caeden went over to join Bentley and I joined Chris on the treadmills.

"Hey," I said.

She smiled and said, "Welcome to the Pack."

I laughed as I started the treadmill, "You guys are like family aren't you?" I asked referring to the Pack.

"Yeah," she said sadly and gave Bentley a look of longing. She shook her head, looked at me, and blushed when she knew that I had seen. She looked back at Bentley and whispered so low I almost didn't catch it, "Is it wrong that I like him?"

"No," I said, "and he likes you too."

She laughed harshly. "You mean like a sister. That's all I'll ever be to him, a sister," she said forlornly.

"No," I said. "I've seen him looking at you like you look at him. You should go for it." I pointed to Charlotte and then Logan. "Poor Charlotte unfortunately has the hots for your brother and he is completely oblivious."

She smiled slightly when I told her about Bentley but then frowned when I mentioned her brother and Charlotte. At first I thought she didn't like the thought of Charlotte with her brother but instead she said, "Logan isn't good enough for Charlotte. He's completely ignorant about everything. It must be true, what they say, about girls being more mature than boys because Logan is only a year older than me and I am by far the more mature one. But Charlotte deserves someone who worships her. She's so kind, and giving, she's my best friend." Chris paused and said, "Charlotte needs someone like Bryce. Someone to make her laugh and treat her like a queen. I mean look at him, he can't take his eyes off of her. Gosh, she's just as oblivious as my idiotic brother."

I laughed. "Poor Bryce, poor Charlotte, poor you, and poor me."

"Why poor you?" she asked. "You have Caeden." I was amazed that she could talk with the pace at which she was running.

I sighed, "Caeden's great but it's all a bit overwhelming, don't you think? One minute I'm a normal kid and the next my whole world is turned upside down."

"True," she said, "I didn't think of it like that."

"It's hard too," I said, starting to breathe heavy as the treadmill suddenly started an incline, "having such strong feelings for someone I hardly know. I mean, I know we became friends when I moved here but it's difficult going from 'friends' to 'meant to be together forever'. It's a lot of pressure."

She clucked her tongue in sympathy and then we lapsed into companionable silence. The treadmill steadily inclined and increased the speed. I began to sweat and huff and puff.

Caeden left the weights and he and Bentley switched places with Logan and Bryce. Caeden took off his gray t-shirt, leaving his chest bare; his boxers peeking out above his navy basketball shorts. His body was slick with sweat, his bronze skin gleaming, a light trail of brown hair cascading down into the waistband of his pants and his well-muscled chest, arms, and abs stared at me.

For a moment I forgot what I was doing and my feet went out from under me and my face smashed into the moving belt of the treadmill. It hurt badly but what hurt more was my pride.

Everyone was silent and then burst out laughing. Everyone but Caeden. He was at my side in a moment.

"Are you okay?" he asked, gently probing the side of my face that had smacked the treadmill. I could feel a headache coming on and a bump forming on the top of my head.

I tried to play cool, "Oh, I'm fine. I do this all the time. I like to give people a good laugh."

He rolled his eyes and stated, "You're hurt."

"Yeah," I said ashamed. "I tried to warn you that I didn't like to exercise."

He helped me up and said, "I didn't realize that was due to your total lack of coordination. Let's go get you some ice."

The others resumed their activities with the exception of Bentley who switched to boxing with the punching bag. Caeden led me around the corner and up the basement steps into the main house.

"I'm sorry," I mumbled as he dug around in the freezer for an icepack. I hopped up on to the kitchen counter and let my feet dangle over the edge.

He found one, wrapped it in a cloth, and held it to my head, "For what?" he asked.

For a moment I lost my train of thought because his naked chest stared me right in the face. I averted my eyes and made eye contact with him but that was just as bad so I settled with looking out the bay window.

"For being such a klutz," I said.

He chuckled. "You don't need to apologize. Accidents happen."

"Have you ever heard of a clumsy shifter?" I asked.

"No," he said grinning. "But you haven't shifted yet," he reminded me.

"I bet stuff like this never happened to the others," I grumbled.

He laughed and said, "No, they're all very coordinated." I frowned and he grinned, "But I on the other hand... Well let's just say riding a bicycle might as well have been climbing a mountain." He leaned down and whispered in my ear, tickling my skin with his breath, "I still don't like bicycles."

I laughed and pushed him away. "You drive a motorcycle Caeden. That's a bike."

"It has an engine," he defended, "that's different."

He removed the ice pack and gently probed my skull. It was only slightly tender now and I could tell the knot had diminished in size. "How does it feel?" he asked.

"It's okay," I said hopping off the kitchen counter. I started to walk out and head down to the basement but his hand grabbed my wrist stopping me. He pinned me back against the counter, one arm on each side, so I was trapped. My breathing accelerated. I stared at his perfect chest and then slowly trailed my eyes up to meet his. Instead of a cocky grin his face was thoughtful.

"Sophie," he whispered and his fingers came up to a brush a piece of hair back from my face that had come loose from my ponytail. He leaned in closer to me and my breath hitched.

"Caeden!" Bentley called from the basement doorway. "Get your butt back down here! You owe me a match."

Caeden chuckled and kissed my cheek. "We'll finish this later," he said with a glint in his eye. My heart raced.

I followed him back down to the basement. Instead of getting back on the treadmill I decided to sit down in the corner where I would have a good view of Caeden and Bentley.

They didn't put on any protective gear and stood at opposite ends of the mat facing off. Bentley grinned and twisted his neck and cracked his fingers. Caeden just stood there. I noticed that everyone stopped what they were doing. Charlotte and Chris came to sit beside me.

"This is the best part," said Charlotte. "I love watching the guys fight."

Chris looked at me and said, "It's so much fun. You should try."

I rolled my eyes. "I can't even stay vertical on the treadmill so I doubt this would be any different."

Chris bumped my shoulder. "Come on, you have to try so you can learn. I sucked when I first started and now I can take down my brother without breaking a sweat."

"That's because he doesn't want to hurt you," said Charlotte. "I bet Bentley wouldn't be so gentle."

Chris looked at me and leaned over to whisper, "Bentley can put his hands all over me and be as rough as he wants." She laughed and Charlotte looked at us questioningly. I just shook my head.

The boys were now circling each other. Bentley glared at Caeden menacingly but Caeden still looked calm.

"Now remember," warned Charlotte, "that we heal fast."

"Why?" I asked but I didn't need to wait for her answer.

A loud thump sounded and Bentley lay flat on the floor. I hadn't even seen Caeden move. Bentley grunted and slowly stood. He spat blood on the floor and when he grinned his teeth were stained red. Bentley threw a punch and Caeden's arms came up to block him. Then Caeden punched Bentley and I heard a bone crunch. More blood dripped onto the floor.

I had thought that Bentley wound have the upper hand simply because of his size. Caeden was tall and broad with large muscles but Bentley was all those things times two. Bentley was taller, wider, and more muscular but still lean, however, Caeden clearly had more skill.

Caeden grabbed Bentley by the elbow and flipped him down on the mat. From his position on the floor Bentley kicked Caeden in the chest. Caeden grunted but then smiled in challenge.

I wanted to close my eyes, I didn't like seeing Caeden get hurt, but my eyes were riveted.

Bentley threw a particularly brutal punch that would have knocked out a normal guy. But Caeden wasn't normal and it only served to spurn him on. He grinned and did a flip in the air and did some kind of complicated kicking and punching sequence. Their fighting was getting much more structured and less street. I knew they both had to be doing some serious martial arts but I had no names to go with the moves. They were both breathing heavy but neither gave up. Someone whistled and I looked away from the fight. It had been Bryce and he turned to grin at me.

Caeden and Bentley began to taunt and goad one another. Before my eyes I could see their cuts and scrapes heal but both had some serious injuries that were taking longer to heal. Caeden's whole left side was bruised a hulk-like green and purple and if Bentley didn't soon set his nose it would heal crooked.

They continued their complicated dance. I could tell they were both beginning to wear down. I looked at my watch and was surprised that they had been going at it for almost an hour. They both took more punches than they blocked, now, and both of their chests were heaving. Bentley through a punch and Caeden fell to the floor. He was slower than normal to get up but I quickly realized it was a show. Bentley didn't though. Bentley grinned and taunted Caeden.

Like a deadly lighting strike Caeden was up and Bentley was the one on the floor. He didn't get up.

Bentley rolled over with his face against the mat. "Match," he muttered into its blue folds.

"Say it," said Caeden with a grin. He stood over Bentley with his arms crossed over his chest.

"Ugh," groaned Bentley into the mat.

"And I want you to look at me," said Caeden, clearly enjoying this.

Bentley groaned and shakily stood. I could see a split in his lip heal before my eyes. "Oh, mighty Alpha, you are great, you are powerful, and you are unstoppable and undefeatable. You, Alpha, are the strongest wolf and I am but a weakling. You win," Bentley said. "Happy now?" he added.

"Delighted," Caeden grinned.

Bentley pulled off his t-shirt and started wiping away the blood with it. I thought Chris would have a heart attack looking at his chest. She gasped and started to breathe heavy. I didn't know how they were all so oblivious to her crush. It was written all over her face, the poor girl. I shouldn't say anything though. After all, I fell off a treadmill looking at Caeden and it wasn't like I hadn't seen him shirtless before. True, he had been covered in blood at the time and that kind of ruined the image. I preferred a slick with sweat Caeden to a bloody one any day.

Caeden came over to my side and grinned. He pulled me up off the floor and held me against his naked chest. I tried not to hyperventilate. "What was that all about?" I asked.

"I won so that was the deal," he said.

"What if he won?" I asked.

"I would've had to rub his feet," he said wiggling his nose in disgust. "So, I had to win," he stated.

I laughed and then noticed the bruises that were still on his side. I hesitantly touched his side. He shivered. "Does it hurt?" I asked.

"No," he said.

"I'm hungry," said Bryce from across the room, breaking the moment. I moved away from Caeden but he kept a hold on my hand.

"Me too," said Bentley.

"Mom, should have lunch ready," Caeden said. He picked his shirt up off the floor and slipped it over his head and then took my hand again. We filed up the steps after the others. Before we entered the house Caeden stopped on the stairs and gave me a quick, toe-tingling, kiss. He grinned and tugged me up the rest of the steps.

Sure enough Amy had prepared a feast for lunch. She had grilled hotdogs and cheese burgers and made macaroni and cheese, cheesy potatoes, and green beans to go along with it. The boys piled their plates high and I was surprised when Charlotte and Chris took just as much. I came along and got a normal, human-sized, portion and joined them. Bryce scooted over so I could have the seat by Caeden.

"So," said Bryce addressing me, "when do you turn eighteen?"

"January sixteenth," I said.

"Oh, so you've got a while yet." He said. He shrugged his shoulders. "I guess it's a good thing though. It gives you time to learn about being a wolf." I paled at the mention of my being a wolf. "Don't worry," said Bryce patting my hand. "You'll love it. It's the best feeling in the world. It's like you're unstoppable."

"Bryce," scolded Caeden, "I think you're scaring her more than you're helping." He gave me a look and asked, "Are you okay?"

"I'm fine," I said and smiled to prove that I was. "And he wasn't scaring me. I'm not as breakable as you think I am."

He grinned and kissed my cheek to a chorus of

"Aww's".

Bentley shoveled some mac n' cheese into his mouth, swallowed, and said, "So, Caeden how does it feel to be whipped?"

Caeden rolled his eyes at his best friend. "I'm not whipped," he said, "you just wait till it's you."

Bentley looked longingly at Chris and then back at Caeden, "Nope, not a chance. I'm a free spirit."

"Aren't we all," said Charlotte softly almost sadly. They all looked sad and I realized that as much as they embraced being wolves it was still like a curse. I knew that most of the time they genuinely enjoyed being shifters but I also knew that at times it had to be a burden.

"So," I said trying to lighten the mood, "does anyone have any embarrassing stories about Caeden?"

Everyone brightened at that and Caeden groaned. "Don't do this to me," he said to me.

I grinned. "Oh, something you don't want me to know?"

"No, I'm afraid you'll decide I'm a complete loser," he said and hung his head in mock shame.

"Not a chance," I said and squeezed his hand and gave him a quick peck on the cheek.

"Okay, lovebirds," said Bentley. He looked at me and said, "Do you want to hear a story or not?"

"Of course," I said.

"Alright well stop sucking face," he said with a grin so I'd know he was joking.

"Zipping my lips," I said and mimed zipping them closed.

Bentley steepled his fingers in front of his face and said, "Hmm, where to begin? There's so many." He was thoughtful for a moment and then said, "How about the time that Caeden and I were just mere pups and we decided to kill a squirrel."

"Oh no," groaned Caeden and buried his face in his hands.

"Oh yes," said Bentley grinning evilly. "Caeden I were about five years old and we got the bright idea to go kill a squirrel with our bare hands. So, we wandered out to the woods and found several squirrels gathering nuts for the winter. We hid in some bushes, bushes that turned out to be infested in poison ivy, and watched the squirrels. We had seen our dad's on many occasions take down large prey when they were in their wolf forms so we thought we'd surprise them by getting a squirrel. Well... the squirrels apparently didn't want to get caught. Caeden and I jumped out of the bushes with our plastic swords, screaming like banshees, and the squirrels fled up into the top branches of the trees. We both tried to climb the tree unsuccessfully. But the squirrels had a plan." Bentley laughed and then continues the story. "They started throwing their nuts and acorns at us as hard as they could. By that time we were both starting to itch and getting pinged in the head with tiny projectiles wasn't helping the situation. So, we ran. Only the squirrels decided to follow. We screamed and ran home with the squirrels right on our heels." Bentley shuddered. "After that we both look twice when we see a squirrel and give it a wide berth."

Caeden laughed and said, "You left out the most embarrassing part."

"Oh, right," said Bentley. He leaned towards me conspiratorially, "We were both butt naked."

Caeden looked at me and grinned. "Bentley and I were convinced that if we ran around naked we'd shift into wolves."

I shook my head and laughed. "That's a good story."

"It is now," said Caeden. "At the time were too preoccupied with all the itching to laugh about it."

"I learned my lesson," said Bentley, "never hide, naked, in a bush of poison ivy. The consequences aren't worth it."

Amy had come into the room and chuckled. "I've got a story," she said.

Caeden groaned. "Please, no, mom."

She smiled and said, "When Caeden was seven he got the bright idea to run away. He packed a bag full of cookies and went outside and sat in the woods."

She paused so I prompted her. "What happened?" I asked.

"I forgot something to drink," Caeden said. He shrugged his shoulders. "I was seven, my plan wasn't foolproof. So, I marched my sorry butt back into the house and surrendered to my punishment."

Amy laughed. "And then all the cookies he ate made him sick."

Caeden looked at me. "I wouldn't touch another cookie for a month."

"So, what did you do to make you want to run away?" I asked.

Caeden grinned. "I made Bryce eat worm pie so to avoid my punishment I ran away."

"Worm pie?" I asked with a smile.

"Yeah, it's like mud pies only with more worms."

"It was good too," said Bryce smacking his lips.

Amy patted Bryce's shoulder. "My strange child," she muttered.

Bryce grinned. "Don't knock it till you try it."

Amy shook her head. "What will I do with you?" she asked exasperated.

"Sell me in the slave trade," Bryce quipped.

"No one would want you," said Caeden.

Bryce feigned offense. "I am very desirable, dear brother."

Caeden pointed his fork at Bryce. "That's Alpha."

Bryce rolled his eyes and threw his hands in the air. "You're still annoying so what difference does it make?"

I found their sibling fights to be very entertaining. I was an only child and had always longed for a sibling to play with. You could tell that the brothers loved each other and that their fights were more at poking fun at one another. It would have been nice to have had a sibling to confide in growing up, especially now, with how much my life had changed.

We finished eating and then Bentley stood. "Come on Christian, it's time for our patrol," said Bentley washing his plate.

She smiled and said, "Give me a second." She finished eating and followed suit.

"I better get going," I said to Caeden. "I have a lot of homework."

"Oh, yeah," he said rather reluctantly. "I'll walk you to your car."

Caeden and I walked out the front door. He had stuffed his hands in the pockets of his shorts. I unlocked my car but before I could get in it Caeden had pinned me against its metal frame.

"Caeden," I said my breath catching. His blue eyes smothered mine.

He leaned towards me. "Don't go," he whispered.

"I have to," I said. "I really do have a lot of homework. I was going to do it yesterday but then we were gone the whole day."

"Please don't go," he whispered against my lips. "I don't like being away from you. It makes me anxious, nervous. I imagine all kinds of bad things happening to you."

I laughed. "You're the one that showed up bloody on my front porch. Not the other way around."

"Still," he said leaning in even closer until his blue eyes dominated my line of vision, "my body doesn't like it. I'm on edge the entire time your away. Last night nearly killed me."

"You've been away from me every night since we met. I think you'll live," I said with a smile.

"That was different," he defended. "That was before we kissed, before we spent the night together, it was before… it was before I knew that you felt the same way about me."

"Caeden," I whispered.

"Sophie," he moaned and closed those precious few

gaps and pressed his lips to mine. He pressed his body against mine. I grabbed the hair at his neck and held on for dear life. Kisses like this should be illegal. My mouth opened underneath his. I could feel my knees going weak. As if he could sense my weakness his hand wrapped around my waist holding me up.

A voice shouted behind us. "Caeden stop sucking face! We have stuff to do!" yelled Bentley.

Caeden groaned and pulled away. Not taking his eyes off mine he said, "Bentley, I am going to kill you."

Bentley chuckled and sauntered over, Chris on his heels.

"Come over for dinner?" I asked breathlessly.

He grinned, his dimple showing, "I'll be there." He started to pull away. "Uh, Sophie?"

"Yeah?" I asked.

"Can you let go?" he grinned.

Somehow, during our intense kiss my hands had moved from his hair to his shirt. I had the fabric fisted tightly in my hands. My cheeks bloomed red and I let go. Two very distinct wrinkles were left behind.

Caeden leaned down and kissed my cheek. "I'll see you for dinner," he said grinning. I watched him follow after Chris and Bentley who were disappearing into the trees. With a burst of speed Caeden jumped on Bentley and both fell to the ground. I laughed and got in my car driving away.

I could hear the sounds of wolves yowling in play and it put a smile on my face.

EIGHT.

Gram wasn't at home when I got there so I assumed she was either meeting with the council again or at her store. I was worried about how much time Gram was spending with the council. It made me think that there was something bad, something major, going on. But then it again it could just be my overactive imagination because Caeden acted as if it was normal. If he wasn't worried then I shouldn't be worried either.

I took a quick shower and changed into jeans and a long-sleeved maroon shirt. I quickly finished my homework before deciding to start dinner. I looked through the refrigerator for something to make for dinner. I decided to make a homemade pizza. I first made only one but then decided with the way that Caeden ate that I should probably make two. Just as I stuck them in the oven the doorbell rang.

I practically floated to the door. A smile lit my face before I even opened the door. I opened the door wide to let in Caeden. His hair was still slightly wet from the shower, the ends curling slightly. He had on jeans and a black pea coat, with a gray scarf. I thought that he had never looked more perfect.

Noticing my gaze he blushed as if embarrassed. "It got cold out," he said quietly. "I may be wolf but I'm not entirely impervious to the cold."

"You look perfect," I breathed. "I feel underdressed," I stated.

I closed the door as he began to shrug out of his coat and pull off his scarf. "Have no fear," he said hanging up his coat, "I wore a plain shirt." I smiled as he tugged at his gray long-sleeved shirt. "Is that pizza I smell?" he asked with a grin. "I thought you Beaumont women felt the need to cook everything?"

I laughed. "I did cook it," I said, "and it should be ready any minute." On cue the timer went off and I strode in the kitchen to get them before they burned; Caeden right behind me.

"Mmm, smells delicious," said Caeden as I removed the pizza's and waved the oven mitt at them to help cool them down.

I shook my head. "You think everything smells good."

He grinned. "That's very true. But I still know the difference between what's good and what's bad."

"Sure you do squirrel-hunter," I mocked.

He groaned. "Can we just forget about that?"

"Oh no," I said, "never."

I cut up the pizzas and grabbed two slices for me and a whole pizza for Caeden. He was already sitting at the table and he grinned when he saw that I had made him a whole pizza.

"You already know me so well," he said and took a bite. "This is really good," he added.

"I'm just waiting to see you eat a whole cow or two," I said.

He laughed. "Next time," he said.

We ate in companionable silence, every little bit one of us voicing an errant thought. Our peace however was disturbed by a scratching at the back door. I jumped. I couldn't think coherently. All I could see was Caeden, only a few days ago, at my door as a wolf dying. Was it possible that one of the others had been attacked?

Caeden stood and sniffed the air. "It's just a dog," he said and sat back down grabbing another slice of pizza.

"A dog?" I asked, still holding my hand over my racing heart.

"Yeah," he said around a mouthful. "Wait," he said holding up a hand. A grin spread across his face. "I think your familiar is here."

"What?" I asked. "How is that possible?"

He chuckled. "We don't control when they come. But it might not be your familiar," he added. "It might just be a stray."

The scratching at the door became more incessant,

harder to ignore. I stood and went to the door. I expected some kind of monster of a dog to jump out at me like Murphy. Murphy was a nice dog though just abnormally large. One of the sweetest I had ever been around so it couldn't be so bad could it?

I opened the door, looking into the gloom, for a big dog. But what I found was a tiny little Boston terrier staring at me with the most adorable brown eyes.

"Aww," I said picking up the tiny dog.

Caeden laughed. "He suits you," he said.

"He's mine," I said. "I can feel it. But how?" I asked cuddling the dog to my chest.

Caeden laughed. "I don't know. It's a weird perk of being a shifter," he stood and petted the dog on top of his head.

I cooed softly to the dog in my arms. He was just so cute with his white and black fur and pointy ears.

"What are you going to name him?" asked Caeden.

I held the dog out at arm's length. "Archie," I said. "His name is Archie."

Caeden laughed and said, "I hope Archie and Murphy get along because if I have my way you'll be spending most of your time with me."

"Oh is that right?" I asked. I looked at Archie. "Do you think they'll get along? I mean, Archie's a small dog and Murphy is the size of a moose."

Caeden eyed me. "He gets along great with Bailey so I don't see why this would be any different."

I set the dog down on the floor and grabbed a bowl from the cabinet. I filled it with water and set it down for him. Within moments he had lapped it all up. "Good boy," I said and stroked his soft fur. "You know this is your home don't you? Don't you?" I asked in that gooey voice that most people reserved for babies.

Caeden shook his head and laughed at me. I didn't care though. This was a new experience for me. I had never had a dog before. I wondered at that. Didn't my parents have familiars? I'd have to ask Gram about that later.

Caeden sat back down and continued eating his pizza. I was so absorbed in my new dog that all thoughts of finishing my meal were gone.

Chomping on his pizza, a little sauce sitting adorably in the corner of his mouth, Caeden said, "How about tomorrow after work I take you to PetSmart? We can get little Archie some toy's and what not."

I smiled. "That would be great. My poor little baby doesn't have anything," I cooed to the dog. I saw Caeden shake his head out of the corner of my eye. I didn't care though. I was going to have my fun.

I heard Gram's car pull in the driveway and then a moment later she appeared at the front door. Archie went running to her, his tail wagging.

She smiled and bent down to pet him. "Well, who is this?" she asked.

"Archie," I supplied. "He's apparently my familiar."

She smiled. "He suits you."

"What does that mean? I'm cute and sweet?" I asked jokingly.

"Of course," said Caeden grinning.

I raised my eyebrows, "So Murphy symbolizes that you're a giant mess?"

He grinned, his dimple showing. "No, silly. Murphy is my familiar because we have the same traits. Passionate, affectionate, easy-going, quiet, fearless, loyal and many other amazing things." He finished with a laugh and a mischievous twinkle in his eye.

"Maybe you should date him?" I said.

"Ugh no thanks," said Caeden and then grinned. "He's not as good of a kisser as you. I don't think I could survive off of Murphy's kisses. But yours... Your kisses are like heaven."

"Glad to know that you've made out with your dog, Caeden," I said and punched his leg from where I sat on the floor with Archie who had curled up in a little ball on my lap.

He puckered his lips. "You seem to like the way I kiss. I guess practicing with Murphy paid off." He laughed and moved his legs to avoid another punch from me.

"Ugh, too much information," said Gram. "You're making me nauseous."

I couldn't help the laughter that burst forth. Caeden started laughing too. A few tears leaked out of the corners of my eyes.

Gram sat down across from Caeden to eat her pizza. "So how did it go today Sophie? I know you were dreading it."

I groaned and Caeden grinned.

"Sophie was fine up until the point where she fell flat on her face when she got a look at my delicious abs," he said and pulled up his shirt rubbing his chiseled stomach.

I blushed and then mocked him, "Delicious huh?"

"Oh yeah," he said jokingly. "My basement floor is now flooded with your drool."

"That's not drool that's your sweat," I chuckled.

"Touché," he replied with a smile. He finished his pizza and stood. "I better get home. I don't want to worry my mom. I'll see you tomorrow at school, babe," he said and bent down and kissed my cheek and rubbed Archie behind his ears.

"Bye," I said and smiled at him.

"Bye Lucinda," he said and hugged Gram.

She patted his cheeks. "Be careful," she said.

"I always am," he replied heading out to the living room to put his coat on.

Gram harrumphed and said, "No you're not."

He chuckled and ducked out the door. I heard his Jeep start and then pull away. "I'm going to head to bed," I said to Gram. "I am absolutely exhausted."

Gram laughed. "What are you going to do, Sophie? We're going to have to whip you into shape," she said with a quiet chuckle.

I grinned. "I guess I'm not cut out to be a shifter."

"Not many of us are," she said. "You have to be tough as nails. You'll get there, sweetie," she said patting my hand.

I smiled up at her. "It all still seems so surreal," I said. "It's become more real since I saw Caeden as a wolf but I don't think it'll actually hit me until I change."

Gram sat down on the floor beside me, crossing her legs Indian style. For a moment she said nothing, only petted Archie, then she spoke. "I knew my whole life what I was. I grew up with my husband and our friends, all of us knowing that one day we would come of age and shift into wolves. We'd seen our parents do it many times and had no reason to doubt them but it was still a scary experience." She patted my knee. "Sophie, you're a strong girl. You're going to make a great wolf. And you have Caeden to help you through it all. I had no one."

I was quiet, thinking, and then I said, "Why were you alone?"

She sighed and looked at me. An ancient sadness glimmered in her shimmery brown eyes, "I never had a mate. I married your grandfather but he wasn't my true mate. I loved him dearly but the bond of a mate is different." She sighed and continued, "Despite the idea of a mate turning into nothing more than a legend we still abided by the old rules. The rules clearly state that a female without a mate must make the change alone. I was scared to death. I was only eighteen and the first female to change in my generation pack. I had no one to talk to but my mother and the other elders. It was so frightening but exhilarating at the same time when I first shifted. I felt like for the first time in my life I was coming into my own skin. I felt free but whole at the same time. It was amazing. After that I felt silly for all the worrying that I had done. So, don't worry Sophie, it's not necessary. Everything will work out perfectly. And you are so much luckier than the rest of us because you'll have Caeden to help you through it. He'll be there to coach you through it." She pulled me against her and began to stroke my hair. "You may be finding out about this after everyone else but you are so much luckier than they are because you have something infinitely more precious, Sophie. You have the gift of the purest, most kind, forgiving, all-consuming, true love. I wish I could have had that. It's a gift everyone wants and few receive it. Human and shifter alike. For whatever reason you and Caeden have been given this gift, just like your parents, I can only hope that the bonds are coming back because everyone deserves to have it."

"Gram," I said and cuddled closer into her comforting arms. I felt like a little kid again, but in a good way, sitting in her arms. "My feelings for him are so strong Gram. It scares me," I whispered.

"I know sweetie," she said. "It'll get worse once you're bonded too."

"Bonded?" I asked. "What does that mean?"

She sighed. "When you find your mate there's a bonding ceremony. It's almost like a wedding but only for the two of you. It's a very powerful, very old, kind of magic."

"Does Caeden know?" I asked.

"Yes," she said. "He probably didn't tell you because he didn't want to scare you further. He's very attuned to your feelings."

"But how do you know all this?" I asked.

"It's written down in our histories. We stopped believing in mates because for hundreds of years there haven't been any. Like I've told you before, fact turned into legend, and here we are today."

"Oh, right," I said embarrassed.

"It's okay, sweetie," she said patting my hand. "You're bound not to remember half of what we tell you. There's just so much that you don't know but you'll get there."

I stood and said, "Thanks for the talk Gram but I really do have to go to bed. I have school tomorrow."

"Oh right," she said. She stood with the grace and

agility of someone much younger than her. She kissed my cheek and said, "Goodnight, Sophie."

I picked up Archie and headed to my room. I changed into my pajamas and climbed under the covers. Archie decided to be a pillow hog so I graciously pillowed my head on my hands despite how uncomfortable it was. I'd let the dog have the pillow. He was too cute to say no to. He made a cute little snoring noise that instead of keeping me awake lulled me into a dreamless sleep.

In the morning, for the first time ever, I woke up ready for school. Not necessarily school but the idea of seeing Caeden. Seeing him now would be different than previous times at school, now we were no longer friends, but more. I dressed in a hurry and rushed out the door, with a piece of toast between my teeth, and Archie barking at the door. I only hoped that Caeden was as excited to see me as I was to see him.

I pulled into my parking spot and a moment later Caeden pulled in beside me in his Jeep. The weather here was like a yo-yo going from high to low quicker than you could blink and today was a particularly chilly day. I was bundled up with a jacket and scarf and saw that Caeden was dressed similarly.

I got out of my car a smile already on my face. Caeden smiled when he saw me, said, "Hey," pulled me into a hug and then kissed me quickly on the lips. He inhaled my scent and said, "I love the way you smell, like, cookie dough and icing."

"Thanks," I said and then added, "I think."

"Don't worry, it's a good thing." He said and bent to kiss my cheek.

Travis Grimm chose that moment to come skidding into the parking lot. He parked his sports car and sauntered over to us. I felt Caeden's muscles tense and I had the urge to grab him and run in the opposite direction.

Travis stopped in front of us and sneered at Caeden, "Don't you think you should date someone within your own species?"

Caeden growled and I tightened my hold on him. He squeezed my hand lightly in a silent reminder to act dumb.

"Travis what are you talking about?" I asked to help ensure that he still believed that I was only a human and not a shifter.

He turned to glare at me. "*Stay out of this*," he snarled and pushed me out of the way. I could see an evil glint in his eye. He was looking for a fight and he hoped that by insulting me he could get to Caeden.

It worked. Caeden lunged at Travis but suddenly Bentley was there pulling Caeden away saying, "He's not worth it man. He's just not worth it."

Travis grinned cockily like he had learned something valuable, stuck his hands in his pockets, and strode confidently into the school.

Caeden was doing that weird, vibrating, shimmering around the edges thing. His breathing was heavy and Bentley was trying to calm him down. I batted Bentley away and took Caeden's face between my hands.

"Calm down," I said looking into his blue eyes. I noticed that his eyes had taken on a distinct wolfish quality. They seemed to glow gold around the edges. Slowly, they began to return to normal. "I'm okay," I added. "He just wanted to get under your skin. You can't let him do that. You're an Alpha you have to be the bigger person," I was thoughtful for a moment, "or wolf, I guess I should say."

He laughed at that and returned to himself. He shook his head, "I'm sorry. When he touched you... I've never felt like that before. I mean he always goads me but this was different. I just *couldn't* stand the thought of him touching you. I'm sorry. I just felt so possessive. You're my mate and I didn't want him messing with you. It's one thing when he messes with me but when he grabbed you, I just lost it. Sorry," he said again.

I kept my hold on his face so he had to look me in the eye. "Caeden, it's okay. Really. But you need to learn to control yourself around him. You can't let him win. You're an Alpha and he's not so he's jealous."

"You're right," he said. "I've got to stop thinking like a little boy and be a man, be an Alpha. I have to put you and my pack first." He smiled. "Thanks for being my rock."

I leaned my forehead against his. "You're my rock."

He kissed me and Bentley gagged. "You guys act like an old married couple."

We both laughed. Bryce pulled into the parking spot next to Caeden's and hopped out. He looked between the three of us. "I missed something and it was big. I know it," he said.

Caeden ruffled his younger brother's hair. "Don't worry. It was just Travis, like always."

Bryce shook his shaggy hair, once again reminding me of a dog, and said, "Want me to teach him a lesson?" he did a karate chop in the air. "I can take him," he added.

"Travis would get far too much satisfaction out of that," I said.

"Too bad," said Bryce. "Maybe one day."

Looking at Bryce I was a little worried that one day might be soon, like first period soon, since we had math today. What I wouldn't give for it to be a day two.

We met up with Logan, Chris, and Charlotte in the cafeteria. They had no idea what had transpired in the parking lot but said they saw Travis come in and take off with the members of his pack and that he looked particularly happy about something. I knew that couldn't be good. I was dreading math more and more. Too bad I couldn't just twitch my nose and it would be over.

The bell rang and Bryce and I headed off to math. Walking down the hallway I said to him, "Don't start anything, Bryce. I mean it. Travis wants a fight so please don't give him one."

Bryce looked at me with his blue eyes that were similar to Caeden's only darker. "I hate him so much," he whispered.

"Why?" I asked.

"Well for starters I think he knows something about the night my dad died and he's always doing something to Caeden. He hates it that Caeden is an Alpha and he's not. I don't know why that bothers him so much. I mean he's the son of an Alpha so he'll get the position when either his dad dies or steps down. I think he hates that Caeden has so much power. The Grimm Pack is small compared to ours. If you only count the new generation it's only three wolves. Travis, Robert, and Hannah."

"So, he's jealous that the Williams Pack is bigger?" I asked.

"I think that's only part of it. The Williams Pack or should I say the Beaumont Pack has always been the most powerful pack of wolf shifters in the world because the first wolf to shift was a Beaumont. Travis hates that. He craves power; I can smell it on him."

"You can smell it?" I asked.

"Yeah," he said. "It's a wolf thing. When people have certain thoughts their body gives off a certain scent."

Oh dear lord, what kind of scents did my body produce when I was near Caeden?

We were at the classroom now so it made talk impossible. Travis smirked at me and Bryce when we came in. I took my seat which was still, unfortunately, in front of Travis. Like he did every math class he played with my hair and touched my skin. The feeling of spiders crawling over my skin appeared at his touch and a sense of wrongness. I always had this feeling when he touched me and I hated it but I was too scared of Mrs. Harding to say anything. She seemed to favor Travis and since she already hated me I didn't see the point in adding fuel to the fire. When the bell rang I gave Bryce a tight-lipped smile and headed to my history class.

Charlotte was already in her seat in the back of the room. She smiled as I took my seat next to her.

"I can't stand him," I said into my hands.

"Who?" she asked. I gave her a pointed look and she

said, "Oh, right. Travis."

"He's just so awful," I said.

"He is," she agreed. "The whole Grimm Pack is like that," she said and pointed to a particular unpleasant girl in our class. "Hannah is just as bad. She's just more subtle about it."

I agreed completely with that.

We quieted when the teacher came in but quickly resumed our conversation when it became obvious that he was oblivious.

Charlotte looked at Hannah and then back at me. "Hannah has more of a reason to act the way she does. When she was little her sister drowned and she's never gotten over it," whispered Charlotte.

I suddenly felt bad for the unpleasant girl. Something like that does change a person. Caeden and Bryce were extremely close and I couldn't imagine the pain they would experience if they lost one another.

The rest of the day went by quicker than I had come to expect. But I still had to survive woodshop. Luckily I had Caeden for a partner. However, that meant he did most of the work. All I was good for was sanding and painting. We were finishing up making bird houses. Next we would be making stools.

I put my bag down on the desk and joined Caeden at our station. He had already cut all the pieces and I had sanded them so today we would be decorating and assembling them if we had time.

Caeden had already gotten the paint, brushes, and water. I sat down beside him and began to paint. I wasn't very good so I planned on painting it a solid green with flowers. Caeden painted some ocean waves on his and I was amazed at how good he was. The waves swirled realistically on the wooden surface.

"You're good," I commented, pointing to his birdhouse.

He laughed. "No, I'm not. But when compared to

yours I'm da Vinci."

I smacked his arm. "It's not that bad," I said.

"You're right. It's worse," he chuckled.

"Caeden," I scolded.

"It's cute," he said. "Is that better?"

"Much," I said and smiled. We put our wooden pieces on the drying rack and gathered up our stuff so we'd be ready to leave.

I would be at the bakery before Caeden since he was always assigned the after school check. Mr. Collins came over and complemented Caeden on his workmanship. He smiled at me and said that I could try harder. I was mortified but then Mr. Collins started laughing so I knew he was joking. He was probably happy that I was too scared to touch any of the power tools anymore. I once screamed and ran from the room when Caeden tried to get me to use the power saw. The metal monster had screamed and sputtered woodchips at me and that was all it took to clear me from the room. The whole class found it very entertaining but I hadn't. Mr. Collins thought it was funny too until he found out that I had broken the saw. I thought that was just justice being served. They should've known not to give me a tool. The only tool I seemed to be able to handle was a screwdriver and that was iffy.

The bell rang and Caeden and I walked hand in hand to the parking lot. He kissed me quickly and then I got in my car. As I left the school parking lot I could feel eyes on me and it wasn't the warm, comforting, feel of Caeden's eyes. These eyes felt menacing and evil. When I turned to look I made eye contact with Travis. I shuddered and drove on.

NINE.

I arrived at the cupcake shop and found Gram icing cupcakes. "I thought I'd help you out," she said.

"Oh, Gram I could have done this."

"I just thought it would be easier if I had all the cupcakes made for the afternoon," she said and with a flourish finished icing the last red velvet cupcake.

"Well, thanks Gram," I said and kissed her wrinkled cheek.

She smiled, patted my hand, and removed her apron. "I'll see you later. I'm making lasagna for dinner."

"Sound delicious," I said.

She smiled and left. I pulled my hair up into a ponytail, put my hat on and my *Lucinda's* shirt. I had gotten in the habit of keeping my work clothes here, Gram didn't mind, and it was easier than carrying them in my backpack or car.

I grabbed up the slats of cupcakes and carried them to the front and began loading them into the refrigerated case. The bell chimed signaling a customer.

"Welcome to Lucinda's. How can I help you?" I asked sliding the case closed. I straightened and looked up into the face of the customer. "Travis," I breathed.

He smirked, his hands in his pockets. "There's something different about you."

I stumbled back a step. Anyone could recognize the predatory glint in his eye. "What can I get you?" I asked trying to form some semblance to normal.

"I want you," he said.

"What can I get you?" I asked in a strained voice. I could feel sweat beading on my skin and my fight or flight senses were kicking in.

"What is it that Caeden sees in you? You seem pretty normal to me. But appearances can be deceiving. I would know. Just look at me. Look at me!" he screamed when I didn't.

I looked at him. At his pale skin, white-blond hair,

and angelic expression. He would have been good looking if it weren't for the scowl on his face and his black eyes. I could tell that his eyes were like his soul. Black, lifeless, and evil.

"Good," he said. I tried to stay strong, to not let him see the fear in my eyes but from the smirk that spread across his face I knew he saw. He came closer to me. I stepped back and was now against the wall. He stretched his arm across the distance, it wasn't far, and stroked my face. I gulped. "Fear," he said and inhaled the air around me. "You should be afraid," he breathed. He straightened and said, "I'll have a devil's kiss cupcake."

For a moment I didn't move.

"Tick tock," he said.

My feet moved forward and I grabbed a devil's kiss cupcake which was chocolate cake, with dark chocolate icing and a cherry. I put it in a box, told him the price and handed it to him. He smirked and threw a ten dollar bill at me. "Keep it," he said and started for the door. Before he opened it though he looked back over his shoulder at me, "I'll be back," he said and left. I had a feeling he would be back for something other than a cupcake. Something like me.

I heard the back door open and jumped.

"Hey," said Caeden, "did I see Travis' car?" It took a moment for me to get my voice back. By this time Caeden was standing in front of me. "Well?" he prompted.

"Yeah," I said and turned away so he wouldn't see the lie in my eyes, "he just wanted a cupcake."

His hand rubbed my arm. "Are you sure? You seem... shaken."

"I'm fine," I said even though I was far from it. I mentally scolded myself. I had to act normal. Caeden didn't need to worry about Travis harassing me. I plastered on the most genuine smile I could muster and said, "He just makes me mad."

Caeden seemed to buy it. "Oh," he said, "don't let him bother you."

"You're one to talk," I said with a smile and bumped him with my hip.

He looked sheepish. "I know," he said. "Sorry."

The bell over the door chimed again and a big group of people came in, effectively cutting of our conversation. I breathed a sigh of relief.

We stayed busy and for the first time I was thankful. Normally I didn't like it when the store was busy because it gave me less time to talk to Caeden. Finally closing time came. I locked the door behind the last customer and set to work cleaning. Caeden helped. He seemed to sense that I didn't want to talk. I was grateful. We finished in record time since we didn't goof off.

I let my hair down from the pony tail and turned to Caeden, "Do you want to come over for dinner? Gram's making lasagna."

"Wish I could," he said, "but I promised my mom that I'd have dinner at home tonight."

"Oh, okay," I said. "Tell your mom that I'm sorry for keeping you from her."

Caeden pulled me against his chest. "It's not that. She's just worried about me because of what happened with the Grimm's she thinks I'm only safe if I'm in her line of sight. She tried to put a leash on me last night when it was time for my duty."

"No, she didn't." I said.

"Oh, she tried all right," he said. "I guess she thought she'd walk around with me all through my shift. But I'm a big boy and can take care of myself."

"Oh, so showing up close to death on my front porch is taking care of yourself?" I asked.

"You've got me there," he said and kissed me. "Oh, my mom wanted to know if you and Gram would come over for Thanksgiving dinner? The whole pack usually comes."

"I know that I'd love to but I'll ask Gram in case she has something planned," I said as I locked up the building and walked to my car.

Caeden grinned, kissed me, and said, "Great." With a spring in his step he got in his car. He let me pull away first before leaving himself.

Gram was excited about having Thanksgiving dinner with the pack so I promised to tell Caeden. I looked at Archie and realized that Caeden and I had forgotten to go to PetSmart after work. Honestly though, by the time we cleaned up after closing there wasn't much evening left. Especially when you had homework to do. I knew we both had tomorrow off. Gram had another woman that worked only twice a week, Tuesday evenings and Friday evenings. Her name was Cate and she was older, in her fifties, but enjoyed her time at the shop.

I called Caeden and told him about Thanksgiving and asked him if he would want to go with me to the pet store.

"I'm so sorry, Sophie," he said, "I completely forgot."

"It's okay," I said. "I'm a ditz and forgot too. How can I expect you to remember something if I can't remember it myself?" I joked.

He chuckled into the receiver. "That's true. At least now I'll get to bring Murphy along."

"Will he fit through the door?" I joked.

"Of course. He's a dog not a horse," he said.

"I couldn't tell the difference," I said.

"You better get used to it," he said. "We're mates and we're going to be spending the rest of our lives together and that includes Murphy and Archie. Oh, and Murphy sleeps on my bed by the way."

"I guess I'll have to sleep on the floor," I said jokingly.

"Murphy will make room, promise," he laughed.

"That's nice to know," I said.

We said our goodbyes and hung up. Archie took over my pillow again. I kissed the cute little dog on his nose and fell asleep.

* * *

Luckily school was just a regular uneventful Tuesday.

For whatever reason I kept expecting Travis to jump around a corner and say, "Gotcha," but he didn't. In fact he wasn't there at all. I felt that this didn't bode well for any of us. He was planning something. I didn't know what but I knew he had to be up to something. He had been far too smug yesterday.

I pulled into the driveway and grabbed my backpack, thankful that I hadn't been assigned any new homework. Archie jumped excitedly at my legs when I entered the cozy yellow house.

"Gram!" I called out. Her car was in the driveway so I assumed she was somewhere around here.

"Yes, Sophie?" she said coming out of her bedroom. Her reading glasses were perched on the end of her nose and she held a large leather bound book in her hands.

"I just wanted to let you know that Caeden was picking me up. I need to get some things for Archie."

"Oh, I'll get you some money," she said, turning and heading back into her room for her purse.

"No, Gram. Don't worry about it," I said. "Remember? Dad gave me a credit card. I think this would apply under emergency. I mean the dog does have to eat something."

Gram laughed, "Yeah, something other than my slippers would be preferable." She looked down at the floor and I followed her gaze. Archie had indeed chewed a hole through both of her slippers. "At least he's cute," she said as Archie looked at us both with big round puppy dog eyes.

"Yeah, he does have that going for him," I said.

"Talking about me?" asked a male voice from behind me. I turned to look at Caeden. Seeing my face he said, "Knock, knock."

I shook my head. Gram laughed. "I'll see you later."

I gave her a kiss on her wizened cheek, scooped up Archie, and followed Caeden outside. Instead of his Jeep he was in Bryce's.

He shrugged his shoulders. "Murphy's a big dog, and

leather and dogs do not mix. The car came with a warning label."

I laughed. "I'm sure it did. Did this one not come with a warning label?"

"No," he said. "It's fabric."

I climbed into the older Jeep and held Archie on my lap. Caeden climbed in and Murphy leaned forward between the two seats to give Caeden a lick on the cheek.

"I missed you too, buddy," he said to the dog.

I laughed and then was surprised when Murphy's large tongue flicked out and licked the side of my face. "Eww, dog drool," I said.

Caeden chuckled, petted the dog, and said, "Good boy." It looked like the dog smiled.

As we drove Murphy and Archie decided to inspect one another. After a few cursory sniffs they must have been satisfied. Murphy lay down in the back of the Jeep and Archie snuggled into my lap. A light little snore filled the car.

We drove into town and Caeden parked in front of the PetSmart. I didn't have a leash for Archie yet so I held on tight to him. Caeden put the back hatch of the Jeep down and Murphy jumped out. The dog sat there and patiently waited for Caeden to put his leash on. Murphy's leash matched his collar, chunky brown leather.

"Come on Murphy," said Caeden. The dog strode purposefully towards the store. Obviously this wasn't his first time. People in the parking lot openly gawked at the large dog. My heart went out to Murphy, it had to suck having people stare at you, but instead he seemed to like it. He held his furry dog chin high and eyed the staring people, his large tongue lolling out the side. At one point I would have sworn he winked. He grinned his huge, wolfy dog, grin at a man who had stopped in the middle of the road. Caeden laughed at his dog. I was quickly discovering that familiars were more like people than dogs.

The sliding doors opened as we entered the store.

There weren't many people there and there was only one person on the registers. Birds chirped loudly and I could hear hamsters twirling in their little metal wheels. Caeden grabbed a cart, which I put Archie in, and headed towards the back of the store.

I immediately grabbed a big bag of dog food. I picked out a dark purple leather collar and leash. I figured since if it was a darker color it was a little less feminine.

"Purple? He's a boy," said Caeden. Apparently Caeden didn't.

"So? Boys can wear purple. Plus, it's a dark purple."

Caeden shook his head and looked at Archie. "Sorry, man. I tried."

I narrowed my eyes at Caeden and proceeded to pick out some dog toys. I held up a toy shaped like a newspaper that crinkled. "Do you like this boy?" I asked the little black and white dog. He sniffed the toy and took into his mouth. "I guess that's a yes."

I tested him a couple more times. He refused to take several of them so I could only assume he didn't like them. He really was like a little person. Caeden got Murphy a couple of new toys too. Murphy found a pack of tennis balls which he took into his large mouth and pulled from the shelf. He walked around the store holding his prize proudly.

After I picked out a dog bed for Archie we were ready to go. We paid and headed back to the Jeep. Dark had already descended and the full moon winked at us like an old friend. I looked at Caeden. "You're not going to go wolf on me are you?"

Caeden laughed. "I'm a shifter not a werewolf."

He opened the back hatch and Murphy jumped with amazing agility for an animal of his size. Caeden unpacked our cart and I climbed in with Archie. I had snatched his collar from the bag so I affixed it to his neck. His blue name tag, that I had made before we left, dangled from it. Archie quirked his head and then licked my cheek.

I stuck my tongue out at Caeden as he started the car.

"See? He likes his purple collar."

Caeden shook his head and looked at Archie. "Silly dog."

Archie stuck his tongue out and licked Caeden's nose.

We stopped and picked up something quick to eat before Caeden dropped me off at home. He helped me unload the car and then gave me a quick kiss goodbye. My stomach fluttered at the touch of his lips on my skin. I hoped desperately that the feeling never went away. I knew that my body and heart were already in love with Caeden and my mind was quickly catching up with them. I just didn't know when I would be able to say those three little words of, I love you.

TEN.

It was Thanksgiving morning and I was completely undecided on what to wear. I didn't want to wear my typical jeans, sweatshirt, and hair in ponytail. I wanted to look nice. No, not nice, I wanted to look beautiful.

I stood in front of my closet with my hair dripping wet down my back and a towel wrapped firmly around my torso. I put my hands on my hips. What to wear?

I finally pulled out a pair of gray slacks that I had once worn for an interview and my cozy red sweater. Satisfied as far as my wardrobe went I headed to the hall bathroom to do something about my flat, straight, hair. Sometimes, my hair dried with a slight curl on the ends and other times it hung lank and lifeless. I blew it dry the rest of the way and then curled it into soft waves. I thought it looked decent enough. I pulled out my makeup and spent more time than usual, adding eye shadow and blush. Normally, I only wore lip gloss and mascara. But today was important. I wondered if Caeden felt it too. One day I would marry Caeden, he was my mate after all, and we would be spending holidays together... as a family. This was the start of that tradition and it sent butterflies flying excitedly through my stomach.

Gram knocked on the bathroom door making me jump. "Are you ready yet?" she asked impatiently. I had heard her feet pacing outside the door for the last fifteen minutes. "I am an old woman and I have to pee."

I fluffed my hair and decided that I was presentable. "Done," I said opening the door. Gram rushed past me and closed the door in my stunned face. "You could have gone outside," I said to the closed door.

From inside she said, "I'm a shifter not a dog. Only dogs pee outside."

"And cats, rats, mice, bears, wolves, which you are I may add, and other various wildlife creatures. Oh, and frequently human males."

"I'm not a male," she said and I could hear the sounds

of her washing her hands. She opened the door. "You just like to argue don't you?"

"It's my favorite pastime," I said with a smile. "Can we go now?" I asked.

She raised her eyebrows at me, "I'm not holding you up am I?" she asked sarcastically. "I was ready two hours ago and you spent the last three getting ready."

"Sorry," I mumbled. "I'm nervous."

"It's dinner," she said.

"Thanks for stating the obvious Gram. I appreciate that."

"Any time," she replied walking out the front door. We took her Nissan Altima instead of my car. The small car handled the William's dirt driveway surprising well. When we reached the gate Gram pulled out a card like Caeden's and slid it through the slot. The wide gates opened beckoning us forward.

"How come you use a card to get in and a code to get out?" I asked as she navigated the dirt road.

"It's just a precaution. That way if someone manages to get in they won't be able to get out." She was thoughtful for a moment. "Unless they shift to a monkey but I've never heard of that so I think we're safe from monkey attacks," she joked.

"Good to know," I said.

We made it to the end of the circular driveway and it was littered with cars. It looked like we were the last to arrive. Thanks to me. Gram parked behind a large truck that looked like it could squish her small car if it felt like it. The butterflies resumed their nauseating dance. I took a deep breath hoping that the urge to throw up went away. I was shy and from the cars parked in the driveway I knew a large crowd waited inside. It was time to put my big girl pants on.

"Come on Sophie," Gram said from the front door.

"Oh, right," I mumbled, trying to remember how to make my legs work.

I made it to the door just as Gram knocked a second

time. The door swung open to reveal Amy, a frilly apron overtop her classic black dress, "Come in you two," she said ushering us through the door. "Lucinda and Sophie are here!" she yelled over her shoulder.

I was shrugging out of my jacket when Caeden appeared at my side. He kissed my cheek and I leaned back to relish in the comfort that his simple presence brought me. His rich scent of pine and cinnamon enveloped my senses. Caeden took my hand and said, "Come on, I'll introduce you to everyone. They don't bite. I promise."

A large group was gathered in the family room and for each person there was a familiar. I saw the rest of the pack standing in a corner with their familiars standing guard at their side. Poor Archie, I had left him at home, he had to miss out on all the fun.

"This is Emily and Grant," he said pointing to a couple in their forties. "They're Logan and Chris' parents." I could see the similarities. Logan and Chris both had their mom's heart shaped face but Logan had his dad's square chin. Their hair color seemed to be in between their parents shades. Chris had her dad's soft pale green eyes and Logan had his mom's hazel ones.

"Hello, it's nice to meet you," said Emily in a high soprano voice. Her honey blond hair was in a fancy up do and she wore black slacks with a gray sweater. Looking around the room at all the fancy clothes I was glad I had chosen what I had.

"Hello," said Grant taking my hand in his. His hand was large and paw like but warm and soft. His blond hair was brushed back from his face.

I smiled at them both and said, "It's nice to meet you too."

Then Caeden whisked me away to another couple. The man wore a dark navy suit and with his black hair and dark eyes he reminded me of 007. But he also looked like an older version of Bentley. The woman looked like a tiny doll next to the large man. She had brown hair and intelligent green eyes. She smiled when we approached. "You must be Sophie," she said and took my hands in hers. "I'm Angie."

I smiled. "Hello, Angie. You must be Bentley's parents?" I asked.

Angie looked at her husband and patted his flat stomach. "Jeremy really marked him didn't he? I swear that boy doesn't look like me at all."

I laughed. "He does look a lot like his dad," I said smiling at the man named Jeremy.

"I hear you don't shift until January?" she asked.

"January sixteenth is my birthday," I said.

"It's also a full moon," she replied.

"I know," I grimaced. Curiosity had struck me and I had looked it up some time ago.

"Did you know that the most powerful wolves, the best Alphas, eighteenth or sixteenth birthday fall on a full moon?" she asked.

"I didn't know that," I said.

"Caeden's sixteenth birthday was on a full moon. You two are going to be dynamic, unstoppable even. In the legends I've heard of one mate's first shift landing on a full moon but not both," she said.

"I guess we just had to break the mold," said Caeden.

Angie squeezed his arm and said, "You always did have to be different didn't you?"

"Yes ma'am," he replied.

For the first time I noticed what Caeden was wearing. He wore navy pants with a light blue and white striped shirt belted into his pants. The affect was astonishing. His bright blue eyes captivated and held me immobile. The pale blue and white of the shirt made his already tan skin look even tanner and his dark brown hair was falling across his forehead and curling at the nape of his neck. His customary brown scruff covered his cheeks. He was perfect and he was mine.

He smiled at me and it helped to break the trance... somewhat.

We said our goodbyes to Bentley's parents and then he glided me across the family room.

The family room had two story ceilings and dark wood beams crossed the ceiling. The walls were a dark wood paneling like what would be found in a library. And speaking of libraries there was shelf after shelf filled with books. The room was shaped like a rectangle with windows covering the right and front wall. A large stone fireplace stood proudly against the left wall and was surrounded by built in shelves stacked with books. Large leather couches surrounded the fireplace. Blue-gray and brown rugs covered the dark hard wood floors in a haphazard arrangement that somehow just worked. A large chandelier hung down from the middle of the ceiling. It looked like it was made of real wood and wired with tiny lights. The room reminded me of the casual library that might be found in a manor somewhere. I could picture myself snuggling onto one of the leather couches in front of the fire with one of the many books in my hand.

"You look beautiful tonight," Caeden whispered in my ear. I looked over at him, my musings of the room completely forgotten.

I smiled. "Thanks," I said. "You look handsome."

"You think so?"

"Definitely," I said. "If another girl looks at you I might have to claw out her eyes."

Caeden's laugh filled the room. "I'd like to see that."

"I'm sure you would," I said with a smile.

He led me to yet another couple in the room. The man had brown hair and brown eyes. The woman had flaming red hair and emerald green eyes. A little boy of about twelve stood next to the woman. He had red hair and brown eyes. Freckles covered his young face.

"This is Keith, Savannah, and Jake," he said motioning first to the man, woman, and little boy. "Charlotte's parents and younger brother. This is Sophie," he said then motioning to me.

The woman named Savannah pulled me into a hug,

squeezing the air out of my lungs.

"Mom!" yelled Charlotte from across the room. "Don't break her."

"Sorry," said Savannah releasing me. "You're gorgeous," she said. "You two will have the most beautiful children."

Red flames devoured my cheeks like they were starving. But I couldn't help picturing a little dark haired boy and girl with Caeden's blue eyes. I knew Caeden would be an amazing dad. I could see him running around the yard after them now, wrestling with our son, and even playing Barbie's if our daughter asked him too. It was a future I yearned to have. But for now I had to make it through the present.

"Thanks," I whispered. I saw that Caeden's cheeks were red too but I thought the expression on his face looked similar to mine and that maybe his thoughts had gone in the same direction mine had.

Caeden introduced me to a few other people and then we joined our friends where I had to be introduced to their familiars.

"This is Lucy," said Logan pointing to the chocolate lab at his side.

"This is Gwenie. She's an English Mastiff," said Chris.

"My familiar Levi," said Charlotte petting the Dalmatian at her side.

"Marilyn Monroe," said Bentley grinning like the golden retriever at his side.

"And you know Bailey," said Bryce.

I petted each of the dogs and said, "I wish I would've known. I'd have brought Archie."

Just then Gram came in from the foyer. "Apparently someone didn't want to be left behind," she said and I saw that she held Archie in her arms.

"Archie," I scolded, "how did you get here?" I took the little dog into my arms. "Poor little baby," I cooed. "You didn't want to be left behind did you?"

Caeden laughed and shook his head. "That is one determined familiar."

I put the small dog down on the ground to play with the others.

"Dinner's ready!" called Amy coming into the room. She had ditched her apron, showing off her black dress.

The large group of people filed out of the room. I didn't see how we would all fit at a table but no one else seemed worried.

My jaw literally dropped when we stepped into the large dining room. This house must be bigger than I had originally thought. The dining room reminded me of something one might find in a castle or another place of magnificence. The dark wood floor gleamed brilliantly. A large chandelier hung above the long wood table it's crystals casting rainbows throughout the room. The table had to be custom made for it sat at least thirty people and the legs of which were four different wolves. The chairs were all wing-backed and done in a rich gray velvet. A large built in dining cabinet was imbedded into the right wall. Two large windows filled the far wall. Caeden took the head of the table and motioned for me to take the place at his right, Bryce took his left, and his mom beside me. Everyone else took their seats around us. Those pesky butterflies made their return when I realized that everyone was staring at me and Caeden. It had never occurred to me that in meeting these people that I would one day be in charge of them. Caeden had obviously already accepted his responsibility as Alpha but I hadn't even come to terms with what it would mean to be a shifter. Now not only were Caeden and I mates, we were leaders too; leaders of an elite group of shifters. We hadn't even graduated high school yet!

For a moment I felt faint. Caeden kept a firm hold on my hand. Everyone else sat while the two of us stood. Caeden cleared his throat. "I'm so glad that we could all gather here today to celebrate Thanksgiving," he gulped and continued. "This is our first without my dad as our leader. I know that I'm young but I hope that I'm doing justice to the role I've been given. I don't take the job of being Alpha lightly. I know that many of you are older and more experienced than I am and I hope that one day I can have half the knowledge you all possess. I love and admire each and every one of you. I will do the best that I can as your leader and I hope that you will all stand behind me."

The people clapped and smiled, nodding their heads in approval. Caeden gave my hand a squeeze. "Say something," he whispered, barely moving his lips.

Scared stiff I thought of something to say, anything, so I could stop standing there looking like an idiot. "Um," I began. Real classy, I thought to myself, 'um', just stick your foot in your mouth why don't you; I silently scolded myself. "I don't really know what to say. I grew up knowing nothing of being a shifter. I've only known about all of this for a month. It's a lot to just have thrust upon you. I don't know what I would do without Gram, Caeden, and the rest of the pack. I'm not going to lie and say I'm not scared because in truth I'm terrified." I looked at Caeden for support and then continued. "I haven't even shifted yet and a great responsibility has fallen on my shoulders. I only hope I'm worthy enough."

Silence met me and then slowly everyone began to clap. Relief flooded my veins. I was going to kill Caeden later though. He better watch his back.

He let me sit down and then he began to carve the turkey. Everyone passed around the various dishes. I found my plate heaping full and that didn't even compare to the people who had three and four plates. Caeden said a blessing over the meal and then we were allowed to eat. Every piece of food burst inside my mouth with flavor. I had thought Gram was a good cook but Amy could give her a run for her money.

The hungry wolves finished their meals in record time. I left half my plate untouched and had to sneakily undo the button on my pants. Caeden saw and heat rushed to my cheeks. Oh, well, I thought.

Everyone gathered in the family room again. I stayed to help Amy clean up from the monstrous meal, no pun intended, and Gram stayed behind as well. Amy had an industrial sized sink and a restaurant style dishwasher so clean up didn't take as long as I thought it might. In record time I was able to join the others in the family room. The adults had taken to wine drinking. Caeden pulled me into his arms when I came in and we collapsed onto one of the plush leather couches. He kissed me square on the lips right in front of everyone and smiled at me like he'd won the lottery.

He nuzzled my neck and inhaled deeply. "Cookies," he whispered. I giggled. "Did you enjoy your meal?" he asked.

"It was delicious," I replied. "but I did not enjoy that stunt you pulled, making me give a speech, you know I'm shy."

He laughed. "That's exactly why I didn't tell you. I knew you'd chicken out if I gave you time to think about it. I had to surprise you."

"Well, you did and don't you ever, ever," I repeated, "do that again."

"Are you throwing a temper tantrum?" he asked with a grin. "Because this is not Toddlers and Tiaras."

"Oh, you haven't seen a temper tantrum yet. You just wait, mister."

He laughed. "You're cute when you're angry."

"And you're annoying when you're smug." I supplied.

He grinned and pulled me tighter against him. "Oh come on. You know you wouldn't change a thing about me. I'm so full of awesomeness it should be illegal."

"Maybe you should be arrested," I quipped.

"I'll be your prisoner anytime. Bring on the shackles baby, I'm your slave," he grinned mischievously.

My cheeks flamed as I pictured Caeden in handcuffs, my prisoner to do my bidding. Oh dear, I thought. Shut up! I screamed to my thoughts. Wasn't there an off button for your thoughts? I needed one desperately.

Caeden laughed as if he sensed where my thoughts were trailing. I could feel my whole body turning red. At least the sweater and slacks hid most of the treacherous red splotches.

I turned my head, to look at anything besides Caeden, and looked at the beautiful night sky outside the window. I hadn't ever seen this many stars. At Caeden's house I always felt like I was one with nature. It didn't feel as if this house had been built by man but instead created by nature. The trees seemed to embrace the civil war era house and the animals darted around outside like they weren't afraid. It was a sight to behold.

Caeden's fingers lightly played with my hair and then skimmed the line of my jaw sending chills up my spine. His scent of pine and cinnamon surrounded me to the point that I wasn't sure I could think straight. Here we were in a room full of people and it felt like it was only us. Caeden did that to me. He always looked at me like I was the only girl in the world and I would always find everyone around me disappearing. There was only him and only me.

His thumb caressed my cheek and I found my lip trembling and my knees shaking. It was a good thing I was already sitting. As the room and the people around me faded to the back of my mind I leaned my head on Caeden's shoulder. He wrapped his arms around me and held me close. I felt his lips kiss the top of my head.

"You look so beautiful tonight, gorgeous, stunning, and a bunch of other adjectives. I can't believe you're really mine," he whispered in my ear, tickling the hair there.

"I don't think I'm that beautiful but when you say it I'm tempted to believe you," I said.

"You should. I never lie," he smiled.

"Sometimes I can't believe that I get to keep you. That we're mates. You're so perfect and I'm just... not," I said.

He kissed my cheek. "Don't worry I'm far from perfect. Ask my mom. I can never remember to put the toilet seat down," he grinned.

I couldn't help but laugh. "You always know what to say don't you?"

"What can I say? I just have a way with words," he joked.

"You sure do," I said and smiled.

People started to leave and say their goodbyes. I was amazed at how the older wolves addressed Caeden. You'd think it would be weird with Caeden being the age of their children but they treated him like I assumed they would treat any other Alpha, with respect and for some admiration. Chris and Logan hugged me and then Caeden before leaving with their parents. Charlotte had said goodbye a while ago, toting an angry Jacob behind her, because he didn't want to go home and go to bed. Bentley tackled Caeden from behind and gave him a brotherly hug before heading out. Finally all that was left was me, Gram, Caeden, Bryce, and Amy.

"I guess we better go," I said standing and calling Archie to me. He had been curled up next to Murphy, hidden in the folds of his long fur.

Caeden's hands snaked around my waist and he pulled me against him. "Please, don't go," he begged.

I laughed. "I have to go home sometime," I said.

"Move in here," he said. "Lucinda can come too," he added and turned to wink at Gram.

"That's okay," she said. "I'm an old woman. I don't want to be roommates with two smelly teenage boys."

"Hey!" said Bryce, "I don't smell."

We all laughed as he picked up Bailey and stormed out of the room and up the stairs.

Caeden chuckled and kissed my cheek. "Fine, I'll let you leave."

"Let?" I questioned.

He grinned and leaned down to my ear. "If I was desperate I could *make* you stay here. Maybe you could be *my* prisoner," he said with a waggle of his eye brows. His grip tightened on my arm but it didn't hurt. "I could shackle you with my hands alone. You wouldn't be able to get away," he grinned against my ear. "But," he said pulling away, "I'm a nice guy so I'll let you leave."

I pushed his shoulder lightly. "You're not that nice," I joked.

"I'm sweeter than peaches and cream," he grinned, the dimple in his cheek showing.

I saw that Amy and Gram had disappeared. "I've got to go," I said motioning to the door. I gave him a quick kiss but then he held me there, deepening it, my mouth opening under his. "Caeden," I pleaded. But he continued to kiss me like I was all he needed to survive. My body relaxed into his strong arms and my hands tangled in his hair.

He pulled away with a grin. "Bye," he said.

"Bye," I whispered breathlessly. He chuckled and got my coat. He helped me into it and then held the door for me. He leaned down to kiss me again and this time I was the one that took it to the next level. My hand rubbed his cheek and then I pulled away before his kisses convinced me to never leave.

ELEVEN.

It was the third week of December with Christmas break fast approaching. The atmosphere in the school was lifted. We were all just about to get a much needed break. With only two more days to go the teachers had been lenient with homework but harsh with tests. Their claim, if they waited till after break we'd forget everything, I found I couldn't argue with this logic. So with that I had my study hall desk covered in math notes while Caeden distractedly played with my hair.

"Stop it," I giggled when he tickled my face with the ends of my hair. "I have to study."

"Please," he said, "you know that stuff inside and out. You'll do fine."

"Mrs. Harding hates me," I said. "I have to do well on this."

"Sophie, you have a 4.0. I don't think that's about to change."

"Caeden," I sighed. "To have a 4.0 you have to work for it. That's what I'm doing," I said indicating the explosion of equations. I could see Travis' dark eyes glued to me from across the room. His glare was menacing, predatory, but relaxed, the snake preparing to strike.

His fingers played with the skin at the back of my neck.

"Caeden," I scolded.

"Make me a deal. Go out with me tonight and I'll leave you to your studies. Deal?" he asked.

"Caeden, I need to study tonight too," I whined.

His fingers played with chin and then trailed down my arm to my hand. He leaned in and inhaled the skin at my neck.

"Ugh! Fine you win! I'll go out tonight," I said throwing my hands in the air.

He grinned like he had just won the lottery. "Swee-eee-eeet." He said making the word into three syllables. I shook my head at him and turned back to my notes.

No more than thirty seconds later the bell rang. "You're the devil," I muttered.

"That's right, never make a deal with me," he said and bent to kiss my cheek as he stood and grabbed his backpack.

"What about work?" I asked but I knew that since it was Tuesday we were both off. I was just in desperate need of an excuse.

He grinned. "You know we have today off," he waggled his finger at me like I was a pesky two year old. I piled my notes together and stuffed them in my backpack. I brushed my hair out of my face.

"I know," I grumbled and slung my backpack across my shoulder.

"Dress warmly. We'll be outside some," he said.

"Are you trying to get me sick?" I asked as we started down the hallway.

"No," he said. "Have you ever been sick before? I'm talking common stuff, cold, flu?" he asked.

I thought his question strange but I thought about it for a moment. "No," I said.

"All part of being a shifter," he said. "We can still get serious illnesses unfortunately. Like cancer."

"My grandpa had cancer," I said. "I never met him. He didn't know about me. Only Gram did."

"I'm sorry," he said.

"It doesn't matter," I said. "It just makes me think that my parent's sacrificed a lot to be together."

"They did," he stated, "and I'd do the same for you in a heartbeat."

"And I'd do anything for you," I replied ducking into my classroom.

Neither one of us had said those three monumental words but we were getting closer day by day. It frightened me and exhilarated me all at the same time. With a smile on my face I took my seat.

* * *

I stood in front of my closet contemplating what to wear. I wanted to look nice, but not too dressy. Which shouldn't have been too hard but my winter wardrobe, well my whole wardrobe really, was limited.

I pulled out a pair of dark wash jeans and a pair of boots. Now for a top… Hmm… Maybe… Nope, not that… Not that one either…

"Aha," I said pulling out an ivory long sleeved billowed blouse. I slipped it on. Perfect. And my black winter coat would go perfect.

I had curled my hair once again and put on only a minimal amount of makeup. Only mascara and a little blush and lip gloss. I fluffed my hair and picked up black fedora.

I twirled in the mirror not quite satisfied. I spied my dark purple scarf strung across the old chair; I had yet to do any remodeling to my room, not even paint. Maybe one day. Archie surprised me by jumping onto the chair and grabbing the scarf in his mouth. He wagged his tail, jumped down, and brought it to me.

I petted the dog's head as I took the scarf from him. "Thanks Archie but I could have done without the dog slobber. The dog licked my hand and wagged his tail at me. "Bye Arch," I said walking out of my room.

I was surprised to find Caeden already in the living room. I hadn't heard the door open. He looked dapper in his dark jeans, navy sweater, and black pea coat. He smiled when he saw me. His teeth flashing a startling white against his tan skin.

"Wow," he said and I blushed.

"I can look nice when I want too," I said trying to hide my face.

"I can see that," he said.

"Jerk," I said but went and kissed him. He laughed against my lips.

"Go, you two," said Gram, "you're making me positively ill," she smiled.

"Bye Gram," I said.

"Lucinda," Caeden tipped his head and then we were out the door. He had driven his dark red Jeep and left it running so it was nice and toasty warm. The temperature had been steadily dropping every day; it had to be getting closer to twenty degrees then thirty.

"Where are we going?" I asked.

"Downtown," he said, "to the historic district."

"Sounds fun," I said and meant it. I loved old buildings and towns. Just history in general. What can I say? I'm a classified nerd.

"I'd say I'm sorry for taking you away from your studies but I'm not," he grinned as we got on the highway.

"If I fail it's your fault," I joked.

"I can handle that," he said. "As long as you have fun tonight."

"I always have fun with you," I said.

He laughed. "I'm just so exceptionally awesome."

He exited the highway and navigated the dark streets of the town. He drove into the heart of the city and parked in a parking garage.

He stopped the car and kept muttering the section we were in to himself. I couldn't help but laugh at him. "Don't laugh at me," he said. "I routinely get lost in these garages and I don't think you want to be stranded out here in the cold do you?"

"No," I said and then shook my head. "Did you ever think to use the panic button?"

He blushed. "No, that never occurred to me."

"Well, now you know."

He chuckled. "We make a good match," he whispered.

I was quiet for a moment before I said, "We do. I guess this freaky wolf thing picked us for a reason."

He leaned his head against the headrest, the soft glow of the parking garage lights illuminating his face, he took a deep breath and said, "I would've picked you without the wolf thing."

I looked at Caeden, at his glowing blue eyes, and the earnest expression on his face, "I feel the same," I whispered. Despite Caeden being my mate I still found it hard to completely relinquish my heart to him. But I was getting close.

We stayed in the car for a few more minutes, not saying a thing, letting our words hang quietly in the air, making them all the more powerful.

Finally Caeden turned to me and smiled his dimple showing. "Enough of this serious talk let's go have some fun."

He got out of the car and went around to the trunk. I hopped out just as I saw him sling something across his shoulder.

"You play guitar?" I asked.

"Yep," he said.

"Why am I just now learning this?" I asked.

He grinned and took my hand leading me out of the garage in the direction he wanted to go.

"I have to keep a few surprises up my sleeve," he shrugged, "You know... just in case you get sick of me or something," he smiled.

"You know that's not going to happen," I rolled my eyes.

"Still," he said, "I have to keep you on your toes."

I laughed. "I'll be on them," I said. "So, what else don't I know about you?"

"Hmm, besides my all around awesomeness? I'm a ninja."

I smacked his arm and he chuckled. "Come on be serious," I said.

"Okay, I'm trained in most forms of martial arts, but you probably already figured that out. I like to play golf, and go fishing. I sing and play guitar," he said, ticking the different things off on his fingers.

"Wow," I said. "I can't sing to save myself and definitely can't play an instrument."

"I know," he hung his head. "You're in the presence of a serious dork."

"I think it's amazing."

"So," he said, "what don't I know about you?"

"Well, when I was five my mom made me do pageants. By the time I was seven I had put a stop to that. I was always more of a tomboy. I used to play soccer and was good at it. If I had ever stayed at a school long enough I might have been able to get a scholarship."

"You're perfect," he said and I laughed. "Maybe you should try out for the soccer team in the spring."

"No," I said. "I don't think so."

"Why not?" he asked.

"I don't know," I shrugged my shoulders. "I don't really have the time. Between school and work."

"What about college?" he asked.

I looked up at him, "I don't think college is really a priority anymore. I'm a shifter now, and an Alpha. I have a pack that I have to learn to lead."

He wiggled around. "I feel bad about that. If you want to go you should," he said.

"I don't see the point in wasting a bunch of money on a pointless degree. I don't think a college degree is going to teach me how to be an Alpha."

"I guess you're right," he said, "I just hate thinking your choices are being taken away from you."

"Caeden," I said. "I was a shifter before I met you. You didn't cause this. I just found out kind of late is all."

"Well, if you change your mind and want to go. I'll follow you. The pack will too."

I laughed. "That would be awfully selfish of me."

"No," he said. "It would be selfish of all of us. We've talked about it before, the pack. We'd all like to go to college we just thought it would never be an option for us. We all come from money and so it's not necessary. Our earlier ancestors built a fortune so we could protect our clan."

We exited onto the street and all talk of shifters

ceased. The skeletal trees were wrapped in twinkling white lights. Old fashioned lights lined the cobblestoned streets. I really felt like I had stepped back in time. There was even a horse pulling a carriage. My breath fogged the air.

"This way," said Caeden tugging on my arm. He pulled me down the street pointing out various places before ducking inside a small coffee shop. I had never liked the taste of coffee but I did enjoy the smell.

"Caeden!" called an older man behind the register. "It's about time you got here."

"Sorry, I'm late, Griff." Caeden said.

The old man smiled. "Just don't make it a habit." The man looked to be in his late sixties. His hair was gray and hung down to his shoulders. His eyes were a light brown. "Who's this?" he asked Caeden, pointing to me.

Caeden squeezed my hand. "This is Sophie, my girlfriend. I would've said, soul mate, love of my life, my everything, but I didn't want to freak her out," said Caeden with a grin.

Griff's laugh filled the room. "I think you just did."

Caeden shrug his shoulders. "Oh, well. Doesn't everybody preach about their undying love in a coffee shop?"

"No," said Griff, "they don't."

"Damn," said Caeden, "I must have gotten coffee shops and grocery stores mixed up."

Griff laughed. "Just get set up boy." He turned to me. "Sit wherever you would like and if you want anything it's on the house," he said.

"Thanks," I smiled and followed Caeden through the coffee shop/small restaurant. It turned out that even though the coffee shop wasn't very wide it was long and stretched on into a dining room. There was even a small fireplace that Caeden sat down by. "So, you play here?" I asked.

"Yep, every Tuesday. I draw quite a crowd," he said with a wink.

"Oh, I'm sure," I said sarcastically.

"You just wait and see," he said. "I have to get set up.

Why don't you sit over there," he said pointing to an empty table in the front left of the room where I'd have a good view.

"Okay," I said, starting towards the table.

"Wait," he said and grabbed my wrist pulling me back. He kissed me lightly on the cheek and grinned. "Now you can go," he said.

"You're so demanding," I muttered loud enough so he could hear it. He laughed lightly and sat down on a stool in front of the fireplace, pulling out his guitar.

Quite a crowd poured in and scanning it I quickly realized they were all girls around my age, some a little younger and some a little older. They grabbed a table right in front of Caeden. I guessed he hadn't been exaggerating.

He turned and winked at me. "I just want to thank a very special girl for being here with me tonight," he said and nodded towards me. The group of girls glared daggers at me and I shrunk back in my seat.

He first did a cover of Swedish House Mafia's, Save the World Tonight, and then moved into a cover of Death Cab for Cutie's, I Will Follow You into the Dark. He then moved into a song that I knew he had to have written. I found myself blushing at his words. He did a couple more original songs and then finished.

As he zipped up his guitar case, one of the girls from the group, a leggy blond, tried to talk to him. My vision blurred red for a moment and I had to breathe deeply to get a control on myself. Girls were going to talk to him just like boys were going to talk to me. It didn't mean anything. But that didn't mean anything to the jealousy that flared annoyingly in my stomach. I tried to douse it with positive thoughts.

Caeden smiled at the girl and she took that as an invitation to puff out her ample chest. I dug my nails into the wood table so that I wouldn't walk over there and rip out her dyed blonde extensions. I knew that this wasn't really like me. This was the bond. The fact that we were mates. I didn't want another female anywhere near him. He was mine.

Breath hissed out through my teeth. I knew in that moment, had my birthday already passed, that I would have shifted right there in the tiny restaurant. My hands shook so I hid them in my lap so no one would see. The girl reached out and put her hand on his bicep.

That was it! I stood up from the chair so fast that it slammed into the back of the wall with a loud thunk. But instead of confronting the girl like I wanted to I ran into the bathroom.

Luckily no one was in there and I had it all to myself. I braced my hands against the sink and breathed in through my nose and out through my mouth. When I looked in the mirror I saw that my eyes had become bloodshot. So, much for my nice evening with Caeden. I might as well have stayed home and studied like I had planned. I ran the water in the sink and splashed it lightly on my face so my makeup wouldn't run.

My hands were still shaking uncontrollably. "Sophie," I scolded my distraught image, "she's just a girl. There is no competition. Stop this now. You're being beyond silly."

I nodded my head at my reflection and looked at my hands. They weren't shaking nearly as bad. Good.

With one more deep breath I labeled myself dignified enough to leave the bathroom.

When I walked back into the dining area Caeden was sitting at the table and the group of girls was gone. "I'm sorry," I said sitting down.

"Are you okay?" he asked concern shown completely on his face.

I shook my head. "Honestly? I don't know."

"I tried to get away from her as quickly as I could. I could see you were distressed and I'm so sorry about that."

"I knew there was nothing to worry about," I said putting my head in my hands, "but I couldn't help it."

"I know," he said. "From what I understand of the

legends it's a hard thing seeing your mate with someone who shows *interest*. You kind of go into 'back off' mode. It's a natural animalistic reaction."

"But I'm not an animal," I cried softly into my hands.

He chuckled. "If it's any consolation I would be ten times worse than you."

"Somehow, that doesn't make me feel any better."

"If that doesn't make you feel better maybe this will... The entire time she was touching me I hated it. It didn't feel right."

"Stop talking about it," I moaned. "I want to stop thinking about it."

He chuckled. "Alright, I'll stop."

"So," I said, "have I completely ruined our evening or can it be redeemed?"

He laughed, "Oh, I'm not letting you off that easy. That's for sure."

I smiled. "Good."

"You mean you're not freaking out about being away from your precious studies?"

"No, I'm not," I said with a smile. "It actually feels good to be a normal teenager."

He leaned closer to me conspiratorially, a grin playing on his beautiful lips. "We're not actually normal teenagers. Aren't you forgetting something pretty major?"

"Hmm," I said thoughtfully. "Are you a wizard?"

He laughed and scooted back to his original position. "Definitely not." He replied. "I run through the woods I don't brew potions."

I smiled. "Thanks for making me feel better," I said.

"No problem. I have a feeling stuff like that is going to happen to both of us pretty often." He was thoughtful for a moment. "And it's only going to get worse," he whispered. After another moment he smiled and took my hand. "Let's go get some dinner."

I suddenly realized just how hungry I was. "Good idea," I said.

"Come on," he said leading me to the front of the building, his guitar case slung over his shoulder. "Bye Griff," he called before we walked out the door. The older man grunted and I smiled.

I saw that while we were in the coffee shop it had started to snow. It covered the cobble stone streets in a light white blanket and fell from the sky in endless circles.

"It's so beautiful," I said breaking away from Caeden's hands and twirling in the streets like a little kid, my tongue hanging out to catch a random flake.

Caeden laughed. "You're more beautiful."

I stopped my twirling and met his blue gaze, my cheeks flushed from cold, I smiled and said, "Suck up." Then I resumed my twirling.

Caeden's chuckle filled the half empty street. "I try to be the least bit romantic and you always shoot me down."

I stopped and fluttered my eyelashes at him. "If you call that romantic you're going to have to try harder."

"You shouldn't have said that," he said.

He came at me and suddenly my legs were swept out from under me. He twirled me around in the falling snow. I wrapped my arms around his neck. Little white flecks stuck to his black eye lashes making the blue of his eyes look cerulean. I took one hand from around his neck and pressed it to his scruff covered cheek.

"I can't believe you're mine," I breathed.

"Always," he said and pressed his lips to mine. The kiss was hot enough to melt the snow around us. Normally the thought of the people watching us would have worried me but with Caeden I didn't care. He made all my other thoughts disappear. He broke the kiss and pressed his forehead to mine. His arms still held me firmly. "As much as I'd like to stand here kissing you all night I really am hungry."

I laughed. "Okay, let me down."

"Oh, no," he grinned and I knew I was in trouble. "I'm carrying you all the way there. That's your punishment for saying I'm not romantic." He laughed and started carrying me down the street.

"Put me down," I laughed beating on his chest.

"Nope," he said, "not yet."

Finally, after persuasion and fighting him didn't work, I just let him carry me. However, with my arms crossed and a pout on my lips. He strode purposefully towards his destination. A smile kept springing on his lips, his dimple showing. His blue eyes looked down at me.

"I hate you right about now," I said.

He grinned. "Hate? I can handle that. Hate is a passionate word."

"You're incorrigible," I said.

We made it to the restaurant after what seemed like forever. But instead of putting me down like I expected he would he maneuvered me so that he could open the door to the restaurant.

A man stood with a stack of menus in his hand. "My word, is she okay?" he asked.

I rolled my eyes.

Caeden grinned. "She fell and I think she hurt her ankle but she was determined to get something to eat. I told her I thought she might need to go to the hospital. So, here we are," he said with a shrug.

I glared daggers at my mate.

"Well, come right this way. Let's get you seated miss and I'll get you some ice," he said striding into the dining room, Caeden trailing behind him with me in his arms.

"Really," I said, "that's not necessary. I didn't even fall," I whispered the last part.

Since it was late there weren't many people eating but enough that we received quite many stares. The man placed our menus down and pulled out a chair which Caeden promptly dumped me in. Once the man was gone with a promise to bring me some ice for my ankle I said again to Caeden, "I hate you."

He grinned at me completely unashamed. "I couldn't

resist."

The man returned with some ice wrapped in a rag. "Thanks," I muttered and when he had disappeared around the corner I lobbed it at Caeden. He laughed and caught in his hands.

I chose that moment to look around the Italian restaurant. Everything was terracotta colored and a red glow seemed to surround the place. I could smell garlic coming from the kitchen but it wasn't overwhelming. The waitress came to get our drink order and Caeden handed her the rag of ice. She looked at it perplexed and then left. Obviously news of our grand entrance hadn't reached the kitchen yet.

I perused the menu and quickly made up my mind. The girl came back with our water and had her notepad at the ready. "Do you know what you want?" she asked.

Caeden indicated for me to go first. "Yeah, I'll have the fettuccine alfredo."

She wrote it down and turned to Caeden. "I'll have the same," he said.

"It shouldn't be too long," she said with a light smile and took our menus. I thanked her and then she was gone.

"So," said Caeden leaning across the table. I found myself leaning closer to him as well.

"So?" I prompted when he didn't continue.

"Are you still mad at me?" he asked, looking at me with those big blue eyes. I was quickly learning that those blue eyes could certainly get him out of trouble.

"No," I said. "As long as it doesn't happen again."

"I'm not making any promises," he grinned.

"Then I guess I still have to be mad," I said with a light smile.

"Too bad," he said. "But it was certainly worth it."

I laughed. "I'm glad my torment is your pleasure."

"What can I say?" he said shrugging his shoulders. "I'm a disturbed kind of guy."

I shook my head, "And here I thought you were more of the jokester type."

"Babe, haven't you ever heard of not judging a book by its cover?" he said in mock shame, hanging his head.

"Have any tattoos I don't know about?" I asked.

He laughed. "Nope, my skin is perfectly clear. But you're welcome to check."

I looked around the restaurant. "I would," I said, "but you see that lady over there," I pointed and he nodded, "I really wouldn't like to cause her to have a heart attack and die prematurely. That seems cruel. Don't you think?"

"I guess so," he replied.

The waitress returned with our food. We had scooted so close to each other across the table that our noses were practically touching. We jumped apart and both gave a nervous laugh. Caeden coughed into his hand to hide his flaming cheeks. It was getting difficult to resist our magnetism. Our bodies were always being drawn together. There was no fighting it. Heck, most of the time we didn't even realize it was happening.

"This smells delicious," I said.

"Oh, it is," he said.

I took a bite and moaned in pleasure. Caeden laughed. "Somehow," I said around a mouthful, "everything always tastes better when you don't have to make it. Don't get me wrong. I love to cook but sometimes it's nice not to have to. This is a treat."

"I'm glad you're enjoying it," he said taking his first bite.

"Oh, I am," I said taking a big bite that I could barely fit in my mouth.

He laughed.

"What?" I asked. I realized I had pasta sauce smeared across my face. I wiped it off my cheeks turning red. I shrugged my shoulders, "I never did claim to be lady like."

"And I wouldn't have it any other way."

"Oh sure?" I mocked.

"No, really. I like you just the way you are. You're perfect."

I pointed towards his food with my fork. "Just eat so you can stop feeding me lies."

He laughed and shook his head. "One day you'll believe me when I tell you how smart, beautiful, and perfect you are."

"Not likely," I said, and then laughed. "But I am pretty smart."

He laughed, its deep sound resonating in my bones, "You make me laugh," he said.

"I try," I said with a smile and fluffed my hair.

"God I lo-," he stopped himself.

"What?" I stuttered. "What were you going to say?"

"Never mind," he said dismissing his previous statement with a wave of his hand. Had he really been about to tell me that he loved me? Now, looking at his stony expression it seemed impossible.

I scrambled through my brain trying to come up with something to ease the awkward tension. I wasn't used to this feeling around Caeden. "I hope this keeping me away from my studies doesn't resolve in a big fat F."

Caeden sent me a thankful look. "You'll do great, you're smart. I have no worries, you shouldn't either."

"Somehow, I'm still worried," I joked.

We finished our meal and Caeden paid the bill even though I begged him to let me pay my half of it.

He took my hand and we walked outside. The snow was, if possible, falling harder. I loved the crispness in the air and the feel of the snowflakes on my cheeks. "Thanks for dinner," I said. "I would have paid for mine. You didn't need to do that."

"I know you would have, sweetie," he said. "But I asked you on a date and that means that I pay the bill. No arguments. I like to spoil you. You're just going to have to get used to it," he said with a grin, his dimple appeared. I couldn't resist it. I had to kiss that dimple. He grinned when I pulled away.

"Not likely," I replied.

He squeezed my hand and said, "I always win."

"I never lose," I narrowed my eyes.

His smile made his blue eyes tinkle. "There's always a winner and a loser and I am not about to lose on this matter."

I laughed. "I think we just like to argue. What are we even fighting about?"

"The fact that you don't want me to spoil you. I thought that was every girls dream?"

"Not mine," I said. "I can look out for myself. Remember, I moved around a lot so I had to learn to be pretty independent."

"But you don't need to be that way anymore," he said. "I'm here and I'm not going anywhere."

I looked down at the snow covered ground. "I know that," I said. "It's just a lot to get used to."

"I know," he whispered and I wondered if he really did.

TWELVE.

I must have fallen asleep on the way home because I awoke to Caeden's arms wrapped around me as he laid me on my bed. I cracked my eyes open and he said, "Hey, beautiful."

"Sorry, I fell asleep," I said groggily.

He started taking my shoes off. "I actually thought it was pretty darn cute."

I groaned and took my hat off throwing it across my room. I felt a slight bounce on the mattress and then Archie lay down next to me. Caeden turned to leave.

"Wait!" I called and he paused.

"Yeah?" he said turning.

"Thanks for tonight."

He smiled. "Better than studying?" he asked.

"Way better," I said smiling.

He started towards the door. "Wait!" I called again. He looked back at me a full blown grin on his face. Despite being half asleep I stood. I took his face between my hands and kissed him slowly and deeply. "Now you can go," I whispered against his lips.

"Not yet," he breathed pressing his lips firmly to mine. My mouth opened under his. When he saw that I wasn't going to resist he gentled the kiss.

Gram chose that moment to walk by my room. I heard her footsteps pause and then she spoke. "If you two keep that up I'll be a great-grandma. You best stop that now."

Caeden chuckled against my lips. "Love you too Lucinda. Love you too."

Satisfied she walked away.

"Bye," said Caeden pressing his lips once again to mine.

"Bye," I said.

He grinned and left.

I changed into my pajamas and climbed under the covers. For once, Archie gave me my pillow. "Thanks," I muttered to the little dog. He wrinkled his nose at me and then started snoring. I laughed and in moments was sound asleep.

* * *

A strange white light filled my room when I woke up. I pushed the quilt off of me and cracked the blinds in the window that was beside my bed. I smiled to myself. It looked like a winter wonderland outside. It couldn't be more than two or three inches but it was beautiful. It covered the various trees outside my window in a fine dust.

A light knock on my door had me turning. "Hey sleepyhead," Gram said.

I looked back out the window and startled at the amount of light outside my window. It had to be after first period. "Oh crap," I said jumping up.

Gram chuckled. "Don't worry. School's cancelled."

"Oh," I said stopping in my tracks.

"Here," she said holding out a cup of hot chocolate.

"Thanks," I said taking it. I took a sip and let the silky, chocolaty, goodness slip down my throat. "You're amazing Gram," I said holding up the cup.

"I'm still planning to open up the shop today. Would you mind working too much?" she asked.

"Of course not," I said.

"Great," she replied. "I'll make you some breakfast and then you can head over."

I finished my hot chocolate and then jumped in the shower. I blew my hair dry and then pulled it back in a ponytail. I put on a black long-sleeved shirt and then put my *Lucinda's* shirt on over it. I was silently thankful for a moment that Gram let her employees where jeans. I put on the hat and tied the laces on my sneakers. All set.

"Just in time," said Gram sliding a cheese omelet onto a plate.

I sat down at the little table and took a bite, "Yum," I moaned.

Gram laughed. "Good?"

"Delicious," I said.

She sat down then with her own plate. We ate in comfortable silence and then I cleaned my plate.

"Alright," I said. "I'm going to head out."

"Okay, be careful," she said.

"I will," I said, already tugging on my winter coat.

I started my car and let it sit for a couple of minutes to warm up. I pulled away and drove as slow as possible the short distance. The neighborhood roads were pretty bad but once I made it to the main drag the road were fairly decent. I still worried over black ice though.

But luckily I made it to the store without wrecking the car. I parked and Caeden pulled in right at the same time.

"Fancy meeting you here," he said getting out of the Jeep; he had his *Lucinda's* baseball cap on backwards.

I feigned shock, "Caeden Williams are you stalking me?"

He laughed. "I'm not prone to stalker tendencies," he said and then appraised me. "But for you I might."

Now I laughed. I unlocked the backdoor and we set to making the day's cupcakes. We still had two hours before the store opened.

In record time the kitchen was a mess. Flour coated the stainless steel island and the floor. I laughed looking at Caeden. "You have batter on your face," I said.

He wiped at it only making it worse. "Did I get it?" he asked.

"Far from it," I said around a laugh. I turned the mixer off and went to help him. I grabbed a rag wiped gently at his cheek. "It's gone," I said.

"Thanks," he said his voice choked.

I went back to mixing when I heard the curse behind me.

"What is it?" I asked, surprised at the string of profanities coming from his mouth.

"We're out of cupcake liners, cream cheese, and a load of other crap. The truck was supposed to come in last night but apparently it didn't," he groaned.

I wiped my hands on my apron. "Well," I said putting my hands flat on the counter. "What do we do? Can you run to the store and get the bare necessities?"

He took his hat off and ran his hands angrily through his hair before replacing it. "I guess so," he said. "We don't have much choice. Will you be okay?" he asked.

I batted my eye lashes and said, "I know I look like a damsel in distress but I'm really going to be okay for the fifteen minutes it'll take you to go across the road to Food Lion."

He laughed. "Alright," he said putting his hands up in defense, "I get it, you'll be fine." He pulled his keys out of his pocket. "I won't be long," he said starting towards the back door.

"I'll be fine," I said with a laugh and then pushed him out the door.

I already had some batter prepared but since we were out of liners there wasn't much I could do. So, I tried to clean up as best I could. I knew that it would only get messy again but I figured some mess was better than a lot of mess.

I was just rinsing out the rag when I heard the door open behind me. A smile lit my face. "That was quick," I said.

"Were you expecting me?" asked a voice that made the hairs on the back of my neck stand up.

Travis.

Stunned I dropped the rag back into the water where it splattered. Little droplets of water sprayed up to cover my arms, the floor, and the counter. I whipped around to find Travis and a man I didn't recognize.

The man had sandy brown hair and black eyes that matched Travis. He had a strong jaw and a button nose. His button nose didn't match the evil look on his face. He smiled a smile that promised pain and suffering. I knew that this was Peter Grimm, Travis' dad, he had to be.

I looked back at Travis. Trying to think about

anything besides about what was going to happen to me, I wondered where Travis got his white blond hair. It must have been from his mother. But it seemed to out of place with his black eyes.

They took a step closer and the time for thinking about mundane things like hair and eyes was over. My flight or fight senses were kicking in and they were screaming *run!* They had the back exit blocked, there was no way to get around them, and they were too big to fight. I had no choice but to run. And so run I did.

I sent up a silent prayer that I had worn sneakers today and then I sprinted to the front of the shop. I pushed a rolling cart behind me and heard it crash followed by their curses. I could hear their footsteps behind me and it was a small place so I ran faster. I flew through the swinging door and then jumped over the counter and probably bruised my leg in the process but it didn't matter. I had to get out of here now. I reached the door, which meant sanctuary, but it wouldn't open.

It was locked.

And with it my fate was sealed.

I gulped once before something smashed into my skull and then everything went thankfully numb.

* * *

It didn't take long for me to come around. They were pulling me into the back of a large truck at the back of the store.

"Help!" I screamed. Their hold on me tightened. I tried to elbow one of them and succeeded. I heard a muttered 'ow' but they still held tight. "Let me go!" I screamed kicking my legs. I was going to make this as difficult as possible.

The man that I assumed was Peter laughed in my face. "Not likely," he sneered and then closed the door of the truck in my face.

I screamed as loud as I could. Tears ran silently down my cheeks.

Travis and the man got in the car and then were screeching out of the parking lot. Obviously, killing us by hitting ice was not a concern.

Idly I wondered how long it would take Caeden to get back and see that I was gone. Would he know what happened? Would he be able to find me?

Or, I gulped, would they kill me before he could?

I didn't want to die. I hadn't even had a chance to live yet. So, many things I had yet to experience. Looking at their faces I had no doubt that they would kill me. I could see it in their eyes. I knew Travis was a bad person but I hadn't suspected him to be a murderer. But hadn't he and his dad tried to kill Caeden? I knew they wouldn't hesitate to end my life. My life was meaningless. As far as they knew I was just a regular human. I squished my lips together to hold in the whimper that wanted to escape.

"Why are you *doing* this?" I asked my voice cracking.

"Bait," muttered Travis. "Caeden seems fond of you."

"What are you going to do to him?" I asked.

Travis glanced back at me and I knew the answer.

"You're going to kill him." I gulped it wasn't a question but Peter answered me anyway.

"We already failed once," said Peter, "we won't fail again."

I bit my lip until it bled so that I couldn't scream. Tears silently leaked out of my eyes. Kill him. They couldn't. I wouldn't let them. I would find a way to escape? Or a way to warn him? I had to do something. I would not let Caeden die for me despite my earlier thoughts of rescue. When it came to life or death I would die a million times over before I let Caeden die for me. I hadn't said I love you, to him, but I did. I was in love with him. Madly. Deeply. Completely.

They drove for a while before they pulled over and put a blindfold over my eyes and tied my hands together. One of them slapped my face and then shoved me forcefully into the car. My knee collided with the metal of the car door. He laughed. It was Peter.

We drove, and drove, and drove. I knew they were trying to confuse me. It didn't matter though. I didn't want to be found. To be found meant Caeden's death and I couldn't have that.

Finally, after hours, the truck stopped. Someone pulled me roughly from the car and I knew that their fingerprints would leave behind bruises.

"What's so *special* about you?" whispered Travis in my ear before he shoved me forcefully in to the ground. "Clumsy thing aren't you? Pathetic *human*," he spat.

Tears sprang to my eyes again and I was suddenly thankful for the blindfold so that they couldn't see. Travis pulled me roughly up by hair and I couldn't help the scream that escaped my throat. He laughed.

We walked a little further before he let me go and then I heard a creaking noise. A moldy smell accompanied the noise.

Rough, callused, hands grabbed me, I assumed it was Peter. He laughed in my ear before throwing me down. Down. Down.

My body was battered by cement steps. I heard the door slam closed before my head collided with the floor. It throbbed painfully for a moment before I passed out.

* * *

When I woke up, I thought I must still have my eyes closed, because it was much too dark. And then the puzzle pieces slammed together in my head. Travis. Peter. Store. Truck. Blindfold. Creaking. Fall.

Thinking of the fall and dull throbbing in my head came to the forefront of my mind. Despite my hands being tied I could move them enough to remove the blindfold.

It didn't help. It was still so dark that I couldn't make out my surroundings. It smelled moldy, rusty, and stale. It made my stomach churn. I was extremely cold. I could feel the Goosebumps on my skin and my teeth rattled. The ground beneath me was cold and dusty, like maybe it was dirt. I shivered and wrapped my arms tighter around me. I wished I had a jacket or a sweatshirt. Anything to keep me warm.

I could feel the dried tears on my cheeks crack when I moved my face. I scooted across the floor until I found a wall to lean against. The wall was cold like the ground but I was too tired to care. I leaned my head against the cool stone and brought my knees up to my chest. My teeth chattered so hard that my jaw hurt.

After hours of just sitting there I tried to fall asleep. It wasn't a good sleep. How could it be?

Every little noise that I heard jolted me from my restless sleep. And there were lots of noises. I started to become paranoid. What if that dripping noise wasn't water? What if it was a snake's tongue sliding between its fangs? That scuttling noise, what if it wasn't the wind but a rat?

With nothing to distract me my thoughts ran wild. I tried to empty my mind and think of nothing but that was impossible. In fact it was worse.

All I could see was Travis and Peter attacking Caeden. Two against one. I didn't think Caeden would be able to survive another attack by the Grimm's. He barely survived the first. A sob escaped my chest when I pictured them hurting Caeden, I couldn't think the word *dead*.

The wind whistled outside and the temperature continued to drop. Night had come.

* * *

Light filtered into the room and I cracked my eyes open. I must have finally fallen asleep. My neck hurt from the ungodly position I had slept in. My whole body hurt like I had been run over by a truck. No doubt from being thrown around like a sack of potatoes. The shadow of a figure began to descend the concrete steps. Enough light filtered in so that I could see that I was in some kind of underground bunkhouse. Something like you might see in tornado country.

The person stopped in front of me, the light was behind them, so I couldn't see their face. The person bent down in front of me, I flinched away. A hand snaked out and grabbed my chin forcing me to look into their eyes.

I tried to pull away but the hand wouldn't allow me to budge. "Look at me!" growled the voice of Peter. When I resisted he slapped me so hard I was surprised a few teeth didn't fall out. I did taste blood though and I quickly spat it at him. "Ugh! You bitch!" he yelled.

"Why are you doing this?" I screamed at him. "Let me go! I haven't done anything to you!"

"No? I think you have." Tears ran down my face and he shook me. "What do you know?" he yelled in my face, spit flying.

"What do you mean?" I choked.

"You know what I'm talking about! Don't play dumb!"

I just kept shaking my head.

Peter disappeared and I was alone once again. I heard the door slam shut sealing me in and then the sound of a lock being closed.

I put my head in my hands and cried. I knew I wasn't coming out of here alive. I would die here by this man's hands. I knew it in my soul. My time was ticking away. My death was looming not far off. At that moment I would've almost welcomed it. Except for the one thing that was holding me back. I hadn't told Caeden that I was in love with him yet. I knew he loved me despite him not speaking the words either and I also was certain he knew how I felt. But I still hadn't said the words and I feared I'd never get the chance.

Hours later the door opened again. It looked like it must be sunset. I didn't recognize the shape of this person. It looked like a woman. Which meant weaker, but I knew she too must be a shifter so she wouldn't be much weaker.

I launched myself at her with a battle cry. We landed on the steps, her head whacking against the concrete. I jumped up quickly trying to make a break for the door but her hand wrapped around my ankle and suddenly I was slammed back against the floor with the wind knocked out of me.

"Don't do that again," she said sternly. "I may not have killed you but the others would not hesitate to do so. Your life means nothing to them."

I didn't say anything.

"Good," she said and then I felt the prick of a needle being stabbed into my arm.

My muscles instantly froze and my eyelids became heavy. With a smile she climbed off of me. And then everything went blissfully black.

* * *

I couldn't move my arms. Or my legs. I was paralyzed!

I jolted awake trying to get my limbs to move. Noticing the straps that held me in place I let out a breath of release, I wasn't paralyzed, and then I panicked for a completely different reason. They had me trapped! I was tied to some kind of metal table, almost like a coroner's table and I wasn't going anywhere. I pulled against the restraints but they only dug painfully into my flesh. Liquid began to trickle down my fingers and I realized it was my blood.

A laugh sounded from the corner and I stiffly turned my head to see Travis standing in the corner. It dimly occurred to me that they had brought a lantern for some light. No one else, thankfully, appeared to be in the room. One person was better than several.

"Did you think that after that stunt you pulled we'd keep you loose? Silly, silly, Sophie. You could have hurt my mom. My dad and I didn't like that. He was very angry with you. Lucky for you I'm a nice guy and I talked him down from killing you."

He moved closer to me and his hand tenderly stroked my face. He leaned down over me, his breath tickling my face. "I want you," he breathed. "It's not fair that Caeden gets to be an Alpha and gets to have you. He always gets everything," Travis ground out.

I didn't say anything. Fear held me frozen more than

the restraints strapped to my limbs.

"You're one of us aren't you? I can smell it on you. It gets stronger every day. Which means..." he said thoughtfully, turning to pace the room, I let out a breath I hadn't known I was holding, "You haven't shifted yet. But you're a stranger... Adopted they said... but what if it was a lie..." he suddenly whirled around to stand beside me once again. His face radiated pure anger. "Who. Are. Your. Parents?" When I didn't answer he screamed, "Tell me!"

I flinched. Lie to him! Commanded my inner voice. "I don't know!" I cried. "I don't know! It's true, I'm adopted! I don't even know what you're talking about!"

"Liar!" he screamed, his voice echoing. A purple vein looked ready to burst in his forehead.

Tears leaked out of my eyes. "No," I said shaking my head back and forth. "I'm not!"

He paced the room again and ran his hands angrily through his hair. "You're lying! I'm going to ask you again, who are your parents?"

"I'm adopted!" I cried. "I don't know!"

I saw the flash of silver metallic before it sliced my skin. It burned and I screamed. The knife kept stabbing into my skin. He grinned maliciously at me. "Now everyone will know what you are!"

The restraint was suddenly gone from my right arm and Travis squeezed it tightly. He shoved my arm in my face. Blood ran down my arms in endless red rivers, stained my arm, and my clothes. But when I looked past the red I saw what he had carved viciously into my flesh like I was some kind of animal for slaughter. *Liar.* He slammed my arm back down on the table so hard I let out a scream of pain. He tightened the restraint around my arm so that it was even tighter than it had been before. He grinned down at me and then before I knew what he was doing he crushed his lips to mine. A different kind of pain radiated through my body. My body was rejecting his touch. An electric current ran through my body. He jumped away like he had been electrocuted. His black eyes leered down at me with puzzlement. Then with a smile befitting the joker he was gone.

And I was awake with the pain.

Hours later they gave me food, if you could even call it that, and water. But I couldn't eat.

* * *

Days later, maybe it was a week, I lost track, my body began to shut down. I hadn't eaten anything since I had been taken. I couldn't stomach much more than the water.

And every day, several times a day, they tortured me. My body was now more purple and green than natural skin color. I knew my lip was swollen and my nose felt misshapen. I knew I was missing a finger nail which Peter had forcibly ripped from my body. And every day Travis pulled out his knife and retraced the word, *Liar*, so that it never began to heal.

Peter and Travis took turns torturing me. Thank God they never came in at the same time or I'd probably be dead. Travis always ended his torture with his lips pressed painfully against mine and every time my body rejected his kiss with a shock. He'd smirk and walk away. Maybe he mistook the shock as 'sparks flying', instead of, 'get your creepy lips off mine'?

Travis' mom stood in the room with me. "Sweetie," she said which made me flinch. Why did she even bother trying to be nice to me? "Eat something. You're killing yourself." I wanted to mutter to her that I knew that, that I was doing it on purpose. I would much rather die and it be my fault than to murdered. "Please, just a cracker," she goaded.

I didn't move. No morsel of food was going to pass between my lips.

"Fine, have it your way," she said, in her oddly pleasant voice. Her pale blond hair shown like a beacon in the darkened room. As she neared me I closed my eyes and swallowed.

Somehow, against my will, my mouth opened. "What

are you going to do to me?"

I don't know why it mattered. I'd already been tortured. I think my body was beyond feeling pain.

"You really should eat something. You don't look good," she said instead of answering my question. I felt her hand stroke my forehead tenderly like I was a small fragile child and she was checking for a fever. I still did not open my eyes. Her hand disappeared and with a sigh I heard her start for the stairs that led above. To sanctuary.

"Why are you nice to me?" I croaked before she was gone.

I heard her stutter to a stop. "Because," she said slowly, "you're my best friend's daughter. You have her eyes," she whispered and then she was gone.

I let her words sink in. I was her best friend's daughter. Gram said that my mom was the daughter of the previous Grimm Alpha. This meant that Peter was my uncle. Why had that never occurred to me before? If I could've laughed I would have. My mother's brother was trying to kill me. And my cousin, yuck, had kissed me. Gross.

But I couldn't dwell on that. That time had come and passed.

I was dying. Now was not the time to think of the negative. I only wanted to fill my thoughts with Caeden. It was a comfort to know that my death would spare his. That made it seem so much more worthwhile. I knew he would be sad, that he would miss me, but his death would be spared. That had to count for something.

I closed my eyes and filled the blackness with his image. His dark hair, tan skin, and impossibly blue eyes. The scruff that always covered his face. His grin and the way his dimple would sometimes peak out.

Sleep began to overcome me and I realized that she must have given me something.

Oblivion was my new reality.

"Wake up," a voice hissed in the darkness shattering my nirvana.

I cracked open and eyelid. Travis' mom, I still didn't know her name, was kneeling beside me.

She smiled tentatively at me. "Sophie, I'm so sorry about all of this."

I turned my head away from her. I didn't want to hear this.

"My husband..." she gulped, "Peter doesn't listen well. Neither does Travis," she ran her fingers roughly through her hair, "I fear he's just as evil as his father. I don't know what to do with him." She sighed, "I'm trying to convince Peter to let you go. Now that I know who you are, it's even worse, the betrayal I feel. It was bad enough when I thought you were a stranger's child. But your eyes, they're the same shade of brown," she said. "I fear that if he finds out who you are he won't hesitate to kill you." Emotion coated her words. "I always suspected that Christine faked her death. But her parents and Peter believed it. Her body was never found. I knew she had been seeing Garrett and it was forbidden." She sighed. "She also told me she was pregnant. That was the last night I saw her. Those were dark times for our pack. I fear they're only growing darker. Peter tried to kill the Williams' boy and now he's kidnapped you, a teenage girl. What am I to do?" Her head hung. I suddenly wanted to comfort her. She seemed so broken.

"Why don't you leave?" I whispered, my voice was no more than a croak.

"It's blasphemy to leave one's pack. To go out on your own? It's suicide. Lone wolves, especially female ones, don't live long."

"Can't you join another pack?" My voice became a tad stronger.

She leaned against the wall and drew her knees up to her chest. "You mean the Williams'? I suppose but do you really think they're going to want a Grimm to be a part of their pack." She laughed harshly, "Not likely."

"I'm sure Caeden would welcome you," I said even though I didn't believe it. "He's a good leader," I said. "But would you do it? Would you really leave your pack? Leave your husband? Leave your son? Could you swear yourself to Caeden and his pack?"

"Yes," she said. "I would do anything to be rid of this evil. Of this blackness that's leeching into my heart. Anything," she breathed.

"What's your name?" I asked.

"Leslee," she whispered.

"Thank you, Leslee," I whispered, staring up at the ceiling.

"For what?" she laughed harshly. "For keeping you here? For letting my husband and son torture you? I've done nothing worth thanking."

"You've given me hope," I said, "and hope is worth being thankful for."

She was quiet for a couple of minutes and then she said, "Please, eat something."

"I *can't*," I said my voice cracking and a tear escaping the corner of my eye. She didn't argue me. She could tell it was pointless. "Can I ask you a favor?"

"Anything," she breathed her eyes lightening. She truly was seeking redemption.

"I don't care if they kill me," I said and she flinched, "but please don't let them hurt Caeden. I love him. He's *everything*." I was surprised by how strong my voice suddenly sounded.

"I'll protect him with my own life," she said.

"Thank you," I said, another tear escaping my eye. A happy tear. I had my guarantee. Caeden would be safe.

And then I heard it. A dog barking, the call of, "Sophie!"

Rescue had come.

THIRTEEN.

Leslee stood. She glanced over at me with pleading in her eyes. "I'm sorry, I must leave you. I have to find Peter. He'll be furious. I don't know what he may do."

"I understand," I whispered. She was almost out the hatch when I called a reminder, "Don't let them hurt Caeden. Please," I begged.

"I won't," she said and then was gone, closing the hatch back up behind her. I noticed she didn't lock it.

The dog's bark stopped. I knew that bark though. It was Archie. Just as I was about to start worrying that something had happened to my familiar he started barking again. This time much louder and much closer.

"Sophie!" several voices called.

I heard Peter yell and then his wife's hushing tones.

"Sophie!" yelled again followed by a grunt and then ferocious animal growls.

"I'm in here!" I screamed as loudly as I could which wasn't very loud. I swallowed several times to moisten my throat. "In here! I'm in here! Help me! Please! I'm in here!" I yelled over and over again. The growls sounded like they were right outside the hatch. I heard a yelp followed by a loud thunk and I feared the worst. Had someone gotten the best of Caeden? Please, God no, anything but that. I heard yet another thunk and it sounded like an additional wolf had joined the fight.

"She's in there!" I heard Leslee say before she cried out in pain. More growls erupted and then the tearing of flesh. I heard her scream again and then her screams were silenced.

Wolves growled at each other. I could hear them pawing the ground. And then someone made the first move and an all-out war was launched.

The fight seemed to go on forever before I finally heard the voice of an angel, the voice of Caeden, say, "Sophie, I'm coming!"

The hatch opened and he descended. "Oh, Sophie,"

he choked. My beautiful angel, my wolf, my mate, my everything, strode forward. "What have they done to you?" He came forward, his hands shaking, and ripped the bands from my arms and legs. Drops of moisture sprinkled onto my bare skin. For a moment I wondered at what they were and then I understood.

"Don't cry," I whispered, stroking his cheek as he leaned over me.

His tears turned to sobs and he knelt beside me. He laid his head beside me. I ran my fingers through his silky brown hair. "I thought you were dead. I thought I had lost you."

"I'm here," I whispered. "I'm not going anywhere."

"I didn't think I'd ever find you and if I did I was sure you'd be dead. Lucinda said that I would know though, if you died, she said I'd feel it," he said putting his hand to his heart. I saw then that his chest was bare and he wore only a pair of jeans.

Tears began to leak from my eyes even as I wiped away his. He stood and gently pulled me against his chest, careful of my cuts and bruises.

I wrapped my arms around his neck. "Caeden," I breathed against his neck. "I love you."

"Oh baby," he said, "I love you too. I thought I'd never get to tell you. But I do. I love you so much. I'm never letting you leave my side again. Never."

"I love you," I whispered over and over again. It felt so good to finally say those words.

After a few moments Caeden pulled away. He looked into my eyes and gently traced a cut on my brow. "Let's get you out of here. It's time to go home."

"I am home," I said folding myself into his arms. "You are my home."

He cradled me in his arms and kissed the top of my head. "I'm so sorry, Sophie," he said and started crying again.

"Why?" I asked tracing his brow. "You have nothing

to be sorry for."

"I have everything to be sorry for. I shouldn't have left you. This is all my fault," he said. I wiped away his tears with my hands.

"Oh Caeden," I breathed. "This isn't your fault. They were waiting for their chance to get me and they took it. They used me to get to you. Caeden," I cried, "they want to kill you." Tears ran down my face with a force akin to the Niagara Falls. Our tears mingled together. "I'm willing to die so they can't have you. I won't let them hurt you."

"Oh baby," he said. "Please, don't talk like that. Your life is so much more important than mine," he pulled away and for the first time really looked at me, "Look what they've done to you. They've hurt you so badly. I promise that I will make them feel everything they've done to you. I *will* make them pay for it. They deserve to be tortured like you have, to be held prisoner, and treated like an animal."

"Caeden, please don't talk like that," I begged. "Please don't."

He ran his fingers through my matted, dirty, hair. "Alright," he said. "Come on, up you go," he said lifting me into his arms.

"I can walk," I pleaded with him.

"I doubt that," he said. "You're no more than skin and bones and you're hurt. How long have you been strapped to that table?" he asked.

"How long have I been here?"

"Almost a week," he replied starting up the steps.

He paused when I said, "Almost that long." Suddenly, remembering something, I asked, "Caeden, what happened to Leslee Grimm? Is she okay?"

He gulped. "She's dead, sweetie."

"What? What do you mean? You didn't did you? Please, tell me you didn't kill her? She promised to keep you safe. She said she wanted to leave her pack that she wanted to join your pack."

"Oh, honey," he said, "I didn't kill her. She... she

died protecting me. She jumped in between me and Peter. He killed her."

"He killed her?" I repeated as he continued the rest of the way up the steps.

"Like it was nothing," he said, and I could tell he was choking on his words, "he didn't even hesitate. Travis saw, he and his dad got into it and then ran off. I don't know where the rest of their pack is. It was only the three of them."

The hatch came open and Bryce smiled down at us. "Hey Sophie. Man, you look like crap."

"Really?" I replied sarcastically, "No one told me this wasn't a five star hotel."

He laughed, "Sorry, thought I'd try and get you to smile."

"Bryce," scolded Caeden, "I don't think she feels like smiling right now."

When the light hit my skin I soaked it up like a starved child. It felt like it had been months, not days, since I had seen the sun. We were in a thickly wooded area. Snow still covered the ground in splotches but I could see it quickly melting. It had to be over forty degrees. Trees surrounded us completely. The only buildings were a small log house, that looked more sinister than it did cozy, and the underground cellar area we had just emerged from.

Then my eyes lit upon an odd shaped formation in the dirt. A strange noise escaped my throat. It was a cross between a sob and a scream.

Her glassy green eyes stared up at me. Her blond hair was matted with dirt, twigs, and other woody debris. A slight smile covered her death frozen lips. Crimson red seeped out of a gaping hole in her neck. I could see the teeth marks around her slender neck and claw marks covering her body. Like, Peter had forcefully held her down and then bit into her throat.

"Sophie," breathed Caeden, "don't look."

"It's kind of too late for that," I replied. He winced and started walking away from her body. Bryce was at our side. I didn't see anyone else but I would've assumed it wasn't just the two of them. "Wait!" I cried and he stopped.

"What is it?" he asked.

"What's going to happen to her? It just doesn't seem right to leave her like that. Can... Can we bury her?"

The brothers exchanged glances and then both nodded, decided.

"Alright," said Caeden, "I can see this is important to you."

"It is," I said.

"Let's get something in your stomach and then we'll worry about that. Okay?"

"Okay," I said and realized that for the first time since I had been kidnapped I felt hungry.

We walked for about a mile while I complained that I was too heavy and he was going to hurt himself. "You're light as a feather," he said. "Don't worry. I won't drop you, I promise."

I huffed and didn't say anything else because I was pretty sure that I *wouldn't* be able to walk. We finally came down off a hill to some sort of a side road. I could hear Archie barking madly. Caeden's Jeep was there, so was Bentley's GMC Sierra. His black truck looked like a big hulking monster.

"The others left," said Bentley stepping away from his truck. "It's just us," he said indicating him, Logan, Chris, and Charlotte.

"It's probably for the best," said Caeden. "They're getting too old for this."

"Old?" screeched a voice. "Caeden Henry Williams, I better not have heard you right. If I recall, you needed our help."

"Gram," I breathed and she smiled.

"I wasn't about to risk anything when it came to removing her safely. I may be young but I'm not stupid," he muttered.

"I know that," she said to him, patting his bare

shoulder, "but you young people always seem to forget that there's still some fight left in us older folks. And your parents' aren't old anyway," she said turning to glare at the various wolves. Her gaze traveled back to Caeden, "Your mom was amazing out there. If I hadn't held her back I think she would've single handedly shredded Peter Grimm to pieces."

"I believe you," said Caeden, "she was pissed."

"Watch your mouth," Gram said with a smile.

"Yes, ma'am," said Caeden with a tilt of his head.

Bryce opened the trunk of the Jeep and Caeden gently set me down. He handed me some crackers. "Sorry, it's all I have."

"That's fine," I said, "I'm not sure I could stomach much else."

Charlotte and Chris came over. "We were so worried about you," said Chris.

"Caeden's been beside himself with worry," said Charlotte.

"We all have," said Bentley. That surprised me coming from Bentley. I didn't know him that well. He was Caeden's best friend and a part of the pack, that was about as far as our relationship went.

Caeden shook his head, "I've never been more scared in my entire life. I thought my soul was gone." He sat down beside me and held me against him while I tentatively nibbled the crackers.

Bentley cracked a smile and looked at me. "He was like a crazy man. I've known him since we were in diapers and I've never seen him freak out quite like that. Not even when his dad was found dead."

"Thanks for bringing that up," said Caeden.

Bryce and Caeden both looked sad at the thought of their dead father. Bryce sniffled and walked off into the woods.

"Sorry," said Bentley and he looked like he truly meant it. I saw Chris lean against him and rub his arm reassuringly.

Caeden looked at me to explain. "Bryce, found our dad's body. He's never gotten over it. Not that I can blame him."

"What happened? If you don't mind me asking, you don't have to tell me," I assured him.

"We don't really know. We thought it was an accident but now I'm not so sure. He... He was caught in a hunter's trap... But... while we were scanning this area for you... I saw the same kind of trap."

"Here?" asked Bentley.

"Yes," whispered Caeden.

"You think Peter had something to do with it," said Bentley, it was a statement not a question.

"I thought it was an accident before, that he had been careless and gotten stuck, but dad never was careless. I think he was lured into it by Peter."

"But why?" asked Bentley.

Gram had joined us. Caeden answered Bentley's question but he was looking at Gram. "Because, that meant I would become Alpha. Once he kills me, Bryce will become Alpha. Once he takes out Bryce the line ends and he can become Alpha. He'd have the control of two packs. He craves power. The power of this pack is the only thing he wants."

Gram nodded her head, "I've suspected as much. It'll only get worse if he finds out that Sophie is a true Beaumont. He still doesn't know does he?" Gram asked turning to me.

"No," I said. "Leslee said she knew who I was. That I have my mom's eyes. He made her test my blood but she lied to him. She told him that I was only a human that I really was adopted. She also said that he still believes that my mom is truly dead. She says the pack has never suspected otherwise."

"That's good," said Gram. "The less he knows the better for all of us. Peter Grimm is not one to be angered."

"Gram," I said looking down at the crackers in my hand so I wouldn't have to meet her eyes, "if all the Grimm's are so evil why is my mom different? She's always been nice to everybody and the best mom anyone could ask for."

"Christine always rebelled against what her parents wanted her to be. She was always a sweet girl. She was different than them. I think that's why they always clashed. I mean, the poor girl, had to fake her own death. When she met Garrett I worried, like any mother. She was a Grimm and I thought she was going to corrupt my son. I thought she was leading him on. Finally, your dad came to me and told me that he believed that he and Christine were mates. We started researching the legends and I was positive that he was right. I had gotten to know her better and genuinely liked her. But I still worried. If her family, or even if my husband, had found out… They would both be dead, of that I'm certain. When she got pregnant with you they had to leave, it was the only way to keep you and them safe. I sent them money every once in a while and they would send me pictures of you to a post office box. When your grandpa died they started sending you here every summer. It was the highlight of my year."

"Gram, was my dad really in the military?" I asked.

"No," she said. "That was a cover for all the moving you guys had to do. Your parents feared that if they stayed in one place too long that the Grimm's might find them."

"They sacrificed everything for me," I whispered.

"No," she spoke softly, "they sacrificed everything for each other. You and Caeden will do the same."

I looked at Caeden and he looked at me, "I know," I whispered, "I'm already there."

I finished the crackers and Caeden said, "Alright guys, let's go bury Leslee so we can get out of here."

I squeezed his hand. "Thank you," I said.

His blue eyes glowed with love. "I'd do anything for you."

"I know," I said.

He grinned. "I assume you want to come," he said.

"Of course," I said. "You didn't think you'd get off that easy by just leaving me behind, now did you?"

"Of course, not," he said, and picked me up.

"I think I can walk now," I said.

"I'm going to carry you," he said. Seeing that I was going to protest, he added, "Please, don't argue about this with me. I don't doubt that you can walk but maybe I just want to hold you close. You've been gone for almost a week. Holding you in my arms means that I know you're safe."

"I understand," I whispered.

"Good," he said. "Bryce," he called over his shoulder, "come on."

I saw Bryce emerge from the woods with red eyes and a puffy face. I was surprised when Charlotte went to comfort him.

We all started the trek back to the encampment, well except for maybe me; I just had to lay there while Caeden held me. When we came through the opening in the trees I hoped to see Leslee sitting up and smiling like nothing had happened. But of course, that wasn't the case, she was dead. Murdered by her husband.

Caeden set me down on the wooden steps of the log house. He went around back and returned with a couple of shovels. He tossed one to Bentley and one to Logan, keeping the third for himself. "Bryce, can you sit with Sophie?"

"Sure thing," he said and hopped onto the step next to me.

The boys set to work on digging the makeshift grave.

Bryce and I talked for a while before he stood and said, "I'll be right back."

I watched him go and he returned with a large rock in his hands. He sat down next to me once again and then pulled a knife out of his back pocket. I flinched. He glanced over at me and murmured, "Sorry."

He set to work carving something into the stone. It took him a long time but the end result brought tears to my eyes. He showed me the carving he had created, LESLEE GRIMM, WHO WAS NOT A GRIMM AT ALL.

"Bryce," I said choking on tears. I hugged him to my

chest. "Thank you. This means a lot."

"She helped you. I understand why you want to do this for her. I thought this would make it as close to a perfect grave as it could get."

"Thank you, really, Bryce," I said again. I was still hugging him and his hand rubbed soothing circles on my back. "How did you guys find me?" I asked.

"Archie," he said. "Your familiars can always find you."

"Oh," I said. "I forgot about that."

He laughed. "So did we or we would have found you sooner. When you panic like we all were, coherent thought goes out the window. We just thought the dog liked to bark at us. Then once we understood that he could find you it took a matter of understanding which way he wanted us to go. You can't exactly talk to them and we didn't want to walk because for all we knew you were halfway to Tennessee."

I laughed, "That's true. Where are we?"

"The mountains of West Virginia," he said. "Deep in the mountains," he said. "We would've never found you if it wasn't for Archie. I think that dog and Caeden have formed some kind of weird relationship," he said with a laugh. "Caeden has talked only to that dog for days straight, only stopping to yell at us, like he was going to answer back or something. I don't know maybe he did. I've always found dogs to be quite human."

I laughed and bumped my knee against his. "Despite all of this," I said waving my arms to cover the entire area, "you still manage to make me laugh."

"I try," he said.

The boys finished digging the grave and Caeden went to get her body. I saw that someone had wrapped her in a blanket. They gently deposited her body into the grave and then started covering her with the dirt they had just dug up.

A few tears escaped my eyes and Bryce wrapped his arms around me. "It's okay, Sophie," he whispered. "Go ahead and cry."

And I did. I cried for me. I cried for Caeden. For all the wolves. My mom and dad. Gram. But mostly for Leslee.

She had lived through hell being married to Peter and then bore a son that was just as evil as his father. She had died to save my mate; not given it a second thought. Leslee had spent her entire life being a part of a pack that was nothing but evil. Yet, she epitomized everything that was good. She was someone to admire. She was a good person and her life had been cut short because of that. I could only hope that she was in a better place now, no matter how cheesy that may sound, she deserved it. She deserved to find some happiness in her death since she had so little in her life.

I wiped away the last of my tears with the back of my hand. "Better now?" asked Bryce.

"Much," I replied and gave him a small smile, but it was forced and he knew it. I didn't really feel like smiling after all I had been put through. But I was safe now. And that's what mattered. The torture was over. I would never have to be put through that again. It was over. It was done.

The boys patted the dirt trying to compound the small hill that had risen. Caeden leaned against his shovel and wiped sweat from his brow. Normally the sight of him shirtless and glistening in sweat nearly sent me into convulsions but not this time. It still made my heart pitter patter but not at the magnitude it normally did. This week had changed me completely. I was forever changed. How could I not be? I didn't want to let what happened to me ruin me but it wasn't something I could just forget either. I hoped time could heal me. And if time couldn't then I hoped Caeden could. "We're done," he said.

"Thank you," I said standing and going to hug him. He wrapped his arms around me but loosely. I was thankful. My entire body was sore. I knew I must look horrible but I had vowed to myself not to look at my reflection.

Bryce came over carrying the large stone. I knew that a normal man would never have been able to lift it, let alone carry it without breaking out in a sweat. Bryce placed the makeshift headstone at the top of the mound. He disappeared into the trees and returned with a bunch of frozen wild flowers in his hand. He shrugged and said sheepishly, "It was all I could find."

He gently placed the flowers on top of the marker and they all turned to look at me.

"You should say something," said Caeden squeezing my hand gently like I was a fragile piece of glass that might shatter if he wasn't careful.

"Um…" I started meeting all the eyes staring at me. I cleared my throat and looked instead at the grave so that I was speaking solely to Leslee. "I didn't know you well. I know you were my mom's best friend and I know that you saved me." I sniffled. "You saved Caeden because I asked you too. You were a good person but you were with the wrong one. You deserved to find peace and since you didn't find it in life I hope you've found it in death. Thank you for your sacrifice. I will never forget what you've done for me."

I stepped away and let out a breath I hadn't known I was holding. I looked up into Caeden's clear blue eyes. "Ready?" he asked.

I nodded my head.

They put away the shovels and then we started back to the car. Caeden let me walk this time but he kept a firm hold on me and lifted me over various obstacles. I was thankful for his solid presence at my side.

We made it back to the cars all in one piece. I didn't tell Caeden but I was still expecting Travis and Peter to come out and attack us. I didn't trust them and I knew they'd be back and with a vengeance. That was both of their personalities. They didn't give up.

Gram had stayed behind and dozed quietly in the front passenger seat of the car. The sun had almost completely set and darkness was slowly taking over. Caeden dug in his pocket and tossed his keys to Bryce, "You drive," he commanded his brother.

"Sweet," said Bryce, running around to take the

driver's seat. Caeden shook his head at his little brother. He said a quick thanks to the others who then hopped in Bentley's GMC and took off.

Caeden gently helped me into the backseat of the Jeep and then laid me down with my head in his lap.

"Home," I breathed.

"Yes," he whispered, "I'm taking you home."

"Not if I can't get this stupid thing to work," said Bryce hitting the built in navigation system.

"Hey, hey," scolded Caeden. "Don't hurt it."

"Stupid Chinese," muttered Bryce, "can't they make anything simple?"

"Don't diss the Chinese just because they're smarter than you. It's unbecoming," Caeden said with a laugh.

Bryce mimicked his brother in a high-pitched voice. "Don't be an ass, how about that?" he grumbled.

Caeden rolled his eyes. "A simple navigation system has your panties in a bunch? What am I to do with you?"

"One: I don't wear panties. I prefer to go commando. Two: why don't you just feed me to the wolves? Oh right, I am one," laughed Bryce.

"Too much information," said Caeden. I sat up so that Caeden could lean forward and fiddle with the navigation system. Five seconds later he sat back and muttered, "Was that so difficult?"

"Very," said Bryce, turning on the headlights and putting the car into gear.

"What's all this grumbling about?" groaned Gram. "Can't you see an old woman trying to sleep?"

The boys laughed. "You're not old," said Caeden.

Gram scoffed. "What planet are you living on? The planet of the completely blind?"

"How about the planet of the completely absurd?" added Bryce. Gram smacked the back of his head. "Ow," he said rubbing his head. "What was that for?"

"For calling me old!" quipped Gram.

I started to laugh but immediately stopped when it

hurt too bad. Caeden noticed and sent me a sad look. He pulled me back down onto his lap and ran his hands through my hair. "I'm so sorry," he whispered.

"It's not your fault," I said. "Don't torture yourself with something that was out of your control."

"I can't help it," he said sniffling, his tears dripping from his chin onto my face. "I'm your mate. I'm supposed to protect you."

"Shh, can we talk about this later?" I asked, my eyes already growing heavy.

"Of course," he said.

"Thank you," I said before sleep took me blissfully for the first time in a week.

FOURTEEN.

When the car stopped I was disoriented for a moment. Then I realized that we weren't at Gram's house but Caeden's.

"Hey, sleepyhead," he murmured when my eyes cracked open.

"Why are we here?" I asked.

"Because I'm not letting you out of my sight. At least not yet. Lucinda agreed, right?" he asked Gram as she was opening the car door.

"Reluctantly," she said.

"She said she'd only let you stay here for a few days if she could supervise. I told her that was completely unnecessary. My mom's here after all."

Gram said something unintelligible and started towards the door. Caeden helped me out of the car and into the house.

Gram and Bryce had already disappeared but Caeden's mom stood in the doorway. "Oh, Sophie," she sighed, "I'm so happy you're safe."

"Me too," I said. She took in my battered body and winced.

"I'm sure you want to get a shower and get cleaned up so we'll talk more tomorrow, okay? I'll make you a big breakfast," she said emphasizing with her hands how big. "You look like you've lost fifteen pounds. You're no more than skin and bones, you poor thing."

"I feel like skin and bones," I said.

She came forward and gave me a light hug, her hands fluttering, frightened to hurt me. "Caeden will take care of you. I'll make you a snack for when you come out of the shower, okay? And don't worry, if you can't eat anything, it won't hurt my feelings, but just try," she said with a mothering look and patted my hand. I saw her disappear into the kitchen.

"Come on baby," said Caeden. He held tightly to my hand and we started upstairs. I had never been upstairs before.

"Where are we going?" I asked.

"To my room," he said.

I couldn't help the blush that flooded my cheeks. "Does your mom and Gram know about this?"

"Mom knows," he said and then grinned wickedly. "And what Lucinda doesn't know won't kill her."

I laughed at that. "You're probably right. I think it'll take a lot to kill her."

"I agree completely. She's tough as nails." He turned down the left hallway and then stopped in front of a door. He put his hand on the knob and said, "Promise not to laugh?"

"I won't laugh," I said rolling my eyes.

"Promise?" he smirked.

"I promise," I said.

He swung the door open, turned the light on, and said softly, almost shyly, "This is my room."

The walls were a blue gray color that instantly calmed me. He had a queen size bed pushed against one wall; it was dark wood with a high headboard with spindles and four posts. The posts at the bottom of the bed were shorter than the ones at the headboard though. His sheets were a medium gray color and the quilt that covered his bed was various shades of gray and blue. The window beside his bed overlooked the backyard and the left window overlooked the side yard. There was one door that I assumed was his closet, the one we came through, and a third door that I assumed to be an attached bath.

A couple of guitars hung on the wall, along with what looked like a violin, and ukulele. The floor was covered in a squishy white shag carpet that felt heavenly against my feet. Several bean bags chairs littered the floor in front of a flat screen T.V. I could see an Xbox and PlayStation. Boys and their games, I thought to myself. His dresser matched his bed and the top of it was surprisingly neat. Even his bedside table wasn't cluttered. His bedside lamp made me laugh. It was a bulldog wearing headphones with a gray shade. I noticed the light on his dresser was a stick figure playing guitar. A dear head made out of twine hung above his bed. An aged wood mirror hung above his dresser. What looked like an old work bench sat in the corner serving as a desk. The top of it was littered with a pieces of paper covered in black ink and in the midst of it sat a very sleek looking laptop. I suppressed a chuckle when I saw the mini fridge beside the desk. Various wall art was hung about, intermixed with sports trophics and pictures of Caeden as a child.

I saw one of Caeden, fishing with his dad; he held his catch proudly in the air displaying his missing front teeth. There was a picture of Caeden holding a newborn Bryce. Another showed Caeden dressed as Superman and Bryce as Batman as they posed on the porch steps. There was a picture of just their dad setting up a tent, his smile was much like Caeden's, but his eyes were a deep rich brown. One picture that made me smile was of their dad, Caeden, and Bryce all lined up in a row playing golf, all were in the same pose. Arms swung back, club in the air, and foot crossed watching to see where the ball would land. There was another one where Caeden was rolling around in the sand at the beach trying to fend off Murphy's massive tongue.

I turned back to look at him taking in all that made up his room, made him, and smiled.

"Do you like it?" he asked sheepishly. "I think my mom might have gone a little crazy at Pottery Barn."

"I love it," I said, "it's very you."

He laughed and looked around. "Yeah, I guess it is."

"I like how you have pictures of your family out. It's nice," I said.

"You can't forget my friends," he said pointing to a recent picture of the pack that looked like it had been taken over the summer. They all smiled goofily as the ice cream they held ran down their fingers in sticky rivulets. He looked at me. "I need to get a picture of you up here," he said.

"Oh no," I said, "no pictures."

"Oh, yes," he said wrapping his hands around my

waist and kissed my cheek. "I have to a have a picture of my girl."

"How about this, you can have a picture when I'm not covered in bruises, deal?" I suggested.

"That sounds fair," he said and moved towards the third door. He opened it and sure enough it was a Jack and Jill bathroom. "There are towels and wash cloths under the sink and so are spare toothbrushes." He looked in the shower and smiled shyly, "I don't think you want my and Bryce's guy smelling stuff so I'll go see if I can borrow something from my mom. I'll be right back," he said.

I proceeded into the bathroom, avoiding the mirror at all costs, and turned on the shower getting it nice and hot. I had just pulled out a towel and cloth when he returned with various shampoos and body washes. He dumped them on the counter and then went to the other door that led to another room. "Bryce," he called. I heard a mutter from inside and then Caeden said, "I just wanted to let you know that Sophie's using the shower so please don't break the door down." Another grunt and Caeden closed the door. "Little brothers," he muttered. He looked around the bathroom obviously embarrassed. "I'll... uh... leave you to it," he cleared his throat, "Take your time and I'll find you something to wear."

"Okay," I said. "And thanks."

He kissed me quickly on the cheek and then closed the door behind him.

Everything in the bathroom was an updated black and white look. Much like the kitchen below. I grabbed a bottle of shampoo, conditioner, and body wash and placed it inside the steamy glass shower. I stripped my clothes and threw them in the trash can. I never wanted to see that outfit again. I climbed in the shower and flinched at the feel of the water beating down on my sore body. Instead of healing it was hurting. Silent tears leaked out of my eyes at the pain. It was a miracle I didn't have any broken bones. I began gently scrubbing the dirt and grime from my body. The water that swirled down the drain was brown and red and nearly made me sick. It took me forever to wash the dirt and tangles from my hair. My hair felt like one big rat's nest. Finally satisfied that I smelled decent and didn't resemble a sewer person I climbed out of the shower.

Upon hearing the shower cut off Caeden knocked on the door. "I found some clothes and my mom gave me a hairbrush," he said through the thick wood.

I made sure the towel was secured tightly around my torso before opening the door. His eyes glazed over when he saw me. "I know," I said, "I still look horrible."

"You're beautiful," he said, "you always are."

"Even when I've been strapped to a table and tortured?" I asked softly.

"Even then," he said. "Oh, here," he said handing me the clothes.

"Thanks," I said, "I won't be long."

I closed the door again. He had brought me a pair of his old boxers and a gray t-shirt. I found myself inhaling the scent of him that wafted off the shirt. A slight smile lifted my lips. Even his scent was perfect. I was thankful for the hairbrush and set to work brushing out the clump of hair.

I was still shocked by my appearance in the mirror but I knew it couldn't be half as bad as what I looked like before. My body was littered with bruises. I resembled a human punching bag. And speaking of bags, the ones under my eyes were the size of Alaska. My lip had a cut in it that was blistering around the corners. And there was no hiding the emblazoned, *Liar*, on my arm. It shone like a beacon. I quickly worked out the tangles in my hair as exhaustion started to take over.

After I brushed my teeth I opened the bathroom door and turned off the light. Caeden was stretched out across his bed in sweat pants and a Cage the Elephant t-shirt. He was strumming his guitar and humming to himself. He put the guitar down and opened up his arms. "Come on baby," he said, "you're home now."

I crushed myself in his arms. He held me closely but still hesitantly. "Oh Caeden," I cried. "I thought I'd never see you again."

His hands tenderly stroked my hair. "When I got back…" he choked on his words. "When I got back to the store and you were gone and I saw the mess… I just knew it was them. I had wondered at the other set of tire marks but it didn't click with me until I came inside and you were gone. Normally, I can contain my wolf but I was so scared for you that I shifted right there in the store and ran out the back. Imagine the people who saw a wolf running down the road? Thank God it had snowed and many people weren't out. I called the others and then we had to meet with the council. It's against our laws to attack another pack without just cause. I was furious. The Grimm's had you and I had to sit around and wait for council approval. It was maddening. Finally we got approval but then were faced with the problem of finding you. We had no idea where you could be. But Archie knew. It's a miracle you already found your familiar. Without him I don't think we would have ever found you but I would have never stopped searching. I can promise you that. I would have searched for you until I was old and gray."

I snuggled closer to him. "I believe you. But I didn't want you to find me."

"Why?" he asked puzzled.

I traced the wrinkle in his brow. "Because they were using me to get to you. They were going to kill you. I could take anything they dealt me if it meant you were alive. It was worth it as long as your heart kept beating," I said putting my hand over his steadily beating heart to reaffirm my point. "Would you not have felt the same?"

He sighed. "When you put it that way I would've felt exactly the same."

I cupped his face with my right hand. "I love you," I said.

"I love-," and then he stopped. He grabbed my arm and sat up so that I was sitting in his lap. He held my arm out. "What is this?" he asked angrily.

I rubbed at the letters like I could erase them. I couldn't though. "Travis," I whispered fearing his anger.

"Why?" he practically growled. He gently traced the word with his finger but it still sent a shiver of pain up my spine.

"Because I lied," I said simply. "I told him that I was really adopted, which of course I'm not, and he didn't believe it. So, he did this," I said holding up my arm.

"I hate that they did this to you," he whispered.

"What's done is done," I said.

"Maybe…" he said, "maybe not."

"What do you mean?" I asked puzzled.

"Well…" he said thoughtfully. "In the legends mates could always heal one another. I don't know how it's done but I can try," he said. "It should be instinctual. I was just scared to try in front of the others," he said looking down at the comforter in shame, "in case it didn't work."

"I understand," I said. "But try. Please," I begged.

"Okay," he said his hands fluttering around my body like a spastic bird. "Um… lay down."

"Alright," I said climbing off of his lap and stretching out on his bed.

"Okay… Concentrate… you can do this…" he muttered to himself. He closed his eyes and a wrinkle formed in his brow. Suddenly his hands began to glow.

"Wow," I murmured. "Amazing," I added when his hands began to glide over my cuts, scrapes, and bruises. Not only did his hands heal me but his breath did too. He would breathe on an injury and it would disappear just as quickly as it did with his hands. The healing process accelerated right before my eyes. Cuts sealed, scabbed over, and then disappeared altogether. Bruises rapidly changed colors and then faded to a healthy pink. His finger skimmed my lip and I felt the split seal and be replaced by healthy pink tissue.

Last he came to the word, *Liar*, engraved into my skin. It turned to a faded white, shimmery scar, but would not disappear beyond that. I watched sweat break out on Caeden's brow as he concentrated. The light flared brighter and still it stayed. He removed his hand and leaned down, as if to kiss it, and breathed on it like he had with some of my other injuries. Nothing.

He sat back and looked at me. "It's okay," I said.

"No it's not," he groaned. "I can heal everything but this, why?"

"I don't know," I said and cupped his cheek with my hand. "But I don't care. You healed everything else and I feel amazing. This," I said looking at my arm, "is nothing."

"It's everything," he said.

I bit my lip to hold back tears. I sat up and looked him in the eye. "Does it bother you that much? Are you grossed out by a scar? Do you… do you see me differently now? Am I forever marred in your eyes? What is it? Why does it bother you so much?" I demanded.

His eyes were full of hurt. He gently traced my jaw. "I could never see you differently no matter what. You could be covered in burns from head to toe and you'd still be the most beautiful woman in the world to me. What bothers me is knowing that Travis did this to you and that it will be forever imprinted on your body. A sickening reminder of what they did to you. That's what bothers me."

I covered the words with my hands. "I don't need this to remind me of it Caeden. It will be in my mind forever. This is just a flesh reminder. But I have to move on. I can't let this break me because that's what they want. I *won't* give them that satisfaction."

He pulled me to him and kissed me. "You're so much stronger than I give you credit for."

I smiled and leaned against his chest. The steady beating of his heart comforted me. It was so strong, just like him. It's steady rhythm began to lull me to sleep. He pulled the quilt and sheet back and tucked me under it and then pulled me against his chest. He kissed my ear and fingered my hair. "Sleep now. I'll be here when you wake up."

"Promise?" I asked fighting my heavy eyelids.

I could feel his smile. "Promise," he said. "I love you," he whispered.

"Love you more," I said and then fell asleep to his soft laugh filling my ear.

* * *

When I opened my eyes Caeden's soft snore filled my ear. A smile plucked at my lips. His arms were wrapped around me and he had me cocooned in his arms like I was some kind of precious childhood teddy bear. I wiggled in his arms so that I could face him. I didn't want to waste this time. I wanted to take in his beautiful, peaceful, face uninterrupted.

I traced his perfectly arched brow, smoothing the chaotic hairs there. Next I moved to his straight and defined aristocratic nose. It was perfectly proportioned to his face and didn't compete with his strong chin and jaw. His lips were sinful. They looked like an ancient sculptor had chiseled them from marble. But instead of cold and immobile they were warm and itinerant. His cheekbones were perfectly sculpted and strong. They contrasted nicely with the dusting of dark brown scruff that always covered his face. I put my hand against his cheek relishing in the way the prickly hairs felt against the soft skin of the palm of my hand. In his sleep, his lips flickered into a smile.

A minimal amount of light sifted in through the closed blinds. I guessed it was a little after seven in the morning. I knew after what I had been through I should still be exhausted but I wasn't. Instead I felt remarkably energized. I figured it was a combination of Caeden healing me and then just sleeping with him. I had felt similar the night we had slept on the couch together. We were more compatible than I had even imagined. I mean, who knew that just sleeping in the same bed as someone could make you feel this good. It seemed impossible.

I watched him sleep peacefully for a couple more minutes and then he began to stir. His eyes slowly blinked open and he smiled when he saw me watching him. He pulled me closer to him and pressed a kiss to my forehead. "Morning beautiful," he said. His blue eyes captured mine and I found myself drowning in their endless depths.

"Morning," I smiled.

"Hungry?" he asked.

"Starved," I replied with a giggle as my stomach began to growl obnoxiously.

He chuckled and sat up. His hair was delightfully ruffled on the side like a birds feathers. He stretched his arms, yawned, and climbed out of bed. "I'll make you breakfast," he said taking my small hands in his larger ones and pulling me from the bed against his chest.

"You can cook?" I asked skeptical.

"Are you dissing my mad cooking skills? I make a mean cupcake and you know it," he grinned.

"What's with all the angry words?" I joked. "Mad? Mean?"

He pouted his full bottom lip. "Don't mock me," he jested.

"Alright, so prove it to me that you can make something besides a cupcake," I said sticking my hip out and placing my hand on it.

"I will," he said, "and your taste buds will explode with pleasure."

We trotted quietly down the stairs so as not to wake anybody. Once in the kitchen he made me sit down on one of the stools while he cooked. He put on his mother's flowery apron and I had to admit that he could pull it off. He pulled out the makings for an omelet and hash browns and set to work. He had to keep brushing his shaggy hair out of his face. "Guess it's time for a cut," he commented.

I rested my face on my hand and said, "I like it like this."

He grinned. "Maybe I won't take too much off. Deal?" he said with a wink. Then he added, "I absolutely despise getting my haircut. It's akin to torture."

I laughed. "Don't talk to me about torture," I joked.

His face instantly paled and he dropped an egg on the floor where it splattered. "I'm so sorry, Sophie. That was so thoughtless of me. Please forgive me. I wasn't thinking. I was being stupid. I can't believe I said that. It was extremely callous of me. I feel horrible." He enveloped me in his arms and soothingly stroked my cheek.

"Caeden, it's okay," I said and suddenly I was the one comforting him. "Really, I'm fine. You didn't mean anything by it and I didn't take it that way. You were joking around and so was I. My intention was not to make you feel bad," I said using my finger to smooth his brow.

"I know that," he said, "but I still should have thought before I opened my big fat mouth. I'm really sorry."

"Stop saying you're sorry, please, it just makes me feel worse," I said into his chest.

"Alright," he said gently stroking my long hair, "I won't say anything else about it, today," he added and I rolled my eyes.

"I'll clean this up while you cook," I said pointing to the egg mess that sprinkled the floor.

He smiled. "Thanks," he said and I knew he wasn't just referring to the mess.

I grabbed a paper towel and wetted it, bending down to gather up the mess. I dumped it in the pullout cabinet trashcan that Caeden showed me. He pointed me to some disinfectant and I sprayed it on the floor.

I had just sat back down when Amy padded into the kitchen. She pushed the button on the coffee maker and yawned. "Ya'll are up early," she commented. She looked at me appreciatively, "And you got him to make breakfast. He hasn't made breakfast since he was in middle school and he's never up before ten o' clock when there's no school. I'm impressed. Maybe you should move in."

I laughed. "I'm sure he'd love that," I said with a smile.

"I would," he grinned sliding an omelet and some

hash browns onto my plate. He fixed a plate, of two omelets and enough hash browns to feed three people, for himself. He then fixed a more decent portioned plate for his mom.

The coffee maker beeped and Amy poured herself a cup. She inhaled it's scent before taking a sip. "I can't accomplish anything without my coffee," she said.

Caeden laughed and whispered conspiratorially to me, "She's a monster without the stuff. You notice how she drinks it black? It's just like her soul," he grinned.

"Caeden Henry Williams," his mother scolded.

He laughed and took a seat at the bar next to me. He shoveled a big bite of egg into his mouth and drenched his hash browns with ketchup. "I only speak the truth," he said.

Amy laughed at her son and sat down in the empty seat next to him. She took a bite and said, "This is good son."

"Thanks," he said taking a sip of orange juice.

Amy leaned over and looked at me quizzically. "You look better," she said. Her confusion was written plainly on her face.

"Um..." I said nervously. "Caeden healed me." However, I rubbed self-consciously at the one thing that wouldn't heal. I could clearly remember the way it felt having that word carved into my skin. I would forever be labeled a liar.

"Oh," she said and looked between us.

"It's a mate thing," said Caeden. "It was mentioned in the legends that mates could heal each other so I decided to try. It worked," he said with a shrug of his shoulders.

"Huh," said Amy, "that's pretty cool."

"Except," said Caeden, "I couldn't heal everything."

I rolled my eyes. Back to this again. "Really?" Amy asked. "What wouldn't heal?"

I sighed and stretched my arm out to her. She flinched when she saw the word carved maliciously into my arm. *Liar.*

"May I look more closely?" she asked hesitantly.

"Of course," I said and hopped down from the stool. I

came over to stand beside her.

She gently took my arm in her hands. Her fingers hesitantly ran over the savage markings. "He used silver," she said. "It won't ever heal. It'll stay like this forever. Just like those marks across your chest thanks to Peter Grimm," She said to Caeden as she ran her hand over the pale white indentations. "Let me guess, you were able to heal it closed and scarred but it wouldn't heal beyond this?" she asked Caeden. "Because I'm guessing it looked a whole lot worse than this."

"Right you are," said Caeden.

Her blue eyes darkened to midnight. "They shouldn't be allowed to be shifters. To do something like this to fellow man. It's sickening. They should be stripped of their powers."

"Can that happen?" I asked. "Can you take away their power of shifting?"

"No, I wish. They are an absolute insult to everything that shifters stand for. They have tainted our reputation. The Grimm's have always been bad but now they are beyond evil. They have no humanity left in them. They don't deserve their gift or their lives. If I ever see them again I will make them pay for this. You didn't deserve this. Neither one of you," she said looking between her son and me. "Neither one of you will ever be the same because of this. I can only hope that it makes you stronger. Find comfort in one another's arms. You both deserve happiness and it frightens me to think about how it was almost lost to you both. But don't let the bad break you, let it make you. It's the only way to go on." Tears pooled in her blue eyes. She looked between us.

"You never know when your last day together will be," Amy said and started crying. Her shoulders shook with her grief. "He said he'd be right back like he always was! But he wasn't! And then your brother found him… Dead. He was dead. I will forever cherish those last moments we had together. I never want you two to take each other for granted."

"Mom," said Caeden and I could hear his voice choking on emotion.

"Amy," I said and hugged her. "It's okay."

"Roger and I may not have been mates but I still loved him with all my heart. You never know how long it may last. I know what you went through was beyond horrible, words can't describe it, but I also saw what it did to Caeden. He was experiencing a completely different kind of pain. I could see the hopelessness in his eyes. He became a stranger to me. I never want to see anyone go through something like that again." She gently tucked a stray hair behind my ear and then took my hands in hers. "I fear if you hadn't been found I would've lost my son forever. But now you're here and you're safe and Caeden is happy again. I never want you to take each other for granted. Never," she reaffirmed.

"I won't," I said. "He's everything." Tears leaked out of my eyes. "I thought I'd never get to tell him that I loved him." I looked at Caeden. "I do. I love you with all my heart. I love you like I never knew it was possible to love another person." I smiled and made a joke to lessen the emotional heaviness that had settled in the room. "I already almost lost you and now you've almost lost me. I think we're even now. Okay? No more trying to get ourselves killed."

He laughed and pulled me from his mother's hold and onto his lap where he sat at the bar. He pressed a kiss to my lips despite his mother being present. He ran his hands through my bird's nest of hair. "From now on we do everything together. Lucinda's going to be hard pressed to have me let you out of my sight."

I laughed as Gram walked in. "Why does everyone insist on talking about me when I'm not present? You'd think I was the Queen of England or something."

We chuckled as she grabbed a cup of coffee. "Gram, would you like some coffee with your sugar?" I joked.

She clucked her tongue at me. "This is how sane people drink coffee," she quipped.

"There is nothing wrong with black coffee," said Amy with a smile.

"You're right," said Gram thoughtfully. "There's something wrong with the drinker's mind."

We all laughed and she puttered over to the omelets that lay prepared. "This smell's delicious, Amy," she said.

"Actually," said Amy, "Caeden made it."

Gram turned to glare at Caeden. "If you put something in this that resembles anything besides edible food I will have your head."

Caeden put his hands up. "Now would I do that?"

"You did make your brother eat worm pie, if I recall," I said with a smile as I took my seat and continued to eat my breakfast.

Gram laughed and took a plate. "So you can make something other than cupcakes? I'm impressed." She looked at me and winked, "Sophie, he's a keeper."

Since all the bar stools were taken Gram took a seat at the kitchen table.

"Well," I said. "This was some way to spend my Christmas break. I should get a medal or something for worst vacation ever. What day is it anyway?" I asked.

"New Year's Eve," Caeden said.

"I missed Christmas," I mumbled. I knew I had but it hurt hearing it. "Christmas is my favorite holiday."

Amy leaned over to look at me. "Well, we were optimistic that we would find you so we saved Christmas until we found you. All the presents are still under the tree."

"Bryce wasn't too happy but I think he was scared enough of my wrath that he didn't say anything," said Caeden.

I smiled. This was the nicest thing they could have done for me. Gram and I had planned to spend Christmas Eve night here and celebrate Christmas morning with the Williams' but of course that hadn't happened.

Choked on emotion I said, "Thanks you guys this means a lot to me. It really does."

"You're family now," said Amy. "We wouldn't have done it any other way."

"And look at this way, we get to celebrate two holidays in one day," said Caeden.

Bryce came into the kitchen rubbing the sleep from his eye. His face perked up at Caeden's words. He turned to his mom. "Does this mean I get my presents now?"

"Yes," she said rolling her eyes at her youngest son.

He whooped with joy and ran from the room shouting. "Santa here I come!"

FIFTEEN.

We followed Bryce into the large library-like family room. A large tree was set up in the corner with a mountain of presents under it. Bryce hopped up and down looking like a little kid. His dog Bailey came into the room and joined him in his jumping motions. He practically skipped over to a fancy stereo setup where he hit a button and the room was suddenly filled with the sounds of Christmas. Caeden pulled me down onto the floor and into the comfort of his arms. He kissed the side of my cheek and inhaled the skin at my neck. "I missed this," he said quietly.

"What?" I asked leaning back to look up into his eyes.

"Holding you, you're smell, you," he smiled.

"I'm here now," I said.

"And you're never going anywhere," he said.

"I like the sound of that," I said.

"Lovebirds you're making me sick," said Bryce.

We laughed at him and Caeden planted a big, fat, sloppy, kiss on my lips. "Alright, enough of that," said Gram. "It's time for presents."

"Presents!" squealed Bryce like a five year old girl upon seeing a Barbie Dream House. I couldn't contain the laugh that bubbled out. Bryce glared at me which just made me laugh harder.

"Here Bryce," said Amy shoving a present at her son. He took it and tore it viciously open. I expected his wolf claws to come out any second.

"Yes, yes, yes!" he said doing a little dance and holding up his present. It looked like a very expensive camera but he was waving it around so frantically that the package became a blur.

Amy shook her head and looked at me, "His enthusiasm amazes me."

Caeden said to me, "We say that he saves his energy up all year just for this one day."

"That's not true!" said Bryce pointing a finger at his

older brother. "I'm just a very energetic person."

"I wish you had this much energy when you have duty," said Caeden.

"Maybe if I wasn't stuck with boring old you I'd be peppier," countered Bryce.

"I doubt it," said Caeden and they both laughed.

Bryce looked at his mom, "I'm sick of talking to this old coot. Hit me with another present."

She tossed him one, hard. It hit him in the chest. He mock glared at his mom. "You said hit me," she smiled.

"It's an expression, mom," he said.

"Oh, I know," she said.

Gram pointed to a pile of gifts, "These are for you Sophie," she said, "from me, your mom, and dad."

"Gram," I said, "you didn't need to get me anything."

"I wanted to," she said, "I've been alone on Christmas for many years. This is special."

"Thanks Gram," I said.

I opened my presents in a less savage way than Bryce attacked his. Caeden opened his presents too. I got a bunch of new clothes and a new laptop. I thanked Gram profusely and called my parents to thank them too.

I pulled out a package that I had wrapped delicately. I had wanted to make it perfect. "Here," I said giving Caeden a small smile, suddenly shy.

He smiled and took it in his long fingers. He shook the box and grinned. "What is it?"

"You'll have to open it," I said. "I'm going to warn you, I'm not good with gifts."

He ripped it open and took the tickets out. "This is awesome," he said holding up the Cage the Elephant concert tickets. "Thanks babe," he said and planted a kiss on my cheek.

"I know you like them so I thought we could go see them live," I said.

"This is really great," he said. "And now, here's your present," he said handing me a small box wrapped in red paper.

I treated this box with even greater care than I had my other packages. The red paper fluttered to the ground and I was left holding a small white box. Caeden smiled encouragingly. I smiled back and lifted the lid off and gasped. I lifted the beautiful leather bracelet out of the box. The brown the leather was soft and metal beads with a Celtic design added to it.

"It's beautiful," I breathed.

Caeden blushed, and smiled, his dimple showing. "It's a Celtic love knot." He pointed to the beads, "It represents infinity and never-ending love. I... uh... I actually made it." He blushed even redder. "I thought it would make it more special."

"You're amazing," I said and kissed him. "Put it on me," I said holding out my wrist and the bracelet. In one smooth movement he had the bracelet dangling from my arm. It looked like it belonged there. I fingered it. I was never taking it off. I leaned back against him and inhaled his special scent of pine and cinnamon. "I love you," I said.

"I love you too," he said and buried his face in the side of my neck. I felt his lips press a gentle kiss against my sensitive skin.

Amy started picking up the wrapping paper and stuffing it in trash bags. "It always amazes me," she said, "how every year you put so much time into this and in a matter of minutes it's over."

"Or in Bryce's case, a matter of seconds," I said.

"Hey!" said Bryce in mock disgust. "I'll get you for that," he said and then held up his camera and snapped a picture of me in Caeden's arms. He appraised the picture. "Too bad this isn't good enough for blackmail. You just look like lovesick puppy dogs. Or I guess wolves."

Caeden grabbed a pillow off the couch we were leaned up against and in a blinding fast motion launched it at his brother. It hit him squarely in the head. Bryce glared at his brother.

"You're going to pay for that," said Bryce and suddenly Caeden's arms were no longer wrapped around me. The two of them rolling around on the floor throwing random punches. All while they laughed.

I stood up and began gathering the trash together. "Thanks Sophie," said Amy.

"You're welcome," I said. "Thank you for this," I said. "It really means a lot to me. I want you to know that. Not just this," I said looking at the Christmas decorations still left up, "but for looking for me too."

She stopped gathering up the wrapping paper and looked at me. "You're a part of this family now and we protect our family. We weren't going to leave you with them. We would've kept looking, forever, if we had too."

I sighed and ran my hand through my hair. "I didn't want to be found if it meant they'd hurt him. They want to kill him. I'd die before I'd let them have him," I said.

Amy looked at her son and then back at me. "I know he feels the same. But you have to remember that your death wouldn't stop them from killing Caeden. It would only lead Caeden to it. He'd want revenge. I'm afraid that we haven't seen the last of Peter and Travis. They left with their tails tucked between their legs. Their pride will get the best of them and they'll be back."

"I know," I said. "They won't rest until they accomplish whatever it is they need to accomplish. They're determined," I said. "I'll give them that."

"No," she said, "they're not determined. They're cocky and I can only hope that will be their down fall. I already lost my husband and I'm not about to lose my son too," she said. A light glittered in her blue eyes that I had never seen before. It was the look of a mother bear protecting her cub. Or I guess I this case, mother wolf.

She smiled at me and I knew it was the end of the discussion. It was time to move on to lighter more happy topics. That was fine with me.

We finished packing up the trash and I followed her

out to the garage. She showed me where to toss the trash and then she turned to look at me. She put her hands on her hip, her curly hair floating around her face. "You know," she said, "I'm so happy that if the mates are coming back that Caeden is getting to experience this. I'm not just saying that because he's my son, I mean that's part of it, but not entirely." She sighed, "He's had to become a man quicker than I would've liked because of circumstances out of his control. He's only been shifting for the past two years and to be thrust into the position of Alpha he's handled it gracefully. He's taken everything in stride, even while he was grieving, he was strong. He's never asked for anything in return even though he has the weight of the world on his shoulders. And then you came along and he smiles more than he ever did. He's happier than I've ever seen him. Caeden was always my more serious child. With you he's discovering a side of himself that I don't think he even knew existed. You compliment him and he does you. Anyone can see that you're a perfect match. It's amazing to watch, breathtaking even. I hope the others might find that but if they don't I'm happy that at least Caeden has." She paused and looked at me. "And I want you to know that I look at you like a daughter. I know you probably don't see me as your mom, and I wouldn't want to replace her anyway. But I want you to know that I'm here for you if you ever want to talk. I know it has to be hard on you living away from your mom and dad and then having all of this thrust upon you. Just know that I'm here. I'm a good listener," she said.

I smiled. "Thanks Amy that means a lot to me. It really does. You may not be my mom but I'd like to think of you as my second mom."

She pulled me into a hug. It was awkward at first but some of that left when I wrapped my arms around her. "I'm so glad you're going to be a part of our lives," she said into my hair.

"Amy?" I asked.

"Yes," she said pulling me away.

"Do you know what the bonding ceremony is? Gram mentioned it but she didn't explain it to me." I asked her.

"Let's go inside. It's far too cold in here for a serious talk," she said.

"That's probably a good idea," I conceded.

I could still hear Caeden and Bryce bickering but it sounded like they had moved it to the kitchen. Amy led me past the staircase and towards the back of the house. She opened a pair of French doors that led into a light and airy office. "This is my office," she said, "the one room in the house that is entirely my own."

The walls were painted an airy periwinkle color. The office looked out at the backyard and for the first time I noticed a swimming pool. Her desk was an off white color and shelves of the same color lined the back wall. Books, pictures, and various odds and ends were placed on the shelves. A very expensive computer sat on top of the desk. Airy, white, curtains framed the window and French doors which we had entered through. Two wing backed chairs done in a similar color of the walls framed the doors. She took one and motioned for me to take the other. Somewhere along the way she'd picked up her cup of coffee.

She sipped at it and said, "So you want to know about the bonding ceremony?"

"Yes," I breathed.

"I don't know where to begin," she said. "Every shifter has heard of the bonding ceremony but like so much else we stopped believing in it. It's just for you and your mate. It's like a wedding but just for the two of you-," she said before I interrupted her.

"That's what Gram said."

She smiled and continued. "But much, much, more powerful than any normal human wedding. You each speak the words of the ancient text in front of nature, meaning in the woods," she clarified. "Once you speak the words, once you bond yourselves, you're forever bound to one another. There's no turning back. Your souls become like one. It's said that once you bond with a mate you develop powers but I don't know if there's any merit to that. I tend to think not."

"You make it sound like we have some kind of choice in loving each other?" I asked.

"You do," she said. "You still have the will to choose but why wouldn't you choose him and why wouldn't he choose you? You're destined for each other. You're like the ying and the yang. You fit perfectly together. But the bond *literally* bonds your souls together. You're forever tied to one another. There is no going back."

"What if I said I'm ready," I whispered. "What if I said I'm ready to bind myself to him forever."

Amy beamed. "I'd say that I know Caeden feels the same way. He's talked to me about it. He's wanted to speak to you about it but I told him not to push you, not to pressure you. It's a very romantic, very tying, thing to do. I told him to let you decided when you're ready. After all it's our kind's equivalent of marriage even if we haven't done it in hundreds of years."

I paused at her words thinking about what I was going to say. I played with my hands to avert my eyes from hers. Finally I looked up into those patient blue eyes that were so much like Caeden's but darker. "But we'd still have an actual wedding right?" I asked.

She laughed. "Of course," she said and smiled.

"Oh okay," I said taking a deep breath.

She patted my knee. "Maybe you should think about this some more before you say something to Caeden."

"No," I shook my head. "I'm ready. Now that I know more about it I'm more sure of it. But I'm scared too. I'm scared about a lot of things right now like my first shift," I said. "I understand what a commitment the bond is and I'm ready but if Caeden's not or he wants to wait, even if he doesn't want to do it at all, I'm fine with that too. I don't want to push him."

She smiled. "Oh trust me you won't have to push him. But you will have to wait until you transform. That's part of the ceremony. You both have to have transformed."

"Does it hurt terribly?" I asked.

She grimaced. "It's bad. Just as bad as child birth, this in a way makes sense. You're giving birth to your inner wolf, to your shape. I don't think yours will be nearly as bad though. You'll have Caeden with you. But look at this way. I'm fine, your Gram is fine. You'll be-."

"Fine," I inserted for her.

She smiled and took my hand. "You really will. I think it might even be special for you. After all you'll have your mate by your side. I think Caeden being there will make a significant difference."

"You do?" I asked, hope in my eyes.

"I really do," she said and shrugged her shoulders, "but I may be wrong so don't go getting your hopes up. If you want to talk about this some more feel free to come find me. Okay?"

"Thanks Amy," I said standing. She followed suit and pulled me in for another hug. There was no awkwardness in this one.

"You're a good girl Sophie," she said. I heard a crash come from the area of the kitchen and Amy groaned. She looked at the ceiling like she was speaking to the heavens themselves, "Why couldn't I have had girls? Why?"

We headed towards the kitchen and the commotion. A large wolf growled in the kitchen. The wolf's fur was a light brown with some gold thrown in and looked back at me with Bryce's blue eyes. Pieces of clothing fluttered to the ground.

"Oh my, Bryce Elliot Williams! Change back right this instance! You're going to ruin the floors!" She turned to glare at the laughing figure of Caeden. "What is the meaning of this? Why is your brother in his wolf form?"

Caeden stifled his laugh. "Because I was proving a point."

"And what point was that?" demanded Amy.

"That he's a hot head," said Caeden calmly. He

pointed to the wolf. "I think I proved my point."

"Caeden," said Amy in that eerily quiet way that only parents can. "Why do you insist on provoking him? You're the Alpha you should know better."

Caeden's smile disappeared. "That's why I did it," he said. "I'm the Alpha now. I can't have my little brother disobeying me simply because we're brothers. And I certainly can't have him not knowing how to control his transformations."

Amy sighed. "Caeden, he's new to this. He's only been sixteen a couple of months."

Caeden hung his head. "You're right. I'm sorry," he directed to the wolf that was his brother. He turned back to his mom. "But he needs to lean to control himself."

The wolf stalked out of the room and a minute later Bryce returned, human, with only a pair of jeans on. I was surprised at his toned chest and arms but I guessed I shouldn't have been too shocked. He was a shifter after all. "I can control myself," said Bryce pointing an accusing finger at his brother. His face was red and his chest heaved angrily with each breath.

"I beg to differ," said Caeden crossing his arms.

"Maybe if you didn't provoke me every five seconds this anger inside me wouldn't keep building until I explode out of my clothes! And you didn't have to stab me with a knife either!"

"Caeden!" Amy and I scolded. "What is this really about?" asked Amy suddenly suspicious and I didn't know why.

Caeden looked sheepish and then he sighed. "Dad's not here to teach him like he did me. I'm just trying to fill that role."

"Oh," said Amy, at a loss for any other words.

"Dad was there for me and since he can't be here for Bryce I have to fill that role. It's my duty as his brother and as his leader."

Bryce leaned against the counter. "That's not really

necessary, Caeden. I'm fine on my own. I know you're just trying to help but I don't need it," said Bryce and I could see the anger drain out of him.

Caeden was quiet for a moment and said, "If dad was here you'd want his help but you don't want mine." He shook his head and disappeared.

"I don't know what I'm going to do with the two of you," Amy said throwing her hands in the air.

"I'll go talk to Caeden," I said putting a reassuring hand on her arm. She nodded and I went off to find him. I had heard him stomp up the stairs so I headed towards his room. That seemed the logical place to look for him.

I found him sitting on his bed with his head in hands. I sat down next to him and put my arm around him. I didn't say anything. Instead waiting for him to open up to me.

He turned to me and said, "I just want to help him. Dad was there for me and he can't be here for Bryce. I feel like Bryce was robbed of something and I have to make it up to him. I don't want him to think he's alone in this. Am I wrong?"

"Caeden," I said, "look at it from Bryce's point of view. He feels like he's a baby compared to you and when you keep treating him like a little kid it just adds to that. He feels in adequate. He feels like he's nothing more than the Alpha's brother. I think being a guy and your brother he feels he needs to prove himself to you."

"I don't want him to prove anything to me," said Caeden.

I laughed, "Caeden you stabbed your brother with a knife to test him. It sounds like you want him to prove something."

"When you put it like that..." he said. He shook his head, "I need to go apologize to him. Wait here?" he asked.

"I'll be here," I said. I looked at the pile of new clothes I had gotten for Christmas that I assumed Gram had brought up. "I guess I'll go ahead and get dressed."

He smiled. "I'll be back." He disappeared out the

door.

    I grabbed a pair of jeans and a long-sleeved green shirt and headed into the bathroom. I washed my face and then braided my hair so it would stay out of my way. I slipped into the new clothes and it felt good to have something on body that was actually mine. Not that I hadn't minded wearing Caeden's clothes. I felt like his scent of pine and cinnamon lingered on me even now. That put a smile on my face. It felt so good to have finally told him that I loved him. I felt like I was whole now.

    I opened the door to the bathroom to find him lying on his bed, now made, much like he had been last night. He smiled and pulled me into his arms. "Did you talk to him?" I asked

    "Yes," he said kissing my ear. "He understands where I was coming from and I now know that he doesn't need me like I want him too."

    "Sometimes you just have to let them leave the nest and fly away on their own," I said.

    Caeden's laugh filled the room, echoing off the walls. "You're right," he said. "Maybe you should be my own personal advisor?"

    "Sure Mr. President. Or should I say Alpha?" I giggled.

    He rolled over so he was on top of me, resting on his hands, "Mr. President will do fine," he said and dipped his lips down to meet mine.

    A fire ignited in my body. My fingers tangled in his hair and my legs wrapped around his body pinning him to me. I felt his laugh against my lips. He started to pull away. "Don't stop," I begged. I was surprised when he listened and pressed his lips against mine once again. He deepened the kiss and I felt my breath hiss out in a gasp. I could spend forever like this. It would be better than any heaven had to offer.

    "I love you," he whispered against my lips. His fingers traced the shape of my hip in my jeans. "Imagine if we had never found each other."

"Fate intended for us to meet," I breathed and tried to hold him tighter against me. I never wanted him to leave. I couldn't imagine my desire to be with him becoming any stronger but according to what I had been told about the bond it would.

* * *

I sat comfortable in the confines of Caeden's arms as we waited for midnight and the New Year to strike. His mom, Gram, and Bryce had retired to another part of the house to give us privacy. That meant we had the whole family room to ourselves.

The leather couch enveloped us like a cocoon and then Caeden had us wrapped like mummies in a fluffy blanket. I knew we were both paying more attention to each other than the TV.

Caeden traced my lips while I traced his jaw line. If we weren't touching then we were kissing. I think the others had gotten sick of it and that was the real reason they had left.

I took a deep breath. "Caeden," I said.

"Mhmm?" he said, his nose skimming my hair line.

"When I change…" I started.

"Yeah?" he prompted when I didn't continue.

I sat up and turned so that I could look in his eyes. "I talked to your mom and I think I'm ready. To bond to you, I mean. If you're not then that's fine. I'll wait. But I want you to know that I'm ready to make you mine forever."

He grinned from ear to ear and I suddenly found myself pressed into the leather couch as his lips devoured mine. He pulled away and his grin was still there. "I am more than ready. I can't wait to mark you as my own." Suddenly he pulled away. "Sophie, are you sure you're ready?" He looked at me with concern.

"I've thought about this a lot and the Grimm's taking me put a lot into perspective for me. I'm not ready to walk down the aisle but I feel like the bond will be away to make a commitment to you."

His jaw tightened. "You don't want to marry me but you want to bond with me? Sophie, the bond is more serious than marriage. The bond is an ancient ceremony that hasn't been practiced in hundreds of years. It's old and very, very, powerful magic. You can't reverse it once it's done. With marriage you can get a divorce but you can't undo a bond."

"Caeden," I said. "I understand what you're saying. And I'm not saying I don't want to marry you. I'm only saying that we're still in high school. What would people think? I'm not going anywhere. We're mates. It's not like we would even get divorced. I just... I need some way to make you mine."

"I'm already yours," he said.

"I want to do this, Caeden. I really do. Like I said before, if you want to wait I will," I said but I wasn't so sure that I meant my own words.

"I'm more than ready," he said. "But I don't want to push you."

"You're not," I said. "This is my choice."

His smile returned. He pressed his lips against mine and breathed, "Sixteen more days and you're mine forever."

He kissed me again and I heard the cheers in the background. The ball had dropped in Times Square. The New Year was here and with it many changes were to come. I could feel it.

SIXTEEN.

Christmas vacation came to an end. Now all anyone could focus on was prom. The babble traveled down the hallway like a high speed train. No one knew of my kidnapping and no one made a comment on the fact that Travis was missing. As were the other two members of his pack Hannah and Robert. I wished I could focus on such petty human problems such as which dress and shoes to wear but my worries were much bigger.

In two weeks I would shed my human skin and transform into the wolf I was always meant to be. I noticed things beginning to change already. I seemed to see things with a new clarity. Everything was sharper, crisper, it was eerie in a way. Even smells were more potent and I knew that it would all only get worse once I changed.

Caeden gave my hand a reassuring squeeze as if he knew where my thoughts had turned. I gave him a small smile. We had reached our lunch table. I sat down and Caeden tossed his backpack down and got in the lunch line. I grabbed my own packed lunch from my backpack. No lunch lady surprise for me.

The others were already seated at the table. I hadn't seen any of them since my rescue. Bentley bit into his pizza and then said, "So how are you feeling? I see your bruises and everything is gone." Chris, who was sitting next to him smacked his arm. "Ow, what?" he said choking on his pizza.

Chris looked at me, shaking her head, "Boys are so dumb."

Bentley narrowed his eyes at her. "Oh come on! Like you don't want to know what happened to all the cuts and bruises! The last time we saw her she looked like the incredible hulk. Only without all of the hulkiness and more of the purple and greenness."

Chris shook her head again. "Bentley, don't you know when to keep your mouth shut?"

"Obviously not," he grumbled.

"What's all this about?" Caeden asked putting his tray

down and slipping into the seat next to mine.

Bentley glared at Chris. "I just want to know what happened to all her bruises," he said pointing to me. "And this thing," he pointed to Chris, "says I'm being rude."

"That's because you are," said Chris.

Bentley shook his head. "That's the last time I ask a simple question."

"It's okay Bentley," I interrupted. "You didn't offend me. Chris is just trying to be nice."

"So what happened to all of *it?*" he asked rubbing his hand in front of his face for emphasis.

I looked at Caeden and then back at Bentley. I saw that Bryce, Charlotte, and Logan were now intrigued. "Caeden healed me," I said.

Bentley choked on his pizza again. Chris beat his back. When he finally had control of himself he said, "Really? I thought that was only a legend."

Caeden and I both laughed before he answered. "According to that Sophie and I should be nothing more than legend. But we're mates. If it's true then why isn't that the same for everything?"

"That's true," said Bentley. "It just makes you think though. Everything we thought was nothing more than legend is real. How much more do we not know?"

I laughed. "This from a group of werewolves, I mean, shifters," I quickly corrected myself. "You guys aren't supposed to exist but you do. So why shouldn't this be any different?"

I was surprised when Logan spoke. "You act as if you're not one of us," he said.

I blushed. "Sorry, I'm still trying to get used to it."

Charlotte glared at him and then turned to me. "It'll become more real once you actually shift."

"We grew up knowing what we are, you haven't. It's been hidden from you for all these years," said Chris. She then slapped the back of her brother's head.

"What was that for?" asked Logan glaring at his

sister.

"For being a freakin' idiot," she said. He rubbed the back of his head and then stared at his tray of food. "So, has anyone else noticed not only Travis missing but his minions as well?" asked Chris.

"Of course," we all said.

"They're planning something," said Caeden. "I can feel it. We need to be one step ahead of them."

"But what can we do?" asked Bryce ripping his pizza into narrow slivers. "It's not like we know what they're planning. I think we have to just wait and see."

"No!" said Caeden slamming his fist on the table. Everyone's stuff jumped about three inches off the table with the force. "They took Sophie from me once I'm not letting them do it again! We *will* act first!"

Bentley looked at Caeden, his brown eyes questioning, "Caeden I've always admired you and even more so when you took your father's place but I won't do this. I will not go on a suicide mission." He looked at Chris and I saw that longing in his eyes just like in hers. "I won't let you do this."

Caeden's chest puffed out. "Are you challenging me?" he hissed.

"Hell no," said Bentley. "But you can't risk our lives for revenge. That's just insane and you know it."

Caeden looked at me and I could see the worry there in his eyes. I put my hand on his cheek. "Caeden, in a couple of weeks I will shift too. I'll be stronger. I won't be so vulnerable anymore. And remember, they still think I'm human. I'll have the upper hand."

"That's true," he said and I could see him calming down.

Bentley let out a relieved breath.

"Now that we're not contemplating our deaths can we talk about something more normal? Like, say, prom?" asked Chris.

I groaned and Caeden grinned. "Prom..." he mused.

"Will I get to see you in a dress?"

I wrinkled my nose. "Prom is still three months away so I don't know why we're even talking about it. And if I have my way I won't be going."

"Oh, we're going," said Caeden a challenge clear in his eyes.

"Do you enjoy my discomfort?" I asked him.

He shrugged his shoulders. "I just want to see you in a dress and dance the night away with you in my arms."

Bryce laughed. "You sound like some kind of cheesy greeting card," he said.

"I don't remember them making greeting cards for prom," countered Caeden.

I groaned. "Can we please not talk about this right now? It's still a ways off and so until then I'd prefer not to talk about the 'p' word. Understand?"

Caeden laughed. "Only if you promise to be my date," he challenged.

I rolled my eyes. "If it means none of you will talk about it for the next three months then I'll go and I'll even wear a dress like a real live girl."

They all laughed at my words even Logan which surprised me. Noticing the time I quickly scarfed down my sandwich.

The bell rang and Caeden and I headed for study hall. Even though I knew Travis wouldn't be there I still found my heart stuttering. I walked into the room expecting those bottomless black eyes to be glaring at me but of course he wasn't there. Caeden tugged me into a corner away from the other kids and the teacher. We sat down but he didn't let go of my hand. He gently traced the lines and swirls of my hand.

"I want you to know that it's going to be okay," he said quietly.

"My shift? I know it will Caeden. You'll be there," I said.

"That's not what I meant but that will be okay too," he said not meeting my gaze. "I meant with Travis. I will stop him. I won't let him take you again. I won't let him hurt you. I won't let him get close enough to touch you. He got through me once and I won't let him do it again. He'll find that I'm better prepared this time. I won't let you out of one of our sights. I will always have one of us keeping an eye on you. He won't get through our defenses."

I took his chin in my hand forcing him to look at me. "This is not necessary. I'll be able to protect myself."

"No," he said shaking his head, "not for another two weeks and even then you will still be weak because you won't be accustomed to your form. It takes a while to get used to your wolf form. Plus, we need to keep the fact that you're a shifter hidden from them as long as possible. It's the only advantage we have."

I sighed. Clearly, I would not be winning this argument. And I wouldn't tell Caeden this but it did feel good to know that they would be watching out for me. I still felt on edge, like I was ready to jump out of my skin at any moment. I didn't like this feeling. "Alright fine. Set up guards. Do what it is that you feel you need to do."

He smiled. "Things are so much easier when you see it my way."

"Don't get used to it," I said.

"Too late," he replied.

* * *

After what happened at Gram's store Caeden didn't trust me to go there alone so Bentley followed me there while Caeden and Bryce took off to do their rounds. His large black truck hulked behind me like an ominous cloud.

He pulled in beside me and hopped out of his truck and followed me in the back door. He brushed his shaggy black hair out of his face as I silently opened the back door. I closed the door behind us and turned to face him.

"I know you'll be honest with me Bentley," I said looking into his golden brown eyes. "Am I really in that much danger or is Caeden just overreacting?"

He leaned against the counter and crossed his arms.

"I'd like to say that Caeden is being a lovesick puppy and just overreacting but that's not the case. How can you even question that after what they did to you and when they nearly killed Caeden?"

"You're right," I said. "I shouldn't have asked. I'm sorry."

"Don't apologize," Bentley said. "It was a legitimate concern. You don't know the Grimm's like we do. You're new to all this," he said while I bustled around trying to icing the cupcakes Gram had left cooling. "You don't know what they're capable of. They killed my little brother," he said and look of pure torture and sadness crossed his face. "And they probably killed Roger. They're murderers and a disgrace to all shifters."

I stopped what I was doing and looked at Bentley. I wanted to reach out and comfort him but I figured he wasn't the type to appreciate the gesture. "They killed your brother," I said softly.

"Yeah," he said. "Sam was five and I was eight. He was always following me and Caeden around, a lot like Bryce. So, one day he followed me and Caeden into the woods. I yelled at him. I was so mean," he said and I could see his eyes glimmering, fighting the tears that wanted to fall. "He turned around and I thought he was going home but he didn't. Sam went wandering and when he got tired he stopped by a little creek in the woods to rest. Travis and Robert found him." He laughed harshly. "Caeden and I heard his scream and went running. Travis was the same age we were, eight, but in that moment he looked much older. His face contorted in rage. His face was turning red and he was strangling Sam even as he held him under the water to drown him. I ran and tackled him while Caeden grabbed Sam. I wanted to beat him to death for what he had been doing and then I heard the words I will never forget Caeden saying, 'Bentley, he's dead,' I saw red and then Caeden had to stop me from doing the same thing to Travis that he had done to Sam. Travis and Robert ran away and I went to Sam. But

Caeden was right. I had been too late. He had killed my little brother. I vowed that day to protect anyone I could from the Grimm's. I vowed to never love anyone. I don't deserve any love or happiness that comes my way. My dad became rigid after Sam's death, closing in on himself, and my mom never mentions him. It's like he never existed." He hung his head. "I'm sorry for telling you all of this. I never talk about it. I didn't mean to dump all of this on you."

"Bentley," I said and this time I did hug him. I was surprised when he hugged me back. "I am so sorry that this had to happen to you. But it's not your fault. You do deserve happiness and love. I'm sure if Sam was here he'd tell you the same thing. But I do have a question," I said pulling away. "Why didn't you turn this into the police? They would have arrested him."

Bentley rubbed his face and said, "Because we don't abide by the same laws that humans do. Shifters have their own laws. We deal with our own. We never involve humans in our skirmishes."

"So, what happened?" I asked. "Did the shifters do something?"

Bentley laughed harshly. "Travis walked away with no more than a slap on the hand. The council didn't see fit to punish an eight year old too harshly even if he did commit murder."

I shook my head and patted his back. "The Grimm's are horrible, wretched, despicable people. They don't deserve to exist," I said vehemently.

"I agree completely," he said. "The council is becoming fed up with them. I think they are close to taking action."

"What will that action be?" I asked.

"Their deaths," he said simply. "They are putting all shifters at risk and that's something the council can't turn away from. A dead five year old boy they can ignore but not the fear of our exposure," he hissed with malice.

"I'm sorry," I said again.

Bentley took a deep breath and said, "Thanks for listening. I don't talk about it. Never really did. But all that has taken place in the past couple of months with the Grimm's has brought it to the forefront of my mind and I just can't let it go any more."

"You shouldn't just let it go," I said, "you're brother deserves to be remembered."

"I wish my parent's thought so. I know they blame me for his death and quite frankly, I do too. If I had just let him come with us he'd be here today," he said looking at the floor. His dark hair flopped over his face to hide his eyes.

"Bentley, this is far from your fault and deep down you know it and I'm sure your parents don't blame you either. When I met your parents they didn't strike me as the resentful type. They seemed proud of you. I'm sure that they're still grieving just like you. That's not something you forget overnight."

"It doesn't matter," he said shaking his head, "what's done is done. I may wish that I could change the past but I can't. The only thing I can do is make sure the Grimm's hurt no one else."

"You're a good guy Bentley. I see why you're Caeden's best friend. But don't lock yourself away from love and happiness. You deserve it more than most people. You have a whole pack that cares for you." I wanted to tell him of Chris' feelings but I didn't feel it was my place and I didn't want to push him. "You'll find someone one day. I know it," I said.

"I hope so," he said, "but I don't know if I'm a good enough man for anyone."

"You are," I said, "trust me."

A smile peeked out on his lips. "I'm glad you're Caeden's mate," he said, "you're insightful."

"Insightful?" I scoffed. I flipped my hair over my shoulder. "More like fabulous," I said trying to get him to smile for real this time. He did. The grin broke out over his face and a light laugh emerged from his lips.

Caeden walked in, slapping his baseball cap on, and said, "What's so funny? What did I miss?"

"Nothing," Bentley and I said simultaneously.

"Whatever," said Caeden shaking his head with a smile playing on his lips, "don't tell me." He turned to Bentley, "Thanks man, you can head out now."

"Bye," Bentley called over his shoulder. He paused at the door. "Thanks for the... uh... talk, Sophie," he said and then he was gone.

"I'm glad to see you two becoming friends," said Caeden. "What did you talk about?"

I looked up from the cupcake I was icing and blew a piece of hair out of my face with a breath. "How come you didn't tell me that Travis killed Bentley's brother? Why didn't you even tell me he had a brother?"

Caeden leaned his elbows on the counter. "It's not my story to tell. He doesn't like to talk about it and I don't like to remind him about it. I know he still hurts because of it. He blames himself and so I don't like to bring it up. He's my best friend and I don't want to hurt him."

I sighed. "I think it hurts him more pretending that his brother didn't exist. From what he said it sounds like he benefits from talking about it."

Caeden rubbed his face. "If he wants to talk about it he can. No one's stopping him."

"No one's encouraging him either," I mumbled.

Caeden groaned. "Why are we even talking about this?"

"Because Bentley's your best friend and even though ten years have gone by he's obviously hurting. He doesn't think he deserves happiness or love. Is that what you want for him? A life of loneliness?" I asked.

"Sophie," said Caeden. "What's really going on here?" he asked moving towards me and putting his arms around me.

I gulped and tried to dam the tears back. My breath came out strangled. I couldn't help it. I wanted to put on a brave face but that wasn't possible. Not anymore. "I'm scared," I whispered so low I wasn't sure he heard me. I knew that Travis and the Grimm's were cold, hardened, people. I knew they wouldn't hesitate to kill me if the opportunity presented itself again. But any ounce of humanity that I may have thought them capable to possess was gone. Travis had killed a five year old boy when he was just a boy himself. He was a sadistic, coldblooded, sociopath. His dad was just the same. I didn't know Robert or Hannah but I was pretty sure they were rowing the same boat. Especially Robert, if he had witnessed Travis kill Sam and not tried to stop it he was just as much at fault. How much blood was on their hands? Sam's we knew. Maybe Roger's. Almost mine. Who else had suffered at their cruel hands?

Silence greeted me. I could feel his muscles working beneath his shirt as he held me close. He rested his chin on top of my head. I thought he might never answer but finally he did. "Me too," he said. "I hate to admit but I'm scared too. I can't let them get to you again. They've already caused so much damage. For years they've tormented us. We've always stood in the background letting them do as they please. The council won't let them continue much longer. Their days are limited. I can guarantee you that. But until then we're all in danger."

"Will you teach me to fight?" I asked. "Once I shift will you teach me to protect myself?"

"Of course," he said. "But it won't be necessary because I'm not going to be letting you out of my sight."

I groaned. "That's really going to get old," I said.

He pulled away from me and held his hands in the air like he was weighing something. "Keep Sophie safe or let Sophie die. Hmm. I think keep Sophie safe is winning. So, bite me."

"Gladly," I chuckled and he pulled me into a kiss.

The bell over the door dinged signaling a customer.

Caeden groaned. "And just when I was going to have my wicked way with you."

I laughed and finished icing the cupcakes while he went to deal with the customer. I only hoped that once I shifted that I would be strong. Strong enough to protect the both of us. Strong enough to protect the pack. It was time I picked up my slack.

* * *

I pulled on my yellow and blue plaid pajama pants and a random t-shirt that I pulled out of the drawer. I yawned and greatly looked forward to getting in the bed. I was so tired I was practically dead on my feet. Archie was already sending out a pleasant little snore from his spot on my bed.

"Come on Archie, move," I said trying to slide the little dog over so I could climb in my bed. But he was stubborn and didn't want to budge. "Alright, no more Mr. Nice Guy," I said and picked him up and scooted him over. He gave me an angry little snort and then fell back to sleep. "Well," I said to the little dog. "You wouldn't do it the easy way so it had to be the hard way. It's your own fault."

I climbed in the bed and pulled up the purple bedspread. The only thing I had taken the time to change in the room. Despite Gram giving me her assurance that I could change everything it just didn't seem right. This was her home after all. I reached over to the nightstand and plunged the room into darkness.

I rolled over on my side and closed my eyes. I was just about to drift off when I heard a wolf howling in the distance. At first I was startled. Picturing Travis coming to find me but I quickly recognized it as Caeden. I wasn't sure how I knew it was him but I did. I wanted to howl back, it was like my wolf wanted to answer to his, and I hadn't even shifted yet.

I heard a scratching at my window which startled me so much that fell unceremoniously out of my bed and landed on my butt. "Ow," I said and then heard the scratching again. My heart leaped to my throat. That scratching was on purpose. Nothing around Gram's house would make that noise.

I automatically pictured a gleeful Travis standing outside my window ready to wrap his hands around my throat and squeeze the life out of me. Maybe Caeden's howl had been a warning?

I was about to tiptoe out of my room to find Gram when I heard, "Sophie, it's me. Open the window."

Caeden. Air rushed back into my lungs and I was grateful for the relief it provided.

I opened my window as quietly as I could. "Are you crazy?" I hissed at him as he climbed in my window.

"Maybe," he replied with a shrug of his shoulders.

"What are you doing here?" I whispered.

"Well," he said, "this would have been your first night away from me since we found you and I told you that I wasn't going to let you out of my sight. So, here I am."

"Does Gram know?"

He gave me a funny look. "I just came in through the window and you're asking me if Lucinda knows? That would be a big fat no." He huffed, "And it took you long enough to go to bed. I thought that light was never going to turn off."

"So, what was your plan? To scare me half to death?"

"No," he said holding up a duffel bag. "My plan was to sleep. Look, I brought Jammies."

I groaned. "Caeden, if Gram finds out she'll skin us both alive and sell our hairy pelts."

He chuckled. "You don't think I know that? I just couldn't stand the thought of being away from you. Plus," he said and blushed, "I get the best sleep when you're in my arms."

I wanted to make some kind of joke but couldn't because he was right. I had my best sleep when I was with him. The wonders of being mates would never cease to amaze me.

"Alright fine," I conceded. "I'm tired so hurry up," I said turning around so he could change.

I heard the sound of the zipper and then of clothes being shed. Despite not seeing anything a blush still crept up my neck and to my cheeks.

"Done," he said. "And thanks for this."

I shook my head and turned around. "Don't thank me. I feel the same way. I don't like being away from you."

He pulled me into his arms and dragged me into the bed covering us with the comforter. "I like your pajamas," he whispered against my ear, tickling the sensitive skin.

I blushed. "Sorry, I know they're not very girly. Or… flattering at all for that matter."

He chuckled lightly. "No, they're cute, really. They're like you, practical."

I smacked his arm. "Practical?"

He smiled and from the dim light of the moon I could see his dimple in his cheek. "You're not fussy," he clarified. "You like the simple things. It's one of the things I admire the most about you."

"Well, when you put it like that…" I said. "I guess it's okay."

He twisted a strand of my multi-hued brown hair around his finger. "Sophie, if we keep talking we're never going to get to sleep and we do have school tomorrow."

"Oh right," I said.

He began to hum some random song that quickly lulled me to sleep. With Caeden there I knew that no bad dreams, nothing bad at all, would happen to me. He was my protector. My warrior. My mate. My destiny.

SEVENTEEN.

The day had come. It was here. My birthday. My shift. The day my life would change forever. I didn't know whether to be excited, scared, elated, or terrified. Butterflies viciously attacked my churning stomach. It was Friday but Caeden and I weren't going to school today. He said it would take a couple of days to get used to the shift so I was even more thankful of the weekend than I normally was. I didn't want to go into school Monday as a big, hulking, shaggy wolf.

I hoped shifting would come as naturally to me as Caeden claimed it would. I hated the thought of being a defected wolf. A part of me thought that I may not shift at all. That maybe since I was finding out about this so late it wouldn't happen for me. But deep down I knew that wasn't true.

Over the last two weeks had already begun experiencing changes. My vision was clearer, my hearing tuned, and I could smell things I hadn't been able to smell before. Caeden told me it would get worse once I changed. Actually his word had been 'better'. I wasn't sure if I could get used to this clarity. It was strange, eerie, to see, smell, and hear things you know you shouldn't. And to think that I wasn't even at the level that Caeden and the others were at.

He rolled over and cracked his eyes open, a sliver of blue showing through. He had shown up every night since the first. I was used to it now and couldn't imagine it any other way. Although, I had taken it upon myself to get some new pajamas. Ones that were a little more feminine and didn't possess holes.

"Hey," he said yawning. "What time is it?"

I chuckled and looked at the clock. "Time for you to go. Gram will be up any minute."

"Why didn't you wake me up?" he said jumping out of the bed and pulling his jeans on over his pajama bottoms. He threw a sweatshirt on over his t-shirt and leaned down to press a light kiss to my lips. "I'll be back in an hour," he said starting towards my window.

"Don't forget to use the front door," I joked.

"Ha, ha," he mocked and ducked out the window.

I grabbed some clothes and headed into the bathroom to get a shower before Gram woke up.

I turned the nozzle so that the water was as hot as I could stand it. I climbed in and let the hot stream beat the tension out of the coiled knots of my back. I felt like every muscle in my body was a tight coiled spring ready to release at any moment. It was as if my muscles were preparing for my wolf form to emerge. I squeezed the pink goo of my shampoo into my hand and lathered my head until I couldn't take it anymore. The scent of strawberries invaded my nostrils. I gaged from the smell. My shampoo had never smelled that strong before. I scrubbed my body with my mango scent body wash and the same thing happened. The scent of mango and strawberry mingling together nearly knocked me down. I rinsed my hair and my body off. As the bubbles ran down the drain some of the smell went with it. The water was now cold and giving me the shivers so I climbed out and wrapped a fluffy towel around me. I pulled out the hair dryer and turned it up as hot as it would go. I didn't know what Caeden had in store today but I didn't want to spend any time outside with wet hair. I pulled on my jeans, a sweatshirt, and put my hair back in its standard ponytail.

Gram was coming out of her room just as I was leaving the bathroom. She smiled at me, "Today's the big day."

I tried to smile but I was pretty sure it came out more as a grimace. "Yeah," I said.

She gave me a sad smile. "There's nothing to worry about Sophie. I went through my transformation by myself and so have the others for as long as we can remember. You'll have Caeden with you. You're lucky," she said patting my hand. "Come on; let me make you a breakfast before you disappear."

I followed her into the kitchen and in no time she had

my plate piled high with toast, eggs, and bacon.

"How am I supposed to eat all of this?" I asked.

"You transform tonight. You need your strength. Now eat," she demanded.

The doorbell rang and she went to answer it. She returned with Caeden and promptly made him a plate too.

His hair was still slightly damp. He wore a hunter green V-neck sweater that hugged all of his muscles. A white t-shirt peeked out underneath when he moved. He was far too perfect. I quickly averted my gaze before either he or Gram noticed the drool pooling in the corner of my mouth. Before he started eating he leaned over and kissed my cheek. "Happy Birthday, baby," he said.

"Thanks," I said with a small smile.

"Are you ready for tonight," he asked while his hands drummed an odd beat on the table.

"I can't wait," I said sarcastically. "Doesn't every eighteen year old girl want a wolf to rip out of her skin?"

He chuckled and shoveled a spoonful of eggs into his mouth. "You'll be fine," he said.

"You usually the word 'fine' implies anything but," I retorted.

"You have an answer for everything don't you?" he asked as Gram sat down to join us.

"Definitely," I said and then laughed, "how else do you when an argument?" I took a bite of crunchy, butter drenched toast, and said, "So, what's the plan for today?"

"Well," said Caeden swallowing, "not much. I know today's your birthday and I'd like to do something special but since tonight is your first shift I don't think that's going to be possible."

"As long as I'm with you it will be special," I said.

He grinned and his dimple peaked out briefly.

Gram chuckled and jumped up. "Sophie, I made you a cake. It's your fav-o-rite!" she sing songed. She pulled out a glass covered cake from the refrigerator and sat it on the table in front of me. The scent of chocolate and peanut butter invaded my senses. I could practically taste it on my tongue.

"Yum!" I said, already salivating.

The two tiered cake was slathered in a thick coating of peanut butter frosting and "Happy 18th Birthday, Sophie," was written on it in chocolate frosting. Gram had even taken the time to sketch a wolf howling at the moon in the frosting as well.

"I know its morning but from the look on your face I'm assuming you want a piece now?" she asked.

"Yes please," I said shaking my head enthusiastically.

Gram chuckled and grabbed a couple of plates and a cake cutter.

"Wait!" said Caeden.

Gram paused in her actions. "What?" she asked.

"Sophie, has to make a wish first," he said as if it would be the end of the world if I didn't blow out some candles.

Gram shook her head. "How silly of me to forget," she said. She turned around and began digging around in a drawer. She found a box of neon colored candles and proceeded to stick them in the cake. Gram pulled a lighter out of another drawer and lit each candle.

She and Caeden broke into a very loud, very obnoxious, very, very, very, off-key version of the "Happy Birthday" song. I was glad no one else was there to partake in my complete and utter embarrassment. I puffed out my cheeks and blew out the candles making a wish in the process.

"Cake time!" said Caeden patting his flat stomach.

"Is there room in there?" I quipped.

He grinned. "There's always room for cake," he said.

"Of course," I replied just as Gram put a plate of cake in front of me. I took a bite and moaned in ecstasy. "I swear," I said pointing at the cake with my fork, "that world peace could be accomplished based just on Gram's baking."

She chuckled. "I'm not sure about that."

"Oh definitely," I replied. "Nothing in the world can

compare to your cakes. It's like heaven in a confectionary." I went to take a second bite and saw that the only thing on Caeden's plate were a few chocolate crumbs. "Really?" I asked. "That quick? That has to be a record."

He patted his flat stomach and said, "Maybe I should join an eating competition?"

"You'd definitely win," I commented. "I've never seen anyone put away as much food as you can. I'm just waiting for you to swallow a cow hole. Now *that* is as an accomplishment."

He chuckled. "I'd try that but I don't think my jaw is big enough to accomplish that feat," he said.

"Snakes do it," I said.

"I shift into a wolf not a snake," he said and crossed his arms. He leaned across to me and said conspiratorially, "You just wait until you shift. You'll be hungry all the time. And you'll have an affinity for rare meat."

"Really? Because I was starting to think that was just an excuse for you boys to eat all the time," I said. "I mean Charlotte and Chris eat normal, human-sized, portions."

"Ugh, you found me out," he said with a grin.

I finished my cake and then grabbed Caeden's plate. I washed them both and placed them in the drying rack.

My phone rang in my pocket. I pulled it out and saw that it was my dad. As soon as I said hello he and my mom started singing happy birthday. It was just as bad if not worse than Gram and Caeden's version.

"We miss you," said my dad.

"I miss you guys too," I said into the phone.

"It's been far too long since I've seen my baby girl. Now you're eighteen, having your first shift, and you've met your mate. You're a woman now," he said getting choked up.

"Don't worry dad, I'll always be your baby girl," I said with a smile.

"I sure hope so," he said. I heard some shuffling and then, "Sophie, I love you. Your mother is demanding control of the phone now."

"Love you too, dad," I said but I wasn't sure if he heard me because suddenly my mom was on the phone.

"Sophie, tonight is your first shift," she said.

"Thank you captain obvious," I said with my usual sarcasm.

"Sophie, don't be smart with me. Now listen here, it's going to hurt. It's going to be the most painful experience of your life. Worse than childbirth and I would know since your head was the size of Pluto."

"Thank you mom for comparing my head to a planet. I appreciate that," I said.

She continued on as if I hadn't said anything. "But when you go through it with a mate it can also be a wondrous experience. You'll become even more connected than you are now. Have you decided if you're going to perform the bonding ceremony?"

"Yeah mom," I said. "We are. I'm ready so don't even try and talk me out of it."

"I wasn't going to do that. I was just going to say be careful. Being mates already connects you but the bonding ceremony brings you together in ways you can't possibly imagine. But I'm going to let you both discover that on your own. Just please be careful."

"What are you implying?" I asked.

She hesitated and I prepared myself for what I knew was going to become a very uncomfortable conversation. "The bonding ceremony can lead to sex. Please don't let that happen, Sophie. Shifters get pregnant the same way that regular humans do you know? How do you think you came into this world? When your dad and I bonded those feelings were so overwhelming and what do you know? Nine months later you were here."

"Oh my God are you trying to have the sex talk with me?" I asked completely stunned.

Caeden had been taking a sip of water when I said this and spewed droplets of water all across the table.

"Well," my mom said and I could tell she was

completely flustered, "yes. Shifters can't shift with clothes. So, you'll already be naked and the temptation might become too great."

"Mom," I said with flaming red cheeks, "let me stop you right there. I'm not ready for *that*. You have absolutely nothing to worry about."

"Oh thank you Jesus," she said upon hearing my complete sincerity. "I've been worrying myself sick."

"You have nothing to worry about," I said.

"Good, good," she repeated. "Well, now that I have thoroughly embarrassed myself I'll let you go. You have a lot to prepare for tonight. Happy Birthday."

"I love you, mommy," I said.

"I love you, Sophie. I miss you so much. But your father and I made the right choice by sending you there. Even if..." she hesitated. "Even if my family did take you it was still the right choice."

"Bye mom," I said and hung up the phone before the waterworks started.

I looked over at Caeden, who was wiping up his water mess, with red cheeks that matched my own. "What was that about?" he asked.

"You don't want to know," I said.

"Probably not," he conceded. "Let's go before I make an even bigger mess," he said tossing the rag into the sink.

"Agreed," I said taking his hand.

"Bye Gram," I called.

She came out of her bedroom and pulled me into her arms and away from Caeden. "Oh Sophie," she said, "so much is going to change after tonight. I'm so proud to call you my granddaughter. I couldn't have gotten luckier with you. You're so special and you're going to make an amazing shifter. You just wait and see. Good luck sweetie. I'll see you tomorrow."

"Tomorrow?" I questioned.

"Yes tomorrow," she said.

She herded us through the door and then stopped

Caeden with a hand on his arm. "If you're going to be sleeping in Sophie's bed at night I'd prefer you used the door and not the window."

Both of our cheeks flamed a brilliant shade of crimson once again. "Yes ma'am," he said hoarsely.

"Now that that's settled, enjoy your day."

* * *

"I can't believe she *knew*," I hissed once we were safely ensconced in the Jeep and backing out of the driveway.

He chuckled, "It was silly of me to think otherwise. I mean she is a shifter after all. Given her age and her status on the council her hearing and sense of smell has to be far superior than most. But I guess she let it slide until now because she knows I'm not going to sneak in and steal your virtue."

I scoffed. "What is it with people and my virtue today?" I asked rhetorically. "And what do you mean her 'status' on the council?"

"Lucinda is the head of the council of elders. She was married to a Beaumont which means she's like shifter royalty and you are too." He cleared his throat.

"Good to know," I mumbled. "But what if I don't want to be shifter royalty? What if I just want to be plain, old, regular Sophie?"

"Sorry but you can't pick your parents and your dad is a Beaumont which means you are too. You can't run from your name."

"I don't even know what that means," I said.

"I know," he said.

"Well, are you going to tell me?" I asked.

He started down the lane that led to his house. He ran his hand roughly through his hair and stopped in front of the gate. A moment later the gate swung open. By this time I had given up on an answer but finally he said, "Yes, but later. Let's have some fun first."

"Deal," I said as he pulled into the garage. I noticed

that his mom and Bryce's cars were gone. Bryce I, of course, knew was at school. But I had no idea where his mom could be. "Where's your mom?" I voiced as he came around to get my door.

"Out. She thought she'd give us the day to ourselves," he said, taking my hand and leading me towards the civil war era house.

"That was nice of her," I said.

He smiled and opened the side door that led into a mudroom. "She figured you'd already be stressed enough today about your shift without her hovering."

"Thanks for bringing that up," I said.

He took his boots off and I slipped off my sneakers. He gave me a sheepish grin. "Sorry, but we will have to talk about it sometime today."

"Well sometime will have to wait," I said.

He pulled me into the family room and onto the plush leather couch. He kissed the top of my head as I reclined against his chest. "I'm sorry I don't have anything special planned," he said.

I turned in his arms to get a clear view of his face. "This is special," I argued. "I'm getting to spend it with you. This is perfect," I said.

He smiled and said, "I love you, more and more every day."

"I love you too," I said. He cleared his throat and wiggled a bit in his spot. "What is it?" I asked.

He gave me a sheepish smile and his adorable dimple peaked out. Caeden was all man but that one little dimple always managed to make him look a cute little precocious boy. I would never tire of seeing it. "Well..." he started. He wiggled again and cleared his throat.

"Spit it out, Caeden," I said.

"It's nothing bad," he said. "But I think that come spring break we should go see your parents. There's more we can learn about being mates and maybe they can help us understand why 'them' and why 'us'."

"That's a great idea," I said. "Why were you so scared to ask me?"

He cleared his throat. "As soon as I came up with the idea I got the insane fear of being on an airplane. I've never been afraid of flying before so I assume it's coming from you. *Are* you afraid of flying?"

I gulped. "Yes." In my excitement of seeing my parents I had completely forgotten their location. Germany. No car could get me across the ocean and boats were just as bad as planes. When I was younger we went on a particularly bad flight that I still had nightmares about. I never quite got over it and so my parents started avoiding planes as much as they could for my sake. "You know... it's kind of weird you knowing stuff about me that I haven't even told you."

He chuckled. "You can do it too you know? I mean, we did already test this theory."

"So what are you afraid of?" I asked.

"Just think for a moment it'll come to you," he said.

I closed my eyes and just thought for a moment. What could Caeden possibly be afraid of?

"Snakes? Really?" I said.

"Flying? Really?" he mimicked and we both laughed. He rubbed my arm soothingly and rubbed his nose against my neck. "Don't worry. I'll be right beside you on the plane. I'll talk you through it. Distract you," he whispered with a brush of his lips against mine. "You won't remember a thing," he said, his fingers rubbing my neck.

"Hmm," I said relaxing against his touch. "I have no doubt that you will be able to sufficiently distract me."

"Good," he said. "Since, that's settled I'll be sure to book our tickets."

I groaned.

"You won't remember a thing," he said rubbing my arm.

I let out a breath. "I certainly hope so or you're in for it, mister."

He chuckled and the motion shook both of us.

A few minutes of comfortable silence passed. I loved the fact that Caeden and I could sit and neither of us felt the need to fill the silence with endless chatter. There are very few people you can be that comfortable with. It was a rare thing to find and I was thankful for it. His long fingers stroked my hair and rubbed my scalp. I felt my eyes getting heavy from the relaxing motion. I wasn't even sleepy but for some reason, even as a child, someone rubbing my head always put me to sleep. I liked to be petted; maybe it was a sign of the wolf in me. Did wolves like to be petted? No, they were wild. Oh well, I just enjoyed it.

I cracked my eyes open as Caeden continued to massage my scalp. "Are we going to just sit here all day?" I asked even though I was pretty sure I already knew the answer.

He sighed. "Yes, we both, but especially you, have to conserve our energy for tonight. It's going to be extremely draining. The more energy you have the easier it will be to shift and then to shift back to your human form. Trust me, I've been through this."

I sighed. "I'm not ready. Maybe next year," I whined.

He chuckled and kissed the top of my head. "Sorry babe but the moon doesn't wait for you."

"I'm scared," I admitted.

"You'd be an idiot not to be," he said. "It's normal to be scared," he rubbed my arm. "But I'll be there. Everything will be fine. I wouldn't tell you so if I didn't think that."

"What did you mean earlier when you said that I'm part of shifter royalty?"

He sighed and mused his hair. "It's hard to explain but whenever the first shift occurred it was by a Beaumont. Therefore the Beaumont's are shifter royalty. Not just among wolves but among all shifters. Beaumont's are more powerful stronger, faster, quicker. You're the best of the best."

"What if I can't live up to that?" I asked. "What if I suck at being a shifter? What if I'm not cut out for this?"

"Whoa, slow down," he said. "Of course you'll be all that. You already possess some of your potential, I've seen it. It'll reach its peak once you shift."

"Caeden," I said quietly.

"Yes?" he prompted.

"Who was the second wolf to shift?" I asked.

He swallowed and I could see his Adam's apple bobbing. "A Williams," he said quietly.

"I figured," I said. "Is that why at Thanksgiving everyone looked at us like we were a King and Queen?"

"Yeah," he sighed. "They're convinced that we're the answer to their prayers."

"Why?" I asked sitting up.

"The shifter community has become very disconnected. We used to all mingle together. Panthers, wolves, eagles, tigers. It didn't matter. Now, we all separate and stay within our clan. But there's even strife among communities of the same species. I mean look at us and the Grimm's. We can't stand each other. I think the council and the other members of the pack are hoping that we can unite us all again. They also hope that if we are regaining mates then the others will too. That was the cause of a lot of the strife. But even once the idea of mates became nothing more than a legend it didn't change things."

"How come I feel like we're supposed to save the world?"

He chuckled. "This isn't a comic book."

"It kind of feels like it," I said.

"It does doesn't it?" he agreed.

Time ticked by and lunch came along. We made sandwiches and ate in the kitchen. After, we cleaned up and headed to his room. He collapsed into a bean bag and sighed. "At least it's not as cold as it usually is in January," he commented.

"That's true," I said. It was an unseasonably warm day today. I hoped the temperature didn't suddenly decide to drop tonight. I didn't want my shift to take place in the freezing cold. "Caeden?" I asked. "How is this going to work? How do I go all *wolf*?"

He motioned for me to sit in the other bean bag and I collapsed into its air beads. It made a scratchy noise as the beads moved around to accommodate me. "The first shift is the only one we don't control. The moon calls to the beast in you and you can't resist it. It's instinctual. You don't actually have to do anything. Your body takes over for your mind."

"I don't know if I want my body to take over my mind," I said.

He chuckled. "We don't have any say in the matter. Whatever magic it is that we possess that makes us turn takes over."

"Magic," I breathed.

"You'll see," he said. "When you change it's like *magic*. Once the pain is gone it's the best feeling in the world. You feel unstoppable. It's freeing. You'll love it. The unknown it what's scaring you. Don't let it."

He had me pegged. There was no avoiding it. I hated the unknown. Not knowing something made me feel blind and I didn't like it for one second. Caeden and the whole pack had grown up with the knowledge of what they were. I had been kept in the dark. True, it was for my own safety as well as my parents but that didn't make it okay. I had deserved the right to know that I wasn't exactly *human*. Now, my full moon was here and my beast was going to emerge. I got the feeling from Caeden and the others that they weren't exactly allowed to discuss the transformation. Not just with me but with each other. Like it was taboo to know about what to expect.

Caeden leaned across and took my small hand in his larger one. He tucked a piece of hair behind my ear. "It'll be okay Sophie. You're not going to go through this alone. I'm going to be there to talk you through it. You have nothing to be afraid of. I promise. I'm sorry I can't tell you more but we're really not allowed to discuss it. It's a very personal experience it and the council really doesn't want us to discuss it with other first time shifters. We're only allowed to give words of encouragement."

"But you're going to be with me," I said, "you're going to see me got through it. I don't see why you can't tell me. It doesn't seem fair."

"It doesn't seem fair to me either. But that's the way it is. Before we change we're only allowed to know the jist of it."

I huffed and pouted my lips like a four year old but I couldn't help it. It was completely unfair to have to go into this whole thing blind. I felt like all I knew was that tonight at midnight I was going to turn into a wolf, it was going to hurt, and Caeden was going to be with me. It wasn't a lot to go on.

Caeden sighed and leaned back in the bean bag. The air beads crunched with the movement. He rested his hands on his knees. "I'm sorry I can't tell you more. But tonight I'll be there to talk you through it. I'll coach you as best I can."

"I guess that's as good as I'm going to get," I said with a small smile.

He laughed. "Yeah, it is."

"I'm sorry if I'm bothering you," I said.

He chuckled. "You're not. I just about drove my dad crazy just before my own change. I was scared to death. But he told me the same things I've told you. Except for the part where I'll be with you."

I rubbed his hand more to calm myself than to do any soothing of him. My mind was on overload. For the past couple of months I had been able to ignore the fact that I was going to turn into a wolf. But now the day was here and I wanted to run in the other direction. I felt like that if I pretended this day wouldn't happen then it would magically disappear. But the only magic in the world that existed was the magic that was going to turn me into a wolf.

Once I got over the initial shock of Caeden and the others being wolves it didn't bother me. I thought Caeden was beautiful as a wolf. But for some reason I just couldn't wrap my mind around the fact that I was going to be this beautiful, majestic, creature too. It just didn't make sense. With the others I could see their wolf shimmering behind their eyes. But with me? I looked in the mirror and saw just plain, old, perfectly normal, brown-eyed, Sophie. Nothing more, nothing less. I could see power in the others but I saw no power in myself. I was a weak, pathetic, human.

What if I didn't change?

As much as I was afraid of the actual changing part I was even more afraid of not changing. What if there was something wrong with me? What if I was defective?

"Sophie, are you okay?" asked Caeden.

"Mmhmm. I'm fine," I murmured.

He looked at me suspiciously. Those blue eyes told me that clearly he knew that I wasn't but he didn't push me to be honest. I was thankful for it. I needed time to sort things out in my head. My hours as a human were dwindling into the single digits. Tonight I would become a wolf. Tonight I would bond forever with my mate. Change was thick in the air like toxic syrup.

EIGHTEEN.

"Alright," said Caeden standing up from the bean bag and stretching his long legs.

"Alright what?" I asked.

"It's time to go," he said.

"It's not dark yet," I commented.

"Thanks I hadn't noticed," he said. He smiled. "Don't worry I have a plan. I want to make tonight as special as I can since we weren't able to do anything fun today."

"Should I be afraid?" I asked.

"Very," he said.

"I'm in," I said. He smirked and pulled me up from the lump on the floor that once resembled a bean bag.

He took my hand and led me towards to Bryce's room. He knocked on his little brothers door. "Come in," said Bryce.

Caeden pushed the door open. The first thing I noticed about Bryce's room was that it was green. The next thing I noticed was that it was a mess. I had been taking Caeden's neat-freakiness for granted. Clothes, shoes, soda cans, and food wrappers littered the floor to the point that there was no floor. Caeden glanced back at me with an apology written on his face. Bryce was sitting on his bed with some kind of game controller in his hands. The sound of gun shots rang through the room.

"What can I help you with?" asked Bryce never taking his eyes away from the screen that his game was playing on.

"I need the keys to your Jeep," said Caeden.

"Her name is Stella," said Bryce pulling out a chain of keys from his pocket. He tossed the keys in Caeden's direction. "Take care of her," said Bryce waving us away.

Caeden chuckled and closed Bryce's door.

"Where are we going?" I asked as Caeden led me down the winding staircase to the main floor.

"The woods," he answered. "That's why I needed

Bryce's Jeep."

"The woods," I repeated.

"Yep, come on," he said taking my hand and leading me out to the garage after we stopped to bundle up and put our shoes on. We climbed into the old green Jeep. It croaked shakily to life. He backed out of the garage but instead of heading towards the gate he veered to the left and down an unmarked, nearly invisible, road. The car bumped along and I worried that my head might hit the ceiling if we hit a bump to hard. I held on for dear life but Caeden was clearly enjoying himself. I thought it was a miracle that good ole Stella didn't lose her balance. I worried that I might get sick with all the bouncing that was going on. There seemed to be no real road that Caeden followed. He just drove and tried to avoid the trees while I tried to not squish my eyes shut and scream.

We drove for about an hour before he stopped the car.

"Are you okay?" he asked me.

"Fine," I mumbled.

"You're green," he said.

"Really? No wonder with all the bumping that was going on," I replied. I opened the door of the Jeep and jumped out. I inhaled the crisp, clean, air like my life depended on it. Which I guess it did. Slowly, I began to feel my head clear.

"Better?" he asked.

"Give me another minute," I said.

"Sit with your head between your knees," he said and guided me towards a stump of a tree.

I ducked my head between my knees and sighed. "That is better," I commented taking a couple more deep breaths. Air flowed freely through my lungs clearing away the remaining nausea. A small brown rabbit scuttled by my feet. It was completely unafraid of me and Caeden. It stopped and twitched its small pink nose at me. I smiled at the critter as it scampered away. Satisfied that I wasn't going to get sick I sat up. Caeden was leaning against a tree watching me. I blushed. "Sorry," I said. "I don't have much of a stomach."

"It's okay," he said. "I'm used to rough terrain. I should have warned you."

He held out his hand and helped me up from the stump. He pulled me against his chest and held me for a moment.

"You're really going to hate me in a second," he said.

"Why?" I questioned, leery of his answer.

"We have to hike from here," he said with a sheepish glance.

I smacked his arm. "You know I suck at that kind of stuff," I said. "I can't even stay upright on a treadmill and that's flat," I cried.

He chuckled. "That was only because you were distracted by my amazing abs," he said patting his stomach. I smacked his arm again. "Ow," he said rubbing the spot.

"You better lead the way," I said, "if you want me to make it to wherever it is we're going before I go all wolf on you."

He laughed and took my hand again. "Don't worry. It's not that far. About a mile," he said.

"A mile!" I scoffed. "This isn't gym class!"

He tugged on my hand so I would trudge along. Which I did; albeit grudgingly.

* * *

The terrain wasn't too hard to trek but I did fall a couple of times. Scrapes littered the palms of my hands and the skin of my knees. Caeden assured me that when I shifted they would heal. Finally, Caeden held back a branch and we broke into a clearing.

I gasped.

Sunset was descending on the sky and the pinks, oranges, and gold turned the clearing into a place of majesty. The skeletal lines of the trees were far from menacing when they were hit with this light. The leaves that crunched beneath my feet were bathed in a shimmering gold. And in the middle of it all was the most spectacular sight I had ever seen. A waterfall fell soundly into the clearing. The roaring of the water filled my ears with a comforting sound.

The water rushed down into a river. It was cold enough that diamond icicles had formed and were glowing in the waning sunlight. Trickles of water dripped off of the icicles as they slowly melted. The affect was breathtaking.

"This is so beautiful," I gasped.

Caeden grinned and his dimple peaked out to greet me like an old friend. "I thought it might make tonight more tolerable if you were able to experience it somewhere beautiful."

"How did you find this place?" I asked in complete awe as I turned in circles to take it in.

"I was out exploring one day and heard the roar of the water. I came to investigate and found this. It's amazing what Mother Nature can accomplish when she goes untouched by humans," he said entwining our hands together. "Come on," he said pulling me to the back of the waterfall. "I have something else to show you."

I couldn't help but let his excitement rub off on me. It was contagious. He brushed away some broken branches of a bush and motioned me ahead of him. I could see that he was leading me into some kind of cave. I had to get down on my hands and knees and duck my head to make it through the narrow opening. It was a tight squeeze and an even tighter one for Caeden. I could feel the rock pressing against my sides and my claustrophobia began to kick in. I inhaled deeply with my nose and exhaled with my mouth. It was pitch black and I couldn't see anything but I trusted Caeden with my life so I kept going.

A gush of air breezed across my face and I inhaled it hungrily. I still couldn't see anything but there weren't any rocks pressing against my sides anymore. I felt Caeden move past me and it sounded like he was walking. I lifted my hand up to see if my fingers would skim rock. When they met blissful nothingness I hesitantly stood up.

I heard a click and then the cave was filled with a bright yellow light. Another click and another light joined the first. My eyes began to gradually adjust to the sudden light. Caeden came back to stand beside me and took my hand.

One more blink and my vision cleared.

Stalagmites surrounded us and I could see water running down their sides. The ceiling surged above us. I looked up and was almost lost in its depths. The lanterns created a yellow glow over the whole place. For some reason the walls seemed to glow deep blues and purples, oranges and red. I felt like I was inside a jewelry box. Various mosses were growing on the rock walls adding green to rainbow of colors. Even through the rock walls I could still hear the roaring of the waterfall. With a gasp I realized that we must be inside the waterfall.

In the corner were plastic bins filled with various objects. It looked like food, clothes, and maybe a couple of sleeping bags.

"How did you find this place?" I asked; my eyes finally settling on Caeden although it was hard to keep them from wandering and taking in the simple majesty of this place.

He chuckled. "Just like I did the waterfall. I stumbled upon it. I thought it was beautiful. Untouched," he said.

I sat down on a natural ledge and patted the space next to me for Caeden to join me. I looked back up and the ceiling and saw a sliver of night sky. Inky blue-black was replacing the earlier gold's, oranges, and pinks. My wolf was getting closer to being released.

"Are you okay?" asked Caeden. Obviously he had picked up on where my thoughts were taking me.

I swallowed and turned to look at him. Even in the terrible light that the lanterns provided I could still see the glow of his blue eyes. I traced the contours of his face with the palm of my hand. The scruff of his stubble rasped against my hand creating a pleasant burn.

"I'm fine," I said. "How many times are you going to ask me that?"

Caeden grinned. "Before the night's over or for the

rest of your life?" he countered.

"Both?" I smiled.

"A lot," he answered.

I leaned my head against his shoulder. "Can we get this show on the road?" I asked with a laugh already knowing his answer.

"No," he sighed. "We must wait for the moon. In the meantime," he said jumping down from the ledge and moving over to the clear plastic bins, "I made us a picnic."

"A picnic?" I asked hopping down from the ledge as well. His hand snaked out to steady me when I teetered.

He popped off the blue lid and set it aside. "Yeah," he said. "I brought all this out earlier. I wanted tonight to be special. It should be something that you look back and remember with a smile," he said pulling out glass containers of food.

"You're so sweet," I said and meant it. Not many boys would think to do something like this, to make tonight easier on me. But Caeden wasn't most boys.

He smiled up at me and gently stroked my cheek with his thumb. "I love you," he whispered.

I sighed at his words. "I don't think I'll ever get tired of hearing you say that," I said.

"I certainly hope not," he said. "Because I plan on telling you every day for the rest of our lives," he said and kissed me. His lips were warm and firm against mine. My hands snaked around his neck holding him closer. He chuckled and pulled away. "There will be plenty of time for that later," he said. "But now we eat." He popped the lid off of a pasta dish, stuck a fork in it, and handed it to me. "Sorry, it's cold but there's no electrical outlets down here for a microwave," he joked

I sniffed it hesitantly. The smells of basil, garlic, and rosemary engulfed my lungs. It smelled heavenly. Caeden twirled his own pasta around on a fork and waited for me to take the first bite. I slid the noodles in my mouth making a very undignified slurping noise in the process.

"Mmm," I said. "This is really good." I twirled another bite around and promptly stuck it in my mouth.

A smile lit Caeden's face making his eyes glow like two blue orbs. "Thanks," he said, "I made it myself."

"Really?" I asked swallowing and taking the water bottle that Caeden offered me.

"Yeah," he said and even with the yellow glow surrounding us I could see red flood his cheeks. "I like to cook."

"Lucky me," I said with a laugh.

Caeden laughed too and said, "I know you probably thought I could only make cupcakes but I am a man of many talents."

"I won't forget that," I said.

He laughed. "I've just gotten myself in trouble haven't I?"

"Yep," I said. "Big trouble," I demonstrated with my hands just how big.

"What am in for?" he asked.

I pretended to ponder. "I think I'd like to see you strap on some yellow gloves and up to your elbows in soapy water and dirty dishes."

"What is it with women thinking it's hot to watch a man wash dishes?" Caeden asked shaking his head.

I quirked my brow, "Why is it men like to watch women mow the lawn? Forget the dishes. I think watching you mow the lawn would suffice."

He shook his head. "Why is that?"

I blushed and finally answered. "You. Hot. Sweaty. Half-naked."

He laughed. "When summer gets here I promise to let you watch me mow the lawn. I really know how to tell that tractor whose boss."

Our easy banter continued until it was almost midnight. At around eleven o' clock I began to become very uncomfortable. My skin began to buzz and my senses became ultra-sensitive.

Twenty minutes away from the time of my shift Caeden grabbed some stuff from the bins and climbed out the opening. I followed behind him.

It was bad enough coming in but going out was ten times worse. With my newfound sensitivity everything around me was spiked. The brush of the hair on my arms against the rock wall felt like a knife scrape. The sound of our shuffling felt like drums being hit right beside my ears. It was too much to take. A small whimper escaped my lips. Everything was too loud. Too sensitive. Too something.

"Don't worry, Sophie. We're almost there," called Caeden and his voice echoed back to me.

I certainly hoped so. It felt like my head was going to explode.

The sounds of Caeden's shuffling disappeared and were replaced by the sounds of scraping and twigs snapping. Caeden's hand flashed white as he reached into the darkness to grab me and help me out. My knees shook as I stood. The cold night air caressed my sensitive skin. My knees shook with the weight of the moon pressing on me.

"Caeden," I whimpered.

"Don't worry. I'm here," he whispered into the night.

He took my hand and when he saw that I couldn't move my legs he picked me up off the ground and swung whatever it was he had brought with him over his shoulder.

He walked around the side of the cave so we were in front of the roaring waterfall. The full moon turned the water white.

Caeden stopped before the rocky ledge and set me down. "Do you think you can change?" he asked.

"Change?" I asked confused. "I didn't know there was any thinking about it. I thought I just turned into a wolf," I cried.

He chuckled. "That's not what I meant," he said. He held up some kind of dark fabric. "You need to change out of your clothes and put this on. Your clothes don't shift with you, remember?"

"Oh right," I said embarrassed. My legs still shook but I thought I could manage. I took the fabric from him.

"Why don't you change over there," he pointed, "and I'll go this way," he said and I saw that he had a matching cloak.

He disappeared into the darkness and I made my protesting legs move in the direction in which he had pointed.

I stripped my clothes and the rasping of the fabric made me feel like my skin was on fire. The word *Liar* etched into my skin glowed a pearly white in the moonlight. I pulled on the red velvet cloak and pulled the top clasp together. There were no other clasps and I knew the reason why. Anymore buttons would restrict my movement once I turned into a wolf. I decided to leave my clothes where they were for when I returned. I slid the ponytail holder out of my hair and let my chocolate brown hair cascade over my shoulders. I knew Caeden preferred it down. I held the red cloak tightly against my body. Hand me a picnic basket and call me Red Riding Hood. After all I was about to go meet the big bad wolf.

I tentatively stepped out from the cover of the trees. He was standing on a rock in the middle of the river. His feet were bare. His red cloak matched the one he had given me. It hugged his muscles and I knew it looked far more exquisite on him than it ever would on me. From the tilt of his shoulders and the twist of his head I knew he heard me but he made no move to turn. There were several smaller rock slabs leading to the larger one that Caeden was standing on in the center of the river. I hopped from one to the other until finally we were both on the same one. Slowly, he turned to face me.

My breath caught in my throat. The moonlight gleamed off of the smooth, tanned, naked skin of his chest. A light dusting of brown hair trailed down from his navel. I forced my eyes upwards to meet his blue eyed stare.

"It'll be okay, Sophie," he said.

With him there I knew that the words he spoke were true.

The orb of the full moon reflected in his azure eyes. I was riveted. I began to pant and my skin began to buzz. His strong arms gripped my shoulders.

My muscles clenched and I lost my grip on the cloak. But I didn't care. The time for modesty had passed.

Pain coursed through my body. A pain like nothing I had ever experienced. My back arched and I thought I screamed but I heard no sound. Caeden's arms continued to grip me as my beast tried to break free.

"Caeden," I whimpered and was surprised that I could speak at all.

"You're doing great, Soph," he said.

"It hurts!" I cried as my muscles jerked this way and that. It felt like I was having seizure.

"I know, baby, I know. It's okay though. This is normal. Just roll with it. Don't fight it. Fighting it will make it worse."

I whimpered again and tried to relax my body. It helped, like he said, but not much. My head arched back against my will taking in even more moonlit rays. A single tear rolled from my eye down my cheek. Caeden's thumb gently caressed it away.

"Almost there," he whispered.

My neck twisted in a contortion that didn't seem humanly possible and I guess it probably wasn't. I screamed and screamed and screamed. My muscles hurt and twisted into shapes that didn't seem possible. More tears rolled from my eyes. How anyone made it out of this alive on their own was beyond me.

"Let go," he murmured.

I snapped the leash on my beast and roared into the night. The periwinkle blue eyes of a gray wolf reflected back at me.

You're beautiful. Sounded a voice that I recognized in my head as Caeden's.

I did it? I thought but it came out more like a question.

You did it. He thought. *You're absolutely exquisite.* He came forward and nuzzled his black nose against my throat. *Mine.* I heard his thought.

I looked down with completely new eyes and saw that I was covered in chocolate brown fur with a golden and red glint to it.

We can hear each other's thoughts? I asked belatedly.

He gave me a wolfy grin, tongue lolling to the side. *Of course. It's how we communicate in this form. Distance isn't an issue and we don't hear every thought. Only the ones we want others to hear.*

This is amazing. I thought.

I knew you'd like it once you got over the shock of it.

I looked down at my furry brown paws and saw the red cloaks lying on the gray rock like a bloodstain.

Can we run? I asked. I had never liked running in my human form but my wolf form? I thought it might be something I would enjoy.

Race ya. He thought and then was gone in a flash. But with my new wolf's eyes I could easily spot him. The power that surged in my muscles surprised me. I effortlessly caught up to him. I tackled him easily in this form. What had I been so afraid of? This was amazing.

Our laughs echoed in my head as we rolled around in the dirt, grass, and twigs. He got away from me and took off running again. I knew that if I lost sight of him that I would still be able to find him. His scent, which had been potent enough when I was just human, invaded my senses and I thought it would never leave. The scent of pine and cinnamonwas now joined with a hint of citrus and wood. It was heavenly.

I surged my legs forward and sprinted after him. His laugh echoed into my head. *Amazing isn't it.* He thought.

Incredible. I thought back.

I felt his smile in my mind.

I'm so happy that I got to experience this with you. He thought.

I wouldn't have it any other way.

I love you. He thought as I caught back up to him.

We stopped. I nuzzled his wolfy neck like he had done to me. *I love you, too.*

I heard his sigh in my mind as he soaked in my words. He nuzzled my neck and thought, *Cookies, cakes, and icing.*

Pine, cinnamon, citrus, and wood. I thought back. I heard his chuckle in my mind.

We took off running again and playfully nipped at each other's heels. We ran for hours and I never felt tired. I sensed it when Caeden began to lead us back to the river and waterfall. I was amazed that I was able to pick up on such a thing.

I stopped when we reached the river. I saw that he was moving towards the robes.

Caeden. I thought and my heart pitter patted.

Yes. He thought turning around to look at me. He was so beautiful as a wolf that I found myself gasping and at a loss for words. Or…um… thoughts.

How do I change back? I don't know how to do this. I thought in a panic.

It's okay Sophie. It's not hard at all. You just have to visualize yourself as a human. You can do that right?

I hope so. I thought.

I heard his chuckle in my mind. *You've done everything beautifully tonight. I have no doubt that this will be any different.*

I was glad that at least one of us had faith in me. We hopped onto the rocks. He shimmered into his human form and pulled the cloak on. We'd both seen everything. There was no need to be polite now.

I closed my wolf eyes and pictured myself human like he said. I pictured my long brown hair, my slender hands, my knobby knees, and ten toes. My body vibrated and when I opened my eyes I saw human hands instead of wolf paws. I grabbed the cloak and wrapped it around myself.

"Are we going to do this?" asked Caeden and he sounded out of breath.

I stood and met his eyes. I knew he was talking about the bonding. "Yes," I rasped.

He smiled. He took my hands in his large ones and grinned. "Do you, Sophie Noelle Beaumont, take me as your mate? Do you pledge your heart, your soul, your very being to me? Will you bond yourself to me?"

The air around us crackled with electricity and I swore I saw flickers of white light.

"You have my heart. You have my soul. You have my being. I am yours forever. I bond myself to you," I spoke with confidence. I didn't know how the words popped into my head but I knew they were the right ones to speak. He smiled.

I swallowed. "Do you, Caeden Henry Williams, take me as your mate? Do you pledge your heart, your soul, your very being to me? Will you bond yourself to me?" I gulped. For a moment I was unsure of his answer.

He smiled hugely. "You have my heart. You have my soul. You have my being. I am yours forever. I bond myself to you," he said with conviction. His lips pressed against mine. One hand cradled my cheek while the other rested at the small of my back. Purple and white lights twinkled around us like fireflies. Magic, like he had said. A very old, very powerful, kind of magic was at work here.

"Amazing," I murmured. Tonight was just full of amazement.

I hugged myself against his sculpted body. I nuzzled his neck much as I had done as a wolf. The scents of pine, cinnamon, citrus, and wood erupted in my nose. "I love you," I said.

His hand gently rubbed my arm. "I love you more than words can express. You're my other half."

I sighed blissfully at his words.

"Come on," he said. "You have to be tired. We'll sleep in the cave and drive back tomorrow morning."

Until he said it I didn't realize how tired I had become. My muscles were sore and my eyes were heavy with fatigue. He led me to the entrance of the cave and told me to go on in and said he was going to grab our clothes. I crawled through and this time the journey hardly bothered me at all. I was growing used to it.

The yellow lanterns were still glowing when I entered the cavern. A minute or so later Caeden crawled through with our clothes. He stuck them in a plastic bag and then began rummaging through the bins. He tossed me a baggy long-sleeved shirt and sweatpants that must have belonged to him. I slipped them on with my back to him as he slid into something similar. The sleeves and the pants legs were too long so I had to roll them up to be able to walk. When I turned around he was pulling out sleeping bags and down comforters. He also had a space heater. I didn't think it would be necessary. Since my shift I felt hotter. Like my skin was on fire. Even the long-sleeved shirt seemed to be too much.

He grabbed two pillows and fluffed them before setting them with the sleeping bags. He pulled out something else and began pumping it. I realized it was an air mattress.

He grinned. "I didn't think the floor would be too comfortable," he winked.

"You've thought of everything," I breathed.

"I wanted tonight to be perfect," he said.

"I has been," I said and he smiled. My stomach flipped at that smile.

Once the mattress was pumped he covered it with the sleeping bags and lay down. He motioned for me to join him. I did and he pulled the down comforter against us. He spooned me against him and kissed my neck.

"Sleep now," he whispered as his hands gently caressed my cheek and then stroked my hair. I felt his soft lips press against my cheek.

I felt my eyes grow heavy. "I love you, Caeden," I said with a sleep heavy voice. "I'm glad you were here."

"Me too," he said but it sounded like he was in a tunnel. Sleep overcame me and I dreamed of full moons, wolves, and little red riding hood.

NINETEEN.

"Hey, sleeping beauty," said Caeden when I finally cracked my eyes open. Light flooded the cave and for a moment I was shocked. I was surprised any light could penetrate in here. But then I remembered the natural opening in the ceiling which explained the light.

"What time is it?" I asked sitting up and yawning. I knew my hair must be a mess but it wasn't like he hadn't seen it.

"It's almost ten," he said.

"Really?" I asked shocked. I normally never slept passed eight.

"Yeah," he said. "It's normal to sleep a lot after you shift for the first time. I slept until almost two after my first shift. My dad was ready to send out a search party."

I saw that he was dressed in the clothes he had worn yesterday. He tossed me the plastic bag that my clothes were in.

"Change over there," he motioned to a dark alcove, "and I'll get this stuff packed up and then we can head home."

I nodded my head and moved into the shadows to dress. Despite the pain of my transformation I had enjoyed the time just the two of us out here in the wilderness. No one was here to watch us or scold us or judge us. It had been wonderful. Despite my claustrophobia I was finding the cave to be a sort of sanctuary.

I pulled on my jeans and zipped the zipper. I slid the elastic band off my wrist and pulled my hair back out of my face. I eased out of the shadows to find Caeden folding the blankets neatly and adding them to the bin. He had let the air out of the mattress and it laid feebly on the floor. I came over to help him. I rolled the mattress up and handed it to him. He smiled graciously.

"Ready?" he asked.

"Yeah, I guess so," I said and I knew he heard my reluctance.

He pulled me against him. My palms rested on his chest and he pressed his lips forcefully against mine. It was a demanding, take-all, kiss and I loved it. My mouth opened underneath his and he took advantage. His fingers twined in my hair. I swore sparks were flying with the heat we were producing.

"Ready now?" he asked pulling his mouth away from mine. His hand was still twined in my hair and his breathing was as labored as mine.

"Definitely not," I said.

He chuckled. "Well, unfortunately we do have to go."

"Darn," I said and he laughed. He pressed his lips against mine again but this time the kiss was tender. His thumb gently stroked the side of my face. He tugged me towards the entrance and climbed out first. I climbed out after him.

The temperature had changed overnight. Fifty degrees had turned into thirty degrees. I didn't know how I knew but I did. But amazingly enough I didn't feel it. It could have been seventy degrees for all I knew. The cold no longer seemed to penetrate me. I wondered what the hot summers would feel like.

Caeden looked back at me and smiled. "I wish we could run as wolves to the Jeep but I didn't think to bring a stash of clothes. Now that you're a wolf we'll have to leave some of your clothes around at various locations. It's no fun shifting without clothes. But your stamina should be better now so it shouldn't take very long."

"Lead the way," I said even though it wasn't necessary. With my new senses I could clearly see the patch from which we had come.

Caeden was right. The mile long trek didn't take nearly as long this time around. I didn't even fall. Maybe being a shifter wouldn't be so bad.

However, the ride back was just as bumpy and I still found myself getting queasy.

"Are you okay?" asked Caeden at one point.

I nodded my head scared of what might come out of my mouth if I opened it up. Caeden seemed to realize this and resumed his silence. When he finally drove out of the woods and parked in the garage I immediately hopped out, sat on a spare tire, and stuck my head between my knees taking deep breaths.

"I'm sorry," said Caeden.

"Just give me a minute," I huffed. I worked the cold air through my lungs getting rid of the lingering feelings of nausea. He waited patiently for it to pass.

"I'm going to have to remember to get you some motion sickness pills," he said with a chuckle.

I looked up and glared at him. "I'm not exactly used to off-roading in the woods for your information."

"Touché," he said.

I stood up slowly making sure the movement didn't spin my head. When it didn't Caeden took my head and lead me into the house. The door had hardly clicked behind us when his mom came running towards us.

Amy jumped up and down on the balls of her feet as she clapped her hands. Her smile was huge and infectious. "How'd it go?" she asked.

I shrugged my shoulders. "I guess the way it does for everybody," I said. I had no experience in this matter so how was I supposed to know whether it was good or bad?

Caeden grinned at his mom. "She's a natural. She was amazing." He nuzzled my neck. "I'm so happy I got to experience that with her, mom. It was incredible. I think she's beautiful now but when she shifted? Wow," he said. "She took to the transformation with ease. I couldn't have hoped for more."

"Did you have any problem shifting back to your human form?" she addressed me.

"No, not at all," I said. "Caeden's a great teacher."

"Did you..." she hesitated.

"Did we what?" I prompted.

"Did you bond?" she asked.

"Yes," I said, "and that was as far as it went," I assured her.

And it was amazing.

I looked at Caeden. "Did you say that out loud?" I asked.

He looked at me puzzled, a wrinkle in his brow, "No," he said, "I didn't say anything."

"Yes, you did. You said, 'and it was amazing,' I heard you," I said getting hysterical.

"I didn't say anything out loud," he repeated.

"He didn't," added Amy.

My mouth popped open in a little O of surprise. "You mean, I heard your thoughts in human form? Think something towards me," I said.

Like what?

"Oh my God," I gasped. "This must be part of the bond!" I exclaimed.

"You think something," he said. "I want to try and hear your thoughts."

Uh, you're hot. I thought directing my thoughts towards him.

His laugh filled the mud room. *I think you're hot too.*

This is crazy. I thought.

More like amazing. Now we can hear each other's thoughts when we're human too. This is great. I wonder if your parents can do this.

I don't know, maybe. I guess we'll find out over Spring Break.

Oh right. He thought.

His mom was staring blankly at us and Bryce had joined her. He leaned down in his mom's ear and said. "Those two are weird." Amy swatted at her son.

"Are you guys… communicating telepathically?"

"Uh… yeah," I said nervously.

"Wow," she said.

"Mom, I need to tell you something," said Caeden.

"Oh dear lord what is it now?" asked Amy shaking

her head.

Caeden looked at me and then at his mother. "Sophie and I think it would be a good idea to go and see her parents over Spring Break to learn more about being mates and the bond and what it all means."

Amy sighed. "I should've known it wouldn't be *that* bad since it was coming from you and not your brother but we always go camping over Spring Break, Caeden."

"I know, Mom. You and Bryce can still go but I think this is important. Sophie and I need to understand what all this means. They're the only other mates. We don't have much choice."

She shook her head and sighed. "Alright, I guess I don't have much choice. You are a man now and I can respect your need for answers. We'll get your tickets tonight. Sophie, does your grandma know about this?"

"No," I said. "Caeden and I just talked about this... yesterday." Had it only been yesterday? It seemed so much longer. So much had taken place in the last twenty-four hours that it didn't seem possible.

Amy ran her hand through her short, brown, curly hair. "Well, call Lucinda and let me know if she's okay with it and if she is I'll go ahead and purchase your ticket as well."

"Oh, that's not necessary," I said. "My parents gave me a credit card and I'm sure they wouldn't care if I purchased a plane ticket to come see them." I gulped at the thoughts of planes. And flying. Turbulence. Shaking. My stomach was getting queasy at just the thought of it. I really hoped Caeden could indeed distract me.

"No, no," she said and patted my hand. "Let me do this. I didn't get you anything for your birthday and this would be a great gift. A chance to see your parents. Please, let me do this."

"It's really not necessary," I said. "But thanks it means a lot to me."

"Oh, you're welcome dear," she said and pulled Caeden and me into a group hug.

"I need some lovin' too," said Bryce and he joined us.

"I'm going to make some lunch," said Amy already heading towards the kitchen. "Call your grandma and your parents."

"I will," I said already pulling out my cell phone.

"Hello?" said my dad. "Sophie? How'd your shift go?"

"It was great dad. Once the pain was gone it was amazing," I said.

"I knew you'd be a natural. You're a Beaumont after all," he said.

"I was calling for a reason," I said. "I have a question."

"Okay shoot," he said and I could picture him reclining back in whatever chair it was he was sitting in.

"Caeden and I would like to come see you and mom over Spring Break? We have a ton of questions about this whole situation," I said nervously twisting a strand of hair around my finger.

I could hear his smile over the phone. "Sure, sure, that's great. I miss my baby girl and I want to meet your young lad. Especially if we're going to be stuck with him."

"Daddy," I scolded.

He chuckled. "I'm sure he's a great boy but you're my little girl so I've gotta make sure he measures up." I could picture him rolling up his sleeves like he was preparing for a fight.

"No one will ever measure up to your standards. If you had your way I'd be a nun," I said with a laugh.

"That's not a bad idea," he said and I could hear his guffaw. He sobered up and said, "But I'm not naïve, Sophie. This boy is your mate and I know he's not going anywhere. I would enjoy getting to know him better. Man to man," he said.

I looked over at Caeden who was leaning against the doorjamb with a quirked brow. "Daddy, don't hurt him," I gulped.

My dad's laugh filled the phone. "I won't hurt him," he promised.

I let out a sigh of relief. "Thank you," I said.

"We'll send you ticket," he said.

"Don't worry about it," I said. "Amy wants to get it for me as a birthday present."

"Well, that's nice of her. Extend my thanks to her," he said.

"Will do," I said

"Your mom will be so pleased to hear your coming for a visit. Hang on a second!" he said. "You do realize you have to get on a plane."

I chuckled. "Yes, daddy I am aware of the plane situation. Caeden has promised to keep me sufficiently distracted."

My dad choked into the phone. "Tell that boy to keep his hands to himself!"

"Daddy!" I scolded again.

"I was an eighteen year old boy once too, you know? How do you think you ended up in this world?"

"Eww, dad! Can we please stop talking about my conception! It's grossing me out!"

He chuckled. "I'm just not ready to be a grandpa, that's all."

"You have nothing to worry about, grandpa," I said. "I'm not ready to be a mommy."

Caeden was snickering in the corner. I glared at him and he quickly shut his mouth.

"Alright, well we'll be seeing you soon, baby girl. I love you," he said.

"Love you too, daddy. Tell mommy I love her too and I miss you both."

"Bye kiddo," he said and hung up.

"I miss them so much," I said looking up at Caeden. He wrapped me in his arms.

"I know, baby," he said.

"It's getting harder to be away from them. I've never

gone so long without seeing my parents."

"Well, you'll see them soon," he said.

"If it's alright with Gram," I said.

"Why would she object?" he asked.

"I don't know," I said.

"Well, call her and find out. I'm going to go see what my mom's whipping up for lunch."

"Okay," I said already dialing Gram's number.

"Sophie," she breathed into the phone her relief evident.

"Hey Gram," I said.

"How're you feeling? How'd it go? Are you sore?" she rattled off her questions.

"I feel fine. It went as well as I'm sure can be expected. And yes I'm a little sore," I admitted.

"I've been so worried," she said breathing a sigh of relief.

"I slept until about ten," I said. "And I just got off the phone with my dad."

"Oh," she said.

"I was wondering if it would be okay if I go visit my parents over Spring Break?" I asked biting my lip.

"Of course, sweetie," she said. "I know you miss them," Gram said.

"Thanks," I said. "I'll talk to you later, Gram. I'm starving."

She laughed. "I'm sure you are. The first shift is always the toughest on the body."

"Bye," I said and hung up.

I followed the delicious scent that filled the hallway. I found Amy stirring something at the stove. Caeden and Bryce were sitting at the island.

"Is there anything I can do to help?" I asked Amy.

"No sweetie," she said giving me her sweet mothering smile. "You have to be exhausted after your shift. Just sit down and relax. I'm almost done anyway. I'm sure you're starving. Have one of these," she said and handed me a wire basket with cheddar biscuits wrapped in a napkin. I snagged one before the boys hogged them down. I took a bite and it was delicious. Gram and Amy should open a restaurant everything they made was *so* good. "Done," she said and shoveled whatever it was she had made into plates for the each of us.

She sat the plate in front of me and I saw that it was shrimp alfredo. It looked far better than any you might find in a restaurant. I took a bite and the flavors exploded over my tongue. "Mmm," I said. "This is delicious."

"Thank you," said Amy grabbing her own plate and taking the chair beside of Bryce.

Bryce was shoveling the pasta into his mouth like he was a starved child. It was a Shark Week moment when the great white jumps out of the water with its jaw wide open. Yeah, that's what he looked like, a shark devouring a poor, defenseless, baby seal. I felt for the baby seal. What a tragic death and now the pasta was experiencing a similar fate. It didn't look like he even chewed it. I turned away and focused on my own plate. I purposefully took small dainty bites.

"So Bryce," said Amy. "It looks like it'll just be you and me this Spring Break."

Bryce groaned. "Do we *have* to go camping? You know I hate it."

Amy shook her head at her son. "You're a shifter," she said, "you're supposed to like the outdoors."

"I prefer to go against the grain," he said.

"I know," she said with a sigh. "Do you do it to purposely drive me crazy? Because it's working?"

Bryce laughed. "I just don't want to spend a week in a tent with my mom."

Amy sighed. "Fine, we'll do something else."

"Like what?" asked Bryce chomping on his food.

Amy shrugged her shoulders. "Maybe we should go to the beach."

Caeden slammed his hand down on the table. "That's not fair. We never go to the beach."

Amy tilted her lips up in a smile. "Maybe you can go over the summer."

"You say that every year," he said.

"I'm not stopping you," she said. "So what do you say Bryce? The beach?"

"Sounds good to me," he said. "Anything's better than a tent."

Amy chuckled. "You're such an optimist."

"I try to find the good in everything," Bryce said and I thought he was ready to lick his plate clean.

"I'll get everything set for us then. The sooner you book the cheaper it is," said Amy springing from her seat and cleaning her plate. She put it in the industrial sized dish washer. "Don't forget to wash your dishes," she called over her shoulder no doubt heading to her office to secure hotels and plane tickets.

I finished my meal and washed my plate. I grabbed the boys as well and then added them to the dishwasher next to Amy's.

"Oh!" I said grabbing my head as I swayed dizzily back and forth.

Caeden's hands were instantly on me supporting me. "Babe, are you okay?"

"Just tired," I said.

"Do you want to go to bed?" he asked. "It's perfectly normal to be extremely tired and sleepy after your first shift. Bryce practically slept for a week straight!"

"Hey!" said Bryce offended. I saw that Bailey and Murphy had joined us and Bryce was petting his familiar soothingly.

"Sleep sounds good," I said and before I could move and inch my legs were swept out from under me.

"Show off," muttered Bryce. Caeden chuckled as he swept out of the room with me in his arms. He easily carried me up the steps and into his room.

He gently laid me on his bed and pulled me against his chest. He kissed my cheek. "Sleep for as long as you want. You need your rest so your body can prepare for your next shift. The next one will be much easier," he said sweeping my hair off my face.

"Will I just picture myself as a wolf like I did to become human again?" I asked scooting against his chest so we were nose to nose.

"Yep," he said. "Pretty soon it'll be second nature and you won't even have to think about switching forms. It'll just happen on the fly."

"That sounds... exhilarating," I mumbled.

He chuckled and tapped my nose with his finger. "It is. You'll see. You'll grow to love it."

"I know I will," I said, "the taste I got yesterday... It was amazing, incredible, insane! And then bonding with you... Caeden, I've never been happier than I was in that moment," I said taking his hand in mine.

He smiled and laced our fingers together. "It was the best night of my life."

I looked at our entwined hands and saw our names twinkling together. *Caeden. Sophie.*

I like it. Caeden thought as he looked at my name tattooed on his skin.

I do too. I thought and traced the skillful lines of his name forever imprinted on my skin as much as he was imprinted on my heart.

He smiled and my stomach did that little flip flop. I kissed his adorable dimple and his stubble rasped delightfully against the smooth skin of my lips.

He began to hum a soft melody and my eyes gradually began to grow heavy. My muscles still ached but once sleep overcame me the pain was gone and my dreams were filled of Caeden.

Darkness had fallen when I opened my eyes. Caeden's arms were wrapped snuggly around me and my face was buried in his neck. His snores softly filled my ears. I couldn't believe that I had slept so long after I woke up so late this morning. But my muscles no longer ached and I felt oddly rejuvenated.

"Caeden," I whispered pushing at his shoulder to wake him. He mumbled something incoherent. "Caeden," I said again. "You're squishing me," I giggled.

He opened his eyes and smiled lazily. "Hey," he said.

"Hey yourself," I said. He gently traced the curve of my cheek bone with his finger.

He pulled me impossibly closer and snuggled against me. His nose skimmed the side of my neck. "I love the way you smell," he breathed.

"I know, like cookies," I giggled.

"The best cookies ever," he said.

I motioned towards the window and the growing darkness. "I should probably get home."

He shook his head in denial. "I mean… you can go if you want but Gram okayed it for you to be here for the whole weekend."

"How on earth did you finagle that?" I asked shocked.

He grinned. "My charm. I'm just irresistible."

"You wish," I said and smacked his arm.

"Do you want to stay or go?" he asked.

"I don't have any clothes to change into." I said and bit my lip.

He gently tugged at my lip so I would stop biting it. I sat up and brought my legs up to my chest and rested my chin on my knees. Caeden reached down and grabbed a small duffel off of the floor. He tossed it to me and I caught it. "Don't worry, Lucinda packed it, not me. I promise I didn't try to steal your panties," he chuckled.

A giggle bubbled out of my chest and turned into a full blown laugh. I wiped tears out of my eyes. "Panties? Did you just say panties?"

"Yes… why is that so funny? Panties, underwear, boxers, briefs… knickers… whatever you want to call em' it's still the same thing," he said.

"It's just funny hearing you say panties," I laughed.

"Woman, you have a strange sense of humor," he laughed along with me.

"I know," I said.

He patted my leg and said. "Well get in your Jammie Jams and we'll watch a movie," he said jumping up from the bed.

"Jammie Jams?" I asked trying to suppress another laugh.

"Yes," he said eyeing me, "that's what our mom calls them and by default we do too."

I laughed and slid off of the bed. I held up the duffel bag and said, "I'll go put my Jammie Jams on."

"Don't mock it," he said with a light laugh. "Jammie Jams sounds much cooler than plain old *pajamas*," he spat the word like it was an expletive.

My laugh floated behind me as I strode into his bathroom. Once in there I decided I'd feel much better if I went ahead and took a shower. It meant using Caeden's guy scented soaps but I didn't care. At least then I'd smell like him.

I scrubbed my scalp and skin until it was a raw pink color. I dried off and towel dried my hair. I didn't want it in my way so I braided it away from my face. Maybe the braid would produce some soft waves. Normally my hair hung limply like a noodle with a slight curl at the end. Other than the ends it was pretty much straight.

I pulled on my pajamas, or Jammie Jams as Caeden preferred to call them, and my favorite cozy sweatshirt that Gram had had the forethought to pack.

Caeden wasn't in his room when I opened the door so I headed downstairs to find him. I could hear popcorn popping so I figured he was in the kitchen.

I found him and Bryce, with an almost empty bag of popcorn, tossing the popped pieces back and forth to see if they could catch them in their mouths.

Caeden caught a piece in his mouth and turned to grin at me. "Sorry, we had to pop more," he said holding up the now empty bag.

"That's okay," I said, "it was cute watching you try

and catch it."

"Try? Try? Baby, did you not just see that? I caught it with my mouth on the first try. That takes skills," he said and we both laughed. Bryce joined in our laughter.

"So, what are we watching?" asked Bryce rubbing his hands together.

"I don't know," said Caeden, "I was going to let Sophie pick it."

Bryce groaned. "Do not pick some girly chick flick," he said. "If you do, you best sleep with your eyes open. I don't do Princess Diaries and all that crap," Bryce said.

Caeden looked at me and smirked. "Don't listen to him. He was obsessed with Beauty and the Beast when he was little."

Bryce rolled his eyes. "Only because dad said that when I was a man I would turn into a Beast. I was curious."

I patted Bryce's arm. "Don't worry. I'm more in the mood for The Fast and the Furious," I laughed.

"Oh thank God," he said and sauntered off with a skip in his step.

"Beauty and the Beast?" I asked Caeden quirking my brow.

He chuckled. "Some parents give their kids the 'birds and the bees' talk. Our dad gave us 'you're going to turn into a hairy wolf beast' talk," he shrugged his shoulders.

"Does that make me the Beauty?" I asked with a smile.

He grinned and his dimple showed. "Most definitely," he said and pecked me on the lips. The microwave dinged and he pulled it out. He opened it and deposited it in a blue bowl that was hand painted with pieces of popcorn and various candies, Williams, was written on it. He stuffed a handful of popcorn into his mouth and mumbled, "Come on," around his mouthful. He took my hand. His were sticky with butter but I didn't mind.

Caeden led me through the endless maze of his civil war era house. There were many rooms that I had yet to discover and I thought for sure I would get lost if I was left to wander on my own.

He led me to a hallway just before his mom's office that I had never noticed. Wall sconces were set at intervals and cast an amber glow down the hallway. Caeden opened a door and motioned for me to enter. Bryce was pulling down a screen and powering up a projector. Four rows of five chairs each were set on diffcrent levels just like in a real theater. The seats were plush red leather. The walls were a thick burgundy fabric. I wondered when it would finally hit me that Caeden had *money*. I wasn't sure it ever would. After all no one ever seemed to work, except for Caeden at the cupcake shop. Where did shifters get their money? Gram lived like regular person. I just didn't understand it.

"Where do you want to sit?" asked Caeden taking another bite of popcorn.

I slid into the back row and plopped down. "Please save me some popcorn," I said kindly.

"You better take this then," he said handing me the blue monogrammed bowl. It was already half empty, or half full, depending on your perspective.

The movie blared to life. My hands instinctively reached up to cover my ears from the bombardment of the loud noise. Caeden grabbed the popcorn bowl before it could fall.

"Sorry," said Bryce turning the volume down. He plopped down on one of the front row seats. His curly head suddenly popped back up. "Uh, can you two please not make out back there? I really don't want to be sick."

Caeden grabbed a handful of the buttery yellow popcorn and tossed it at Bryce. His little brother ducked out of the way but not before most of it hit its mark and lodged in his hair.

"At least it's not gum," said Bryce. He pulled a piece of popcorn from his hair and stuck it in his mouth. He chewed and swallowed. "Still good," he said and shrugged his shoulders before hitting play.

I cuddled against Caeden's side. I was right where I wanted to be. Nowhere was more perfect than in his arms. Of that I was certain.

TWENTY.

"Ew no," I said to the puce dress that Charlotte held up.

"Sophie!" she groaned. "You have to pick a dress! You did agree to go you know!" she squawked.

I was really beginning to regret my decision to go to prom with Caeden. The whole thing had turned into my worst nightmare. I didn't like dresses. I didn't like to dance. And here I was being forced into both.

I groaned and put my head into my hands. "I'm not going to wear that," I said. "I'm already going to be miserable I at least want to be miserable wearing something I sort of like."

"You haven't even tried anything on," said Chris holding up a silver dress against her slender frame. I would never be as model thin as her. I was too curvy. At least Caeden seemed to like my curves.

"I don't see the point in trying on something that I hate on a hanger. If I hate it on a hanger I'll despise it on myself," I reasoned.

Charlotte sighed and said, "You're hopeless."

They scanned through the racks while I laid back against the velvet covered ottoman I was sitting on. I tapped my black converse against the floor. They had dragged me to this ginormous mall in the hopes of finding a dress. But I knew it wasn't going to happen.

The annoyingly helpful sales lady came by yet again. Her white blond hair was pulled back into a ballerina style bun. She wore a black pencil skirt with a tucked in ivory blouse. Her pale blue eyes bore into mine and she pouted her red lips. "Are you sure there's nothing I can help you find?"

"We're good thanks," I said rudely. I wished she'd leave us alone. Didn't she see that it was my plan to not find a dress? Could the annoying blond not take a hint?

Chris and Charlotte came screeching after her before she could take three steps. I groaned. This was bound to be bad.

"Actually," said Chris, "we do need your help."

"Certainly," the sales lady said in a high soprano voice. "What can I do for you?"

"Our friend here," Chris pointed to me, "needs to find a dress. Do you have any recommendations for her?" Christian asked politely.

Recommendations? It was a prom dress not a college application.

The sales lady put her index finger against her plump red lips and silently appraised me. I desperately wanted to roll my eyes. Suddenly her eyes lit up and the put her finger in the air in an 'aha!' moment.

"I'll be right back," she said and disappeared into the racks of dresses.

"Christian I'm going to kill you," I said in a monotone.

"Ooooh!" said Chris mockingly. "She uses my whole first name. I'm so very scared. I'm quaking in my little boots."

The sales lady returned with a deep green dress in her hands. I sat up intrigued. She held it up and asked hesitantly, probably afraid I'd bite her head off, "Do you like it?"

"It's beautiful," I said reaching out to feel the green fabric between my fingers.

Charlotte clapped her hands together and said, "Yes! She has some fashion sense."

"Are you sure it's not more your color?" I asked.

She glared at me and I swore flames sprouted from her red hair. She put her hands on her hips and said, "Having red hair and freckles does not make me a leprechaun."

"Sorry," I mumbled.

"Would you like to try it on?" asked the sales lady.

"Sure, why not," I said and followed her to a dressing room. I eased out of my clothes and slipped the shimmery emerald fabric down over my hips. I gasped at my reflection.

"Let us see!" I heard Chris' voice outside the door.

I opened the door. Chris, Charlotte, and the sales lady

peeked hesitantly at me.

"Oh my God," said Charlotte and Chris simultaneously.

"You look beautiful," said the sales lady, clearly proud of a job well done. "It's a one-shoulder draped goddess gown," she said to the girls having obviously decided that I had no fashion sense.

"I like it," I said.

Chris and Charlotte gasped.

"I never thought I'd hear those words escape your lips today," said Chris.

"We have the perfect shoes and earrings to go with that," said the sales lady.

"My ears aren't pierced," I said.

"Oh," she said clearly crestfallen. She asked me my shoe size. I rattled it off and she disappeared. A moment later she returned with a gold spiked gladiator looking heels in her hands. I thought they looked like a death trap.

I slipped them on to appease the three staring women and wobbled.

"You'll get used to them," said Charlotte.

"I doubt it," I said. "But I'll take them both anyway."

The girls cheered and high fived the sales lady. As I pulled on my jeans and t-shirt I heard them asking her for suggestions with their own dresses.

The sales lady found a short gold dress for Charlotte. I thought it looked stunning on her. The corset top was fully beaded and accentuated her small figure and the gold skirt was a three tiered tulle ruffle. She also found a stunning dress for Chris as well. The dress she found for Chris was a midnight blue with intricate silver and black beadwork. It was ruched with a sweetheart neckline. The color of the dress made her honey blond hair look blonder and her pale green eyes striking. The sales lady disappeared to find them appropriate shoes and jewelry.

By the time we finally left the store Charlotte and Chris had befriended the sales lady. Her name was Cheryl. I thought it was funny. The three C's. Charlotte, Christian, and Cheryl. They could start their own club.

We had ridden in my car because it had the most room but Chris had driven since I didn't know my way around the city.

We got in the car and I started programming the navigation system to be set for home.

Her chipper British accent demanded that we turn left and then right up ahead.

"Thank you, Beatrice," I said kindly to the colored screen displayed before me. Chris did as Beatrice said and snickered at me.

"Beatrice? You named your navigation system?" she asked trying to contain her giggles. Charlotte was currently in a fit of hysterics in the back seat.

"Well, she is a woman and she's British. I also like the name Beatrice and I thought if we were going to be spending a bunch of time together she deserved a name."

"You are aware that you named and are referring to an inanimate object like it's a person. You must have been one strange child," she commented.

I crossed my arms over my chest. "Laugh at me all you want but Beatrice has never failed me. Unlike you two," I added.

Chris guffawed, "When have we ever failed you?"

I pointed back behind us at the large mall. "Case in point, you declared you could find me a prom dress. If I recall correctly Cheryl found my dress."

"That's because you hated everything we pulled," said Charlotte from the back.

"It was all ugly. Even my grandma wouldn't wear the stuff you were trying to put me in," I said.

Our carefree laughter filled the car. I had never felt better. I had real friends and a boyfriend and an extended family that loved me. My wolf family.

We stopped on our way home at a Red Robin and got burgers and shakes. Night had fallen by this point and we still had a forty-five minute drive home. I was exhausted by the time I walked in the door. Shopping can do that to me.

"Did you find a dress?" asked Gram from her perch on the couch. She hit the mute button on the television and Fox News stopped blaring through the room.

I held up my dress that was currently wrapped securely in a garment bag and my bag of shoes. "This dreadful day was a success," I muttered.

Gram laughed. She took the bags from me and hung them in the closet. "You look dead on your feet," she said and kissed my cheek. "Go to bed Sophie. Oh, and Caeden's in there," she said.

Sure enough Caeden was spread out across my bed in his pajamas. Or... um... Jammie Jams...

"How was it?" he asked. "As bad as you thought?"

"Worse," I said and he pulled me into his arms. He kissed the top of my head.

"But you found a dress," he said having obviously overheard my conversation with Gram.

"Yep," I said.

"Can I see it?" he asked.

I raised up and glared into his blue eyes. "Absolutely not. I want you to be surprised."

"It's not like it's a wedding dress," he said.

"So," I said, "I don't wear many dresses and I want to have as much an effect on you as I can."

"You always have an effect on me, Sophie," he said and his voice was thick.

"I want it to be a surprise," I said.

"Fine," he said. "But you can't see me in my tux until the day of," he chuckled.

"Deal," I said and we shook on it.

* * *

"Hold still," admonished Chris as she smeared some kind of glittery substance across my eyelids. I tried to wiggle away from her. "Charlotte!" she called and the leggy red head appeared in the bathroom. I was sequestered on a stool where I wasn't supposed to move. The not moving wasn't working out to well. "Hold her arms," said Chris.

Charlotte's hands clamped down on my arms holding me in place. Chris looked at me with an evil glint in her eye. She had me now.

She had already forced me to scrub my scalp and my skin raw. Once I was buffed to her specifications she filed my nails and painted them in a shimmery gold. She painted my toes as well. I didn't see the point. My dress was long and would cover them, no one was going to see them, but she insisted.

Chris finished dabbing on a shimmery gold eye shadow onto my lids and then plucked my eyebrows. She put a smoky gray eyeliner underneath my eyes and then attacked me with a mascara wand. She made me pout my lips and swiped a pale pink gloss across my lips. She then attacked my cheek bones with a bronzer.

"Now for your hair," she said attacking my locks with a hairbrush. Once it was smoothed out she curled it. She braided one side and then swept my hair into a side up do.

"Voila," she said standing back and surveying her handiwork with her arms crossed over her chest. "What do you think?" she asked pointing to my reflection in the mirror.

I gasped. There was no way that the goddess in the mirror could be me. The foreign creature in the mirror stared at me with large caramel brown eyes and pouty pink lips. Her chestnut brown hair was styled to perfection and cascaded down her slender bare shoulders. Her skin was flushed a pleasant pink and shimmered under the lights. The green of her dress made her look like a mythical creature. She was glowing and her smile was breathtaking.

"Is that me?" I asked hesitantly.

Chris smiled, clearly pleased with my reaction. Charlotte released my arms having decided that I wasn't going to run screaming for the hills.

"Yes, that's you," said Chris.

"Thank you," I said.

Chris threw her hands in the air. "Finally! A thank you!"

I laughed and the other two joined in.

Chris had done an amazing job on me but how could I compete with her and Charlotte's perfection. Chris' hair was coifed in an elegant do that rivaled those you'd see on the red carpet and Charlotte's deep red hair cascaded like a red river down her back. Charlotte's gold dress brought out hints of gold in her red hair.

Chris looked like she could compete with actresses and royalty. Charlotte looked like she should be on the pages of a magazine. It was completely unfair.

Charlotte looked at the clock on the bathroom counter. "The guys should be here any minute," she said. "Grab your clutch and put your shoes on," Charlotte said. Before I could stand and get them she disappeared into my room and grabbed them.

I slipped on the death trap heals and took the beaded gold clutch that Chris had leant me.

"Do you have your phone? Camera? Lip gloss?" Charlotte ran through a check list.

"Yes, phone, yes, camera, no to the lip gloss," I said checking the clutch.

Charlotte sighed and grabbed the pink lip gloss off of the counter and put in the clutch. "There," she said, "you're all set."

"Thanks," I said.

The doorbell rang and Charlotte and Chris squealed in delight and raced out of the bathroom. I reluctantly followed behind them trying to hide in the background. I was not as attention seeker.

"Oh dear, don't you look lovely," said Gram from the kitchen.

"Gram," I said looking at my feet.

"Well you do," she said. She patted my cheek and her wise eyes sparkled with tears. "You're growing up so fast, Sophie," she said. "And don't complain but I promised to email your parents a bunch of pictures. They feel bad that they can't be here."

I groaned.

"Now, now," she said flicking her finger back and forth at me. "Now you better get that tush of yours out there before that young man of yours comes barging in here."

I laughed and headed out to the living room. I noticed that Chris was standing beside Bentley and I idly wondered if they were going together. Bryce and Logan were collapsed onto the couch, tired before the night had even begun, Charlotte stood off to the side staring longingly at Logan while he looked at his fingernails. I didn't miss Bryce's glances at Charlotte.

Standing proudly in the middle of the room was Caeden grinning from ear to ear. The look he gave me sent blood coursing through my veins and straight to my cheeks. I glanced self-consciously at my feet. He *of course* looked absolutely stunning in his tux. The black and white of the tux against his tan skin and brown hair made him look like some kind of Adonis. Although I thought that even when he wore a t-shirt and jeans. He looked perfect and I felt unworthy in comparison to the god that stood before me. The adjective that came to mind to describe Caeden was delectable. Yes, unquestionably delectable.

"Wow," he said, "you look amazing. Stunning, incredible, gorgeous, exquisite." He shook his head and simply said, "Wow," again.

"Thank you," I said trying to hide the blush flooding my cheeks. I was scared that the heat in my cheeks would melt my makeup. Could that happen?

"Beautiful," he said and came forward and took me in his arms. His thumb circled my cheek and I leaned into his palm with a sigh. His touch alone could always calm me. My love for him grew every day and every time I saw him. I thought when you loved someone that was it. You just loved them. But that's not true. When you love someone that love changes and grows. It becomes more. More than you can comprehend. "I love you," he whispered in my ear. I wondered if he had heard my thoughts but I didn't think so. I hadn't been directing them at him.

"I love you too," I said.

He smiled. "I can't believe you're mine. I'm the luckiest man alive."

I'm the lucky one.

He grinned hearing my thoughts. It was so much more intimate speaking without words.

"I got you a corsage," he said.

"And I told you not too," I said even though I had gotten him a boutonniere.

He laughed. "When do I ever listen to you?"

"Never," I said with a smile.

"So why start now?" He asked.

"Good point," I said and tried to contain a giggle.

He grabbed the plastic box off the coffee table and took the delicate flower out and slid it onto my wrist.

"It's beautiful," I said softly touching the delicate petals. Three small white orchids surrounded a pale green carnation and there were several large leaves.

He blushed which surprised me and said, "Chris helped me pick it out. Since you wouldn't let me see your dress I had no clue what to get."

"It's perfect," I said and pulled out his matching boutonniere. Chris had helped me pick it out as well. No doubt all about her plan to have the perfect prom. I pinned it onto his tux and when I finished he pulled me against his chest and kissed me on the cheek.

"Pictures!" squealed Gram producing a small silver camera from somewhere. "Smile!" she said. Caeden looked down and smiled at me while I smiled up at him. Flash! "Ooh! That's a good one!" said Gram. "I'll have to put this up in the house. Okay now look at me," she said going into photographer mode.

We looked at the camera. Flash! I blinked my eyes and little white balls of light danced behind my lids. Flash!

Flash! Flash! Gram was having way, way, way, too much fun with this.

"Everyone now," she said, "come on squish together. You too Logan!" she said when he didn't move. "Any day now Logan. I'm not getting any younger!" Logan reluctantly stood next to Charlotte. Poor girl. I didn't think he was worth her time when clearly Bryce thought she was everything. Gram positioned the camera and then cried in frustration, "Bryce! Can you at least act like your happy!"

"No," said Bryce.

Gram sighed and held up the camera once again. Just before the flash went off Caeden swept me into his arms and planted a dramatic movie star kiss on my lips.

Gram chuckled. "Alright, I'm done. I promise," she said and put the camera down on the table beside the door to prove her point. "Have fun, ya'll." Her eyebrows knitted together. "Maybe not too much fun," she amended.

"Bye Gram," I said with a smile and kissed her soft wrinkled cheek.

She patted my arm. "Love you, Sophie. Go on now before prom ends," she said. "Plus, I have to send these pictures to your mom before she has a bloody conniption."

I chuckled at her. Caeden took my hand and we followed along behind the others. A large, long, stretch SUV limo was stationed outside my house.

"Oh no!" I said and turned to go back inside. "I said no limo, Caeden."

He grabbed me around the waist and held me firmly so that escape was impossible. He chuckled in my ear, "You said nothing about limos. Besides the pack is splitting the cost."

I raised a lone eyebrow at him, jutted out my hip, and placed my hand on it. "Really? How come I didn't pay my share?"

"Because I paid it," he said giving me a, duh!, look.

"Caeden," I whined. "Why do you insist on torturing me?"

"Sophie, you're going to have fun. I promise," he smiled.

"You better hope so or you're in big trouble, mister," I laughed.

"You're cute when you're trying to be tough," he said and humor sparkled in his eyes.

I feigned indignation. "You better think I'm cute all the time," I said.

"Oh, I do," he said and held me around my waist. "I love you no matter what you wear, what your clothes look like, you're always perfect to me. And I love looking at you in your wolf form. Your fur is so beautiful."

"I think your fur's beautiful too," I said and nuzzled his neck much like we did in wolf form.

He grinned.

Bentley stuck his head out of the limo. "Love birds! You have three seconds or we're leaving without you!"

Caeden laughed and pulled me into the limo. The driver closed the door. "Sophie, has an aversion to limos," he told his best friend.

"I do not," I pouted. "I simply don't like you spending unnecessary money one me. It's ridiculous. You know there *are* starving children in the world," I said.

"I am aware of that," he said, "that's why we frequently donate to various charities."

I crossed my arms over my chest. He had me trapped.

"Fine," I said, "spend your money any way you want."

"I will and I do," he said. "I do work you know," he chuckled.

Of course I knew that. We worked together, for lord's sake. I rolled my eyes at him.

The limo smoothly rolled forward and out of the neighborhood. It was still early and the plan was to eat at the hotel prom was being held at before it began. The ride was pretty short further proving my point that the limo was completely unnecessary. The limo rolled to a stop in front of the old historical hotel downtown. I knew we were near the coffee shop that Caeden played his guitar. The driver opened the car door and we all slid out.

The hotel was brick with cream and gray stone accents. A black metal type canopy covered the door. I knew the hotel had been built in the twenties and even though it had been recently remodeled it still carried hints of that time period. A bellman graciously opened the door for us and we filed in. Caeden took my hand and we lead the way into the restaurant. I noticed other kids from our school there in their prom dresses and tuxes. I thought Caeden out shone all the males in his tux. Maybe it was all with how you carried yourself. Caeden wore his tux with confidence where most of the guys scattered throughout the restaurant tugged uncomfortably at theirs and you could see their intense dislike for the garment clearly on their face. Even Logan didn't look nearly as uncomfortable in his tux. I wondered why he even came. He seemed even more unhappy to be here than Bryce was and I was pretty sure I knew Bryce's reason for being unhappy and it could be summed up in one word. Charlotte.

"Can I help you?" asked the woman behind the podium.

"We have a reservation under Williams," said Caeden looking completely in his element in this elegant restaurant that was no doubt very expensive.

The woman checked her list and nodded her head. "Right this way," she said leading us to a table already set for the seven of us. Caeden pulled out a chair for me and I sat.

"Thank you," I said to him as he sat down beside me.

He smiled and picked up the menu that had already been set on the table. "I'm so glad you came with me," he said.

Reluctantly I admitted, "I am too. Don't make me regret before the nights over," I smiled.

He chuckled and entwined our fingers together. He brought my hand up to his lips and kissed my knuckles.

"Never," he said.

I turned my attention to the menu but he kept his hold on my hand. The waiter came and got our drink orders by the time he returned we had all decided. I had settled on the salmon meal.

Our meals came and we joked back and forth. In the moment it was easy to forget the danger we were all under. But Travis and his dad were out there somewhere.

My meal was delicious and I was thoroughly enjoying myself. When we finished and paid for our meal prom had been going on for a good forty-five minutes.

Caeden grinned and took my hand leading me from the restaurant into the ballroom. A huge grin was spread across his face. The others followed along behind us. Caeden pushed open the ivory door into the ballroom. A deep base thudded and purple lights pulsed. A deejay was set up in the corner. Different colored fabrics teepee the ceiling.

I noticed the way some of the kids on the floor were dancing and blanched. I sincerely hoped Caeden did not expect me to dance like that because no way in hell was that about to happen. Nope, nope, nope! It was more like dry humping than dancing! I had never been to a dance before and couldn't believe that the teachers allowed students to dance like that. My parents would kill me. I wrinkled my nose in distaste.

With my new keen sense of smell I could smell alcohol emanating from half of the boys on the football team. I was getting a headache just smelling it. How on earth did I let Caeden talk me into this? I'd rather be at home in my pajamas curled up in his arms with a good book. That situation was more to my liking but I had promised to come so I was stuck here. Maybe it wouldn't be so bad. I hoped but I doubted it.

Caeden found and empty table and Logan and Bryce promptly plopped themselves in two of the chairs. They sure were happy campers. I think I was having more fun than those two combined. Chris, Charlotte, and I dumped our clutches on the table so we wouldn't have to hold on to them all night.

"Dance with me?" Bentley asked Chris.

Her face lit up like she'd just one the lottery. "Yes!" she squeaked. He smiled which surprised me and took her hand and led her onto the dance floor. Maybe he had taken my advice and finally realized he deserved to be loved.

Charlotte stood awkwardly off to the side her face contorted in some kind of inner turmoil. I really felt for her. She had feelings for a jerk when a really sweet guy had feelings for her. It was a complicated triangle and they were all oblivious to it.

I still didn't really like Logan. I thought he came off as a standoffish jerk to be honest; the complete opposite of his bubbly younger sister. But maybe it was just shyness. He seemed to only hang out with us as an obligation to the pack. I got the feeling he didn't really like anyone. He probably preferred his own brooding company.

Charlotte twiddled her thumbs and her face scrunched up as she came to some obvious conclusion.

"Logan," she said hesitantly and he grumpily glanced at her.

"What?" he asked his brow wrinkled in disgust. What on earth did she see in him?

"Do... you... want to... dance... with me?" she gulped going pale. Bryce looked up at her with hurt in his eyes. How could she be so oblivious to his feelings? The boy wore his heart on his sleeve!

"No!" he snapped grumpily and abruptly stood and headed to the refreshments table. His blond hair glowed different colors in the pulsating light.

Charlotte's bottom lips quivered. She looked at me with panic and scurried quickly out of the room like a rabbit. My heart went out to her.

I plopped into one of the chairs in a very unladylike fashion and Caeden sat down beside me. I leaned conspiratorially across the table towards Bryce like we were sharing a very important secret.

"Bryce," I said sweetly.

"Yes," he said leaning across towards me. I felt like we were spies planning some king of mission.

"Go after her," I said sweetly and twisted my head to the side.

"Why?" he ground out thickly through his teeth. "She doesn't like me."

"She doesn't know your feelings there's a difference," I said.

Bryce flicked his floppy hair towards Logan who stood by the table broodingly. "She likes that jerk not me."

"You have to show her that you're worth noticing," I said. "If you like her, prove it," I said.

"That's not fair," he said.

"Life's not fair," I countered. "Just go talk to her. Ask her if she's okay? Ask her if she wants to leave or stay and dance with you? Trust me, she'll want to stay and dance with you. I'm not telling you to confess your undying love for her, Bryce."

He narrowed his eyes at me and stood. "Fine, I'll go find her and when she completely ignores me it'll be your fault."

"We'll see," I said leaning back in the chair with a grin.

He shook his head and disappeared out into the lobby of the hotel in search of Charlotte.

"That was hot," said Caeden with a grin.

"What was?" I asked puzzled.

"You," he said, "being all determined matchmaker."

"I just want to see people who deserve to be happy find that," I shrugged my shoulders.

"You're really good at picking up on unsaid things," he said.

I sighed and looked down at the table I traced random patterns on the white linen with my pinky finger. "Before I found out about being a shifter and the…uh…no college rule

I wanted to be a therapist. I like to help people find their way."

"You amaze me more every day," he said. He pondered something for a moment. "Maybe you should still go to college," he said.

I sighed. "You're the one that said shifters don't go to college. Our job is to serve and protect."

"That's true," he said, "but maybe it's time we do more than that. I hate to see you lose out on your future and like I told you before the rest of the pack and I would like to go to college too. I mean, we couldn't go away for college, we'd have to go to the community college but it would still be an education."

I smiled. "Do you mean that? Can I really go?"

He nodded his head and smiled hugely. "We're going to college!"

I squealed and jumped into his lap throwing my arms around him. I kissed him soundly on the lips. I didn't care who saw. Teachers beware. "Thank you, thank you, thank you! I love you!"

He laughed. "Wow, it really doesn't take a lot to make you happy," he said and his eyes crinkled.

"Nope, it doesn't," I said. "I am a simple girl."

He chuckled. "You are far from a simple girl. You're amazing, not simple."

"We'll agree to disagree then," I said as Logan, having apparently decided the coast was clear, took his seat again.

"Dance with me," said Caeden brushing his lips against mine. His body was tensed for a fight.

"Yes!" I said enthusiastically surprising him. After the news I had just received I thought nothing could bring me down from my high. I climbed off of his lap and he led me to the dance floor.

Some kind of upbeat European song was playing. I didn't exactly know how to dance to it but then again I didn't know how to dance to any kind of song. Fast or slow so I just rolled with it.

"'Can you spend a little time, time is slipping away, away from us so stay, stay with me I can make, make you glad you came. The sun goes down. The stars come out. And all that counts, is here and now. My universe will never be the same. I'm glad you came. I'm glad you came,'" played the song.

Caeden began dancing expertly to the music and soon he had me swaying to it too.

He grinned as he listened to the lyrics. "I'm glad you came," he said into my ear so I could hear him over the music.

"Me too," I admitted. "I never thought I'd be happy I came to prom but with you... Yeah, I'm glad I came," I grinned.

"Success!" he joked. "She admitted it!"

I laughed and smacked his arm.

The song finished and switched to something slower. Caeden pulled me against his body and moved us slowly to the sway and beat of the song. Across from us I saw Bentley holding Chris in a similar pose. I hoped they got together. They were as perfect for each other as Caeden and I were.

Over my shoulder I saw Bryce and Charlotte come back into the ballroom. He was holding her hand and led her out onto the dance floor. I wanted to do a little happy dance but I settled for grinning like a fool as a constellation prize. Bryce held her tentatively in his arms. He caught my eye and grinned. He then gave me a thumbs up behind Charlotte's back. I smiled. My work was done for the night.

I laid my head against Caeden's chest. Its steady beat and the heat he always carried calmed me. I didn't think life could get more perfect than this moment.

EPILOGUE. TRAVIS.

"You bastard," I ground out through my teeth.

My father grinned at me. "She was useless. Just like you. Who would want you as a son you worthless piece of shit!" he spat blood on me.

I narrowed my eyes. He was pushing his limit. My hands curled into fists as I tried to block the red haze from my eyes. I could feel my veins engorging with blood as my adrenaline spiked. I hated this man more than I hated life itself. But he had something I wanted and I was just about to get it. I twisted my neck from side to side to relieve some of the tension coursing through my body. I was like a live wire ready to ignite at the slightest provocation.

"You really shouldn't have said that," I growled in a deadly calm.

My dad's eyes narrowed to calculated slits.

"You wouldn't dare," he hissed.

"Oh, I would father," I said and lunged the silver made knife that I had hidden in my pocket, straight through his heart. I twisted it to make sure it hit home.

His eyes widened in shock. Shock and astonishment.

"Sleep tight papa wolf," I said with a smile.

He took a last gurgling breath, blood spilling from his lips, and finally the bastard died.

I grinned and then licked his blood off the knife. It was done. He was dead. It had been so much easier than I thought it would be. I had wanted a fight and had not received one. I was disappointed to say the least.

I bent down and cut a hole through his plain t-shirt and then used the knife to dig out his heart. Satisfied, I thrust the knife through the door of the shed with his heart attached to it still dripping with his warm blood.

Joy.

That was the emotion I felt seeing his heart pinned to the door like a sacrifice. Its sticky dark rivulets dripped satisfyingly down the door.

I turned and sauntered into the woods not bothering to

glance back at the man that was my father. He deserved no pity.

I shed my clothes and shifted into my wolf form. I felt stronger than I ever had before. Unstoppable.

I howled into the night to call my pack.

My pack, I thought smugly, to call and let them know that there was a new Alpha in town.

Yes, I Travis Grimm now had what I desired most.

I was Alpha.

Things were about to get interesting.

I smelled the scent of bloodshed nearing. I sincerely hoped it was Caeden's.

I howled once more in victory and ran off into the moonlight.

ACKNOWLEDGEMENTS

First off, I want to thank my amazing family for putting up with me and my dreams of writing. Honestly, most of ya'll believed in me even when I didn't, and I thank you for that.

Thank you to my best friends Shelby and Amanda (Manders!) for being there for me. Seriously, most friends wouldn't stick around like ya'll have. Hopefully one day I'll learn not to put writing first.

Thank you to my junior and senior high school teachers, Mr. Partington and Mr. Painter. Even though I didn't really talk about my dreams of becoming an author you both helped me greatly and helped shape me into the person and writer I am today. You have no idea how much both of your critiques and praises helped shape me… even if they were my crappy essays' you were reading.

Most importantly, I want to thank my fans. If it weren't for you guys, I wouldn't be where I'm at. Thank you for loving my characters as much as I do, and thank you for your encouraging messages/emails, music suggestions, etc.

BOOK 2 IN THE OUTSIDER SERIES
NOW AVAILABLE

INSIDER

Nothing will be the same.

MICALEA SMELTZER

TURN THE PAGE FOR TWO EXTRAS FROM CAEDEN'S POV
(MORE EXTRAS CAN BE FOUND ON MY WEBSITE)

CAEDEN'S POV
MEETING SOPHIE

I squeezed the icing onto the cupcakes in a swirl. Over and over again. In a way it was almost hypnotizing.

If only my mind could be cleared so easily.

Instead of worrying about normal, teenage guy things, I was thinking about my pack and the slaughtered deer we had discovered last night while on patrol. This deer hadn't been killed by anything normal. It had been killed by a shifter and viciously at that. Most shifters, being part animal themselves, respected nature. But whoever had done this... They were sick. I knew who it was. The Grimm's. But it was against our laws to accuse another pack of doing something without *solid* proof.

I had howled my arrival and shown up Lucinda's. She had been... less than helpful. Her granddaughter had arrived, who was one of us but knew nothing of us. Apparently I had frightened her but how was I supposed to know? Lucinda had kept her arrival a secret even from me despite my being Alpha. I knew I needed to speak to her about it, about her needing to communicate with me, but that was difficult. She was my elder and we were taught to be respectful. It was a delicate matter and I was new at this. My dad hadn't been gone long. I was new at this whole Alpha thing and young at that. How was I supposed to tell people my mom's age what to do? People my grandparents age? They were supposed to tell me. But since my dad was Alpha the responsibility had passed to me with his death. I questioned myself every day of whether or not I was ready for this. How could I live up to the kind of leader my father had been?

I finished icing the last cupcake and began to hum a House of Heroes song under my breath. Pleased with my handiwork I picked up the tray and rounded the corner, ready to head out front and display them, when a noise startled me.

I turned, my muscles tensing for a possible fight and for the change from man to wolf when everything but *her* disappeared.

The walls, the floors, everything, melted away. It was as if the entire world disappeared. Nothing was left except for her and me. Her presence held me to this spot, to this earth, not gravity. She stood in front of me with dark chocolate hair and brown eyes to match. She smelled like freshly baked cookies. She was perfect. She was everything. And she was *mine*. My wolf howled inside me. My mate.

And then, in a very unlike myself maneuver; I dropped the dang gone cupcakes on the floor. Icing arced across the floor in a spray to cover my shoes, jeans, the floor, and then her.

Crap.

Graceful Caeden. I scolded myself. *Letting a girl make you lose your cool.*

But this wasn't just any girl. My soul recognized her as mine. She was my mate and my wolf was howling happily and running around like a pup. Mine. Mine. Mine.

I looked at the mess I had made, a very big mess, and then back up at my mate. I felt heat flood my cheeks which made me feel like a bigger dork.

Now you're blushing like a freakin' school girl? Get it together Williams.

My mind seemed to clear of anything to say to the angel before me so I simply bent and began to clean up the mess. Maybe I could think of something clever to say while my hands were occupied.

"Don't worry I've got it," said the girl bending down to help. She tightened her ponytail in a movement that I was certain was unconscious. Her fresh cookie smell nearly overwhelmed my lungs. How could someone's natural scent smell that good? It didn't seem possible.

"It was my mistake I'll get it," I said. I'd say anything to stall for time now. I didn't want to leave her. Maybe dropping the cupcakes had been a good thing.

"I can get it," she said. "I'm sure you probably want to get out of here," she smiled. Her smile lit the whole room. I swallowed thickly but found myself smiling back. I saw her muscles quake a bit and felt a bit smug. I wasn't the only one affected.

"Why don't we do it together?" I suggested and heard her heart beat a bit faster.

"Sounds like a plan," she said and dumped several ruined cupcakes into the nearby trash can. "I'm Sophie by the way. Lucinda's granddaughter."

It figures. The head elder's granddaughter. Put a silver bullet through me now.

"Caeden," I said. "I didn't know you were coming," I added unnecessarily. I had known someone was coming in to the shop I just hadn't known it would be *her.*

"Should you have known?" she asked and quirked a brow. It was the cutest expression I had ever seen.

I waved my hand. "I didn't know anyone was coming and as you can see you gave me quite a fright," I motioned to the mess I had made. I tried to act as nonchalant as possible. I didn't want her to see my emotions so plainly on my face. She'd think I was a creeper.

But the look on her face made me think she could see how I felt.

Despite not wanting to leave her I knew I needed to get out of there as soon as possible. If I had to inhale the scent of cookies much longer I'd be proposing marriage.

We finished clearing the cupcakes off the floor. I watched her wipe up the floor and then wash her hands.

She was so beautiful and completely unaware of it.

She turned around and I tried to wipe my face of expression and failed epically.

"So," she said in dismissal. "You can go now."

Was she that ready to get rid of me? Did she not feel this? Was it one sided?

I shook my head to clear my thoughts and to help

hide my face. Not quite ready to leave her I said, "I'll go after I make some more cupcakes to replace the ones I dropped. You can cover the front."

She looked like she was about to protest when the door at the front chimed.

Saved by the bell.

"Okay fine," she said. "Showtime."

I watched her disappear through the swinging door. Her cookie scent lingered in the kitchen. Shaking my head I started another batch of cupcakes. I drew out the process as long as I could but eventually I could no longer stall. I placed the cupcakes in the refrigerated unit in the front. Sophie was busy with a customer and paid me little attention.

Although, from the slight tick in her cheek and the way she kept looking out of the corner of her eye I knew she wasn't quite as oblivious as she pretended to be.

"Bye Sophie," I whispered under my breath. I knew she didn't hear me. Louder I said, "Bye Sophie."

"Bye," she said and flicked me a glance. Her brown eyes, the color of nature, captivated me.

I moved into the back room, cleaning up so she wouldn't have to, and shucked my apron and baseball cap. I ran my fingers through my hair to fluff it back up.

Once I exited the building and climbed on my motorcycle I began to doubt everything that had just happened.

Mates? Was it possible? I only knew of mates happening in the legends. Was it just my hormones going nutso over a hot girl? I didn't think it was the last one but who knew?

Well, there was one person who would know.

* * *

I parked my motorcycle in the driveway of the little yellow house. I was lucky to catch Lucinda at home. Normally she was occupied with the council. As I pulled off my helmet she walked out the door and locked it behind her.

"Caeden? What are you doing here?"

"I have a question for you," I breathed.

She walked towards me. "What is it? I need to leave. The council just called. Is this about the slaughtered animals?"

"No, it's not," I said.

"What's the matter boy? Come on, speak up. You look ill," she added.

"Is it possible-" I swallowed thickly before continuing. "Are mates possible?" Saying the words hurt me. I braced myself for her to scoff in my face and tell me I was being silly.

Instead she surprised me by saying, "Sophie?"

I nodded. "It was just like the legends said. I saw her and it was like- like-" I fought for words. "Like wow," I shook my head. "I saw her and bam! It just hit me like a semi-truck. Is it possible?" I repeated.

"Yes," she said. "It is."

I sunk to the ground on my knees. I lay my hands flat on the asphalt driveway.

She's yours Caeden. I told myself. *Yours.*

CAEDEN'S POV
SOPHIE'S MISSING

I didn't understand why Lucinda was making us work on a snow day. I mean, no one was likely to show up. But I agreed to go in and I knew Sophie was going to be there and there was no way I was going to let her go in there by herself. Any time with Sophie was better than no time. I loved her with every fiber of my being, had since I first saw her, but I knew she was frightened of that and I didn't want to give her a reason to run from me. I needed her to say it first. I needed her to know that I wasn't forcing her into this.

She pulled into the back of Lucinda's and I pulled in right next to her. Perfect timing.

I stuck the baseball cap on my head, backwards, and hopped out of the car. I knew I was grinning like a fool when my gaze met hers but I couldn't help myself. The girl made me crazy.

"Fancy meeting you here," I said as I closed the car door.

She pretended to be shocked. "Caeden Williams are you stalking me?"

I laughed and said, "I'm not prone to stalker tendencies," I appraised her perfect body, "but for you I might."

She laughed as she unlocked the backdoor. Her laugh was the most precious sound in the world to me. I wondered if she knew how much I cared about her.

Together we set to making the days cupcakes. We had two hours until the store opened and my personal opinion was that we'd do all this work and no one would show up. At least I might get to spend some time getting better acquainted with her lips.

Sophie laughed and I looked up from mixing the

batter to see what had caused that giggle. From the look on her face it must have been me.

Oh no, was my shirt on backwards? Inside out? What had I done?

"You have batter on your face," she said as if she had read my mind.

I wiped manically at my face. "Did I get it?"

"Far from it," she said with a laugh. She turned off the mixer she was using and grabbed a rag. She came towards me and her scent of freshly baked cookies assaulted me. She gently wiped my cheek. I held my breath and clenched my fists so I wouldn't reach out and grab her body to me. I wanted to feel her pressed against me. I wanted my lips on hers. I just wanted *her*.

"It's gone," she said softly and stepped away.

I let out the breath I had been holding. "Thanks," I said and hated the choked sound to my voice.

She went back to mixing and for a moment I allowed myself to watch her. Her chocolate brown hair was pulled back in a ponytail and stuffed into the black baseball cap. A stray piece escaped and she tucked it behind her ear in an automatic response. Her full pink lips were pouted and her coffee colored eyes were more gold, like a latte, this morning instead of their usual dark. Her cheeks were flushed a pale pink from working and flour sprinkled her shirt and arms. She was so effortlessly beautiful and completely unaware of it.

I turned away from her, in the hopes of actually accomplishing something, when I discovered that we were now out of cupcake liners and a bunch of other stuff. *Great.* Lucinda really thought this through.

I cursed in frustration and then did it again just 'cause I could.

"What is it?" Sophie asked from behind me. Her voice was soft like a whisper.

"We're out of cupcake liners, cream cheese, and a load of other crap. The truck was supposed to come in last night but apparently it didn't," I groaned and rubbed my face with my hands.

She wiped her messy hands on her apron. I could see the wheels turning in her head, looking for a solution.

"Well," she said and leaned against the counter, "What do we do? Can you run to the store and get the bare necessities?"

I took the baseball cap off and ran my fingers through my hair before replacing it. "I guess so," I said roughly. "We don't have much choice. Will you be okay?" I asked. My Alpha was howling inside me at the thought of leaving my mate. It was actually painful. I knew being separated didn't hurt Sophie the way it hurt me. For me it was not only emotional but physical as well.

She batted her long black eye lashes at me. "I know I look like a damsel in distress but I'm really going to be okay for the fifteen minutes it'll take you to go across the road to Food Lion."

I laughed even though I didn't feel like it. "Alright," I sighed and put my hands up in defense. I pulled my car keys from my pocket and started towards the door. "I won't be long," I said. It sounded like an assurance for her but it was really for me.

"I'll be fine," she smiled and took my breath away. When I didn't move fast enough for her she put her hand on my back and pushed.

She closed the door behind me. I didn't hear it click and I wanted to open the door back up and lock it but I figured she'd think I was being an over protective pain in the ass. Which I was but that wasn't the point.

I stood there for a moment, debating on whether or not to tell her to lock the door.

Stop being an idiot Williams. You're only going across the street. You'll be gone for ten minutes. How much trouble can one girl get into in ten minutes?

I sighed and climbed in my car and drove across the street to Food Lion. I only saw one person working and maybe three people besides myself shopping. I grabbed what I needed and hauled butt to the check out. I looked at my watch. I had already been six minutes.

I was pretty sure the guy checking me out was a sophomore from school. I guess Sophie and I weren't the only ones that had to work on a snow day.

I handed the kid my debit card and bounced from foot to foot. He handed me back my card and I grabbed the bags and ran out to the parking lot where I then slipped on ice. The bag went flying and I began to cuss like a sailor. I don't think I had ever cussed so much in my life as I had today. I grabbed up the bags and this time I tiptoed to the jeep to avoid another fall. I'd probably break my ankle this time. If I did, I could always change to a wolf to heal it but I don't think anyone wanted to see my standing naked in the middle of the Food Lion parking lot. I also think the sight of a wolf might scare the few people out and about.

I reached the jeep and held onto the door handle when my feet hit another patch of ice. Once my feet were steady I threw the bags onto the passenger seat and started the engine. I drove around the bank that was across from Food Lion and stopped at the stop sign. I was about to go forward, across the street to Lucinda's, when a truck came screeching around the corner from Lucinda's and straight into traffic. Well, if there had been any traffic.

I watched the Chevrolet Silverado skid a bit when it hit the ice and then it was gone. The truck looked strangely familiar. I checked traffic yet again to make sure there were no more idiots speeding and then I was in back of Lucinda's. I grabbed the bags and was almost to the door when I realized how I knew the truck.

Peter Grimm.

I dropped the bags on the ground and ran into the store.

"Sophie! Sophie!" I called and looked around wildly. I hoped against hope that she would peek around a corner, say I was silly, and we'd have a big laugh. But that didn't happen.

The place reeked of Peter and Travis. Sour lemons and vinegar. Not pleasant at all.

The kitchen was a mess and I followed it to the front of the store. I found a small pool of blood by the door. I sniffed and Sophie's scent bombarded me.

They made her bleed!

With that thought I couldn't control my transformation. My body morphed into a wolf right there in the little shop. My clothes exploded everywhere.

I hopped over the counter and ran out the back door. I didn't care if anyone saw me.

Caeden? What's going on? You're not on duty. Bentley.

My thoughts were too scattered to answer. He could sense my distress.

What's happened? He asked.

They took Sophie. The Grimm's. They took her from me. She's bleeding and she's scared and she needs me! I stopped and howled at the sky. Even in their human form they'd know the call of their Alpha.

Caeden? Bryce.

What? Logan.

Charlotte and Chris hadn't turned yet so she wouldn't be coming.

Meet me. I said and gave them my location.

Four wolves bound towards me. I saw Bentley's black form first. Logan's white wolf came from the left and Bryce's chocolate form came from the right. They skidded to a stop in the snow.

The Grimm's have taken Sophie.

Bryce whined at this news.

Why? Asked Logan. *What is she to them? They don't know what she is and they're forbidden to harm humans.*

This is the Grimm's. I said. *They don't follow the rules. We need to alert the others. The longer she's with the Grimm's the more dangerous it is for her. I already can't sense her anymore. She's too far away.*

We'll do whatever you need us to do. Bentley said.

Thank you. I said. I looked at each of them. *Get your parents and Bryce you get mom. I'm going to the council. Meet me there.*

They raced off.

Someone get Charlotte's parents'. I added.

Don't worry. Said Bentley. I knew his words were only for me but they did little to comfort.

* * *

I found some clothes hidden in the woods. I think they were Bryce's. They were a bit too short and snug but now was not the time to be picky.

I walked up to the door of the small two-story brick house. The council met at the abandoned house in the woods. No one but us knew its location and for now it was still hidden from the Grimm's. The house was in disrepair. Broken windows, rusty doors, the place looked abandoned but I guess that was the point.

I braced myself before I rang the doorbell. You never, *ever*, interrupted council meetings.

The door opened.

"Alpha Williams?" said Cody Mathers, Charlotte's grandfather. I hated how he said *Alpha Williams* in a condescending tone. Most of the Elders were against me being Alpha. They thought I was too young. Sometimes I agreed with them but I wouldn't let my pack go without a fight if it came to it.

"I need to speak with the council. It's an emergency."

"We are in the middle of council business. You can wait in the hall until we are done and then you'll have your chance to speak."

I pushed the door open all the way and stepped inside. "*I* am your Alpha, Cody, or have you forgotten? I'm speaking to the council *now*." I had never forced my status as Alpha to get something I wanted but when it came to Sophie I'd do whatever it took.

"This way," said Cody and led me down the hall.

The house was nicer on the inside than the outside. They had done a good job of cleaning it up but I could still smell the traces of mold and the animals that were the previous tenants.

He opened the door at the end of the hall and addressed the room. "Alpha Williams requests an audience with the council." They murmured and he motioned me inside.

I looked around at the elders. How did they all fit into such a small room?

I took my place at the empty head of the table. I was supposed to attend council meetings but since I had no desire to sit in a room with a bunch of old people all day I usually skipped. Across from me, at the other head, was Lucinda. She was in charge when I didn't show up which was often. My eyes locked on hers and I said, "The Grimm's have taken Sophie."

Her eyes darkened and I watched her body tense. The others began to murmur.

"We need to find her, quickly, before they do something irreparable."

"When did this happen?" asked Cody.

"Thirty minutes ago. We were at Lucinda's store. We were out of a bunch of stuff so I ran across the street to Food Lion. When I got back Sophie was gone."

Cody chuckled. "Maybe the girl simply left. Do not place blame on the Grimm's when none is do."

"I saw Peter's truck and the place reeks of them. Sophie's blood is on the floor. They *hit* her. As far as they know she's *human*."

Cody swallowed but kept his mouth shut.

I appealed to Lucinda. "Help me find my mate."

Lucinda looked around the room. "You old, foolish, farts. They've taken my granddaughter and you want to sit here and argue about whether the Grimm's deserve blame? If they hurt her…" She didn't finish her sentence. She simply stood and started to leave the room. "Come on Caeden. Let's get our girl back."

I followed her to the front door. When she opened it I was surprised to see my whole pack there. Lucinda looked back at me and smiled. "Good job, boy."

* * *

The whole pack was squished inside Lucinda's tiny, one-story, house taking turns sniffing Sophie's clothes. Archie barked like a maniac at my feet.

Sitting here in the kitchen I felt like I wasn't doing anything productive. I needed to be out there looking for her. She was alone and scared and she needed me. I should have protected her.

"Caeden," said my mom.

"Go away," I said. I knew it was no way for an Alpha to treat a member of their pack, mother or not.

Sophie had been gone for hours now. I felt like I was going insane. I kept imagining all kinds of different scenarios. All of them ended with Sophie dead.

I felt her fingers gently run through my hair like she used to do when I was little. "We'll find her Caeden. I promise you."

"I know we'll find her," I said, "but what state will she be in when we do?"

"Caeden-"

I stood and went out to the backyard. The cold didn't touch me. Nothing could when I was in this state. Nothing else mattered except finding Sophie. I wrapped my arms around myself, not from the cold but from a need to hold myself together, and sunk to the ground. Tears spilled out of my eyes and sobs raked my body. My fingers dug into the ground. I pulled up icy handfuls in my frustration. I dropped my head into my hands not caring if I got dirt on myself. I tried to stop my sobs. My pack shouldn't see their Alpha lose it like this. I needed to be the one with the level head but I just couldn't do it. I needed Sophie and she needed me and I couldn't get to her. I shouldn't have left her. This. Was. My.

Fault.

I continued to sit on the cold ground and cry. I hadn't cried since my dad died and even then I hadn't cried like this.

Finally I picked myself up off the ground. I wiped the dirt from my clothes and straightened my shoulders with a new resolve. I wouldn't breakdown again until Sophie was home safe because she had to be safe. I couldn't imagine the other possibilities anymore. I had to be positive. As of right now, she was still alive, I knew it and I also knew I'd know if she died. Lucinda had been over this with me. Even if I hadn't wanted to listen to her at the time her words were now a comfort.

I opened the door and my pack glanced at me. They said nothing of my breakdown and I was thankful.

Bentley gave me a sympathetic glance and then looked at Christian. I didn't know why those two didn't just give it up already. They weren't exactly hiding their feelings.

"What do we need to do to find my mate?" I said. Everyone began speaking at once. Maybe just maybe she'd be home tonight.

* * *

Five days.

Sophie had been gone for five days.

The longest five days of my life.

A school week had never seemed *this* long and it was the same length.

I hadn't slept in the last five days and barely eaten. Maybe a cracker or two and a sip of water. I knew my mom was right, that I needed to eat and sleep to keep my strength up, but I just couldn't. Not until Sophie was back.

Archie barked like he had non-stop for the past five days. He scratched my leg and when I didn't move he bit my ankle.

"What is it?" I snapped at the dog. He looked up at me with those intelligent brown eyes reminding me painfully of his master. When I didn't make a move he whimpered and pawed at my leg. He whimpered again, turned in a circle, went to the front door and scratched. Stupid dog had to pee.

I opened the door to let him out. When I went to close it he barked. I opened the door wide and watched the dog go to my jeep. He better not pee on my tire. Instead, he pawed at the door and gave me a look more human than animal.

Holy flying monkeys! How had I not realized this before!

"Mom! Lucinda! Bryce!" I called. The rest of the pack had gone home.

"What?" they all asked as the came running to my side.

"I've been so *stupid!*" I pointed to the dog. "Archie can take us to Sophie." The dog barked in agreement.

Bryce was standing there in a long-sleeved waffle-knit shirt, basketball shorts, and white socks pulled up to his knees. "How on earth is the dog going to take us there? Last time I checked dogs can't drive."

"We'll put him in the car and he'll tell us which way to go," I answered.

"So, he can talk? Bella's never talked before." I resisted the urge to punch my infuriating younger brother. "Seems like it would be easier to just strap him to the front of the car and have him pull us there."

"Yeah, because a ten pound dog can pull a car," I said.

"That's more believable than the dog talking."

"Boys!" snapped mom. "Get it together. Sophie's still out there."

"We'll need the others," I said. "The Grimm's aren't going to go down without a fight."

"Already done," Lucinda said, hanging up the phone. I hadn't seen her leave.

"Let's get my mate back," I said.

* * *

I drove and Archie sat on my lap. The rest of the pack followed behind me. In my car, was Lucinda, Bryce, and my mom. They didn't say anything which I was thankful for.

"Are we going the right way?" I asked the dog. Under normal circumstances I might feel stupid talking to a dog but not when the dog was my answer to finding Sophie. We were getting closer. I could feel it.

Archie yipped which I took to be a good sign. Once, when I turned the wrong way, he growled and bit my hand. I still had the blood dried on my arm as evidence. Archie signaled with his head for me to turn onto a narrow dirt road. When the road ended I parked the car and climbed out. I left Archie inside. Once I changed to a wolf I'd be able to find Sophie by scent.

I turned to address my pack even though I wanted to strip my clothes and find my woman.

"Sophie's here in these woods. I have no doubt that the Grimm's will be guarding her. I don't know whether it's just Peter and Travis or their whole pack. Therefore, I think we should anticipate the worst. Are you ready?"

"We're ready!" cried out Bentley and Bryce and the others followed.

I smiled.

I turned into the woods, stripped my clothes, and wrapped my jeans around my ankle. I switched forms and my senses were immediately heightened.

I sniffed the air.

Standard woodland smells invaded my lungs. Leaves, dirt, grass, birds, rabbits, and finally *wolf*. I recognized Peter's scent and my feet were moving before I made a conscious decision.

As I was running a spark of something metal caught my eye and made me hesitate. I slowed myself to a walk and hesitantly approached the object. It was covered by snow and dead leaves and I began to paw it away. What I uncovered was a trap for a large animal. Like a bear or a *wolf*. I filed that bit of information to the back of my mind and took of running again. I was careful in case there were any more traps. I quickly warned my pack to be on the lookout.

I caught a scent in the leaves. *Cookies.*

Sophie. Sophie. Sophie. I knew she was near. *Sophie. Sophie. Sophie.* I stopped and howled towards the sky to bring my pack in this direction. Once I heard the patting of their feet I took off. They could follow my scent. I stuck my nose to the ground. I now smelled Peter, Travis, and one other wolf but I didn't know who it belonged to. I didn't smell Sophie but I could feel her and I couldn't get to her fast enough.

I burst through the trees, into a clearing. A small house, more like a hut, was all that seemed to be in the clearing. Peter and Travis came bursting out of the small cabin and a woman came from a cellar. I shifted momentarily to human form. "Sophie!" I called and hoped she could hear me so she'd know I was coming.

The others followed suit and called for Sophie as well.

A noise assaulted my ears and I realized it was Archie barking. I thought I had locked the dog in the car but apparently Archie was a bit of a magician. The dog crept towards the cellar door and barked incessantly. Peter spared a quick glance at the dog and then his gaze was locked on mine.

"Caeden," he said but the words came out funny. His teeth were already elongating. "You're mine!" was the last thing Peter said before he fully became a wolf.

"Peter," said the woman in a voice that I assumed was meant to calm.

"Sophie!" I called. Peter lunged at me and I feinted to the side. My pack joined the fight.

"I'm in here!" I heard her voice. She was alive! But I didn't have time to rejoice in that fact.

Peter was about to lunge for me again so I switched to my wolf form.

I bit viciously into Peter's side and was satisfied when I heard him yelp.

"She's in there!" the woman that had been with Peter

yelled and pointed to the cellar. Her gaze fell on me and Peter. Peter was on top of me, my shoulder in his mouth, and I scrambled to switch the position. The woman came towards us and I wondered how I would be able to fend off two of them. She kicked Peter roughly and he fell off of me.

She sunk to the ground in a predatory stance. I wondered why she didn't change.

"You son of a bitch," she said, staring into Peter's bottomless eyes. I backed away slowly. "You've ruined my life! You've ruined our son! But I won't let you ruin anyone else." I saw her prepare for the change but not quick enough. Peter lunged at her and tore her chest viciously open with his claws. She screamed, it was a high-pitched, jarring sound. He sunk his teeth into her throat and she was silent. The whole thing was over in a matter of seconds.

I saw Travis' wolf form pause as he watched the gory scene.

My pack descended on Peter. They clawed, howled, yipped, and tore. I did nothing to stop them. Sensing defeat he took off into the woods. Looking around, I saw Travis jump from behind a tree and tackle his father to the ground. I kept my sight trained on them until they disappeared.

This had been my first battle as Alpha and I knew it wouldn't be the last. I felt sick to my stomach and I probably would've thrown up if I hadn't had Sophie waiting for me.

Bentley, Logan, and Bryce, I want you guys to stay behind. The rest of you are free to leave. I felt like a teacher dismissing students from class.

I'm staying. The voice in my head belonged to Lucinda.

Of course. I said. *I shouldn't have forgotten. I want you all to wait by the vehicles then, except Bryce.*

Can I at least get my pants? I don't think Sophie wants to see my junk. Bryce; always trying to make us laugh.

Go get your clothes and come back here.

You got it.

I watched them all disappear before I switched to

human form and lost my means of communication. I pulled on my jeans, called to Sophie to tell her I was coming, and then opened the cellar door. I looked over at the body of the woman who had saved me. I didn't know her but in my book she was a hero.

I descended the steps and heard her choked sobs. There was little light but my eyesight was heightened even when I was human.

"Oh Sophie," I choked when I laid my eyes on her for the first time in days. She was strapped to a table, dirty, and crying. "What have they done to you?" I asked as I ripped off the restraints.

My hair fell over my face and tears leaked from eyes and onto her skin. The woman had made me cry more in the last five days than I had in my whole life.

"Don't cry," she said and her hand came up to cup my cheek. Her touch was light and I could since her weakness.

Her simple words sent me to my knees as sobs coursed through me. I should be comforting *her* not the other way around. I lay my head on the table. I rested my hand on her stomach and felt her own hand tangle into my hair.

"I thought you were dead. I thought I had lost you," I said.

"I'm here. I'm not going anywhere."

"I didn't think I'd ever find you and if I did I was sure you'd be dead. Lucinda said that I would know though, if you died, she said I'd feel it," I said and put my hand over my heart.

Sophie began to cry as she wiped my tears away. I stood and pulled her against my chest. I was careful with her, treating her like a breakable doll, because she was so cut up and bruised. I wanted to kill Peter and Travis for doing this to her. Her small arms wrapped around my neck and she buried her face there are well. "Caeden, I love you."

I closed my eyes and savored her words. "Oh baby, I love you too. I thought I'd never get to tell you. But I do. I love you so much. I'm never letting you leave my side again.

Never."

"I love you," she began to whisper over and over. I could hear her say it all night.

I finally pulled away. I looked into her brown eyes, traced a cut above her brow and said, "Let's get you out of here. It's time to go home."

"I am home," she said and wrapped her arms around my middle. Her cheek pressed against my chest. "You are my home."

Those words were just as powerful to me as her saying she loved me.

I wrapped my arms around her back and held her close. I kissed the top of her head. "I'm so sorry, Sophie," I said and started crying again.

"Why?" she asked and pulled away a bit. She traced my brow line. "You have nothing to be sorry for."

"I have everything to be sorry for. I shouldn't have left you. This is all my fault," I sobbed. She gently wiped my tears away.

"Oh Caeden," she breathed against me. "This isn't your fault. They were waiting for their chance to get me and they took it. They used me to get to you. Caeden," she began to cry anew, "they want to kill you." She leaned her forehead against mine and our tears mingled together becoming on entity. "I'm willing to die so they can't have you. I won't let them hurt you."

"Oh baby," I said. "Please, don't talk like that. Your life is so much more important than mine," I pulled away and surveyed the damages caused by the Grimm's. "Look what they've done to you. They've hurt you so badly. I promise that I will make them feel everything they've done to you. I *will* make them pay for it. They deserve to be tortured like you have, to be held prisoner, and treated like an animal."

"Caeden, please don't talk like that," she begged. "Please don't."

I looked into her eyes for a moment and ran my fingers through her hair. "Alright," I said. "Come on, up you go," I lifted her into my arms.

"I can walk," she pleaded.

"I doubt that," I said, not about to put her down. "You're no more than skin and bones and you're hurt. How long have you been strapped to that table?"

"How long have I been here?" she asked softly.

"Almost a week," I replied.

"Almost that long," she said which gave me pause. She had been strapped to a table for nearly five days? I felt sick. "Caeden, what happened to Leslee Grimm? Is she okay?"

I swallowed. That had to be the woman that attacked Peter. Only his wife could hate him that much. "She's dead, sweetie," I said.

"What? What do you mean? You didn't did you? Please, tell me you didn't kill her? She promised to keep you safe. She said she wanted to leave her pack that she wanted to join your pack."

"Oh, honey," I said softly. "I didn't kill her. She... she died protecting me. She jumped in between me and Peter. He killed her."

"He killed her?" she repeated.

"Like it was nothing," I said, "he didn't even hesitate. Travis saw, he and his dad got into it and then ran off. I don't know where the rest of their pack is. It was only the three of them."

The hatch came open above us and for a moment I prepared to fight, assuming it was Peter and Travis that were back. Instead Bryce smiled down on us.

"Hey Sophie. Man, you look like crap," Bryce said.

"Really?" Sophie said sarcastically from my arms, "No one told me this wasn't a five star hotel."

Bryce laughed. "Sorry, thought I'd try and get you to smile."

"Bryce," I scolded, "I don't think she feels like smiling right now."

Bryce said nothing but moved out of the way as I

climbed up the steps with Sophie in my arms. The sunlight seemed to startle her. Her eyes opened and closed rapidly as they adjusted to the light. Her gaze focused on the body of Leslee a noise like a startled cat came from her throat. I was too late to shield her from the gruesome sight but I couldn't stop myself from saying, "Sophie, don't look."

"It's kind of too late for that," she said. She said the words softly but I couldn't help but flinch. I couldn't protect her from the Grimm's and now I couldn't even protect her from the sight of a dead body. I was a complete and utter failure of a mate.

I started to walk away, Bryce at my side, when Sophie cried out, "Wait!"

My body tensed and I scanned the area quickly thinking that the Grimm's had returned.

I didn't notice anything amiss so I asked, "What is it?"

"What's going to happen to her? It just doesn't seem right to leave her like that. Can… Can we bury her?"

I looked over at Bryce. He nodded his head and I nodded back.

"Alright," I said, "I can see this is important to you."

After what Sophie had been through I'd go to the ends of the earth for her to have whatever she wanted.

"It is," she said and her voice sounded the smallest bit stronger.

"Let's get something in your stomach and then we'll worry about that. Okay?" I asked. I knew I would feel ten times better once she had eaten something.

"Okay," she agreed and seemed to brighten.

Bryce and I began to walk through the woods. We had hardly covered any ground before Sophie was complaining that she was too heavy for me to carry.

"Caeden," she whined while she wiggled in my arms, "How much farther do you have to walk? I'm too heavy for you to carry. Put me down. I can walk."

Up until now I had ignored her but now I said,

"You're light as a feather. Don't worry. I won't drop you, I promise." I flashed her a smile.

She huffed and crossed her arms over her chest. At least she didn't complain anymore. I knew she was too weak to walk on her own and I didn't want to have to watch her struggle. It would only break my heart further.

We came down off the embankment where we had parked the cars. Sophie's dog began to bark like crazy sensing that she was close.

Bentley was leaning against his large black truck with his arms crossed over his chest. "The others left. It's just us," he indicated Logan, Christian, and Charlotte.

Charlotte hadn't been able to participate in the fight since she hasn't changed yet but she had still wanted to some to be here for Sophie.

"It's probably for the best," I said. "They're getting too old for this."

"*Old?*" someone screeched. "Caeden Henry Williams, I better not have heard you right. If I recall, you needed our help."

Drats, rats, and kittens! I should've known Lucinda wouldn't have left. I knew she'd chew me out later over that comment.

"Gram," Sophie breathed from my arms, oblivious to my discomfort.

"I wasn't about to risk anything when it came to removing her safely. I may be young but I'm not stupid," I muttered under my breath to Lucinda.

"I know that," Lucinda said and patted my shoulder, "but you young people always seem to forget that there's still some fight left in us older folks. And your parents' aren't old anyway," she looked around at the others before her wise gaze locked on me again. "Your mom was amazing out there. If I hadn't held her back I think she would've single handedly shredded Peter Grimm to pieces."

"I believe you," I chuckled, "she was pissed." I hadn't paid too much attention to the fight but I had noticed my mom tearing into Peter. I hoped he didn't forget.

"Watch your mouth," Lucinda said with a smile and the skin around her eyes crinkled.

"Yes ma'am," I said and pretended to bow my hat to her.

Bryce opened the trunk of the jeep and I sat Sophie down inside it. My arms didn't even feel tired from carrying her, contrary to what she believed. I found some crackers and handed them to her. "Sorry, it's all I have," I said and combed my fingers gently through her hair.

"That's fine," she said and nibbled hesitantly on the end of one, "I'm not sure I could stomach much else."

Charlotte and Christian came over. I knew they were both eager to see Sophie.

"We were so worried about you," said Christian.

"Caeden's been beside himself with worry," said Charlotte.

I groaned.

Great, everybody was going to tell Sophie what a lunatic I was. Couldn't they just zip they're lips?

"We all have," said Bentley. I exchanged a look with my best friend. I wondered if what happened with me and Sophie would influence him in regards to Christian. I knew he felt like he didn't deserve love but I didn't think that way about my best friend. He deserved love more than anyone I knew.

I shook my head and said, "I've never been more scared in my entire life. I thought my soul was gone." I climbed into the jeep beside Sophie and put my arms around her. I was afraid that if I wasn't touching her she might disappear. I needed to reassure myself that she was here and she was finally safe. After days without her this all felt so surreal.

Bentley smiled at Sophie and said, "He was like a crazy man. I've known him since we were in diapers and I've never seen him freak out quite like that. Not even when his dad was found dead."

"Thanks for bringing that up," I said to my best friend.

My dad's death was still a sore spot for me but especially for Bryce. I looked up and met my little brother's gaze. His blue eyes were misty and he looked four years younger. He turned and disappeared into the woods.

"Sorry," said Bentley and unlike when most people said it he actually meant it. Christian came up to him and leaned against him. Her hand gently rubbed his arm. I wasn't sure she was aware of it. They were like magnets. One always seemed to attract the other.

Sophie was looking up at me with a question in her intelligent brown eyes. I sighed. I knew I'd have to have this conversation with her eventually. I might as well get it over with now.

"Bryce, found our dad's body. He's never gotten over it. Not that I can blame him," I said.

"What happened? If you don't mind me asking, you don't have to tell me," she said.

"We don't really know. We thought it was accident but now I'm not so sure. He... He was caught in a hunter's trap... But... while we were scanning this area for you... I saw the same kind of trap."

"Here?" asked Bentley.

"Yes," I whispered back. A chill went up my spine that had nothing to do with the cool air.

"You think Peter had something to do with it," Bentley said.

"I thought it was an accident before, that he had been careless and gotten stuck, but dad never was careless. I think he was lured into it by Peter."

"But why?" asked Bentley.

Lucinda came over to see what was going on. I looked into her eyes when I said, "Because, that meant I would become Alpha. Once he kills me, Bryce will become Alpha. Once he takes out Bryce the line ends and he can become Alpha. He'd have the control of two packs. He craves power. The power of this pack is the only thing he wants."

Lucinda nodded her head thoughtfully. "I've suspected as much. It'll only get worse if he finds out that Sophie is a true Beaumont. He still doesn't know does he?" Lucinda asked Sophie and worry etched the lines of her face.

I held my breath as I waited for Sophie's answer.

"No," she said. "Leslee said she knew who I was. That I have my mom's eyes. He made her test my blood but she lied to him. She told him that I was only a human that I really was adopted. She also said that he still believes that my mom is truly dead. She says the pack has never suspected otherwise."

"That's good," Lucinda said thoughtfully. "The less he knows the better for all of us. Peter Grimm is not one to be angered."

"Gram," said Sophie softly. She looked down at the crackers in her hand. "If all the Grimm's are so evil why is my mom different? She's always been nice to everybody and the best mom anyone could ask for."

"Christine always rebelled against what her parents wanted her to be. She was always a sweet girl. She was different than them. I think that's why they always clashed. I mean, the poor girl, had to fake her own death. When she met Garrett I worried, like any mother. She was a Grimm and I thought she was going to corrupt my son. I thought she was leading him on. Finally, your dad came to me and told me that he believed that he and Christine were mates. We started researching the legends and I was positive that he was right. I had gotten to know her better and genuinely liked her. But I still worried. If her family, or even if my husband, had found out… They would both be dead, of that I'm certain. When she got pregnant with you they had to leave, it was the only way to keep you and them safe. I sent them money every once in a while and they would send me pictures of you to a post office box. When your grandpa died they started sending you here every summer. It was the highlight of my year."

"Gram, was my dad really in the military?" Sophie asked. I began to play with her fingers.

"No," she said. "That was a cover for all the moving you guys had to do. Your parents feared that if they stayed in one place too long that the Grimm's might find them."

"They sacrificed everything for me," Sophie said and I could hear the threat of tears in her voice.

"No," Lucinda said softly, "they sacrificed everything for each other. You and Caeden will do the same."

Sophie looked up at me and I met her gaze. I loved her so much and I hoped she knew that. I would tell her every day, every hour, every minute, and every second, of the rest of our lives. She was my mate and I loved her with every fiber of my being. Nothing would ever change that.

"I know," she whispered and her brown eyes swam with emotion, "I'm already there."

My breath caught and I licked my lips. I wanted to kiss her, right now, right here, but I didn't want to hurt her so I restrained myself. She was looking better but I could still see how utterly exhausted she was. I was afraid that if not for my arm around her she'd fall over.

When she finished the crackers I said, "Alright guys, let's go bury Leslee so we can get out of here."

She squeezed my hand and said, "Thank you." I could see how much this simple act meant to her and it made me fall more in love with her. Leslee had been a part of Sophie being tortured but Sophie still held compassion for the woman. We could all learn something from Sophie.

"I'd do anything for you," I said and nuzzled her neck.

"I know," she said.

I pulled away and said, "I assume you want to come."

"Of course, you didn't think you'd get off that easy by just leaving me behind, now did you?" she asked.

"Of course not," I said and hopped down out of the trunk. I picked her up.

"I think I can walk now," she said and pushed at my

chest.

She could be so dang gone stubborn.

I tightened my hold on her. There was no way I was about to let her go.

"I'm going to carry you," I said. She opened her mouth to protest so I quickly added, "Please, don't argue about this with me. I don't doubt that you can walk but maybe I just want to hold you close. You've been gone for almost a week. Holding you in my arms means that I know you're safe."

"I understand," she whispered and her arms wound around my neck. Her fingers tangled in my hair and I lost my breath.

"Good," I said to her. "Bryce!" I called over my shoulder. "Come on."

Bryce bumbled out of the trees. He'd obviously been crying, his cocky smile and swagger now gone. Charlotte hurried to his side. I hoped she didn't give him false hope. Bryce had had a crush on Charlotte for as long as I could remember. I hated to see my brother have his heart walked all over.

The pack and I trekked through the woods. Lucinda stayed behind. When we emerged in the clearing Leslee's body still lay in the same spot. From a distance it seemed like her body was a natural formation in the land.

I sat Sophie down on the steps of the log house, kissed the top of her head, and went in search of shovels. Surely there were shovels around here. I didn't really plan on digging a grave with my bare hands.

You really thought this one through, huh Williams?

Luckily there were a few shovels in the back. I grabbed three and headed back to the front of the cabin. I tossed a shovel to Bentley and Logan and kept the other for myself.

"Bryce, can you sit with Sophie?" I asked. I hoped Bryce would be able to cheer her up.

"Sure thing," he said and hopped onto the step beside

her.

Bentley, Logan, and I set to digging. Between the three of us it wouldn't take long. I saw Bryce disappear into the woods and return with a large rock. What was he doing? As I dug I saw him pull a knife out of his pocket. Sophie flinched and my heart lurched. I started to go to her but Bryce seemed to be handling it and I didn't want her to think that I was clingy. As I watched Bryce began to carve something into the rock. Sophie began to cry slightly and then she wrapped her arms around him. Bryce seemed surprised but hugged her back.

We finished digging the hole and I went to get Leslee's body. One of the girls had thought to bring a blanket and had wrapped the body. I carried the woman's body like one would a child and laid her gently in the dirt. This woman had protected me from her husband. She had befriended Sophie. There was more to Leslee Grimm than anyone had ever realized.

The guys and I picked the shovels back up and began to cover her up. At least the ground wasn't frozen anymore or it would have made our job a lot more difficult. When the ground was covered we patted it down. I leaned against the shovel and wiped sweat from my brow. I turned to find Sophie watching me. "We're done," I said unnecessarily but I felt the need to fill the silence.

"Thank you," she said and bumbled her way towards me. She hugged me and I lightly hugged her back. I was so afraid I might hurt her. She was so bruised and I knew there were many more bruises, emotional ones, that I couldn't see and it broke my heart. No one, least of all her, deserved what she had endured.

Bryce came over with the stone and placed it at the head of the grave we had created. I read the words.

LESLEE GRIMM, WHO WAS NOT A GRIMM AT ALL.

He disappeared into the woods and came back with a handful of wildflowers. Dirt was still clinging to their roots.

"It was all I could find," he shrugged. Who knew my

annoying brother had a heart?

"You should say something," I said to Sophie and squeezed her hand gently.

"Um..." she said nervously and bit her lip as she met everyone's gaze. She wiggled slightly beside me. She straightened and spoke solely to Leslee's grave. "I didn't know you well. I know you were my mom's best friend and I know that you saved me." She sniffled and wiped her nose. "You saved Caeden because I asked you too. You were a good person but you were with the wrong one. You deserved to find peace and since you didn't find it in life I hope you've found it in death. Thank you for your sacrifice. I will never forget what you've done for me."

She swallowed, stepped back, and took a deep breath.

She looked up at me and I asked her, "Ready?"

She nodded.

I handed Bentley the shovels and he put them away. Once he came back we started into the woods.

"Do you want me to carry you?" I asked.

She shook her head. "I can walk, really," she added when she saw my doubtful expression.

Despite her words I almost picked her up anyway. *Almost.*

Instead I comforted myself by keeping a hold on her. Sophie kept glancing around like a startled bird and I had a feeling she was looking for either Travis or Peter to return. It broke my heart.

The cars appeared through a break in the trees. The sun was almost gone and the moon was already out. A few stars glimmered above. Or maybe they were planes?

We reached the road and I dug my keys from my pocket. I tossed the keys to Bryce and said, "You drive."

"Sweet," Bryce drew out the word. He scurried to the driver's side and hopped in. Lucinda was asleep in the front passenger seat. I shook my head at my brother.

I clapped Bentley on the back and said, "Thanks man."

"I'm here for you," Bentley said and a significant look passed between us. I knew he was remembering Sam. He climbed into his truck.

"Bye," I said to the others as they got in. The truck left as I was opening the back door of the jeep. I waved.

I helped Sophie into the car and then pulled her head down to my lap so she could lie down.

"Home," she said but it sounded like a plea.

"Yes," I whispered, "I'm taking you home."

"Not if I can't get this stupid thing to work," Bryce said and hit the navigation system. Was he *trying* to break my car?

"Hey, hey," I scolded. "Don't hurt it."

"Stupid Chinese," Bryce muttered, "can't they make anything simple?"

"Don't diss the Chinese just because they're smarter than you. It's unbecoming," I laughed.

Bryce mimicked me in a high-pitched voice before saying, "Don't be an ass, how about that?"

I rolled my eyes at his antics. "A simple navigation system has your panties in a bunch? What am I to do with you?"

"One: I don't wear panties. I prefer to go commando. Two: why don't you just feed me to the wolves? Oh right, I am one," laughed Bryce.

I smacked him in the back of the head. If there was an award for most annoying sibling Bryce would win hands down.

"Too much information," I said. I helped Sophie sit up so I could set the navigation system. For a math whiz Bryce could pretty dense. Seconds later I sat back and said, "Was that so difficult?"

"Very," Bryce said and flicked on the headlights. He put the car in drive and I breathed a sigh of relief. I was finally going to take Sophie home.

"What's all this grumbling about?" Lucinda said, coming awake. "Can't you see an old woman trying to sleep?"

Bryce and I laughed. "You're not old," I said.

Lucinda turned around and scoffed at me. "What planet are you living on? The planet of the completely blind?"

"How about the planet of the completely absurd?" Bryce added. Lucinda turned around and smacked his head like I had. "Ow, what was that for?" he asked, rubbing the spot.

"For calling me old!" Lucinda said.

Sophie began to laugh but abruptly stopped. I could see the pain in her eyes. I pulled her back down to my lap and ran my fingers through her hair. "I'm so sorry," I whispered into her ear. My breath seemed to tickle her.

"It's not your fault," she said. "Don't torture yourself with something that was out of your control."

"I can't help it," I said and began to cry again. My tears ran down my face, off my chin, and splashed onto her skin. "I'm your mate. I'm supposed to protect you."

"Shh, can we talk about this later?" she asked and her eyes began to close.

"Of course," I said and brushed her hair back from her forehead. I wiped my tears with my other hand.

"Thank you," she said and her eyes closed again. I began to sing the lyrics to *Your Guardian Angel* by The Red Jumpsuit Apparatus softly under my breath. A smile quirked her lips and my body finally relaxed for the first time in days.

ABOUT THE AUTHOR

Micalea Smeltzer is an author from Virginia. She is permanently glued to her computer writing one of the many books swirling around in her head. She has to listen to music when she writes and has a playlist for every book she's ever started. When she's not writing, she can be found reading a book or playing with her three dogs.

You can email Micalea at:
msmeltzer9793@gmail.com

Like her facebook page to stay updated on all the latest book news:
http://www.facebook.com/MicaleaSmeltzerfanpage?ref=hl

Follow her on twitter:
https://twitter.com/msmeltzer9793
NOTE: She rarely uses her twitter, so you're better off to contact her another way.

Website:
http://micaleasmeltzer.com/

Printed in Great Britain
by Amazon